FIRST, THE FIELDS

First, The Fields

BY

CHARLES WOOD

CHAPEL HILL

The University of North Carolina Press

VAN REES PRESS · NEW YORK

PJ

TO THE MEMORY OF MY FATHER

CHARLES TURBIVILLE WOOD

FIRST, THE FIELDS

Part One

HUGH set his lantern down beside the rabbit trap and cupped his hands around the warm globe. This time he was taking no chances. Only yesterday he had lost a rabbit because his hands were so numb from cold that he could not hold the squirming creature when he drew it from the box. Two long scratches on the back of his right hand bore witness to yesterday's failure. They could kick like a mule, he mused, as he viewed the red scratches in the dim light.

No sound came from the closed trap.

"Found out he couldn't get out, I s'pose," thought Hugh. "Quit kickin' then, I reckon. Just crawled in the back and took a seat to wait and see what would happen. Soon as I get my hands warm, you'll find out, all right, old fellow."

No sound came from the forest either. Crouching there before the little, flickering light, the boy became nervously aware of its awful stillness. The puny lantern seemed to accentuate the frightful darkness, and now that he thought about it, his imagination peopled the surrounding air with monsters of mythical size and ferocity. The darkness itself seemed animate now, like a horrible black monster, slinking, silent, drawing its breath for a scream. Hugh picked up the lantern and held it high above his head. The darkness crept back a few feet, like a cat before a whip, and crouched beyond the circle of light. Hugh was no longer afraid. His lantern was a weapon before which the black beast always cowered. Movement restored him to reality and to the business of getting the rabbit out of the trap. He raised the door and peered inside. There in the far end of the box squatted the rabbit, its front feet placed meekly together, as prim and modest as an old maid's. One ear hung dejectedly from its head. The other had more spirit; some hope of succor supported it. Its face bore a mask of utter resignation, but back of this touching humility lurked two powerful hind legs, ready to scratch their way to freedom. And Hugh knew this. Cautiously he extended his arm toward the prisoner. His fingers disregarded the suppliant ears, went around them and beneath them, and under the soft belly to the rebellious back legs. When he had grasped both of these firmly, he drew their owner from the box and slew him by a sharp blow on the back of the head.

Swinging the dead rabbit from his left hand, he made his way deeper into the woods, still carrying the lantern, holding it as far ahead of his feet as he could because it was yet dark. None of the other traps yielded anything, however, and soon he found himself at the fringe of the forest with only a wide field before him. The sun played along the edge of the woods, glazing the frost on the grass with every color of the rainbow, and making a crimson bow of the crest of the hill. Hugh could taste the crisp, sweet air as it stung his cheeks.

He shook the lantern violently to extinguish the flame, then hurried toward the house. Here was beginning a day among days on the farm—hog-killing-day. For this event he had arisen earlier than usual this morning, one of the first cold mornings of November with winter near enough to insure the preservation of meat. These were gala days for the very young, days of plenty and feasting, of rich, red gravy, and the aroma of sweet, fresh food. In the seasonal index of his mind this was a period of marked importance, on a par with Christmas and the week of annual revival. For many months the hogs had been fattened, actually goaded, in the attempt to lay on every possible pound, into a consumption of food which exceeded mere hoggishness. All farmers held the poundage of their hogs a matter of pride, and a friendly competition existed between neighbors. A small, lean pig was something of which to be ashamed, a direct reflection upon its owner, since its very leanness bore evidence to a lack of surplus food at his table. Hugh's father had selected the time for slaughtering several days before, after due deliberation with the almanac and portentous readings of weather signs in the sky at evening. His judgment had proved good, for the day was cold and clear, with a salty tang in the air. All preliminary preparations had been made on the preceding day; a huge boiler had been banked with rocks, and near it a pole had been erected on which the hogs would be hung and quartered.

The smoke from the boiler was visible now, coming from behind the woodpile. Hugh ran toward it, saw hastily that no one was attending the fire, and still running, veered toward the pig-lot behind the stable, where his father and the negroes were already at their bloody work. Suddenly a shrill scream of pain and terror split the air around his ears and, halting, he saw his father rise from behind the rail fence, bringing into view as he stood erect the long, glimmering blade of a knife. Through the cracks in the fence, Hugh saw the negroes holding another pig to the ground, one holding its rear feet, the other grasping a front foot and an ear. Cleve Winton strode toward the struggling hog, his face set in grim distaste. As he bent with his knife he saw Hugh, straightened in his tracks, and said, "Go right back to the house, young man."

"But, Daddy, I want to see."

Cleve bent behind the fence. "The house is the best place

for you," he replied without looking up again.

Hugh kicked disconsolately at a cob, turned and walked toward the house. As he entered the yard he heard another wild scream.

He waited for his father at the boiler, warming his hands in the steam. A slight wind played with the rising vapor, whipping it into spirals and nebulous ribbons. Through the shifting vapor he saw stretches of frost-laden pasture, and beyond, the glistening border of the woods. How good the morning was! He thrust his hands deep into the warm steam, breathed deeply of the cold air. In the child's mind the farm seemed like a world, a world shut in and bordered, but complete, nevertheless, complete and satisfying. It had depth and distance enough. Around the house there were noise and activity and teeming life, yet, beyond the woods, like a vast blue wall on the horizon, there was an inhuman solitude. Walking there in the early hours of morning, scouting his line of traps, the dark silence frightened him, and yet he loved it. There was an alien realm which did not vanish entirely with the bright coming of day.

His mother's voice calling Cleve to breakfast dispersed these thoughts and he walked toward the house behind his father. It would have been exciting to stay and watch the negroes quarter the hogs, to see their deft hands trim the great, round hams, and to speculate, meanwhile, on the quantity of sausage they would derive from the lean trimmings. But breakfast was waiting. There were no jaded appetites at breakfast. It was the official beginning of a new day and a serious matter. Rather solemn it was, too, Hugh thought, as Cleve bent his head above his plate and invoked a simple blessing.

"Our Father," he begged, "please accept our thanks for this our daily bread."

The door from the kitchen swung open and Sally Winton

appeared bearing a dish of smoking ham. Its pungent aroma filled the room. Hugh sniffed it hungrily and shoved his plate along the table toward the platter which now rested before his father. Cleve ignored him, his eyes following his wife who turned again toward the kitchen.

"Sit down, Sally," he said. "I'm hungry."

"You can't eat without biscuits," she laughed.

"Where's Aunt Mathy? Why can't she serve?"

"I've got her getting ready to take care of the meat. You know how busy she'll be today."

"Lord, yes," Cleve replied, "but I'll be busy, too, so bring the coffee back with you and let's get started."

Cleve's hunger pleased his wife. She returned with the coffee and biscuits and passed her own plate to him. Hugh watched his mother as she sipped her coffee. He could feel the pleasure it gave her, and he could feel like a sheltering arm around him her satisfaction and contentment with her household. She had a warmth and happiness that was not Cleve's. Hugh knew this without thinking, without consciously appraising them, just as he knew that ice was cold and fire was hot. He looked to his mother for love. His father was kind, but it was a kindness with little sentiment, and a strong leaven of justice.

"Did you catch any rabbits, Hugh?" his mother inquired.

"One."

"What did you do with it?" asked Cleve.

"I left it at the kitchen door."

"For Aunt Mathy to clean, I suppose?"

Hugh sought his mother's eyes. His father had warned him before about leaving rabbits for Aunt Mathy to clean, but Hugh felt that cleaning rabbits was kitchen work, woman's work, Aunt Mathy's work. His father should understand. He knew his mother did.

"Aunt Mathy can find time to do it, Cleve," she said.

"No. Hugh ought to do it."

"Aunt Mathy can clean 'em in half the time I can, Daddy."

"Makes no difference," Cleve replied, "if you catch them you ought to clean them. You enjoy trapping them, don't you?"

"Yessir."

"Well, you can't have pleasure without responsibility. You can't do just the things you want to do. For that matter I hate hog-killing. You can't raise a hog from a little shoat, feed him until you have his confidence, then cut his throat instead of giving him his breakfast and feel exactly good about it. You just can't do it."

"It's the truth," said Sally. "A little pig is just as loving as a dog, if you'll let him be. They'll come and lie under your feet like a playful puppy. I raised one from a little runt when I was a girl. I remember I cried all day when they killed it."

"Still, this ham is mighty good," Cleve laughed.

He spoke no more, finished his meal hurriedly, and went to join the negroes at the boiler.

"Hurry off to school, Hugh," said Sally Winton, rising. "I'll take care of your rabbit."

The sun had set when Hugh returned from school. Its last weak rays had lighted the path through the woods dimly, but darkness was so complete before he crossed the pasture that he was unable to see his father whom he heard in the stable-lot feeding the stock. He called to him and continued along the path toward the house.

He found his mother and Aunt Mathy working in a room of noble proportions, a great, wide room with a high, dark ceiling, beneath which there was space for several cooks to ply their art. He remembered many days when rain and storm had kept him indoors and his pent-up energy had become such an annoyance to his mother that she had allocated some remote corner of the room for the pursuit of his own activities. It had the proportions and structural strength of an engine-room, and in truth, it may be supposed that the builder planned it as such: as the engine-room of a great house, the source of power and comfort and movement for all who went into the world from the shelter of that house. The kitchen was illuminated only by the great fireplace in which several five-foot logs were crackling. The ashes from this fire crept out on a hearth built not of smooth tiles, but of slabs of stone as big as flue-caps. The hearth, as well as the face of the fireplace, glistened from an application of white clay with which Aunt Mathy polished it each morning. Resting on a bed of coals at the edge of the fire was a deep iron pot into which the old woman was pouring a pan of fat, stirring the boiling contents, meanwhile, with a long stick. Near the pot, arranged in orderly fashion along the hearth, stood a row of stone jars in which grease from the melting pot was cooling. It would be rich, white lard. From the mantel were suspended strings of red pepper and bunches of onions, and an assortment of bags whose contents were known only to the old woman. A row of cabinets and bins, large enough for a game of hide-and-seek, built into one wall, advertised their contents by bold lettering across their fronts. The words were formed in the flourishing script of another age, and beneath each label, placed there, perhaps, in a charitable recognition of illiteracy, were little squares of glass through which one could peer into the bins. Here was a large one marked "Flour," and another "Meal," and one, apparently empty, marked "Hominy."

In the center of the room, standing as if it might have grown from the floor, was an oak table of rude worklike appearance. Here Hugh's attention rested, for piled high and wide upon its bare boards rested a mound of lean cuts of pork, each destined to descend into the gaping mouth of the sausage grinder clamped to the table's edge, and to emerge a plastic material which Aunt Mathy's cunning fingers would knead into a sausage of neighborhood fame. Her proficiency brought scores of solicitations each year from people who sought her help in preparing their own meat. She was also blessed with a tongue which provided rare entertainment. Her nimble mind had become, during the course of her long life, a repository of the queer tales and the sub-rosa affairs of the community.

To his mother's summons to supper Hugh explained that he preferred to wait until the sausage had been ground and make his meal from the sample cakes Aunt Mathy would cook in a pan on the coals.

"You'll be mighty hungry by that time," she objected.

"Let me wait, please."

"All right, Son," she agreed, smiling. "But don't get in Aunt Mathy's way," she added as she left the kitchen; "and don't make a pig of yourself."

"No'm," he assured.

Taking pains not to upset any of the jars, Hugh moved to the fireplace and posted himself in the warm glow of the flames. The old woman went silently about her work, but she regarded his position with considerable skepticism. The fire was very hot and soon he began to wriggle from one position to another, too infatuated with the heat to get entirely away from the fire, and too near the flames to stand still long at a time. This went on for several minutes until one of his maneuvers knocked a tin plate from the top of a jar and sent it rattling across the hearth.

"Is you done yit?" flared the old woman, with a fine semblance of scorn. " 'Cause efen you ain't I'd better call yo mammy."

Hugh stooped to replace the plate, but her voice interrupted him.

"Dat fiahplace is ur dangus place wid all dat lard ur bilin'," as if in apology for her harshness. She watched the boy's face illuminated in the flickering light.

"Sho de spit an' image," she muttered to herself.

"Mam?"

"Jest talkin' to mysef, chile, jest talkin' to mysef, but efen you wants to know, I wus thinkin' uf yo granpappy. You favors him mo evy day, you do."

Hugh never tired of hearing her talk of his grandfather, and it was a favorite subject with her. She was devoted to the old man's memory with the unreasoning loyalty of a slave. His wildest escapades became in her account but the privileged doings of a superior person.

"Old Marse was sumpin', efen you gut him started," she said, chuckling. "He didn't take no triflin' offen nobidy, he didn't. Black or white, hit didn't make no diffunce. I remembers 'twan't long atter he come back from de war, mebbe free or foah yeah, 'long 'bout de time dat niggers wus runnin' fur de govinment and ur passle uf 'em wus gittin' kilt fur deir high-falutin ways, dat he fixed old Mose Barnett. Yassuh, he cuored old Mose uf sassin' white folks, sho. Mose had been one uf his niggers fo de war, but atter dat, he took an' set out to croppin' fur hisself. Marse Bob, he wus good to Mose, took an' giv him ur heifer fur his farm, and treated him jest like dar hadn't ever been no slavey-time ur tall. Well, one day we wus plantin' 'baccer, ur way down de road whar yo pappy is gut ur wheat patch now. I wus jest ur gal den, drappin' plants an' sassin' de men-folks. We wus awful rushed, 'cause de season wus dry an' we wus plantin' fast as we could while de groun wus wet. 'Long 'bout ten o'clock Mose, he come ridin' by de field on his mule goin' up toward de sto'. Old Marse, he seed him, an' he sed, 'Mose, tie yo mule an' help us wid dis 'baccer plantin'.'

"But Mose jest kept on ridin' ur little ways, and den he sed, 'You is crazy; I gut to plant my own 'baccer.'

"We all knowed Mose wus lyin', 'cause Marse Bob done giv' him some plants to finish plantin' wid de day 'fo. Marse Bob, he jest looked at Mose, kind uf unbelievin' like fur ur minit, den he say, 'Mose, efen you come back dis way, I'm gwine kill you.'

"He wan't foolin' neither, 'cause he went straight to de house an' gut his gun an' brung hit back to de field. 'Twan't long 'fo Mose come ridin' back, big as life, an' sho' nuff, jest like he sed, Marse Bob let him have dat gun. He stung him good, I reckon, 'cause dat mule wan't fast enough fur Mose. He gut down ofen dat mule, an' he flew, I tell you. Yassuh, he flew. We all jest laid down in de row an' laffed 'til Mose wus plum outen sight."

"Did he kill him, Aunt Mathy?" asked Hugh.

"Naw, but he sho cuored him. He skeered de lights outen dat nigger."

"I reckon he did," said Hugh.

Then they both laughed at this ridiculous memory.

Old Robert Winton had become a legendary figure among the negroes, even before he died. They had loved him and feared him. They told tall tales of his strength, and unbelievable stories of his drunken pranks. Once, they related, he had thrown a man into a well, angered because the fellow had drained the bottle from which he had offered him a drink, had picked him up bodily and dumped him down the well, shouting after him, "Drink your fill, you damned hog."

Then, his anger gone in a flash, he was the first man at the rescue of his sputtering victim. All of his passions were violent and explosive, even his pleasures were fiery, and he indulged them with the fierce abandon of a child, or of a savage.

It was he who built the house in which the family now lived, and it was to this house that he had brought his wife as a bride. Cleve had been born in the house and was no older than Hugh was now when Old Robert went away to join the Southern armies.

With his curiosity whetted by Aunt Mathy's tales, Hugh plagued his father with questions about Old Robert. But Cleve spoke of his father and his own boyhood reluctantly, even with a subdued bitterness.

"Farming," he mused, "it's all I've ever known. I was thrown headlong into it as a child. Why, your grandmother and I ran this farm when I was no larger than you."

It was true that as a child he had borne his mother's messages and commands from one end of the plantation to the other, and had seen that her orders (some of which he himself failed to understand) were carried out. There was pride in Cleve's account of how he had served her, and in spite of his bitterness over this period which had frustrated his education and bound him forever to the farm, he was proud that it was his will and work which had held the farm together even after Old Robert's return.

"I did it," he said, "but God knows whether I should have or not. Even now I believe I would have been happier if I could have studied medicine. I am not a natural farmer, and it has never satisfied me fully."

He had made a success of his occupation in spite of his disinclination for it. There had been a time when even to survive seemed a success. Before the war his father had owned a thousand acres on which most of the arable land was devoted to the cultivation of tobacco. But under the hard times which followed the war these thousand acres had become eight hundred, then six, and finally four hundred. At four hundred Cleve had held it. He could take a just pride in having retained that much, because most of the time he had been forced to put up a lone fight, and being so young he had not the necessary experience with which to withstand the sallies of older and less principled men.

There was a note of bitter accusation in the way he said, "Your Grandfather wasn't much help to me."

In later years Hugh came to understand his father's bitterness, but at the time these stories of his grandfather filled him with nothing but reverent delight.

Old Robert hadn't been much help. Indeed, he made no serious attempt to help. In his last years he drank consistently, cursed the farm roundly, swore that he would never be a patch farmer, and turned the plantation over to Cleve completely. Old Robert, swashbuckling slave-owner, never tried to reconcile himself to the changed times. His world had died at Appomattox, and he accepted the fact, not graciously, but definitely. At times he still swore against the Yankees, cursing them for a pack of ignorant vandals, but he brought no constructive intelligence to bear upon his plight.

His mind turned, instead, to the prodigal days of his youth, days of unearned plenty when the earth, it seemed, had offered up its treasures free for the taking. Life had been like a campaign then, each new day a conquest and an adventure. From the wide shade of his porch he had watched his slaves in the fields, toiling under the supervision of white overseers who carried out his orders with military precision. Although he had been educated as became a gentleman of his station, had read the law and qualified himself for practice, he had chosen, instead, to live the life of a planter, finding that his hearty spirit bore the confines of streets and offices with poor grace. Cleve's farming was hardly more than the sparse tillage of the tenant whites before the war, patch-farming, Old Robert thought. Cleve had their fear of weather, their half servile respect for the tobacco buying companies, and their lack of profane indifference to adversity. One year couldn't have ruined him (already he had begun to think of his own life in terms of the past). Watching Cleve load the wagons for market, he contrasted the spectacle with the marketing days of his youth, when they had packed the tobacco in hogsheads and rolled them to market with a mule train. This, too, had been like a campaign, for sometimes he had taken his tobacco to the Virginia warehouses, rolling it often through snow and mud for days, sleeping at night by campfires, and as apt as not finding his blankets covered with snow in the mornings. Market towns had been romantic places then. Pretty girls ran after the wealthy farmers, and prostitutes hung around the warehouses at night, like women of harbor towns waiting for ships to come in, furtively snatching a precarious living from the poorer farmers who were taking a riotous holiday from domestic restraint. In the hotels card sharps abounded, cheating each other and any stranger whom they could inveigle into play with them. Old Robert had thrown one of these through a window once, pitching his crooked cards after him. He never knew the fellow's name. It made no difference—no one had thought much about it at the time.

In those days it had been the buyers and the warehousemen who were eager to please; but now it was all changed. He had sold his tobacco; Cleve took his to be bought.

But neither his dreams nor his drinking quelled his love of action. Even after Cleve had taken full charge of the farm, the old man would be up every morning, tramping around the fields and barns before anyone else was awake. He kept a jug of whiskey in the stable and always visited it before breakfast.

In a manner quite consistent with the abrupt and hazardous incidents of his life he met his death. One morning he came into the dark barnyard and stumbled against a young bull. For some reason the animal charged him. Still very strong for his years, he seized the bull by its horns and literally twisted him to the ground. Each time the animal tried to regain its feet he forced it back to the ground bellowing with baffled rage. The negroes found him, holding the bull down, and cursing a blue streak. They got him out of the lot safely, but the bull remembered his encounter with the old man and displayed viciousness whenever he came near. Cleve tried to persuade him to give up his morning visits to the barnyard, pointing out the danger, but Old Robert only looked at him in amazement and exclaimed, "What, let a damned cow keep me away from my liquor!"

A few mornings later one of the negroes found him, a bloody, gored mass, clutching in his cold hand the ring which he had torn from the animal's nose.

There was something vaguely shameful in Cleve's account of Old Robert, but Aunt Mathy's stories restored him to Hugh clean and strong again. He was still alive because she loved him and remembered. She spoke of the deaths of those who had gone before her, not as the ends of their lives, but as incidents in the greater, continuous life of the farm. She had no fear of death as a termination, and no conception of its terrible muteness.

"So de bull, he kilt Marse Bob," she said, "and Marse Cleve, he run de farm den."

There was the benign indifference of a god in her dismissal of the dead, an attitude, neither kind nor cruel, which one might attribute to a god, who, surveying humanity from a great distance, could, conceivably, mistake it for a sort of vegetation, constantly renewing itself, sending out new sprouts in the spring, scattering its seeds to the winds of storm, and perpetually flaunting a new leaf in the face of the sun.

Old Robert's wife had been Eunice Williams before her marriage, and everyone said that Cleve Winton was his mother's child. Aunt Mathy remembered her, but it was from Cleve, Cleve who did not like to talk of the old days, that Hugh learned of his grandmother.

She was a small woman, Cleve said, quiet and resolute. She had an old trunk filled with scented dresses, a painted fan, a gold watch which she never wore, and a little cow-bell that gave a lonely, silvery peal. All these things she kept in the trunk as though they did not really belong to her any more.

Her family had lived in a part of the country which was now a wilderness, Cleve said. In the days before the Revolutionary war, and for a long time thereafter, the section from which she sprang had been the domain of the great families of the county and their enormous colonial houses, a land of huge, primitive plantations, stretching for verdant miles along the circuitous valley of the Sligo river. The first settlers had come into this country, following the natural path of the river, and for years the river had been their only means of transportation. Small, flat-bottomed boats, loaded with provisions, were poled along its route far toward its inland source. Tobacco and grain were shipped to harbor in this fashion long before there were roads from the interior to the sea. When the roads came, this country, half wilderness even then, had rapidly returned to its original state. The hills and narrow valleys along the river were rich, but hard to cultivate, and the younger people sought the more tractable land that was laid open by the new roads.

Small towns sprang up away from the river, and people herded in them and around them. Plantation homes appeared along the roads connecting these villages, and the sons and daughters of the old river families became the masters and mistresses of these new homes. The river fields became swamps, seemingly overnight; the forest enveloped the lowland houses like a monstrous green octopus, reaching out tentacles of ivy and honeysuckle to reclaim its own. Here and there along the river some planter had built a mansion, high on a bluff. These elevations had suffered from erosion until they were bare, ugly and red, seamed from top to bottom with ragged gullies, along which scraggy cedars and pines sent their roots down to starve in clay. Upon these withering hills the ruins stood like enchanted guardians of a lost land, lifting their proud old heads above the surrounding waste.

From the porch of their house Cleve pointed out to Hugh, far on the horizon, the blue outline of this region, spread like a hazy veil at the juncture of earth and sky. Eunice had lived there before her marriage, but after Cleve's birth she never returned, for her family had scattered, the old house had been deserted, and for the first time she had felt in her son some tie to this new country. Her character, however, retained much of the river's silence and somber isolation. Cleve remembered how she used to sit of a summer afternoon with her needle-work and gaze at the distant fringe of blue with the intense detachment of a dream. She had a peculiar trick of talking to one, a habit which irritated her husband to the point of profanity, of talking calmly and distinctly, without apparently noting one's presence. She used to speak to Cleve about simple, childish matters in this fashion. "Run and wash your hands, Cleve," she would say, her eyes fixed in distant meditation as if she had not observed him at all, not to mention the condition of his hands. Although it seldom became articulate, there had been a deep affection between them; Eunice was not a demonstrative woman. Indeed, Cleve thought it strange that Robert Winton should have loved her; they had so little in common. Her aloofness, her imperturbability, the unpretentious way in which she went about every matter of living enraged her husband by their very inoffensiveness. His brusque, direct life was essentially a matter of momentary experiences, of quick, devouring pleasures, and gunpowder rages. There was no calmness in him. He could not understand it and he resented it in others. Cleve, on the contrary, demonstrated many of his mother's traits while very young. Even as a child he had felt that he and his mother were united in a strange, tacit alliance against his father. This never came to open conflict, but the feeling remained buried in his heart. He was a little ashamed of it. Old Robert sensed it at times. Once he had said to his wife, "Eunice, you and Cleve, with your damned patience, make me feel that there is a conspiracy against me in my own house."

She died soon after her husband returned from the war, suddenly, and as unpretentiously as she had lived, rather like a stranger slipping unobtrusively from a company which she had found cold and alien. Cleve never understood his father's wild grief, for he had not credited him with a strong love for her. Had Robert Winton talked of such matters, he could have explained that with death she left him an unsolved riddle, a love which had never reached understanding, a surging, baffled emotion which had battled unvictoriously against her serene soul.

Cleve had not married until after his fortieth year, long after Old Robert's death. Hugh remembered his mother from his childhood as a strong, optimistic, happy woman, younger than his father, and by nature an excellent counter for his sobriety. These were his parents, whom he loved in the thoughtless way of a child, but it was to Old Robert, his grandfather whom he had never known, that all the hero worship in his heart went, to Old Robert who stalked through his dreams clothed in the brazen grandeur with which Aunt Mathy's tales had endowed him. Indeed, what he knew of his family, gleaned as it was, piece by piece, from the old woman's rambling tales, constituted a fabulous kind of history, whose figures moved against a landscape with which he was familiar, but against a landscape, nevertheless, which basked in the twilight of a forgotten day, dim and splendid.

The old woman had started to tell him of his father's wedding day, but before she finished she was talking about Old Robert again.

"Marse Bob wus ur smart un," she began; "hit didn't take no long moufin' fur him to say his say, an' when he sed hit, you knowed whut he wus talkin' 'bout. I remembers whut he tole old Mose Barnett, dat yeah de crops wus drownded. 'Twus long fo you pappy married Miss Sally, an' Lawd, hit rained frum de fust uf July to de last uf August. 'Baccer jest rotted in de field; 'twan't no use to think uf cuttin' hit ur tall. De wagons would uf miahed up to de couplin' poles eben efen de trash had uf been wuth cuttin'.' 'Twus all rotten, eby bit. Mose, he didn't have nothin' but ur pore mule an' ur passel uf raggedy chullun. He wus sho' wearied uf farmin' fur hisself, an' he took an' come up heah one day jest 'fo Christmus an' ast ole Marse efen he couldn't give him some work to do. Dis wus way atter he done shot him dat time.

"Marse he say, 'Mose, you kin move yo' crowd up heah in one uf my cabins, an' cut flue-wood fur me dis winner. I'll see dat you gits rations an' fiah wood.'

"Money wus so scace dem days, dat efen anybidy had ur piece dey wus scaid to show hit. Jest de same, Mose 'lowed, 'Looks like ur free man oughter have some wages.'

"No sooner 'an he gut de words outen his mouf, Old Marse say, 'Mose, you ain't free, you is hongry.'

"Mose knowed whut he wus talkin' 'bout, too, 'cause fo
night he done took an' moved all dem chullun up heah an'
started cuttin' dat wood."

2

Old Robert's virility was extended not only through
Aunt Mathy's memory; many of the customs of the farm
which had come down unchanged from his time gave him a
kind of monumental existence. Hugh saw in his father's
dealings with the hands the same humor and pathos which
colored Aunt Mathy's tales, and many of these little dramas
were enacted in the very spot where Old Robert had once
reigned—a small office built in the yard. Here the hand of
his grandfather was still heavy. He had built the office when
he built his home. Its furniture consisted of pieces discarded
from the house, an old secretary standing higher than a
man's head still holding his books and musty letters, a high
straight-backed chair bottomed with oak strippings (a rainy
day's work of some dark fingers now long dust), and in one
corner an old cavalry sword frozen in its scabbard with the
rust of half a century.

It was Saturday and Hugh had just built a roaring fire to
warm the office for Cleve's weekly interviews with the
negroes and he stood before it now watching his father who
was checking a cropper's account. Cleve closed the ledger
and sighed wearily.

"It takes the strength of Samson and the patience of Job
to keep these croppers from running themselves into debt,"
he said. "And running me in as well," he amended.

Cleve had, in addition to a wage hand who worked about
the house as well as in the fields, four families living on his
land. These were croppers who worked not for wages, but

for half the proceeds of the crop. Many of this class moved from farm to farm, making new bargains each year, taking with them to their new homes, as the accumulated capital of their previous labor, a few cheap articles of furniture, a stove, a dresser with the glass cracked, perhaps, and several cane-bottomed chairs. Other than these they brought minds familiar with the routine of tobacco growing, and hands able and willing to work. Knowledge that required supervision, and hands that required direction were their only assets. Their food and clothing for the year were provided by a local store with which Cleve carried an account. He indorsed this credit, of course. In addition to assuming this risk he provided mules and implements to till the soil. He provided the house in which they lived. In the fall when their tobacco was sold he received half of the selling price. In those years when poor prices and poor crops prevented the negroes paying their accounts, he paid the difference himself. Sometimes it was possible to reclaim this money if the following year were profitable. Often it was regarded, not as a debt, but as a tribute to an economic system under which the worker's liability was determined by the forces of nature and circumstance. Cleve knew that the credit which he supplied his croppers was virtually a gambling stake, made in the hope of favorable seasons and fair prices.

"Oh well, it's all in a year's work," Cleve grunted as he locked the ledger in a drawer.

His weariness and complaint did not reach Hugh, whose body was warm and comfortable before the fire, and whose thoughts were of a new rabbit trap he planned to place that afternoon. He knew exactly where it should go. He had seen the rabbit's path that morning where it crossed an old rail fence.

Reality came to the office at this moment in the form of a knock at the door. Hugh opened it and saw a negro man of middle age whom he did not know. The negro scraped his feet rigorously on the doorstep and entered, hat in hand.

"Mawnin' Cap'n," he said, as Cleve turned toward him.

"Good morning, Uncle," replied Cleve.

Hugh judged his father did not know him either. The negro edged around to the fireplace and thrust his bare hands into the blaze, holding them there until it seemed they must have been blistered, but he withdrew them apparently unharmed. Then he took his hat which until this moment he had held under his arm and laid it by the door, as if it were an impediment to whatever business had brought him there.

"Cap'n," he said at length, "I wants to talk ur little bizness wid you."

"What's your name?"

"I'm Lige Johnson. I been workin' down on de river, me an' my crowd. Been down in dem Sligo bottoms 'till tiahed uf 'em, plum wone out wid scratchin' dem hills, I is. So las' fall I started lookin' roun', an' nachally I done hyead whut ur good farm dis heah is, an' dat you is ur good man to work fur, so I 'lowed I'd come up heah an' see 'bout ur bargain wid you. Is you needin' any mo help?"

"That all depends," Cleve answered. "It's true, I'm planning to take on another cropper. How big is your force?"

"Well, lemme see now. Dar's me an' de ole 'oman, but she ain't much good in de field on account uf ur misery in her back, an' I gut three boys an' ur gal."

"Boys grown?"

"Yassuh, two uf 'em is, de udder, he's just ur chap, 'bout de size uf dis little genlmun," he replied, indicating Hugh.

"A right good force," Cleve reflected, "but why do you want to move?"

"Well, suh, you see, I been rentin' ur farm frum Mr. Dannel Long fur 'bout five yeah, an' de fust yeah de crops wus drownded, an' hit done took me de rest uf de time to git outen debt on dat yeah, an' las' yeah one uf my mules up and died, an' I don't like dat country nohow. De hootin' owls comes right up and roostes wid de chickens down dar."

"So you stayed until you were out of debt," commented Cleve.

"Yassuh, I paid outen debt, but looks like nobidy kin git urhead uf Mr. Long. I ain't so sharp at figgin', nohow, an' I'd jes like to be rid uf de 'sponsibility uf rentin'."

"Will it take much to run you?"

"Nawsuh, Cap'n, 'twon't take much. I's gut plenty corn to do me, an' ur big barrel uf 'lasses, an' I raised free hogs. I'll need ur little wheat flour now an' den, an' ur few close. Dat'll be 'bout all, I 'spect."

"Well, Lige," said Cleve, "I believe I can give you a home, but I can't promise until I make some investigations. Come back next Saturday and I'll let you know."

"I'll be heah, Cap'n, I'll sho be heah," cried the negro, picking up his hat, "an' thank you, suh."

Cleve resumed his work, and Hugh threw another stick of wood on the fire, thinking to himself that this was a likable old negro, and hoping that Cleve would make a bargain with him.

Hugh had known most of the farm negroes as long as he had known his parents; they were, indeed, like a part of the family, some of them having lived there all of their lives. These people represented the best among the local colored people, for untouched by the disorder attendant upon the life of the transient cropper they had developed a strength of character and industry which was as rugged as the soil on which they lived. They loved the farm. They had a vague sense of possession. The land had meaning beyond that of sustenance; it was home. Their white folks were not masters, but protectors, a bulwark against the years of famine, and a tower of strength between them and the law.

Cleve's investigation reflected credit on Lige, and when the negro came for his answer the following Saturday, he was told to get ready to move. Exactly a week later, Cleve sent his wagon to bring the new tenant and his family to the farm. As Hugh was free from school that day, he was allowed to accompany the driver. This was his first trip into the heart of the river country, but he had heard enough about it to make him regard going there as something of an adventure, and no traveler journeying through a foreign land ever had his eyes more open for strange sights than Hugh, perched by the side of the stolid driver on the long rumbling wagon. The borders of the farm really touched on the woods which ran in an unbroken growth to the river's course, and they were soon out of sight of the house, picking their way slowly along the rocky road which led deeper into the forest. What arable land there was in this country lay near the river, plantations which the first settlers had cleared, and on which they and their descendants had lived while that region prospered. Their desertion of the valley had not been one of expansion, but rather, one of abrupt departure; so Hugh now saw on both sides of the road pines whose roots had never known the exploring point of a plow, giant oaks and hickories, older than the road at their feet, and here and there, a rocky knoll where only broom sedge grew.

They passed through several miles of this virgin growth before any signs of habitation appeared. At one or two places narrow roads, hardly more than paths, rambled off through the trees, and presently a sharp turn in the road brought into view the first open field for miles, a field whose rows of corn stubble led to the very door of a rickety old house. Hugh saw no outbuildings at all, but this did not appear so strange when he was able to view the place from another angle, for it became evident that the one structure served as both house and barn. From the paneless windows of the stone cellar, mules and cows stuck out their contemplative heads. Several little blacks sprawled in the sunlight on the wide porch, beside them two lean, black hounds. Along the tumble-down railing of the porch some sets of plow-gear were hanging, left there to rot at the end of the summer's work.

They found Lige and his family awaiting them eagerly. In fact, his youngest boy who was, as Lige had said, about Hugh's size, was waiting for the wagon at some distance from the house. He seemed undetermined, when they rolled into sight, whether to fly home and announce their coming or to board the wagon and accompany them. Hugh settled his quandary by inviting him to ride.

"What's your name, boy?" he demanded.

His passenger settled himself securely between two of the upright standards before answering.

"My name's David," he replied, "but dey jest calls me Dave."

"Well, Dave, do you want to move?"

"Yassuh, I likes to trabel. I went to Granville oncet. I knows whar yo place is."

"It sure is different from these woods," Hugh stated critically. He felt important, like a visitor from another world.

"Dat's whut Pap says. Hit sho is diffunt he says. He don't take to dis country."

Dave dismounted with this observation and disappeared into the cabin. Lige and his two grown sons set about loading the wagon with furniture which they had already stacked in the yard. His wife and daughter busied themselves with various bundles and bags which they thrust in between the pieces of furniture. All of their possessions were loaded in less than half an hour.

The last thing they brought from the house was a grandfather. He hobbled toward the wagon bending upon a venerable, crooked cane. Although his progress was slow, and evidently accomplished with some pain, none of his relatives offered to help him. He hobbled along, his woolly gray head bobbing up and down with each step. Behind him, at a respectful distance, walked his two oldest grandsons.

"Dat's Granpap," Dave explained.

"Why don't they help the old man along?" Hugh asked.

" 'Cause he won't 'low hit," was Dave's obscure explanation.

"Won't allow it?"

"Naw. He's sumpin'."

"Huh?"

"He's sumpin', he is. He's ur hunnerd yeah ole," Dave added proudly.

The old man reached the wagon and with the help of one hand he hoisted a foot to the brake shoe, and then grasping a standard, he undertook to pull himself aboard. Twice he failed. His grandchildren stood behind him, ready to catch him if he fell, but not daring to offer any aid. Hugh attempted to ease his ascent by a timorous hand at his ragged elbow, but the old man shoved him away.

"I'll make hit, chile," he said, not unrespectfully.

He paused before trying again, and turned his dim eyes upon Hugh. They were like two black sloes beneath a film of cream and coffee. They took in Hugh's bewilderment.

"I don't need your help, chile," quavered the owner of the dim eyes, "I don't need nobidy's help. I's gut wooden eyebrows and chain guts an' I don't need nobidy's help."

Having thrown this light on the source of his ancient prowess, the old negro essayed the wagon frame again, and this time he managed to clamber aboard.

"See dar!" he exclaimed, triumphantly.

"Yes sir," said Hugh, "I see."

" 'Tain't nothin' wrong wid me 'ceptin' my eyes," stated Granpap, "but dey bofers me right smart, dey do."

"Yes, sir," was all that Hugh could say.

"I hurt 'em back in de war," the old man explained, "back in de Cibel War, dat wus. I uster put gunpowder in 'em to keep me frum sleepin' when de old marse left me on guard, an' dat didn't do 'em no good. Hit makes 'em hurt now. But dat's all dat's wrong wid me," he added with a toothless cackle.

"Yes, sir," said Hugh for the third time in honest and amazed admiration.

"Evybidy ready?" yelled Lige. "Whar's Dave?"

Dave appeared at this moment from the edge of the thicket behind the cabin, tugging at a rope, on the end of which hung a recalcitrant hound, which, he explained, had been deterred by a last-minute engagement with a rabbit. He tied the dog to the rear of the wagon frame, found a berth for himself among the cluttered family belongings, and the wagon creaked up the road.

The rough wagon-track climbed from the valley of the Sligo here, and as they mounted Hugh's eyes took in the desolate stretches through which they passed. The long sloping meadows between the broken red hills seemed alive with a creeping silence. The phantom of a memory and a race shadowed this region. Even the midday sunlight seemed thin and retreating, and Hugh could see that night would fall quickly here. The country had a kind of beauty when viewed from the high distance of his home, but here its beauty seemed the fixed beauty of death, its peace the terrible languor of stagnation. It was, in reality, a desert, a great green desert, which threw a deceiving blue mirage on the edge of his world.

Hugh stayed with the wagon until they reached the cabin where Lige and his family would live. He watched the old grandfather lower himself to the ground. Dave pulled a chair from the wagon and placed it for the old man, who sat in it until the others had carried the furniture into the cabin and started a fire. When the chimney was flying a pennant of smoke he raised himself on his stick and began his slow march toward his new home.

The sun was low in the sky and Hugh was hungry. He deserted Dave and raced across the fields toward his house.

3

During the winter months the work on the farm was too heavy for a child's help, so Dave was free to play with Hugh much of the time. But often their play was only an imitation of their elders' work. Hugh had a small ax which his father had brought him from Granville, and Dave had an old one which Lige had given him. Armed with these they trudged along behind Cleve and Lige as they walked toward a growth of pines which Cleve had selected for his year's supply of flue-wood.

This was really the first step in making a tobacco crop, this preparation of a huge store of wood for the curing barns. Hugh remembered these "cutting frolics" from other years. In the distance he could see several hands from neighboring farms waiting at the edge of the woods. Neighbors piled in and helped each other cut wood, just as they helped raise each others' barns. But this was all new to Dave, who had lived in the isolation of Sligo. Hugh had told him how the negro axmen vied with each other on the bodies of the felled trees. He understood about this.

"Cuttin' de butt," he exclaimed. "Pap kin cut hit fur my brudders."

"If he can cut it for some of those men waiting there, he's plum' good," said Hugh.

"I bet he kin," said Dave.

Lige stopped and looked at the two boys.

"Shet yo mouf, Dave," he ordered; "you talks too much."

Dave grinned at Hugh.

"You watch Pap," he whispered.

The waiting men were busy whetting their axes and bragging about their skill. A giant negro who bore the name of Sugarfoot issued a broadside challenge.

"I cuts de butt fur eny man heah," he laughed, "den seconds fur de next best."

"You sho b'lieves in wukkin' fur yo sumpin' t' eat," jibed one of the group.

"I'se eatin' white folks' rations dis night," he rejoined.

Lige took no part in their banter. Most of them were strangers to him, and he whetted his ax silently.

Sugarfoot watched him derisively.

"Whut dat thing you whettin' so, nigger?" he demanded with a swagger.

Lige's black face betrayed no emotion. He whetted his ax.

The other negroes were not laughing now. They felt a challenge with none of the good humor which had stirred them a moment before. Their watchful silence prodded Sugarfoot.

"I say, nigger, whut is dat thing you is whettin' so?" he persisted.

"Hit's ur ax, fool," Lige answered, "jest ur ax."

Cleve's voice silenced them.

"Let's get going boys. Hugh, you and Dave get back out of the way."

The negroes moved into the woods in pairs and fell on the trees, one on each side, each cutting toward the heart. Sugarfoot went with Lige.

"Soon as dis tree falls, I'm gwine show you who's a fool," he taunted.

Hugh and Dave waited impatiently for the tree to fall. Dave was nervous.

"Dat Sugarfoot is sho ur big un," he said.

Soon the great pine leaned against the sky, then came crashing to earth.

"Now jump on dat butt," Lige cried to Sugarfoot and took his own position about twenty feet above his opponent.

Sugarfoot leaped on the trunk, his ax poised above his head. Lige mounted the trunk and swung his ax aloft.

"Ready," yelled Cleve, and their axes sank into the pine together.

Sugarfoot cut like a demon. His blows almost buried the ax from sight, and they fell with the precision of a machine. But Lige struck blow for blow. At the heart they both whirled like dancers and tackled the other side of the trunk. Again their axes rang like bells, and as they bit into the hard heart of the pine the blows sounded like iron beating iron.

"Come on, Pap!" yelled Dave, unable to contain himself.

Somehow Lige managed to increase the tempo of his strokes and his last blow severed the log while Sugarfoot's ax was still in the air descending for the stroke which finished his cut.

The others acclaimed Lige with a shout in which Sugarfoot joined. He and Lige cut together for the rest of the afternoon.

Before the wood they cut that day had been mauled, Cleve cleared a space of brush and roots, fertilized it, and sowed tobacco seed there. He covered the bed with canvas to protect the young plants from cold and insects and left it secure in his mind that when his fields were ready for the plants in May, nature would have the plants ready in the bed.

In March and April the fields were prepared for the resetting of the plants, furrowed and refurrowed, then laid off in long beautiful rows, each folding a powerful vein of fertilizer in its bosom. Planting was a precarious time. The soil had to be wet enough to nourish the tender plants making their bow before the late winds of spring. Morning cold and midday heat were their enemies; many would not survive. Cleve wanted to plant his entire crop during May, but a scarcity of rain prevented this. Finally it became necessary to pour a dipper of water into each hill destined to support a plant, and this tedious business prolonged the completion of planting far into June.

Hugh and Dave could help in this work, and they could help in the battle against grass and weeds which tried to choke out the less virile tobacco plants. All natural forces are the enemies of tobacco. Rain and sun are its life; rain and sun are its death. Too much or too little, one way or the other, and it is finished. It grows rapidly and ripens quickly, and develops at no time during its life a strength of fiber sufficient to withstand any caprice of nature. Winds blow death and destruction among it. Hail is a plague. Insects and huge, green worms assail it in swarms, as if directed by some malevolent Moses.

In August the tobacco had ripened. The plants were then shoulder high, had spread their broad leaves from row to row . . . the fields were like billowy green-and-yellow carpets. Harvest was a period of incessant vigil. The ripe tobacco would soon begin to rot. Cleve inspected the fields daily now, because the plants should be cut when the first full tint of gold had spread through the topmost leaves.

Here again was work which Hugh and Dave could do. Cleve called Hugh some mornings as early as four. Autumn was already in the air and he shivered by the stove while Aunt Mathy cooked breakfast so they could beat the sun to the fields. There the plants drenched him with dew which

made a sopping blanket of his overalls and stung his bare
ankles like ice. It was best to cut the plants in the cool of the
morning in order that the sun might wilt their brittle
strength before they were transported to the barns.

Hugh loved the tobacco curing season. The fires were
kept burning day and night, and the nights were so cool
now that the heat from the flues was very pleasant. He could
lie on the ground before the mouth of the flue and look for
twenty feet down the flaming interior. The rock walls were
red hot. Little poisonous tongues of flame licked them with
darting, serpentine speed. Hell, and brimstone, and the torture of the damned were only twenty feet away. God became too real and watchful when Hugh looked into this
man-made inferno. It was much better to lie on a cot and
watch the blue smoke pour from the flue chimney, to watch
it curl upward, scatter in dim spirals, and vanish, finally, in
the wide high sky.

Aunt Mathy, too, enjoyed these summer nights around
the barns. All the negroes congregated there after the day's
work was done, to bask against the warm foundation walls,
or sprawl on a dirty quilt before the mouth of the flue,
where they sang hymns or bawdy ballads with equal fervor.
One night Aunt Mathy started a song in which all the negroes joined:

> *"Ole Gen'al Lee surrendered,*
> *Under de apple tree.*
> *Hit bust de band of slavery*
> *An' sot de niggers free."*

"Yas," she cried when their voices had died down, "free
to starve, and git kilt fur not doin' hit wid no politeness!
Ole Mose wus de freest nigger I eber seed 'till he gut
hongry, den he would crawl on his empty black belly, jest
like ur snake."

And then she launched into a history of Mose and his children, telling how he had tried to make a preacher of his oldest boy, Amos, how by prayers and threats he had prevailed upon him to learn to read and write.

"But hit didn't do Amos no good," she exclaimed. "Amos wan't bawned no scholar, an' he wan't bawned no preacher. I neber will fergit," directing her remarks to Hugh, "de time yo granpappy left Amos to look atter de barns, endurin' de time he went to de house fur to git hisself ur dram. Amos wus ur big boy den, 'bout twelbe yeah ole, I reckon, an' he wus stayin' at de barns fur to help Ole Marse pull de wood to de flues.

"Ole Marse say, 'Amos, kin you read?'

"An' Amos, he 'low, kinder proud like, 'Yassuh.'

"Den Ole Marse go in de barn and show de thermomety to Amos an' tole him to read hit, an' sho 'nuff, Amos read hit. Den he make him read hit backards to see efen he wan't foolin'. Atter he wus satisfied dat Amos knowed whut de thermomety wus fur, he tole him to keep de heat at two hunnerd 'grees, to put in some wood efen hit gut 'low dat, an' to pull out some efen hit gut 'bove dat.

"When he come back he look in de barn fust thing, an' say, 'Amos, hit feel mighty hot in dar to me.'

"An' Amos say, 'Yassuh, dat whut I thought, an' I look at de thermomety, an' hit say two hunnerd an' thuty, so I brung hit out doahs an' let hit come down to two hunnerd, like you said.'

"Ole Marse picked up a cheer an' started to kill Amos den an' dar, but he gut tickled an' started laffin', an' he laffed so long dat Amos took scaid an' run home."

The negroes rolled with mirth when Aunt Mathy told this tale. Hugh felt sorry for Amos. He could picture his grandfather laughing at the little negro, and he could see him running home in bewildered fright.

One afternoon during the rush of harvest, a negro fell in the fields and cut himself badly with his tobacco knife. Cleve had to take him to Granville to have the wound sewn and Hugh was left in charge of the barns.

"Just keep the heat in all of 'em where it is," Cleve instructed him. "I'll be back as soon as possible."

"Can Dave stay with me?" Hugh asked.

"Yes, run to the field and get him," Cleve answered; "you'll need him to help you pull the wood to the flues."

Dave left the field laughing at his older brothers sweating under the August sun. "Don't y'all fergit to call me to supper," he said; "I'm lible to drap off to sleep up dar under dem shady trees." With this taunt he turned and raced across the fields toward the barns with Hugh.

There was little for them to do. Cleve had been firing only three curings, and under these steady fires were burning. A fresh stick in the flues every half hour held the heat where it stood. Nevertheless, Hugh, burdened with a sense of responsibility, read the thermometers every few minutes. From one of the barns in which a curing hung ordering, Dave brought several golden leaves.

"Kin you roll ur segar?" he asked Hugh.

"I don't know. Can you?"

"Tain't nothin' to hit," said Dave loftily; "you jest rolls 'em an' licks 'em, den you smokes 'em."

"I can't smoke."

"How you know you can't?" his tempter demanded. "Is you eber tried?"

"Naw."

"Me neither, but I bet I kin."

"I can if you can," said Hugh, sensing a dare.

"Heah den, roll one fur yosef."

They sat down before the flue and rolled the leaves into clumsy cigars and licked the soft, gummy edges fast.

"Dat's a sho' 'nuff segar," said Dave proudly.

"Now let's see you light it," Hugh said.

Dave hesitated. Hugh thrust a pine sliver into the flue and applied the blaze to his cigar, then held the burning stick before Dave's nose. Dave stuck his cigar in his mouth and slowly sucked against the flame.

The sharp fumes of the raw tobacco burned Hugh's nostrils and throat, bringing tears to his eyes. He choked a cough and looked at Dave. Dave casually blew a cloud of thin blue smoke. Encouraged, Hugh took a gentle draw, and blew forth a cloud of his own.

Suddenly, and invisibly, as the force of a wind, a giant hand lifted him. He was flying now above the barns, above the tall pines. He became larger and larger, and a small world swam away from him. For a moment he noticed that Dave was flying with him, but strangely Dave had brought the flaming flue of the barn along. It floated, a tunnel of flame in the air, beside them. Higher and higher they rose. Just when it seemed that there could be no end to his flight, Hugh crashed before the mouth of the flue and the great, solid earth rocked him at its feet. Dave was still with him, prostrate, and ashy in color.

4

Summer was now over and the tobacco fields were bleak acres of stubble and brown grass. Hugh left for school each morning carrying his lunch in a small tin bucket. Beyond the woods he joined Lonnie and Helen Galloway, children of Henry Galloway, who owned the adjoining farm. Their attendance was irregular, because old Henry kept them at home whenever he needed them. Lonnie was a big, husky boy, inordinately proud of his young strength and inclined

to be a bully. A certain sectional patriotism shielded Hugh
from his impositions. Indeed, Hugh courted his favor subtly,
since small boys fared badly in the rough-and-tumble play
of the schoolyard, unless they exercised the wisdom to ally
themselves with some larger group or individual. Three
miles is a long distance in the country, quite far enough to
breed tribal feeling. Hugh's companionship with Lonnie
really amounted to no more than a feeling of clanship, for
the boy was uncouth in both manner and heart. Helen was
a creature of far greater delicacy than her brother, and
unlike either of the boys, genuinely concerned with her
studies.

The schoolhouse was a single large room heated by an
iron stove, and flanked by a long hall which was used as a
cloakroom. The first person to get there in the morning had
to build a fire in the stove. This task had fallen to Hugh
many times, and on those days when Lonnie and Helen failed
to accompany him, it was one for which he had little liking,
for the empty schoolhouse was a ghostly place. Winds
howled through the loft, beginning in a low mournful
plaint and rising to a shrill scream which sent chills up and
down his spine. It was frightful. Aunt Mathy's ghosts stalked
in his mind, fearful figures swathed in white, rattling unseen
bones beneath the folds of their garments. Aunt Mathy had
seen scores of ghosts. Every violent death in the community
had produced one. They had a strange clannishness. All
appeared in the spotless robes of another world, but they
retained their human bones, dry, bloodless bones which
creaked when they moved. Some carried trailing chains.
These usually frequented deserted houses. The great houses
along the Sligo, those with the deep stone cellars, were their
particular province. Woe to the mortal who tarried there
after dark. Some inhabited the roads, never wandering far
from the spot where, as mortals, they had met death. Travel-

ers had seen them at night. They emerged from the woods emitting hair-raising groans, reminiscent of their painful death struggle after some runaway wreck in which a terrified horse had pitched them headlong into eternity. Moving like mist, they passed through fences and bars, neither under nor over, but straight through, as if a fence were only the unsubstantial stuff of a dream. Some ghosts, Aunt Mathy said, could be laid with silver bullets. Hugh reflected that he had never seen a silver bullet.

Miss Alice, a lonely and embittered old lady, conducted the school. Her family had once owned one of the Sligo plantations. She had taken the children to the ruins one autumn afternoon, and they had all gone in holiday spirit, but it turned out to be a pretty sorry picnic. Miss Alice had spent most of the afternoon crying softly. The place was a wretched sight. The woodwork of the house had been burned away, leaving ragged brick walls over which vines had grown in tangled masses. Boxwood mingled its odor with that of cedar and pine, and far down toward the river stretched a winding path of moss-covered stones which now bore no footprints.

Like most of the children, Hugh found the confining hours of school irksome, and on cloudy days his eyes searched the dull sky for some scurrying snowflake, heralding a coming storm, for the weather often gave them a week's holiday. Each flake flying diagonally across the window was a mounting hope. Soon a transformed world spread toward the contracted horizon, an almost forgotten world of billowy, white beauty. Home seemed more distant, and very dear. His mother would be watching for him anxiously. A prodigal supper would be steaming hot, bowls of fiery sausage floating in red gravy, hot, brown biscuits that crumbled at the touch, and pones of golden cornbread, bearing within themselves the heat necessary to send butter melting to their very crusts.

Fried apples dusted with cinnamon, and generous rashers of crisp bacon were waiting for him. Time moved too slowly.

5

Hugh returned home one afternoon and found his father loading the wagons with tobacco which had been prepared for market. For several days the negroes had been stripping it steadily. He had watched them in the evenings when they brought the bright cured stalks from the pack-barn and placed them in a cellar where the moisture would make them pliable overnight and ready to be stripped in the morning. The leaves had been pulled from the stalks, graded and tied in bundles, tied with one of their own number, as strong and as soft as silk. An acre of field tobacco, diminishing in the course of its handling, became in the end a wagon-load of finished, marketable material, a wagon-load of heart-rending effort, a year of diligent care. Here were sweat and fire, labor and art, nature and skill, going to market. The bundles of stripped tobacco had been strung on sticks and packed down to prevent the escape of moisture, for moisture meant weight. The negroes bore these sticks to the side of the wagon and passed them to Cleve who stood in the wagon-bed. Reaching over the side he pulled as many bundles as he could hold in his two hands from the stick. These he arranged in the bottom of the bed until it was covered. One of the men then passed him a bucket of water from which he sprinkled the layer of bundles, using a cedar bough as a brush. Layer after layer was treated in this fashion until the bed was filled. Hugh could not fail to observe the satisfaction on Cleve's face as he packed these fat bundles into place. It was the last thing they would do for it on the farm. When, at length, he drew a canvas cover over the load, and sprinkled it, too, with the cedar bough, he was through with that tobacco forever. It was rather like seeing a ship safe in harbor after a voyage fraught with perils, for it meant the end of fearing storms, and blight, and fire. It was ready for market.

Although Hugh had been to Granville many times with Cleve, he had never seen a tobacco sale. The sight of the loaded wagons ready for the morrow's trip excited his imagination, and at the supper table he asked eagerly if he might go.

"And lose a day from school?" asked Cleve.

"What's one day, Daddy?" Hugh answered. "Lonnie Galloway misses a week sometimes."

"Well, you aren't a Galloway," was Cleve's flat reply.

"But Daddy, Miss Alice says you don't learn everything from books. I've never seen 'em sell tobacco."

"I think you ought to take him, Cleve," his mother said. "It would be educational."

"All right," Cleve laughed, "he can't get too much education."

In the morning Hugh heard the wagons rumbling across the yard long before he got out of bed. Later, after they had eaten breakfast, he and Cleve followed in the buggy. There had been rain on the preceding day, rain followed by a sudden cold, and now the ruts in the road were covered with ice. At places the ice had been broken by the wagons, but most of it was still unbroken although the hard rims had marked it all with a powdery track. Bitter, clear cold nipped Hugh's ears and nose. Clouds of vapor rose from the trotting horse, and steam from his nostrils, like the pictures of fire-breathing dragons. On by the church they went, and around a curve where the briar-grown cemetery wall shut in Old Robert, waiting in unwilling peace for Judgment Day. Now pines crept up to the roadway, their branches forming a green arch above it, through which shafts of sun-

light fell upon them as they passed. Here the bleached,
brown rows of a corn field curved down to meet them.
Summer rains had left a neat little delta of white sand at
the mouth of each. High on a hill a lone persimmon tree
stretched its gaunt arms like a scarecrow.

Granville lay fully ten miles from the farm. In the beginning it had been only a few scattered houses gathered
around two country stores, facing each other diagonally at
a cross-roads, but with the exodus from the river country,
in the early days of Old Robert, Granville had taken on new
life. A county courthouse appeared, a rambling, mud-
tracked abode for justice. A church and a saloon had followed, and by the time Old Robert died, the town boasted a
population of three thousand. Its borders had long since
encompassed the hill which had been its nucleus, and now
they took in the surrounding lowlands. In the summer cattle
still wallowed in the stream on the south side, and a long line
of maples flanked the main street. A railroad flanked the
north, and beyond the tracks lay Milltown, the settlement
that made the railroad possible. Four trains passed daily, two
passenger, two freight, morning and evening, eastern and
western. The inhabitants of Milltown had come from the
farms, landless and homeless whites, living from day to day, a
lazy, shiftless, unimaginative lot. Poor whites who had never
known a surplus of anything except misery, those who had
existed on the bounty of nature when nature was kind, and
on the charity of neighbors when she was not, found in the
cotton mill a deadly security. Here season and storm were not
important. The wheels ground in rain and sun, in winter
and summer. Wages were small but constant. They ate, they
slept, Sunday still came every seven days. A man with many
children could put them all in the mill, and retire upon their
income. Mill life had its advantages.

Four tobacco warehouses graced the four principal streets

of Granville, huge spreading buildings, covering an acre each. Beneath them were endless stalls for horses, above them windowed roofs.

Breakfast smoke was curling from the chimneys of the town when Cleve and Hugh arrived. They drove straight to the courthouse, behind which was a large lot equipped with hitching posts. To one of these Cleve tied the horse, leaving him as much slack rein as possible, since the tobacco sale would take most of the day. Three hundred feet distant, squatting on the ground like a great red frog, was the Planters' Warehouse. Its name stretched in letters three feet high across the front. Beneath were smaller letters which advertised it as the home of good prices. Before its gaping entrance two men were pacing the sidewalk, yelling to the drivers of the passing wagons, calling many of them by name, and exhorting them, one and all, to take advantage of the merits of their house. They knew Cleve and shook his hand warmly.

"Saw your wagons inside, Cleve," one of them said; "prices are tip-top. John Weaver averaged twenty cents yesterday."

"A fair price," Cleve agreed.

The other man pulled Hugh to him, holding him by the lapel of his coat.

"Getting any work out of this little man, Cleve?" he asked.

"No," Cleve replied jokingly, "I'm going to make a preacher out of him."

At this moment a wagon rumbled by, and the two men began their spiel. Cleve took Hugh by the hand and entered the warehouse in search of his wagons. The negroes had not unloaded; Cleve always superintended that. From the wagon the bundles were passed off into wicker baskets resting upon small hand trucks. The loaded trucks were then pushed on a floating platform behind which a small office housed the dial of a scales and a clerk in charge. Here a card denoting the owner's name and the weight of the pile was stuck into the tobacco, and it was displayed upon the auction floor. The building hummed with the noise of this activity, the creaking of wagons, and a medley of hoarse shouting. Suddenly the din abated, and an expectant hush came over the crowd. A group of men marched out from an office in the corner of the building and the sale began. The buyers and bookkeepers marched to the first row of tobacco, and the crowd shuffled around them, treading the tobacco underfoot in their eagerness to keep abreast the buyers. Cleve held Hugh tightly by the hand and mixed with the throng.

The auctioneer, a giant man whose mouth looked like a ragged hole in his face, began a queer, high-pitched, wordless song. Catching his breath between the piles he proceeded down the row; in his wake followed the buyers. A bookkeeper brought up the rear, marking a card on each pile with the buyer's name and the price. All this was done with incredible speed. The auctioneer's voice became like the drone of an engine. The bookkeepers worked with strained intense accuracy. At the end of each row the auctioneer gave a shout like a field hand, and with no pause another row was started. Row after row gave way before them, and finally with a triumphant crescendo, the auctioneer stood by the last pile. Deserting his unintelligible jargon for a moment, he cried, "Open her up, boys; baby needs a new pair of shoes."

A few bids higher than the average came in response to his plea. Cocking his hand to his ear he shouted, "Come on; you can't steal this tobacco."

Finally, having cajoled the buyers into a ridiculously high price, he stooped over the pile, grasped a bundle of tobacco, and thrusting as much of it as he could into his mouth, he bit off a hunk of it, and walked away, working his jaws like a great, ugly mule.

The sale was over. Checks were made out in the corner office and all day farmers presented them at the bank for cashing.

Hugh was glad to get outside after being in the crowded stench of the place so long. The streets were almost as noisy as the warehouse, however, for the buyers were moving their purchases from the sales floor to redrying plants where the tobacco would be stored awaiting shipment. Several long flat-bedded wagons passed him and Cleve as they walked toward the bank. These were loaded high with baskets of tobacco, stacked one on top of the other, like pancakes. Each wagon carried two or three negroes who stood between the baskets and held them in place. In the street behind each wagon walked another negro who picked up the bundles which toppled at his feet.

They found their horse tugging impatiently at his halter, the hard ground beaten into dust by restless pawing. As soon as they had unhitched him and got into the buggy he turned homeward. Near the edge of town Cleve pulled up at a store.

"Your mother told me to bring Aunt Mathy some snuff," Cleve said as he stopped.

"Aunt Mathy told me the same thing," said Hugh.

Cleve bought the old woman's snuff, and buoyed by the roll of bills in his pocket he bought five yards of calico which he handed to Hugh.

"Make Aunt Mathy a present of this," he said.

"She'll like it," said Hugh, " 'cause it's red."

Soon they were in the open country where the roads were muddy, now that the sun had thawed them. The ride home was dull and a bit regretful, the end of a day and of an adventure.

6

Aunt Mathy saw the years fulfilling her early impressions of Hugh. He was Old Robert in new flesh, impetuous, generous, quick to anger, quick to forgive. His companionship with Dave, that arrogant and demanding affection with which he bound him, flashed across her mind like a remote sequence of memory.

These traits she saw in Hugh were not creations of her imagination. Cleve had observed the same things, and they had not pleased him. The boy had the same turbulent love of life which had been Old Robert's. A prancing horse, a negro song borne on the damp night air, the sound of an angry oath, all filled him with a nameless joy. At seventeen he was almost six feet tall, and his walk was strong and confident. Dave knew this strength better than anyone else, because since he had come to the farm there had been few days when Hugh had not used it against him, playfully when they had been children, seriously and competitively as they had grown older, and lately not at all. Dave knew that it was now the strength of a man and that it would never again be playful. The freedom that had existed between them was strangely lacking; a tacit kind of indifference had supplanted it and Dave knew that this tenseness would remain, and that it could not have been otherwise. To say "Mr. Hugh" had been embarrassing to him and to Hugh, but neither questioned the propriety of the prefix; both accepted it as a symbol of their manhood.

The world was changing, too; its growing pains ran with disturbing little quirks into the country around Granville. Sand-clay roads radiated from the town—roads on which no one gave a second look at a passing automobile. Each rural township now had a high school. People talked about education as if it were a new religion. They talked about taxes, too, for taxes had doubled. Farmers planted larger tobacco crops. Some stopped planting grain and corn altogether, put all of their land and energy into tobacco. Flimsy breakfast foods appeared on their tables. Many gave up raising hay for their stock, bought it from merchants in Granville instead, and hauled it to their farms. Tobacco became the only important crop. Tobacco buying became a science and a tragedy. Prices, over which the growers exercised no control, were forced lower. They had no defense. Foolishly they tried to balance increasing costs and diminishing returns by increasing their acreage. Somehow this failed to work.

The papers were full of European war. Each day some new combatant set ineffectual little human props against the German juggernaut which moved slowly toward the sea. Granville saw prosperity in the war clouds. Farmers became optimistic about prices. Preparations were made for larger crops in the coming year.

Cleve failed to share this optimism.

"It's probable," he said to Hugh, "that prices will be higher next fall. War throws everything out of balance. But no war has lasted forever, and this one will come to an end, too."

He had been on the farm too long to pin his hope to the temporary relief offered by a foreign war. One couldn't count on this as a perpetual blessing. Nevertheless, when the high winds of March had driven winter from the land, Cleve, now sixty-seven, began to set his agricultural house in order. Many of the important duties could be intrusted to Hugh. He knew the business as well as Cleve, and unlike him, he had a native love for the work. Turning the great, fallow fields was always like opening a new secret to him. Strength flowed down his arms, down through the oak handles and into the plow, down through the plow and into the warm earth. The sun on his back urged him onward. Even the horses seemed to pull with pleasure, seemed fired with the wine of spring. Existence was good. Hugh could work without thinking of the fruits of his labor. It was enough to work and sweat, to hunger and thirst, and to be satisfied.

Cleve saw in Hugh's love for the farm and its work qualities for which he could not criticize the boy, but at the same time he felt that he should curb them. In his mind other plans for Hugh were shaping, plans framed in the mold of his own life and experience and they were altogether out of harmony with the boy's passion for the land. Cleve could understand Hugh's feeling, but his understanding was not necessarily approval. The sight of Hugh's body filling the doorway as he left for the fields one day impressed him anew with his son's approaching manhood. Turning to his wife he tried to put before her the thoughts which had agitated him so long.

"What are we going to do with that boy, Sally?" he asked.

"Do with him?" she repeated, not understanding.

"Yes, he's almost a man. Shall he stay on the farm, shall he go to college, or what shall he do?"

"To tell the truth, Cleve, it hasn't worried me. He seems perfectly satisfied here."

"Yes, yes, I know that. But is that best for him?"

"What do you think?"

"It's a hard question," Cleve answered slowly. "I can see that he loves the farm. And he'll make a good farmer, too. It's still harder for me to judge because I've never loved farming—not in the impulsive way that Hugh loves it. Its work has always been like—well, *duty,* to me. And as I've grown older my dislike for it has become distrust."

"We've had a good life, Cleve. I've been happy. I am, now —happier than ever, I think."

"You misunderstand me, Sally," said Cleve gently. "We have had a good life. You made it so. But it's been a hard life, too. We haven't accumulated anything. We've lived well, but not as well as my father lived. This farm is six hundred acres smaller than it was two generations ago, and right now all we are assured of is another year's living. I'm sixty-seven years old and all I've got is a farm which will feed and clothe us for another year—God and the tobacco companies being willing."

His wife said nothing.

"That's my life's work," Cleve sighed, "and my life is nearly over. It's not enough. Not the life I'd like to see my son live."

"His future is in your hands, Cleve," replied Sally, "and I will trust it there."

Cleve pressed her hand and gave her a grateful smile.

7

From his place at the breakfast table Hugh saw through the window that Dave had his horse saddled. He watched him tie the rein to a branch and give the animal's rump an affectionate slap as he walked away.

"Dave sure loves horses," he said to his father.

"He's a good boy," Cleve answered. "Like Lige."

Now that Cleve had turned over much of the supervision of the farm to him, Hugh was able to return from school an hour earlier by riding. He also gained an hour in the mornings, although there was little that he could do in this time other than dispatch the hands about whatever farm tasks were pressing. Just at this season there was no particular work to occupy their consistent attention, because the plants were as yet mere buds in the beds, it was too early to drill fertilizer, and what heavy plowing there was to be done had been postponed in the hope that the showers of April would soften the hard, winter-packed soil.

Although each cropper had separate fields, there were certain tasks in which all joined. They planted together, they harvested together, and when they stripped the tobacco they pooled their efforts again. At slack seasons, such as the present, Cleve felt free to direct any of them to whatever work required attention. At his order Hugh had sent most of them about repairing fences and cleaning ditches. He had made them clean the stables and scatter the manure over a worn spot on a hill which he intended to plant with corn. This work had kept them busy for the past week, but now there was not much to be done anywhere. The negroes hunted.

"Would you like a crop of your own this year?" Cleve asked suddenly.

Hugh's mind seized the idea at once.

"I certainly would," he replied.

"You might hire Dave as a wage hand," Cleve offered.

"Dave would like that. Lige can't give him much. I gave him a dollar last Saturday and his eyes were as big as the dollar."

Hugh came to his father within a week and asked permission to clear a new-ground for his crop. As there was plenty of open land on the farm, far more than they ever cultivated in one year, the boy's request amazed Cleve.

"Why do you want to go to the trouble of clearing a new-ground," he demanded, "when there is more open land now than we ever use?"

"I may be wrong," Hugh answered, "but it seems to me that if this war is going to shoot prices up, as everybody believes, why then the weight of tobacco will count more than in normal times. When prices are high weight is just as important as color, isn't it? You know what heavy stuff these new-grounds make, even if it is dark. I don't dread the work of clearing it, not at all; besides, we haven't any too much wood for the barns. Dave could have that bottom and slope opposite Spring Hill cleared in a few weeks, that is, if I help after school."

Cleve considered the matter maturely before replying.

"Go to it," he said at length. "I believe your judgment is sound. Heavy tobacco should sell better this year. Your selection of ground is all right, too, only I wish you would dress the larger trees for barn-logs instead of flue-wood. We need a new barn. Put Dave to work there whenever you like. You ought to get at least three cuttings out of that hill."

Clearing the hill came near causing Dave to regret his new position. No other work on the farm could have been as hard. Hugh took him there immediately after Cleve gave his approval, and directed him to start cutting the underbrush which grew along the banks of the spring branch. Dave took one look at the jungle of briars, dogwood, and ash, and groaned.

"Can't I commence up dar on de hill, whar dar ain't so many little trees, Mr. Hugh?"

"Why, Dave?"

"Den I would hab time to git my wind up fur dis mess."

"No, let's start with the worst first. I'll be back this afternoon. We'll be through before you know it."

Hugh's optimism failed to impress Dave.

"Wust fust," was all he said.

He was a sorry spectacle when Hugh returned that afternoon. Briars had scratched his face and hands, had ripped his overalls, and torn his jacket in several places. His legs were caked with mud to the knees, and his shoes were like two sponges. His disposition, too, was in tatters.

"Mr. Hugh," he wailed, "can't us hab ur crop out in de

open like ebybidy else? I'd ruther fight ur cross-cut saw 'an dis heah thicket."

"It's got to be cleared," Hugh replied, and waded in with a mattock.

It was tedious work. The thicket in the bottom was about a hundred feet wide, and Hugh meant to clear a space extending five hundred feet along the creek bank. To have cleared only thirty feet in one whole day's work seemed hardly a beginning. Although Hugh put in three full hours each afternoon digging roots from the soil which Dave had cleared of brush, it was more than two weeks before they finished in the bottom. The work on the slope was easier and more pleasant, because they progressed faster. None of the trees was huge, and most of them were pines which yielded readily to the axes, although the pine roots gave as much trouble as hickory or oak. They did not bother to remove all the stumps; they could plow around them. The fire which he and Dave built to burn the brush might well have been a bonfire of celebration, because they both felt elated that the most difficult phase of tilling the hill was past. Cleve had visited them at their work often, and while they were burning the brush from which Hugh had salvaged every stick worth saving for wood, he impressed Hugh mightily by telling that in his youth he had seen farmers roll, not only the brush, but whole trees into a pile, and burn every limb to save themselves the trouble of cutting it.

"That was when most of the country was in timber, though," Cleve explained, "before farmers had to watch their woodpile as they do their crib."

All the other tobacco fields on the farm had been prepared for planting before Hugh was ready to drill his fertilizer. These were fields which had been tilled for years, land free of stumps, roots, and rocks, soft soil through which a plow slid like a knife through butter. This did not alarm Hugh, however, because he knew that once his field was arable it would bring a crop to maturity quicker than the less virile fields, so he continued to remove roots and stumps, even after some of the croppers had planted tobacco. Finally, he thought it ready for the plow, and he put Dave there one morning with a two-horse dagger equipped with a sword hanging from the beam. The sword split the soil in front of the point and severed some of the roots which they had failed to remove. It was this work which Hugh had dreaded most, because the shock of snagging a large buried root was enough to tear the plow-gear from the mules, severe enough to throw the plowman head-over-heels above his plow handles. Dave got several bad jolts before the field was finished, but only the plow was injured. Two points had been broken, Hugh found when he returned in the afternoon, but he had antici-pated that this might happen, and had supplied Dave with extra ones before he left.

He saw for the first time the soil which they had been working so long to reach, spread in rippling folds behind the powerful dagger. It was rich, black, and strong, full of a strange vigor which a thousand years had compounded for his use. He took it in his hands and crumbled it between his fingers. How weak and pale the soil of the older fields looked beside it! There was little use of putting much fertilizer here.

Dave's interest in the field increased as the strenuousness of preparing it lessened. He was eager to have it bedded now, and to see the plants flourishing there. Nevertheless, Hugh ordered him to continue breaking it, and he spent the re-mainder of that week turning the black soil. Hugh wanted to lay off the rows himself, therefore he reserved this work until Saturday, when he laid them off straight and clean with a shovel-plow. Dave followed him with a small dagger throwing up beds along the lines his plow had marked. On

Monday he had Dave drill the fertilizer, and by Tuesday at dusk he had reversed the beds, covered the fertilizer, and the field was ready to be planted. The weather had been dry for fully a week, and the turning and returning of the soil had taken so much moisture that Hugh thought it best to wait for rain before setting out the plants.

"Let's water and plant hit," suggested Dave after waiting several days for rain which failed to come. "Dat won't be nothin' side what we already done."

"No hurry yet; rain will come."

Rain came, but only after a week of waiting, a week in which the older fields became so dry that all the croppers were busy hauling barrels of water to them, forced to water each hill as they pegged in the tender young plants. Hugh had almost decided that he would have to do the same thing, but the dull patter of rain on the roof as he awoke one morning assured him that he had not waited in vain. He found Dave waiting for him when he came down to breakfast, and before the sun was up they were in the plant-bed selecting well-grown, uniform plants. After filling two baskets with these, they broke wet branches from the trees and covered the baskets so that the plants would not wilt if the sun broke through the clouds. Then they carried the plants to the new-ground. Dave had used the foresight to persuade two small boys, children of one of the croppers, to accompany them. Each of these little negroes took a basket of plants and swung it over one arm, dropping a plant at each hill, previously designated by a flat smack of a hoe. Hugh and Dave followed them armed with pegs made of lightwood knots. They thrust the smooth pegs into the wet earth, withdrew them and inserted plants into the holes they made, pressed the earth firmly around the roots of the plants, and swung to the next hills. This soon became a rhythmic, mechanical movement, which they executed so rapidly that the two little boys had difficulty keeping ahead of them. Whenever he overtook the one who was dropping for him, Dave rapped him on the bare heels with the hard peg, and the boy would fairly dance down the row until he had put a safe distance between them. They planted the field that day, finishing the last rows by moonlight.

Although the following day was wet, too, Hugh could not refrain from returning to the field. He wanted to look at it studded with plants, this fine field which he had carved from a wilderness, this growing thing which was altogether his own. He had done his work, he realized proudly, as he surveyed the little green shoots, nearly all that he could do other than keep them free from grass. From now on they would be at the mercy of forces largely beyond his control.

The croppers were taking advantage of the wet season to replant their fields; many of the plants which they had set out with only a dipper of water poured on the hill had not survived the week of dry weather. They went about this work gleefully, filled with that reciprocating hope which is the only weapon that farmers have to combat the despair of bad seasons, reasoning that a dry planting season presaged a good growing season, that Nature was a compromising dame, following a snub with a caress, and in the end endearing herself by her very powers of perversity. The belated rains fell steadily for a week, days of murky downpour, followed by days of slow, cold drizzle, until the fields were muddy and the soil like a sponge in which the plants hung limply, some of them in the lowlands pale and dying from a surfeit of water. Hugh's new-ground fared better than the other fields because the soil was firmer, and the rows curving with the hill carried off the surplus water. While the tobacco in the older fields sickened and died, grass flourished. One could almost see it spreading, covering the rich beds like a green disease, entwining itself with the plants, and here and there hiding one altogether. There was nothing to be done about it, Hugh realized, absolutely nothing until the soil was dry enough to cultivate.

The rains came to an end at last, and a few sunny days made the soil fit for cultivation. Then all hands tackled the grass. The negroes made play of the work. Their swift, careful guiding of the hoe became automatic after a few rows of practice, allowing each worker to carry on a conversation with his neighbors on the other rows. They moved across a field, synchronizing their movements to the cadence of a song, their hoe handles moving like the kindred parts of a giant machine, their bodies swinging from hill to hill in an undulating rhythm.

Tobacco, unlike other crops, exercises a dictatorial power over the activities of those who grow it. Indeed, one can construct a calendar by simply denoting the phases of its handling from the time it is planted until it is sold on the auction floor, and this calendar could very well show how infrequent and how beset with anxiety are the holidays of a tobacco farmer; their very lives are gauged to conform with its needs. It is no respecter of the Sabbath; when it is ripe it must be cut and cured. Schools open and close with respect to its demands, and the churches time their revivals to coincide with the slackest period of its cultivation. The perversity of the seasons may alter these schedules at the last moment. And should it grant a holiday it does so with such abruptness, that there is little chance to plan how it may be spent wisely; one must snatch, on the run, what leisure has to offer. Too often the holiday is only a holiday from the fields. Tobacco demands many collateral attentions. Curing barns must be repaired each year. Their flues crack, and clay must be daubed into them before they are fit for firing. Roofs leak, and even in the barn water can ruin tobacco. One never gets through with a tobacco crop; people desert them sometimes.

The croppers regarded Saturday afternoon as a holiday. It had always been so, even in Old Robert's time, and yet they quit work only if the condition of the crop warranted it. Hugh himself thought that work should terminate for the week at noon Saturday, but it would have spoiled his Sunday to leave a field half plowed when it could have been finished before sunset. Grass grew too fast for anything like that.

He finished work in the new-ground about three o'clock one Saturday, left his plow there, and rode the sweating mule to the house. He was surprised to find his mother busy in the kitchen, since it was too early to begin supper. She was alone, Aunt Mathy having gone to a "big baptizing."

"What's up, Mother," he asked, "company coming?"

"Yes, Brother Baily is taking supper with us," she responded.

"In that case I'd better eat now," Hugh said, laughing.

"Now don't go poking fun at Brother Baily. He's a good man."

Hugh patted his mother's shoulder and sat down by the table where she was dressing a chicken.

"I could eat that whole chicken right now if it were fried."

"And you criticize the preacher's appetite!"

"He's a powerful eater, Mother."

"Don't worry. I'm preparing a powerful meal. I've got another chicken salted away. If we don't need it we can have it for breakfast."

"Is he staying for breakfast, too?"

"Of course, and I think it would be hospitable of you to ask him back for dinner, tomorrow."

"Your chicken is all the invitation he needs."

"He's delivering his annual missionary sermon tomorrow," she told Hugh. "It's probably his longest and hardest sermon of the year. I've heard him say that it always taxes his strength to the utmost."

"Mine, too," said Hugh.

"Missionaries do a great work, Son."

"He'll probably work his appetite into a lather talking about the starving heathen," Hugh chided.

"That's enough. You are getting sacrilegious now," she reproved him.

But, laughingly, Hugh took the last word.

"I wonder," he mused, "what scheme he has worked out to get another couple of chickens."

This brought a smile to his mother's face. Only two weeks before Brother Baily had visited the farm, and as he was leaving Mrs. Winton had presented him with a chicken. He placed it in the back of his car, turned to her, and said, "Sister Winton, I have observed that the chicken is a gregarious fowl. Loneliness seems to make its wings itch, and often it lifts them and flies in search of company; therefore, I fear that this one, for which I am truly grateful, will not remain with me long, unless he has a companion."

She had laughed with him and given him another chicken.

"I would have taken back the one I had given him," Hugh told her.

"But he was only making a joke, Hugh."

"At your expense," Hugh replied.

Hugh left his parents to entertain the preacher after supper, and went to the store a mile up the road, where the young men of the neighborhood met on Saturday evenings. His mother thought poorly of these visits to the store, because there lived adjacent to it a man to whom she pointed as an example of wretchedness and evil, a sinner and a sot, old Ed Dixon, the community blacksmith and drunkard. Rumor held that he had been born drunk, but this was probably an exaggeration which had its origin in the fact that in sixty years there were few who could remember having seen him sober. Physically, he had stood his drinking well. Despite the fact that his face seemed perpetually to reflect the fires of his forge, his body was erect, and he moved quickly, with a peculiar scuttling motion, as if life itself were some molten metal which he must rush from fire to anvil in order to forge while it was still hot. As a young man he had inherited his father's wagon and harness shop, to which the smithy was merely an adjunct, attended by a negro. Even at this age he was a heavy drinker, yet he managed to hold the business for several years after his father's death. He even got married. To the normal misfortunes of her position his wife brought a greater one; she had an instinct for reformation, a passion which got her no success, unless the persecutions of the righteous, and the raw pains of martyrdom be success. Her efforts in this direction (she went as far as refusing to prepare anything for him to eat, at times, serving him instead of food a large Bible, opened at the seventh chapter of 1 Corinthians) finally brought several beatings upon her before she left him. Not an unkindly man except when deadened with drink, Ed had taken her desertion badly, had buried his sorrow, as the old song goes, deep in his bottle. One after another his possessions had slipped through his fingers until only the blacksmith shop remained. He discharged the negro and hung on to this. Drinking became his daily food. Reality interested him no longer. His conversation emphasized this, there being nothing one could say which would arouse a contradictory spirit within him. If it pleased one to call the moon a cake of green cheese, it pleased Ed to confirm the statement. Of all the realities only food aroused him. Attracted by the free dinners, he was a regular attendant at revival meetings. The pious ladies of the community had satisfied their evangelical longings for twenty years by converting him. Cornered by a group of these women, he offered no resistance; meekly, and with no apparent embarrassment he suffered them to lead him to the altar, where he confessed his besetting sin, rather, he confirmed the zealous female description of it, and had salvation showered upon his sodden soul. Once each year they set him upon the right track. Once each year, during that bountiful week, he remained sober.

Hugh accompanied his parents to church Sunday morning, taking a seat with his father in the congregation, while his mother went to her customary place in the choir. The choir began a low, sweet hymn. Brother Baily sat behind his pulpit, his hands clasped, meditating upon the heathen.

John Wesley Baily, consecrated by name and his mother's wish, had done his work well. A zealous and able spokesman of the Lord, he guarded his flock with parental care, giving praise where praise was due, and administering criticism and warning to those who fell by the wayside. He had married them and christened their babies, buried their dead, and consoled the living. A powerful man in stature and voice, his was no weakling's gospel. Borne on the swelling tide of his eloquence, simple rural souls were swept to the very shores of hell, left suspended there, like driftwood between the ebb and the flow, in awful contemplation of its horror, before the recoiling surge of his voice lifted them again, high and happy toward the blue skies of heaven.

The hymn rolled to a slow, echoing end. The preacher arose and looked at his congregation, regarding them so long and so silently that an embarrassing sense of guilt agitated some in their pews. Had he accused them, singly, of their secret crimes of the past week, few would have been surprised. But after this terrible pause he launched into the remote history of the church. Beginning with Christ's commands to his disciples to spread the gospel into the four corners of the world, he sketched rapidly the pioneering story of Christianity, dwelling at some length upon Paul's journey to Macedonia, and the troubles which beset poor Peter in Rome. It was a smooth, convincing sermon, and would have resulted, no doubt, in a successful plea for the unwashed hordes of China, had not an untoward event occurred. Just as he was concluding his description of Peter's miraculous delivery from prison, two figures straggled down the center aisle and stumbled into seats. Their conduct, once they were seated, was irreproachable, although their entry had undone the solemn work of an hour's earnest preaching. Interrupted in the middle of a sentence, Brother Baily never completed it. He stared at the two interlopers. They were not strangers. Old Ed Dixon and young Tom Ferrell, both carrying their usual load of whiskey, had come to church. They sat in their places very quietly, stilled by an air of expectancy. A similar spirit hushed the others of the congregation. A moment later all were justified. In a fierce, impassioned voice, Brother Baily swept into a violent denunciation of whiskey and its evils. Words rushed over each other to do service to his theme. The force of righteousness was now allied with the terrible force of anger. Those of the congregation who sat between the preacher and the objects of his wrath, turned in their seats and leveled their gaze upon the unfortunate pair. Old Ed sat with his eyes fixed on the ceiling, the words of the preacher falling on his ears, a mighty but meaningless roar. It had not dawned on him that he was the object of this sermon. Tom Ferrell, however, soon caught the point. Brother Baily had used the word "blockade-still" several times in the course of his fierce outburst. Suddenly, taking his cue from a repetition of the word, Tom asked in a clear voice, "Are you talking about me and mine?"

A deathly silence followed this question. Many of the congregation expected to see Tom struck dead by divine power. The preacher himself gave Divinity an opportunity to interfere. Words failed him. Nothing like this had ever happened before. He stared in amazement at the man who had mocked him in the house of God.

Ed had betrayed only a momentary interest when he heard Tom speak, then he had resumed his inspection of the ceiling. At length silence accomplished what words had failed to do. Tom got to his feet, took his docile companion by the arm, and walked, with difficulty, from the church. The preacher pronounced a hasty benediction, and the heathen were left to their dark ways for another week.

The incident afforded the Winton family a topic of conversation, but one which they discussed only after the preacher had departed. Sally was horrified.

"To think," she exclaimed, "to think that any man would dare interrupt the preacher in the course of his sermon."

"Well, it was Tom's sermon, too, wasn't it?" Cleve asked dryly.

"Cleve, how can you joke about such a thing! I'm ashamed of you. I have never heard of anything like it."

"I think they were both wrong," said Cleve soberly. "Tom shouldn't have come to church drunk, he shouldn't have brought poor old Ed, anyway, but once they were in the church Brother Baily should have ignored them. They behaved until he gave them a tongue-lashing. Not even a sober man likes that in public. The preacher invited trouble."

"That doesn't excuse it."

"No," Cleve agreed, "it doesn't, but it explains it, I think."

"It was plain enough," said Sally.

Hugh wisely refrained from any comment, although he was certain that there must have been many in the congregation who, like him, found the happening more amusing than profane. It would have hurt his mother's feelings to learn what he really thought about it. The church was very much

in her mind at this time, for within a few days the annual
revival would begin, and already she had started preparations
for it, baking cakes and old hams. The revival was scheduled
rather early this year due to the heavy rainfall which had
hastened the growth of the crops. Some of the croppers had
laid their fields by, had split each row with two drives of the
dagger plow and thrown a final furrow around the plants.
They would not cultivate it with a plow again because it had
attained a size which rendered it impregnable to attack by
grass. A great many fields had been topped. All the farmers
topped their tobacco in the cool hours of early morning, and
late in the afternoon, because the midday heat makes the
plant tough and leathery. The top can be snapped out easily
when the plant is cool and brittle. There was more leisure on
the farm at this time than at any other, and since these leisure
hours were confined to the middle of the day, farmers could
well afford to utilize this period for the edification of their
souls and appetites.

When the revival began, Hugh attended it with his people,
not because he was much interested, not because of the excellent dinners, but simply to avoid hurting and puzzling
his mother. His father, he imagined, came for much the
same reasons. Hugh counted himself fortunate that his
mother's coaxing had persuaded him to join the church as
a child, because those young people of his acquaintance who
had not joined were all targets for the many proselyting
ladies among the congregation.

With the detached sense of security which his membership
gave him, he watched less fortunate youth squirm and wiggle
under the torture of these relentless champions of the Lord.
Surrounded by a sea of curious eyes, frenzied by the tearful
pleadings of friends and relatives who had been saved, a
sinner stood a poor chance unless he possessed a character
like rock.

To Brother Baily God's justice was manifested not only by the sharp retribution he visited upon sinful men, but by the warnings and threats he gave for their guidance. His text, this day, leveled the Lord's finger directly at his congregation. Into the silence which he always imposed upon his audience when he arose to preach he hurled that dreadful verse from Saint Matthew: "Then shall two be in the field; the one shall be taken, and the other left."

Hugh surrendered to the preacher's spell. He saw himself with others working in the tobacco fields. The day was hot like any other. Men laughed and talked and made plans for the future. In the woods the jarflies sang. Above their heads buzzards sailed and swooped toward Sligo. Then suddenly they were not alone. A stranger appeared among them, picked one from their midst, and was gone.

Brother Baily bore down upon his hearers. There had been few converts in this revival and he felt in his heart that the sinners within sound of his voice should be warned that even God's patience has an end: "Watch therefore," he quoted, "for ye know not what hour your Lord doth come." His sermon had apparently frightened all the sinners into immobility. Not one came to the altar.

"One more verse," he called to the choir; "just one more." The choir lifted its voice:

> *"Why do you wait, dear brother,*
> *Why do you tarry so long?"*

An agony of exhortation strained the preacher's voice. Here and there in the congregation tearful women pulled at their doomed friends, trying to drag them down the aisle to salvation. But the sinners stood their ground.

Brother Baily's eye found old Ed Dixon, sitting obscurely in a corner. Fixing his gaze upon him he said, "Two shall be at the forge; the one shall be taken, the other left."

As if the words were a command, two ladies gave up their struggle against the man with whom they had been pleading for half an hour and rushed to old Ed's side. They took his arms and guided him toward the altar. He went submissively. At the altar they handed him over to Brother Baily and turned proudly to their seats. Old Ed Dixon had been saved once more.

8

It was very hard, sometimes, to start a tobacco plant growing, to tease it into sending its root down into the bed where it could draw strength from the rich fertilizer which was there waiting for it, but when it did begin to grow it leaped, like Jack's beanstalk, toward the sky. Hugh allowed the plants in his new-ground to reach to his shoulders before he broke out the tops, leaving twelve and often fifteen leaves on a stalk. All the energy which the roots drew from the ground would now go into these, widening and thickening them until they would cover the little valleys between the rows. Breaking out the top seemed to arouse the perverse nature of the plant, which threw out suckers from the base of each leaf in a frantic effort to produce seed. Unless broken out immediately, these rapidly unfolded themselves and became spreading duplicates of the parent plant, defeating the whole purpose of the topping. This spirit of expansion was not quelled by removing these suckers once. The plant pushed forth new ones as long as it lived, and even after it was finally cut the very stubble broke into a bouquet of blooming suckers unless frost quickly followed the knife.

Hugh went to his field in the cool of the morning when the suckers could be snapped easily. He had to work far into the middle of the day, however, because the rich soil of the new-ground accelerated the growth of the parasitical shoots. He detested the work. It was a labor of destruction, necessary, but unpleasant. He began in the rows high on the hill, and worked toward the cooler bottom, in order to defeat the sun as long as possible. This procedure met with Dave's approval readily, for he was no sun lover. By ten o'clock the field was like a furnace; heat danced in the air visibly, like millions of gnats. As seductively shady as an oasis in the desert were the trees at the end of the rows. Straightening to rest his eyes upon their cool shadow, Hugh saw Cleve standing beneath them. He worked toward him, having decided that it was too hot to remain in the field longer.

"Pretty hot this morning," said Cleve by way of greeting.

"It's hot enough out there," said Hugh, weighing his words, "to fry eggs, and that's no joke."

It was hot. The dancing waves of heat covered the entire hill now. Hugh watched them, crawled deeper into the shade, and propped his back against a great trunk. Distant fields of tobacco were black smudges on the landscape. Far away he heard a rooster crow. Jarflies sang their queer songs in the woods behind him, beginning with a slow, unruffled, clicking sound, their noise becoming higher and faster, reaching a mad, staccato buzz, then slowly dying to silence. He felt very lazy, very sleepy, and strangely content.

Cleve's voice broke the spell.

"I've been over the whole farm this morning," he said, "and I never saw better crops."

"It looks like we have just about done it," Hugh interjected. "Everything is coming on fine, corn, too. But you ought to make Lige get after those suckers on Spring Hill. They are as long as my arm."

"I spoke to him. He put up some excuse about a pain in his back."

"He'll have a pain in his back before he gets them out of

there. Looks like he would keep the suckers out, now that the crop is made."

"No, not made; it's too early to say that yet," Cleve objected cautiously. "That's the trouble with farming: you can never count your chickens until they are sold. Hatching them is only the beginning. I had such a crop as this when you were a baby. Hail destroyed it in thirty minutes, every bit of it."

Cleve winced at the memory.

"Worse than hail," he resumed, "prices can make so much trash of it. You never can tell. It's just a gamble."

"You are crossing too many bridges this morning, Daddy," Hugh protested. "We aren't going to sell it today. It's a good crop. Let's be satisfied with that right now. We can't sell it but once, and that's the time to worry."

Cleve regarded him thoughtfully.

"You are just like your granddaddy," he reflected. "I always said that he didn't know one day from another."

"He got along all right, didn't he?" Hugh demanded.

"I suppose so," replied Cleve. "If he ever worried he did it in his sleep. He said nobody but fools talked about the weather. But just the same, it hails, once in a while."

Neither spoke for a space, although Cleve continued to regard his son thoughtfully.

"What's on your mind, Daddy?"

"You."

"I haven't been up to anything."

Cleve disregarded his levity, and when he spoke again it was in a serious tone.

"You are almost a man now, Hugh. Next year you will finish high school, and your playing days will be over. I have been wondering a lot about your future, lately. Have you thought about it any?"

In reality Hugh hadn't given his future much consideration. Cleve's question surprised him, but he replied quickly:

"I think I'm a pretty good farmer right now; look at that field."

"That's just what I feared you thought," said Cleve, "and that's what I want to talk to you about."

Hugh waited for him to continue.

"Of course," Cleve reasoned, "I can't make you be anything, but you are old enough to take advice, and the Lord knows I am old enough to give it. A man sees a lot in sixty years. I've seen enough to make me afraid of tobacco farming. Nature isn't the only the thing a farmer has to fear; he's prey for men, too. Now you take the tobacco companies. They can break us any time they choose, and the better farmer you are, the worse you will be broken. Why, since I was your age I've seen farming change from an easy hit-or-miss proposition to the dangerous gamble it is now. And it's still changing. No, you mustn't count on it too strongly. Your mother and I have talked it over, and we think you ought to go to college. That will give you a better chance than this farm ever can. Hugh, you can be anything you set your head to be."

Hugh laughed.

"If I listened to Mother, she would have me being a preacher. You wouldn't have to worry about me starving then."

Cleve was angered by this attempt at humor. When he spoke again Hugh caught the stern seriousness of his voice.

"Listen to me, Hugh," he commanded. "I'm not talking to hear my tongue rattle. Come here."

He drew Hugh up beside him and pointed toward the hazy rim of the Sligo.

"That's what I mean, Hugh. There lies our yesterday, a wilderness. It wasn't always a wilderness. Your ancestors thought they had a permanent kind of life there. But what happened to them? My grandfather lived like a lord in those hills. He had everything, land, leisure, slaves. He thought I'd have them, too. But it didn't last. Your own grandfather thought he had a plantation that would stand forever right where we live now. But it blew away like dust. We have been getting weaker and weaker, smaller and smaller. I don't think we have seen the end yet. Sometimes I think that the Sligo country is not merely a reminder of our past, but a prophecy as well, a prophecy of a desolate future. It's our tomorrow as well as our yesterday, Hugh, that's what it is."

Hugh was impressed. He remembered the horrible ringing silence of Sligo. It lay before him now, and in all that vast spread of wilderness there was nothing that seemed alive.

"You scare me, Daddy," he admitted. "I'm beginning to see what you mean. And I will think about all you have said. I certainly will."

"All right, Hugh," said Cleve, well pleased. "You think about it."

9

The croppers' fields ripened more quickly than Hugh's new-ground, because the soil was shallow there, the plants sucked it dry of sustenance quicker, and the sun found these leaves less resistant to its gilding than those thick, green leaves in Hugh's field. He and Dave deserted their crop and helped the others harvest.

There had been a great scurrying of preparation going on for a week. Cleve had superintended the repairs to the barns himself. For days the negroes had dug into the clay bank near the spring, tearing out the glutinous stuff, mixing it with sand and water, and daubing the mixture into the cracks in the flues. Cleve stayed at the barns and kept the fires going. Wherever any smoke escaped he located the crevice and ap-

plied a new coating of clay. At the same time he tested the
flue-pipes and replaced rusty ones from a wagon load of new
pipes he had bought in Granville; one can never be too sure
about these things, because when a barn is full of tobacco,
dry as chaff and inflammable as powder, the tiniest flame may
send one off in a flash. Cleve had seen many of them go up
like that.

Some of the negroes split new tobacco sticks from heart
pine and added them to the huge pile of old sticks under the
pack-barn shed. Others constructed a new wagon frame,
building it of cedar which they had cut earlier in the year
for that purpose. The mules were sent to Ed Dixon's to be
shod. The wagons which had hardly been used all summer
were pulled to the spring branch and left standing in the
pool below the spring. The water would cause the wood to
swell in the wheels, making them strong and sturdy. Saturday night found everything in readiness. On Sunday Cleve
walked over the farm and decided which field they should
begin cutting in the morning.

Early Monday morning the wagons were loaded with
sticks. Men, women and children climbed in and rode away
to the fields; there were tasks for all. The men cut the tobacco and hung it across the sticks which the women bore
along behind the knife, and children brought more sticks
from the wagon. Although the plants had to be selected, one
here and there being ripe, they cut and housed a curing before
midday. Another was in the barn by dusk.

Cleve took charge of the tobacco as fast as they put it in
the barns. He stayed busy all day refueling the flues, and
only the urgent necessity of sleep forced him to relinquish
their care to the negroes at night. Hugh was sole master of
the fields, now, selecting the tobacco which needed cutting
immediately, and keeping his eyes open for the appearance of
rotting spots in those fields which had been allowed to stand

ripening too long. Once during the week he stole a chance
to inspect his own field. It was still green and glossy, with not
a yellow tint in it.

A spirit of comradeship moved everybody. Even after the
day's work was over and night had fallen, this spirit brought
the hands together once more around the bright fires of the
barns, where they met to regale each other with tales and
songs, with wild dances in the moonlight, and the wicked
twang of guitars.

Old Lige Johnson held a group spellbound with a tale of a
ghost he had encountered in the Sligo lowlands:

"I seed him movin' ovah de treetops. Evy Gawd's night I
passed dar I seed him, clear as daylight. But he neber made
no fuss, jest swishin' midst de trees."

"Aw, gwan, Lige," remonstrated a dubious listener, "efen
you had uf seed dat thing, you'd be runnin' yit. Ain't no
hant gwiner swish 'round me but oncet."

"Well, I sho seed him, jest swishin' 'long 'bout his bizness."

"How come you ain't daid from runnin', den?"

"Ain't no hant gwiner hurt me when I gut dis," Lige explained, running his hand into his pocket.

"Gut whut?" demanded the skeptical one.

"Dis heah black cat's bone," Lige replied.

"Man, you ain't gut no sho 'nuff black cat's bone, is you?"

"Sho I is. Look heah."

"Lawd, I don't wanter see hit. Efen you is gut hit, you
is gut hit, but don't be draggin' hit 'round me. I ain't no
hant."

"De man whut giv me dis bone," said Lige, "wus ur
cungion doctor frum way back. He say dat cat didn't hab
eben one white har. He cotch him an' slapped him in ur pot
uf bilin' water, an' let him stay dar 'til de skin bile offen his
bones."

"I heah you, brudder."

"He take dem bones," Lige recounted, "he take dem bones an' throw 'em in de creek. Atter while one bone, just one, float up de creek. Dat's de bone."

"An' you gut dat bone?"

"I gut hit."

"In yo pocket?"

"In my pocket."

"Man, you gut sumpin', an' you kin hab hit. I wouldn't eben war de britches whut hit's been in ... ur black cat's bone!"

"Pappy sho gut de bone," affirmed Dave, "I seed hit oncet."

Hugh had listened to this debate silently.

"You don't believe that stuff, do you, Dave?" he asked.

"Yassuh, Cap'n," the boy replied, "I seed de bone."

Lige's talking brought forth other tales of ghosts and trickery, and of "cungionin'." Hugh lay on his cot and listened.

A strange disease had taken a man known to them all. He had accused a "cungion doctor" of placing a spell on him. Only by a doctor with a more intricate knowledge of trickery could he be cured. There were those who made spells and those who broke them. It was a terrible thing to fall beneath one of these spells, your enemy unknown, your disease beyond the power of orthodox drugs. The man would certainly die, the negroes asserted, unless a doctor could be found who could baffle the creator of the spell, or better still, turn his own spell back upon him.

"Yes," agreed Hugh, "that would be the best thing to do, all right."

There were few purposes, he learned, which could not be realized through a knowledge of conjuring. Aided by it one negro could steal another's dog, make him lie at his door and guard it against the approach of its former master. Even wives could be stolen. Filled with a wayward passion they would desert their homes and husbands, to wander where the will of the spellbinder directed. His power effaced the weaker powers of conscience and fear. Mania overcame his victims. The good and the evil alike suffered from his incantations. Only those who laughed were safe.

Some of the young negroes tired of this serious talk of the elders. They withdrew to the side of the barn, and one of the lot began to strum a guitar. Another sang:

> *"Massa bought a yaller gal,*
> *He bought her way down Souf;*
> *She wropped her hair so devilish tight,*
> *She couldn't shet her mouf."*

"Heah, heah," the old folks shouted, "cut out dat scandalous singin'. Dem sassy songs gwiner git us all turned outen de church, fust thing y'awl know."

Obligingly, the young folks sang "Swing Low, Sweet Chariot." Far into the night they sang.

Hugh lay on the cot and listened, enraptured by their husky voices. Finally he drifted off to sleep beneath the stars, their soft crooning a faint lullaby in his ears.

10

Although Hugh was eager to see his own tobacco cut and cured, he took Cleve's advice and let it stand on the hill until most of the croppers had housed every wisp of their own, until a month of 'tending the barns at night and working in the fields at day left him haggard and hollow-eyed, constantly sleepy, and sadly out of temper with the everlasting labor of taking in the crop.

The appearance of his own crop and his father's delay in

cutting it aggravated his ill disposition, vexed him to argument at times. He persuaded Cleve to walk through the field with him once again. It was getting yellow in places now, and near the edges of the field all the bottom leaves were shriveled, some of them completely browned by the fierce August sun.

"Daddy, don't tell me that tobacco doesn't need cutting," Hugh expostulated. "Look at this leaf! Burned clean to the stalk."

"Have patience," Cleve protested. "This isn't the first new-ground I ever saw. The other fields can't stand this heat; it will burn them to the tips in a week, ripe as the stuff is. Yours is not suffering. What's a leaf or two at the bottom? They would only make sand lugs, if cured. The body of the plant can stand another week of ripening. You'll see. You think it's ripe now, but if it's cut, there'll be green spots in it as big as my hat when it comes out of the barn."

There was nothing Hugh could do but wait, but it was a torment to him to spend his time helping the negroes cut, thinking all the while that every hot minute wasted some of his own crop. Cleve was adamant in his decision, however, and another full week passed before a knife touched it. He and Hugh walked through it again on Sunday. The plants were as yellow as gold, but with the exception of the bottom leaves, they were firm and healthy, unmarred by the rotting spots which had been common among the late tobacco in the other fields.

"It can wait no longer," Cleve said when he had surveyed it.

Back at the house he gave instructions to the negroes, when they came to feed the stock, to begin clearing three barns of the cured tobacco early the next morning.

"And have them clear by sunrise," he ordered.

Sunrise found six knives busy in the field. Everybody

worked intensely, talked little, because Cleve's parting in-
junction had been to clean the field that day.

"Don't leave a plant," he had said.

This was the first field in which there had been no need
for selecting the ripe plants. They were all ripe, every plant.
It had been uniform in size since it was planted, none of it
had died and had to be replanted, and the rich soil had
brought it all to even maturity. One row after another they
leveled, leaving nothing but brown grass and dry stubble in
their wake. All day they cut, keeping one wagon busy moving it to the barns. At noon two barns were almost filled. At
night when they returned with the last stick, Hugh found
that the last barn had to be packed to contain it all.

"Three big ones," Cleve said, smiling, "and they'll be
beauties when I get through with them."

Hugh didn't remain to see him start the fires. He went
straight to the house, took a hurried bath, ate a little supper,
and literally fell into bed, too tired, even, to tell his mother
how well his crop had turned out.

II

The completion of tobacco harvesting meant the end of
the year's work to Hugh, but to the others it marked only
the beginning of another harvest; the corn had ripened during the month they had been occupied with the tobacco, and
was now slowly burning in the fields. So predominant was
the general interest in tobacco, however, that not even Cleve
seemed to care greatly about the wasting fodder. The negroes
went about cutting and shocking it in a lazy, indifferent
fashion, taking time from their work to follow the baying
of their hounds in the woods, and spending most of the nights
in the lowlands, hunting 'possums by the light of the moon.

They kept their hounds tied during the day, that is, their 'possum dogs, lest they dissipate their ambition by chasing rabbits. Hugh overheard Dave lecturing his dog after a fruitless hunt.

"You stick to 'possums, you heah, an' I'll stick to you, dawg. You gwiner be mighty hongry next yeah, an' who you 'spec gwiner feed ur triflin', no-count, rabbit hound?"

Hugh returned to school, awkwardly out of place in the small desks and rather contemptuous of the frail teachers, he who had wrestled with a new-ground all summer. These teachers seemed conscious of his growth; they studied his black head as he bent above his books, found his blue eyes more appraising than questioning. Even Helen Galloway, with whom he had walked to school for years, treated him like a stranger. On the first morning her silence, as they walked through the woods, provoked him into wishing that Lonnie was along. But Lonnie was through with school. Old Henry had stopped his son's education as soon as Lonnie was big enough to do a man's work. Old Henry had never gone to school himself, and he felt that any knowledge beyond that of reading and writing was wasted on a farmer. He had made out pretty well with less than that. He thought that allowing a grown boy to loaf all winter was encouraging the habit of laziness, and with that he had no patience whatever. Henry Galloway had been the first of his people to own land, his family having been one which followed a transient and precarious tenant life before the war. After the war, while still a boy, he had worked for wages and his board, had saved all but the board and bought land with the wages, adding an acre as he earned new dollars. Land sold for almost nothing then, bringing no more than a dollar an acre at times. By industry and strict attention to his business he managed to add to his farm until it became large enough to support him. After that he had continued to add to it and he was still doing so whenever an opportunity presented itself. Now that Lonnie could do the work of a man, Old Henry saw no reason why he shouldn't extend his borders faster and easier.

Helen was able to continue in school only because of an incessant fight on her mother's part. Old Henry had wanted to take her out when she reached an age which demanded an increased expenditure for clothes, and he would have done it had not her mother hit upon a plan which relieved him of the expense. She had saved a little money from the sale of chickens and eggs, so when her husband offered economy as a reason for taking Helen out of school, she simply told him to forget it, that she would attend to the expense herself, and glad to be rid of a bitter subject so easily, Old Henry forgot. This was the nearest she had ever come to defying him, but in this case she was determined. Ignorant, like her husband, she had, unlike him, a genuine respect for the mysteries of education.

Hugh had seen Helen at church several times during the summer, but he had not noticed then that she was no longer a little girl. Now he remarked the change, marveling how suddenly girls came to look like women. Her new, unchildish silence gave him time to speculate upon this change fully. She was blonde, tall, and slender, not beautiful in any perfection of features, but healthy and clean. Her manner was neither gay nor restrained, but was rather one of simple friendliness. She had a presence and there was something calm and satisfying in it. Hugh had always liked her; his feeling now was one of distinct approval.

Other boys and girls joined them on the way to school, the older ones entertaining the young children who were making their first fearful journey with tales of the terrors awaiting them. An examination of the books he would need revealed to Hugh that, with the exception of geometry, all of his studies were only continuations of the past session's work. He had heard about geometry from those who had gone before. This had put him on his guard about it. Helen had heard the same stories, and they discussed the matter on their way home. Not knowing the exact identity of this new puzzle which awaited them, their conversation was confined to vague guesses concerning the nature of the stumbling-block. However, they finally consoled themselves with the observation that Walter Hassell, one who had been graduated with great difficulty the preceding year, had not fallen before it. They let it stand at that. It was the most comforting thought they had hit upon in their speculations.

When they got their textbooks Hugh felt that geometry was a silly business—a matter of making mountains out of mole-hills. All this talk about facts which he had known all his life, this intricate proof of self-evident truths, impressed him as a waste of time and a bit ridiculous. His first impression remained. Freed of his fear of the subject he found it not only easy but interesting. Helen had more trouble. This was the first subject in which Hugh had ever excelled her, and he took an undue pride in assisting her with a tricky problem.

Since he had made a crop of his own, Hugh felt that he should bear the expense of his clothes and books, and although Cleve said it was not necessary, Hugh persuaded him to set Dave stripping his tobacco for market. Cleve had some of his own stripped, and when the markets opened those who had expected high prices were not disappointed. The stagnant treasuries of the world were being rifled by the careless hands of war. The whole of Europe, locked in the greatest battle of history, had cast monetary discretion to the slow-moving winds of peace. Victory, victory at any cost was the dominant

thought of every combatant. There was not time to haggle.
America was reaping a harvest of gold. Tobacco prices followed the course set by more standard commodities. Farm
costs had not been greater than in other years, and for once
farmers were receiving a favorable turn of chance. There
were blocked sales daily; warehouses kept going far into the
night. All feared that these prices would not last, suspected
that they were the fruit of speculation rather than evidence
of profitable demand. Harassed by this suspicion, they were
unloading their crops on the market as rapidly as they could
strip the tobacco. There was the atmosphere of a gold strike
about the whole business, a getting something for nothing,
a mad, frenzied rush to cash in before the bubble burst.
Cleve had talked of this stampede in the evenings after returning from Granville.

Hugh accompanied Cleve when his own tobacco was ready
to be sold. It was a hectic day, the town a scramble of rushing
farmers and high-strung buyers, men worn out from doing
two days' work in one. Prices were still sky-high, and people
were spending money as if it grew on trees. Even the poorest
farmers, even the negroes, were handling their money in this
way. To many of them money had been just so much script
previously, something which came into their hands and remained in them only long enough to be taken to the merchant
who had carried them over the year. It had not been something to hold, to count, to spend freely or to store away. It
had never been really theirs before; they had simply handled
it for a moment and then it was gone, gone back into that
strange outer world from which it had appeared like a brief,
green dream.

Standing with Cleve in the bank while they waited their
turn to cash their checks, Hugh watched the farmers pressing around them. Their frantic behavior, their amazed satisfaction over the good prices, the way they thrust the money

into their pockets and rushed from the building, all these things confirmed his father's advice with regard to his education and the future of farming. In Cleve's face he thought he could see the same shame that he felt as he admitted to himself that they were members of a class which had been so long without economic liberty that this first taste of it made them drunk. These prices, which represented for once in many years a legitimate profit, they were accepting thankfully, in a sense furtively, for none thought that their good fortune would endure. No. They were the blind recipients of a gift from the god of war, manna carelessly thrown, which they must gather up and devour before the error was discovered and corrected.

Hugh felt Old Robert's blood driving him to violence and protest at the shameful sight of men taking their rights gratefully. But there was no body to suffer his blow, no ear to hear his complaint.

Winter came on and Hugh observed with some surprise that he was growing up. He assumed an adult reaction to circumstances naturally, and marveled at it later. For the first time he took an aggressive interest in his studies. Language, which he had regarded hitherto, when he thought of it at all, as a convenient array of symbols, as useful and prosaic as the links of a chain, impressed him now with its plasticity of meaning and arrangement. Words, he realized, were more than labels; they were fuses which fired in his mind magazines of meaning and emotion.

Under the weight of these reflections he consciously imposed checks and restrictions upon the impetuosity of his nature. His respect for Cleve and his sober deliberate manner grew enormously. He turned their conversation about college in his mind daily, but with his faculties aroused he thought just as often of the problem which had fostered that conversation. Why couldn't there be some balance between the farm and the buyers? What set men so against men? There lay the problem, he realized. Their farming was right he knew, and all his thinking served not to change his love for it; his love became stronger as a parent's does for an afflicted child.

His changing nature expressed itself to his parents through the reserve which began to mark his bearing. His mother mistook it for melancholy. He was unlike himself now, and she was secretly puzzled and unhappy about him. Cleve, too, remarked this change in his son, assigned it to its proper causes, and was secretly very happy over it. While he had admired his own father's faculty for intensive, vital living, he had observed the same tendencies in Hugh with an uneasy alarm, fearing that they might cause him to place a disproportionate value upon elementary things. The present trend of the boy's development would result in an admirably balanced man, he felt, one who could enjoy life, not like a savage appeasing an ignorant hunger, but with an intelligent sense of moderation and discrimination. Cleve was confident, now, that Hugh would welcome a chance to go away to college.

The entire crop was marketed two months before the expiration of school, and Cleve had, for the first time in many years, a gratifying surplus. There was no indication at this time that the war would end soon, and many farmers were bent upon investing all of their profits in an enormous crop for the coming year. Cleve discussed the wisdom of this course with Hugh, who concurred in the opinion that it would be wiser to plant a crop of normal size rather than risk their surplus against the double hazard of weather and circumstances. Cleve's principal objection to embarking upon an agricultural gamble was the fact that he now had a substantial amount of money toward sending Hugh to college the following fall, a thing which he did not wish to jeopardize under any circumstances.

Hugh came downstairs one cold February morning, built a fire for his parents who would follow, and hurried to the kitchen where Aunt Mathy's stove would have warmed the room. But it was cold and empty when he entered. Feeling that illness or accident had delayed her, he paused only long enough to light a lantern, then rushed across the yard to her cabin. She did not answer his call, and his blows upon her door brought not even an echo.

He knew the door was bolted from the inside and did not try to force it. There was little doubt in Hugh's mind as to what he would find in the silence behind it, and because of his fear he went back to the house and called his father.

He saw the light from the lamp in his father's room throw a path across the dark yard and soon Cleve came hurrying down it. They stopped before the cabin door.

"We'll have to break it in," said Cleve.

They threw their united weight against the door several times but it did not budge. Fearing that his father might injure himself, Hugh thought of the window at the back. They moved behind the cabin and Cleve held the lantern while Hugh smashed the panes with a rock. Once inside he found the bolt in the darkness and opened the door where Cleve stood waiting with the lantern.

Hugh followed his father toward the old woman's bed. She seemed to be sleeping peacefully, but he could see in the dim light that no dream had composed that dark face.

Cleve tried to pull her arm from beneath the quilt but he knew when he touched it that he would find no pulse.

"She's dead, Hugh," he said, "and I'm glad she could go this way."

Hugh was unashamed of his tears, and the knowledge

that she who living had never feared death, in dying had not known it, did not check the sorrow swelling in his throat.

12

Hugh observed that the intimate life of the school produced many love affairs, some of which eventually developed into marriage. The greater part of the students conceived their diplomas to be official seals upon the completion of their education. In leaving school they accepted adult life abruptly but fully. Many married in the spring of their graduation and put away beyond resumption the prerogatives of youth. The life of the farm, where sustenance was wrung daily from the soil, permitted this early venture into matrimony.

Helen had attracted an ardent but somewhat clumsy admiration early in the term from James Carroll, the son of a small farmer who had rested an ignorant hope upon the magic of education and the ability of his son. James had limited his courtship to a few rough-hewn compliments delivered in the form of furtive notes during class hours, and a few bashful words during the noon recess period. He lived in a part of the country some distance from the Galloway farm, and was therefore deprived of the pleasure of walking home with Helen. He did bring her home from church occasionally, but wasted these rides in a dumb admiration which embarrassed Helen a great deal. Hugh's evident companionship with her was a source of torment to poor James, who saw in it not a natural, friendly exchange of admiration, but a superior manifestation of his own emotions. His jealousy expressed itself in a strained and silent attitude toward Hugh; he avoided him as much as possible. Although this amused Hugh because of its utter lack of warrant, he felt a kind of sympathy for poor James. It was a matter on which he could not set him right, however, since neither had ever spoken of it, it had never been born in words, and to speak of it might provoke trouble. Hugh mentioned it once to Helen, and her reply had puzzled him for days.

"He simply has a vivid imagination," she said; "so many people have none at all."

This remark stuck in his mind, and often as they returned from school along the lonely path it reasserted itself as a challenge. She never said or did anything else which he could interpret as an invitation, yet that one cryptic statement kept his mind in a ferment of speculation. He began to appraise her good looks, to wonder what intimacy with a girl would be like; almost imperceptibly his bearing toward her became more thoughtful. He extended her small courtesies and considerations which he had never thought of before, but he was unable to detect any response other than a natural gratitude. From speculation his mind turned to anticipation. He found that he dreaded to reach her home in the afternoons, that he waited eagerly to see her again in the mornings. Her casual movements, walking through the woods, excited him unreasonably; he searched her most commonplace utterances for some meaning which was not there. When he was away from her she was constantly in his thoughts, and quite vividly, too; he had an exact mental picture of her eyes and the delicate curve of her lips. He thought of her lips often, hungered for them unknowingly.

He spent a month in this speculative ardor before his natural boldness of spirit prompted him to a definite move. But when he had decided to satisfy his curiosity about her and his own new emotions, he found that no time seemed quite propitious for the experiment. He could think of no graceful approach, was embarrassed at the prospect of blundering, and although he devised plans at home to bring about what he wanted, in the light of day and Helen's presence they seemed calculated to make a fool of him. But his desire to touch her remained, increased, tormented him finally. He wanted to kiss her, wanted to feel her submit to his kiss and cling to it; there was no doubt about his feelings now. What actually happened came about without the aid of any plans.

One day a fierce March shower left the path wet and muddy, although the sun shone brightly after the rain. Helen picked her way along the sloppy path, leaping small puddles and taking advantage of the firm borders wherever she could. Hugh plodded along behind her carrying her books. When they reached the creek it was still swollen and rushing angrily over the rocks which, customarily, they used in crossing. Helen stopped and surveyed it critically.

"Well, you can't leap that," Hugh thought with satisfaction.

Helen looked helplessly at the foaming water.

"Let's go farther up the stream and search for a crossing," she suggested.

"Let's not," said Hugh suddenly, and without another word he threw the books down and picked her up in his arms. She was startled into a little scream by his abruptness, but he strode into the water before she could protest. He was tempted to stand there, such delight her warm body gave him as she clung tightly with excitement. It took but a moment to wade through, but in that moment Hugh lost all the timidity which had frustrated him for weeks. It was all burned away when her hair brushed his cheek.

When he had reached the other bank he lowered her to the ground, but he still kept his arms around her.

"We've landed," she exclaimed with a nervous laugh, and looked at him questioningly.

There was an answer in the look he returned, but she failed to acknowledge it. Instead she stirred gently, but resistantly, in his embrace. Her hands were resting on his shoulders, and now they pressed against him sharply, as if she had suddenly realized that it was an embrace from which she sought to withdraw. He drew her nearer. Again she raised her eyes.

"Kiss me, Helen."

"No."

"Yes, please."

"No. Let me go."

She struggled against his attempt to reach her face, slipped out of his arms, and ran along the path.

He overtook her quickly, contrite and abashed now that he had blundered so miserably.

"Don't run away," he begged, "I . . . don't run away like this."

She walked along silently, her face flaming. Hugh began to feel that he had made a mess of things.

"Please, Helen, don't act like I have insulted you. I meant no harm."

"You haven't insulted me," she replied slowly, "I don't know what you have done to me."

He could think of nothing to say, although his mind wrestled with a desire to lay some verbal balm upon her distraught feelings.

Suddenly she stopped and exclaimed, "You forgot my books."

"Of course I did," he answered, "but I'll get them."

They were some distance from the stream now, and he walked back slowly, trying to think of some way to expiate his clumsiness. He had retrieved the books and was almost back when he noticed that she was not waiting for him. Her home was not more than a quarter of a mile distant and she was running along the path toward it. As soon as she came in sight of the house she stopped running, knowing that he would not run and overtake her, because her people would wonder at his haste. Feeling very foolish, Hugh followed her, making no effort to lessen the distance between them. Her mother was in the yard talking to Helen when he came up, and he proffered the books without explanation, heard her cool thanks, and beat a hurried retreat. It seemed the best thing to do.

Before he reached home he was already wondering how he would resume relations with her in the morning, what he should say, how he should act, whether they could go on talking placidly as if nothing had happened. They could not, he decided. The situation demanded some kind of action now. He had to repeat his attempt, or conduct himself as if he had never made one. Neither course of action appealed to him at the moment, and he reached no decision that night, although he was terribly aware of a growing desire for her, a desire fed on the delightful memory of holding her in his arms at the stream. When morning came he still had not made up his mind, so he purposefully left for school late, and walked all the way alone.

Helen did nothing that day which indicated that the situation worried her, and when school was over they left the grounds together as usual. There were other boys and girls in the little company, but these took various branching paths along the way, and before they reached the stream Hugh and Helen were alone again. Her manner was so disarming that Hugh forgot his anxiety, and glad to be rid of it so easily, he talked gaily until they came to the stream. Brought face to face with this scene, Helen betrayed, by a sudden lack of conversation, that the previous day's event was fresh in her mind.

Hugh took her hand while crossing the rocks, and since she made no effort to withdraw it when they were across, he held it, his own trembling at the prolonged contact.

"I've felt terribly since yesterday," he told her.

"Why?"

It had been in his mind to say that he was sorry for what he had done, but he knew that he was only sorry that he had failed. So he told her the truth.

"Because I really wanted to kiss you."

"Is that all you regret?"

"I'm afraid it is."

"I thought at first that you were going to ask pardon."

Hugh had taken a position, and he decided that the best thing he could do was to hold it.

"Why should I ask your pardon?" he demanded. "I meant you no harm. I certainly did you none. Anyway, if you had known how I felt you wouldn't have minded, you wouldn't have minded my trying to kiss you, I mean."

"How do you know that?"

"Because you would have to feel as I do to know."

"What do you feel, Hugh?"

"Oh . . . don't you know, Helen?"

He still held her hand, and now he placed her palm against his cheek, felt it linger there caressingly.

"I think I know, Hugh," she answered.

She had drawn nearer, and he could see that her eyes were warm and welcoming, that her whole body was leaning toward him, that there was no resistance in it. Her lips were raised to his, and he kissed them hungrily, finding that amazement clouded the pleasure which he had anticipated. Amazement is a momentary experience, however, and they had an abundance of time before them.

13

During the remaining months of school Hugh and Helen maintained an air of friendly indifference while in the classroom, or at any time when other people were present. They did this because they were yet young enough to feel themselves the possessors of a sweet secret, and to feel, moreover, that maintaining secrecy was not only delightful but important. So neither confided in any friend, nor did Hugh display his feelings by calling at her home on an evident love-making mission. Their free moments were confined to the long walks from school. Each day, before they reached her house, after their companions had taken leave of them at various points along the way, there was left fully a mile of wooded path which they traveled alone. Along this mile the path followed the valley of the stream which was full and rushing at this time of year, swollen with the pent-up winter rains which the spring sun was thawing from the hills.

Flanking the stream were some open fields, covered with tall grass, waist high, and golden in color, like ripe wheat when the wind ripples it in the sun, "broom sedge" the negroes call it from the use to which they put its tasseled ends. Nearer the stream and along its banks grew a wavering line of sycamores and willows, still in their winter bareness. Only the pines and cedars were green with life. Where no broom sedge grew, the pines stretched away from the path, so thick that their trunks seemed like pillars supporting a vast, dark roof. Here had once been cultivated fields, and even now the shape of old furrows curved beneath the matted pine needles. The stream sought the course of the Sligo, winding even here along the borders of the river wilderness, among the pines which ran in an unbroken green wave to the deeper forest which hid the river.

The little valley seemed very old and lonely, and so deep had the stream worn it, that the hills which climbed from its bed seemed at length to have tired of climbing, and to be resting at the forest's edge. There were places where bluffs towered, precipitously, half a hundred feet high. From the faces of these, revealed by long erosion, jutted forth huge boulders, sticking in the clay as though some giant had hurled them there when the world was young. From one of these bluffs projected a ledge, accessible by climbing the bluff at a point lower down the stream and then descending to the shelf.

Hugh and Helen often climbed to this spot since it afforded a wild security, shutting off entirely the view of anyone following the path beneath. An overhanging fringe of undergrowth shielded them from above. Lying here together they talked in low whispers, not louder than the faint wind moaning in the pines above them. Once Helen let her hair fall about her shoulders. Hugh pulled her down beside him and lay with his face against the warm curve of her throat, her hair covering his eyes like a veil, shutting out all the world except her sweet nearness. This day they remained there until the sun sank beyond the opposite hill, repeating each other's names and finding music and madness in their sounds.

Love suffused their bodies slowly. At first it had been a new wonder between them, and they had saluted it with a few chaste kisses, as though it were a lovely image which they had created from themselves, but was itself something other than their flesh. And that was true; it had no flesh, not yet, but they were breathing upon it warmly. Suddenly, one day, their image dissolved, and in its place they had only each other and a hot madness in their veins. They hardly knew what had happened to them, and although they looked at each other with naked eyes, neither acknowledged this stranger in the other.

Helen was generous. Her lips were warm and eager. When Hugh's caresses were too impetuous, she curbed them, but with forgiveness. The spring days grew warm and languorous. The valley flushed lustily. Even the bare walls of the bluffs seemed to bloom with a crimson freshness. When they left the valley each evening their last kiss was a promise and a postponement.

14

During the month of April the United States declared war on Germany. As the attitude of the school and the discussions between the teachers and students had been anti-German for months, this intelligence was hailed with sympathy and a strange pride. It was, they all felt, a delayed vindication of righteousness. Patriotism arose, like a flame from the soil, and swept the country. A few old soldiers, a few who had seen service under Lee, and some who had served in the Spanish-American War, polished up their old glory, and became again, through virtue of experience, men of consequence. They had seen war, had watched hostile banners unfurled to the breeze, had followed their own standards into the raging dust of battle. They knew the taste of powder, and the feel of warm blood, and had seen, it appeared, men who hurled themselves at death as if it were a goal, and a fine thing to gather steel into one's heart. Some displayed ancient wounds and warmed their old souls in the reflected glory of this new crusade. Gathering from the far corners of the county, a little band of volunteers assembled at Granville and entrained to offer their services to the country. Most of these were men who had distinguished themselves as roisterers, gamblers, or drinkers, wild and reckless fellows, willing to try anything once. Among the band were some who had never earned reputations for boldness, calm, thoughtful men, who had nursed secretly a thirst for adventure and the call of far countries. There were others who had been impelled to action by the rising fire of patriotism, men who could be driven to hysteria with words. But to the people of

Granville they were all, at the time, splendid crusaders, marching to the rescue of an outraged world. They departed in a blaze of prophetic glory, followed by the cheers of those who remained behind.

Hugh lent his full approval to these proceedings, and by the time school ended, Old Robert's violent blood agonized his veins daily. He filled his mother's heart with fear by his talk of enlisting; although not quite eighteen, he was a man in stature, and began to feel resentment at his mother's plea that he was only a boy. It was Cleve's reasonable arguments which detained him, Cleve who pointed out that there were millions of older men from whom armies could be formed, that the enemy was already hard-pressed and that should there be need of him there would be plenty of time in which to express his loyalty. Moreover, he offered as a deterrent his own advanced age, which compelled him to rely upon Hugh's assistance in running the farm. Finally, a little ashamed of himself, Hugh promised to remain at home and say no more about being a soldier. Cleve wisely kept him busy, turning over all management of the farm to him and feigning indispositions of one kind or another which shifted the farm's responsibilities to Hugh's rebellious shoulders.

For the first time he found the duties of the farm irksome. His heart was set on battle, and he went about his work with the meticulous precision of distaste. Lying in his bed at night he engaged in imaginary combat with a host of phantom enemies.

Hard-pressed by two huge Germans with fierce, bayonet mustaches, he fought, backed against a muddy trench wall. Now they rushed him simultaneously, both intent upon ripping him to shreds. He evaded their charge cleverly, causing them to bury their bayonets to the rifle muzzles in the hard trench clay. Before they could disengage them he sank

his own bayonet in one brute where to his dismay it lodged
and broke. With a mighty flourish, worthy of Old Robert,
he seized the other before he could turn, seized him with his
naked hands, and choked him until he gasped. It was remarkable that in all these encounters his opponents were men of
middle age, huge beast-like men whom it was a pure pleasure
to slaughter. Not once did he find impaled upon his mur-
derous bayonet the agonized form of a boy whose dying eyes
haunted him with an innocent despair.

From the newspaper accounts of the enemy's atrocities,
it was conceivable that among the Germans there were no
young. One could imagine that the process of becoming a
German was one of metamorphosis in which a man suddenly
became a beast. Dave, who had no knowledge of geography
to protect him, kept a constant watch for them and was as
upset as if a swarm of "hants" had been loosed in the community. Hugh told him that Germany was far across the
sea, and that he was safe.

"Whar is dis ocean at?" he asked.

Hugh pointed eastward.

"How fur dat-a-way?"

"Thousands and thousands of miles," Hugh replied.

"Is dar any of dem in dis heah country?"

"Probably."

"Is you eber seed air un?"

"Not that I know of."

"Do you reckon dey is folks like us?"

"There is not much difference."

"How you gwiner know when you see air un, den? I'd
ruther dey wus like ur snake or ur bar, in case I wanted to
shoot air un. Efen dey is mens, how do dey keep straight
who's gwiner shoot who?"

"They wear uniforms, Dave, the Germans one kind, and
we another."

"Dat's so dey kin keep de shootin' an' killin' straight?"

"Well, not entirely."

"How come den?"

"Well, you see, Dave, it's the law—for us to wear a certain kind of uniform. And the Germans have a law about theirs, too. See?"

"Sho, sho," said Dave. The law was just the law, and that's all there was to it.

There were hours, however, when Hugh's love for Helen conquered his warring instincts, for he still saw her. When school had closed and they were deprived of the companionship which it gave them, he had been unwilling to call at her home. It was a silly feeling, she had protested, assuring him that her parents would not object, yet she had yielded to her desire to be with him, and with full consideration of the danger she dared, she had consented to furtive meetings at the edge of the woods between the two farms, going there at dusk and explaining her absences from home by a number of unplausible reasons. The nature of their meetings, she realized, cast false implications upon her, and would have been damning if they were discovered by Lonnie. And he was as suspicious and sneaking as a cat.

Hugh's refusal to come to her house angered and hurt her, but he met her renewed requests with stubborn evasions. The simple truth of his attitude lay in the fact that he had become so fond of those hours of wild security in their little valley, that he could not bear to think of being with her within the restraining walls of a house, particularly her father's house. Instinctively, he knew that an open courtship would provoke friction in his own home, since neither of his parents could have forgiven Old Henry Galloway for his ancestry. The thing would not have set with them at all. With that pagan loyalty to the moment which had been his heritage from his grandfather, he enjoyed Helen's love with no sense of obligation. Helen's anger always took the form of tears in the end, tears which drove him to a momentary shame over his selfishness. The ease with which he had won her love, as if it had been a gift, encouraged his lack of consideration, made him too demanding. And she held no weapons against him, because he regarded the continued courtship of James Carroll as nothing more than a joke, refusing with all his native arrogance to consider that this constituted a rivalry. Helen's words failed to move him; only her tears shook his brutal indifference to her pleading. He had once kissed her wet cheeks, had rebuked himself, and made a half-hearted promise to call at her home, a promise which he failed to keep in any full measure, because when he went there he had talked at random to the assembled family, had become disgusted with their slovenly talk, and had left quickly without making Helen the ostensible object of his visit. Just a neighborly call. Lonnie made him sick, the great hulking ignoramus. And old Henry was up to his ears in the land. He cared for nothing else, and this love was purely an avaricious one. The house was clean enough, but Mrs. Galloway had been almost humble to him. It was sickening.

Helen had not seen him again for a week, a miserable week during which she fought her desire to seek him in another clandestine meeting. He had passed near her in the churchyard Sunday, had paused and said a single word: "Tonight."

And after a moment of weak hesitation she had answered: "Tonight."

This had been the only struggle between them, and he had been ingloriously victorious.

15

That his acceptance of Helen's love imposed obligations beyond his temporary and voluntary allegiance did not occur to Hugh. He had not pursued her, he had begged no favors, nor had he made many demands upon her. Her devotion had followed their first caress as naturally and as completely as night follows day, as though it had always existed and had come, like the night, at its appointed time. Those furtive meetings, to which she conceded reluctantly, were not, he told himself, demands; they were rather pleasures which she could choose or forego, for he had not learned that love can effect shameful compromises with pride.

This was his first adventure in love, one in which he had been spared the sting of jealousy and the cut of defeat; there was little gratitude in its realization. That Helen's honest response, free of cajolery and wiles, was in itself a fine and rare thing, he did not know, nor was he aware that her devotion had become an insistent passion which would not leave her content with a transitory and frustrated expression. He did not know this of her, yet he knew that it was becoming true of himself. In the beginning, baffled by the newness and power of his emotions, he had talked much and with little satisfaction. Anger, he knew, and fear and doubt and sometimes shame could be eased with words. Love, he found, refused to yield to these symbols. Even caresses, he realized, were only symbols with all their attendant confusion, and they had exhausted them. As far as he knew love itself might be only a symbol, a name which men had given to an unattainable peace and loveliness. It seemed so. It always held something back. It fed on hunger. In all of its loveliness there was a subtle hint of deeper loveliness. There was no peace in seeing Helen, only a delicious riot of hot curiosity.

How strongly Helen felt these same burning questions he did not know; but their relationship, incomplete as it was, delighted him, and he pursued it with no full reckoning of the significance of their growing intimacy. They had not discussed marriage, and he had considered it only in the most remote way. He was not satisfied with their restricted companionship, but he did not feel that his emotions as yet demanded a fixed and permanent adjustment.

To Helen, reared in a family where caution was a formula of action, where all things came by labor, love was not just a happy and inconsequential incident. Her very acquiescence to Hugh's wishes grew not so much out of weakness as from what her heart had established as supremely important. Love was inseparable in her mind from the corollary of marriage, and through a reliance on the evident mutuality of their affection, she believed that marriage would in time ensue. She hoped so fervently. For this reason she had discounted the hazards of their clandestine courtship.

Although she knew that her father regarded the Wintons with a kind of deferential distrust she attached little significance to his attitude, sensing that it was a remnant of servile suspicion which he had retained from his boyhood. Of her ancestors she had heard little, but enough to impress her with the value of holding the subject silent. Her father's patrimony had been only the strength of his hands and the faculty of retaining a part of every trifle that came his way. Although his life's effort had been directed to but one end, that of expressing himself in the medium of possession, of acquiring by right of acquisition a surface parity with the old landowners, his very distrust of these families, his fear of learning and leisure, branded him, she perceived, with the unalterable mark of that class which he strove to escape. Fortunately, she shared little of his feeling, and felt no shame in the company of people from older families. That she realized the practical advantages of a union with a Winton was true, but it was merely recognition, not ambition.

There were times when she felt that her emotions would no longer contain themselves, when it seemed imperative that she make a confidant of someone. She wished to unburden her heart to her mother. Meditating this, she was unable to recall ever having seen an expression of affection between her parents. She had never surprised them in a caress. Somewhat dubious about her mother's ability to understand her relationship with Hugh, she stifled her impulse to tell her anything. With Lonnie she had no companionship at all. His early bullying nature had developed into a surly, brooding contentiousness. Though he had shown no interest in going to school himself, he resented his mother's persistence in keeping Helen there as a mark of partiality. Unwillingly on Helen's part the rift between them had widened over this very thing, and Lonnie widened it further by taunting her constantly with being too good for her family. He had an ill-tempered, ignorant sense of martyrdom, and he scowled at the whole world. He was big and strong and cleverly brutal, and Helen feared that she hated him. Her natural desire to love her brother had long since given way to a feeling of enforced toleration for the sake of kinship. On the whole her family life was drab and lonely.

That very education which Mrs. Galloway had made possible served to exclude her in many respects from Helen's life. It had opened to Helen avenues of thought and delicate pleasures in which her mother could take no part. The conversation of the kitchen, the little recurrent affairs of the household, the simple array of daily trivialities, these were time and substance to her mother, time and substance, hope and reward. The borders of her imagination extended only to Granville and to yesterday, and even there they were a bit vague. But she was immensely proud of her daughter.

Helen had come to feel an intense dissatisfaction with her life and home. There was no corner about this long, dank ell of a house where one could pin a bright ribbon of romance. It stank with the odor of graceless reality. Hugh was right: love flourished only in the fields. Dull, mud-tracked halls and battered kitchens were no harbor for it, nor could it go gaily in the company of resolute and earth-bound families. The wind and the stars, the gentle dew of evening, and the soft sighing of the pines were the music to which it danced, and these alone, she felt, could sustain it, these or some enormous room into which the night could enter, into which the kind light of the moon could steal, like a long caress, and lose itself in its vastness.

She began to look to love for an escape from the unhappiness of her home and from the distasteful permanences which it represented. James Carroll, whom she still saw, became a breathing symbol of all she wished to escape. He was sincere, and speechless. He desired her love, but what, she wondered, would he do with it? He wished vainly for favors which Hugh had gathered as the fruit of impulse. He begged for love and she gave him pity. He would beg from life, she knew, and it would give him a few stones from which to conjure his daily bread. He would live in a small house and dream small dreams, and be thankful, each day, for something or other. He would construe his misfortunes as blessings in disguise, and would torment her with his implacable resignation to an inherited adversity. He would be kind and blundering, industrious and short-sighted, and altogether ineffectual.

16

"Tonight," he had said, and now the day was hastening toward the west.

In the dim light of her room she surveyed her body as she rubbed it dry with a rough towel. It pleased her, straight and clean and gleaming in the faint light. It pleased her to touch it, to remember, in the sense of her own hand, the pleasure of his caressing hands.

On the bed her dress lay folded neatly. It was the one that she had worn all day. Although she longed to change into a fresh one, she dared not. Lonnie would wonder why she had to dress twice in one day. She had been at great difficulty, since she first consented to these meetings with Hugh, to invent suitable excuses for her absences from home. At first she had met him only on Wednesday evenings, pretending a late return from prayer-meeting. Later she had hit upon the ruse of borrowing books from the Wintons. This had proved a good plan, because each book offered another opportunity for a meeting when she returned it. Hugh usually met her with a new book which she brought home and, sometimes, read. Once, in a spirit of fun, he had brought a small dictionary, and again a volume of Roman law, untranslated, which he had found among his grandfather's books. She had taken care to hide these where Lonnie could not see them. She feared that he was not taken in by her excuses, and more than ever she put herself on guard against his ferreting suspicion.

Next her body she put on only fresh garments, her finest dainty things of silk and lace which she had bought in Granville. She dressed herself with care, drawing her stockings smoothly over her knees and fitting her breasts with a creation of her own hands. In her mind she was already at Hugh's side and her heart raced toward him as she slipped on her dress. She paused to take a last look in her mirror, adjusted an invisible wisp of hair, and descended the stairs.

As she left the yard the western sky was still glowing with the retreating fire of the sun, and long slits of crimson broke through the blue clouds which hovered along the horizon.

Whippoorwills sounded their weird calls in the woods between the two farms. Here and there along the hedges which bordered the fields she saw timid young rabbits emerge to browse in the open, dewy meadows. They scurried back into their retreats as she passed. The soft dusk of twilight lay over the meadows, but in the woods it was already dark. Everything was indistinct in this fog of blackness which the ascending moon would soon disperse, for here huge oaks and hickories grew, not profusely, but royally and apart, with the generous strength of age, each having settled itself upon its own proper and inviolable estate. Between these regal trees were open spaces, into which the moon could throw the splendor of its rays. They would guide her home.

Following the path which wound around the ancient trees Helen soon saw, along the border of the woods, the lesser darkness of the open sky in which had appeared now several early stars. There where the path entered the woods Hugh would be waiting. She hurried.

She saw him before she reached the open field, pacing impatiently along its edge. Halting, she called to him softly.

"Helen," he cried, joining her, "it's been such a long day!"

"A long week, dear," she corrected.

He held her close, toying with time, postponing for a moment the delight of closer union. Then he kissed her again and again until she clung to him, limp and speechless with passion.

Taking his hand she led him away from the woods toward the crest of the hill where crimson clover was growing in full bloom. Its heavy, sweet incense filled the damp night air with intoxicating fragrance. Hugh pulled her down beside him and held her head in the curve of his arm. Closing her eyes, she inhaled the clover-laden air, breathing it luxuriously, as if it were an exhilarating drug. He could see the scarlet thread of her smile as she drank in the night like a rapturous wine, trembling with beauty, her lips quivering with love. It seemed profane to talk. Hugh lay with his face in her hair. Through his right arm, lying supine across her bosom, he felt her heart racing.

From a long silence she spoke slowly, looking toward the sky.

"Our love is like the stars, Hugh."

He caught the shamed sadness in her voice, and stilled by it he made no reply.

"We hide it in the day," she continued, "like something too weak to face the sun. It belongs to the night, our love. Strange, silent, as impossible as a star."

Her voice sank to a trembling whisper. She was weeping.

Baffled by her grief, Hugh still said nothing. Beneath his arm a spasm of sobs racked her breast, but soon she spoke in a calmer voice.

"Is our love to be a summer's love, Hugh?"

"What do you mean?"

"You know I can't continue seeing you like this. Haven't you thought of that? I can't help thinking of it, all the time. It spoils everything. If it were just one night I were snatching from time like a greedy child, I wouldn't worry about tomorrow. But I'm not a child. I'm a woman, Hugh, and I love you, and you do nothing but break my heart."

"Helen," he protested, "you know I love you."

"How do I know it?" she demanded fiercely. "Life's just a big minute to you, nothing but *now, now, now!* I can't trifle about this. We aren't playing post office."

Her outburst moved him greatly, and the sight of her wet face sent a wave of compassionate tenderness through him. She was right, he realized with a hot flow of self-reproach: he had been selfish, inconsiderate, even cruel. But this strong tide of remorse did not sweep him to an offer of marriage. He felt for the first time that he was being borne in that direction, and the sudden realization frightened and confused him. He tried to temporize.

"Winter is far away," he said in his perplexity, "and there'll be other springs."

In her overwrought mood Helen took his words as a callous dismissal of all her love had come to mean. She sprang to her feet, rigid with anger and indignation.

"Winter has come already!" she cried. "We'll not talk of spring. What a fool I've been!"

Anger could not sustain her long. Heartbroken sobs rose in her throat, and ashamed to weep before him now she ran blindly towards the woods.

Hugh's own torment spurred him to overtake her. He would explain. She had to understand.

"Helen!" he called, "I didn't mean that! I can't let you go believing I did. Helen ... please ... Oh Helen .. !"

But she was gone, running like a wild thing and deaf to all but her own crying heart.

Hugh picked up the two books she had left, and turned homeward, ashamed and miserable.

17

Helen ran until she reached the meadow beyond the woods, finding her way by habit, so blinded by tears and outraged love that she hardly knew what she was doing. The light from her own house distracted her attention momentarily, and impressed her with the necessity of controlling her emotions before confronting her family. She sat on a stone by the path and tried to dry her eyes, but Hugh's brutality was too fresh in her mind; she wept convulsively. After what seemed an age she attained some semblance of control, and walked toward the house hoping that she would be able to enter it and reach her room unobserved.

This hope was destroyed as she entered the yard. Her mother and father were seated in the hallway with the door flung open to the breeze. Lonnie sat on the porch, his legs sprawled along the floor, his back jammed against a pillar. She had a horrible premonition that they were waiting for her, waiting in judgment. Masking her fear as best she could, she entered the hall.

Lonnie allowed her to pass, allowed her to reach the stairs before he spoke. Then, employing a tone of guileless innocence, he called after her:

"Where have you been, Helen?"

Before she could answer, her father repeated Lonnie's question.

"Yes, where have you been?"

Sensing the import of these questions, she sought her mother's face in the dim light. Her worst fears were confirmed, for her mother sat weeping dumbly.

"Did you hear me, Helen?" Old Henry shouted; "where have you been?"

"I thought I told you that I was going to the Wintons'," she replied, knowing that this answer would provoke him into a declaration of whatever he knew.

"So you have taken up lying, too?" he snapped, staring up at her as she stood on the stairs.

Lonnie had come in from the porch, and stood behind his father. He, too, scowled up at her.

"I know where you were," her father accused; "I've been suspicious of this book business, all along. Lonnie followed you this time."

She looked at Lonnie, bewildered. She had not thought him that mean. His face was hard and ugly. She saw no sympathy there, no mercy, nothing but a stupid pride over having spied upon her successfully.

"Lying 'round in the woods with Hugh Winton," he charged.

"Like a common nigger wench," supplemented Old Henry.

"Don't say that, Henry," her mother interceded, taking a place near her at the foot of the stairs. "I know you're a good girl, Helen."

"You git away from her," Old Henry ordered, thrusting them apart. "That's what comes of your schooling her, and slaving to make her a lady."

There was no answer but a defeated sob.

At any other time this tirade would have unnerved Helen completely. Just now, coming on the heels of her bitter parting with Hugh, it found her numb, already dazed by grief, and passively resigned to their accusations. It was evident that Lonnie and her father had set no limits in their imagination to her transgressions. Unprotestingly, she allowed them to bluster on.

"Too good fur your own kind," Old Henry railed, "but you ain't good enough fur a Winton, 'less you come crawling in the dark."

Knowing that her meetings with Hugh lent themselves to this kind of interpretation, she had accepted, so far, the combined charges of Lonnie and her father with a sense of guilt almost proportionate to their suspicions. Now slow rising anger prompted a denial.

"Yes, I admit it. I met Hugh tonight. I love him, and until tonight I believed that he loved me. That's all; I swear it."

"That's enough," Lonnie sneered.

Her denial afforded Old Henry another chance to berate her. He went off in a tirade, releasing his imprisoned hatred of the Wintons and all they represented.

"I know what the boy is like. I knew his old granddaddy. A woman wasn't safe in the same county with him. The boy is just a chip off the old block, lying 'round in the woods with poor white girls, poor fools, like you."

Although she realized that hatred exaggerated her father's remarks, his outburst, coupled with the memory of Hugh's rudeness which still burned in her mind, kindled a doubt in her heart. Was it true, then, that he had merely played with her, trifled, planned a loveless seduction? The thought filled her with a sick shame, and overshadowed her immediate trouble with her family. Slowly, unmindful of her father's reproaches, she mounted the stairs. At the top she paused and addressed them briefly.

"Lay your minds at rest," she said; "nothing has happened, and nothing will. We broke up tonight. But you know that already, don't you, Lonnie?" she added bitterly.

She locked herself in her room. Stretched across her bed in her virginal and unruffled finery, she wept, exhausted her tears, and finally slept, the fragments of her romance crushed under the sick weight of this doubt which robbed even memory of beauty.

The following day brought with it a morning hope that Hugh would come to reassure her, to remove this growing feeling of deception which ate at her heart like a disease. But he did not come that day, nor in the days which followed. His absence confirmed her father's statements, she felt, and reluctantly she yielded to the conviction that she had been duped, that she had given her love for something that was not love, but only an ugly shadow of it. To support this conviction her imagination revived the ghosts of old fears which she had buried in her heart; the fact that Hugh had not talked much, had never mentioned marriage, and the whole of his ungracious courtship became so many evidences against which the faltering hope in her breast proved a poor defendant—before which it sank into submissive silence and at length died completely.

The atmosphere of a shamed family trust, made more unbearable by her mother's attitude of mute forgiveness, hung like an accusing pall over the house. Slowly, under the oppressive gloom of suspicion, the sick resignation of her soul, and a weakening fortitude in her resolve not to seek Hugh again, she formed a mad resolution, born of defeat and a sacrificial despair.

18

Hugh walked the fields Monday with a heavy heart, repenting the grief which he had caused Helen and himself. It became clear that there was nothing for him to do but go to her and make apology and if possible amends, and during the day he resolved to go that night. But he hesitated before the attendant explanations to his family and to hers that such a move would make necessary. Wishing to know his mind fully, he postponed his visit and decided to wait until he saw her at church. Then he would ask if he might come to her house. They could settle the rest there. He knew now that his desire for her was so urgent that some kind of reunion was imperative, and since it was out of the question to hope for a resumption of their hidden meetings, there was nothing he could do but make an open breast of the matter, face his family, and accept the unpleasant consequences of his decision. Several times during the week he was at the point of making a full declaration to Cleve, but he postponed this also, thinking it wiser to make his peace with Helen first.

He hesitated to take his problem to his parents, because he knew that it would conflict with their plans for his education, as well as offend their pride. When he considered his own dislike for Helen's father and brother, he who loved her, he could see no reason why his parents should accept the match gracefully. It was asking too much. Now, had he been one of many sons, he told himself, he might expect a more tolerant attitude, but he was their only son, their hope of continued existence, and, in a manner, a standard-bearer, one to defend and preserve their way. That this feeling rested upon a rightful pride of long family endurance and accomplishment, upon a mastery of land and adversity which had been a blood heritage, he felt strongly. His destiny was in a sense a family thing, and not altogether his own. His allegiance to these things was no denial of his love for Helen, and their recognition involved no shame of her; he simply saw clearly that her people were forever alien to his, that they were foreign and opposed to all that his name meant in the simple annals of the community.

Hugh searched the church with eager expectancy Sunday. Helen was not there when he arrived, but people often came late. Seated in the back of the building, where he could observe all late comers, he surrendered himself to the mellow peace of the house. At the far end of the building on his left the choir sang, sustained by the somber tones of the organ. Brother Baily's gray hair appeared above the pulpit. Hugh thought irreverently of the two chickens. The hymn came to a reverberating close, the minister rose and delivered a long prayer, concluding with a repetition of the Lord's Prayer, in which by custom the congregation joined, their voices rising and falling like the drone of many bees.

The minister's sonorous voice reached his ears, expounding a text:

"Go to the ant, thou sluggard. Consider her ways, and be wise."

"Go to Helen," thought Hugh; "I have considered her ways and found them lovely. Today I will be wise. Tomorrow she will be mine, all bickerings over, all explanations made."

Like the voice of a cosmic threat the preacher continued: "In the summer of your feasting, prepare against the hunger of winter. Consider the days in passing, and know that verily they have an end, when reckoning shall be taken of their hours and deeds, when rewards shall be harvested, and punishments dealt to those who deserve them. Consider to-morrow and yesterday, and know that today is at once the two. Although you plant with the rising sun, yet may you reap with the evening star. Our time and our place are not promised to us; prepare for the ultimate gathering of the sheaves."

It all sounded woeful and awe-inspiring, but Hugh refused to allow the scriptural words of doom to curb his full spirits. He thought of Helen, and rejoiced in his thoughts.

He searched for her in the churchyard after the services, but she was not there. Disappointed but not alarmed, he started home, leaving his parents to attend to the little social amenities of the churchyard, to speak to everybody and to join everybody in congratulating the preacher, and then to join everybody again in inviting him home to dinner, where he might emulate the worthy ant of his sermon, and take temporary reinforcement against his eternal appetite.

At home he read until four o'clock, when Cleve asked him to walk with him through the growing fields. They walked away from the house, together, down by the well, and through the cedar-shaded valley behind the stables, by the spring and the tobacco barns, and into the road which led through their fields to the blue devastation of Sligo. Cleve appraised the growing crops, remarking that new ground should be planted the next year to rest the fields through which they were passing. Hugh listened, but his mind was not on his father's words.

"We must let Spring Hill grow up next year," he directed; "it has been in cultivation since you were a baby."

"All right. We can enlarge my new-ground."

"Good. That timber is large enough for building logs. We need another barn, anyway."

"I expect we will," Hugh responded, his mind on Helen.

He ate little supper, and excused himself hurriedly, saying that he was going for a walk.

"But you walked this afternoon," Cleve exclaimed.

"I'm going for another," he answered, and left abruptly.

In the week which had passed since he had seen Helen, they had cut all the clover from the hill, going there each evening with a wagon and scythe. He walked over the brow of the hill, found the path at its edge, and entered the woods. When he had passed through them he saw the lights of her house. He wanted to run toward them, but restrained his impatience. As he entered her yard he saw that no one was on the porch. That pleased him. Perhaps she would answer the door and he wouldn't have to ask for her. But Lonnie came at his knock, stared at him sullenly for a moment, and then invited him in. He followed Lonnie's dark bulk down the narrow hall and into the living room. In the dim light of the kerosene lamp he saw Old Henry and his wife. Helen was not there.

The old man did not ask him to take a seat. Instead he demanded gruffly:

"What brings *you* here?"

"Only a desire to see Helen," Hugh replied, angered and puzzled by their rude reception. "Where is she?"

"What you got to see her 'bout?" Old Henry asked.

"I'd rather tell that to her," Hugh replied, trying to hold his rising temper.

"Well, she ain't here."

"Where is she, then, tell me?"

"Mebbe you won't have so much to tell her," said her father, "since she married Jim Carroll today."

Hugh checked an exclamation of incredulous protest. He looked in their faces. Mrs. Galloway confirmed her husband's statement, sobbing:

"It's so. It's so."

He stumbled from the house and walked blindly down the path, trying to reconcile this impossibility with his senses. Not his Helen, not Helen of the clover kisses. Rage and grief clouded his mind; his heart sickened with the knowledge that he had brought it all upon himself. And yet his mind refused to accept what he had heard as reality. With the unbelief with which one looks on death, the human inability to comprehend that which is not human, his senses balked at this thing which he knew was so utterly false.

He reached the clover hill, threw himself on the earth, and wept the long bitter sobs of youth. It was his first taste of sorrow, his first defeat, and it seemed like the dissolution of his world. Here just a week ago he had held her vibrant with love for him. Here he had kissed her and felt her heart race at his touch, her heart which even now throbbed with a grotesque lie.

19

Now that Helen was irrevocably gone his love for her, which had been a restraining influence against his desire to join the army, became a reason for wishing to carry out this desire. The familiar fields, the sight of her house across a naked hill, the empty intimacy of the woods, all seemed to mock him. Hitherto, twilight, the time of their appointed meetings, had been a welcome hour, a happy veil which a kind earth drew over the sad inconsistencies of day, a veil which shielded, among many things, love. "Dusty dark" as the negroes called it now provoked his memory into a train of self-torturing thought.

The crops were being laid by, and whether he was working in his own or directing the negroes he could not escape the dull pain of memory. Her name was in every sound, and it went up and down the rows with him. The solitude of the fields was not solitude but a mocking silence, and clinging with habit-bound hands to his plow, as if it were some animate thing which pulled him along with it, he covered row after row with only a vague comprehension of the work he was doing.

In France, he thought, strange action and strange faces would offer some relief from these bitter surroundings. Formerly he had looked on this as adventure; now it was escape. With the crops laid by, he could leave without deserting Cleve in a time of urgent need. Cleve could handle everything after that. Each day he came nearer a decision, and finally, when he was quite sure that their protests would not deter him, he announced his decision to his parents.

They were thunderstruck. His mother broke into tears immediately, but Cleve's patient reserve turned to quick anger.

"That's the biggest fool thing I ever heard of," he cried.

"I'm going," Hugh said stubbornly.

He had known how they would take it and had steeled his heart against their protests, but the sight of his mother's face forced him to look away. He began to wish that he could have simply gone without facing them.

"In God's name why are you doing it, Hugh?" Cleve demanded. Hugh knew he could not tell him.

"I think I ought to," he replied.

"The government will call you when you ought to go."

"I'm going now."

Cleve turned and walked across the room, whirled in his tracks with some new argument on his lips, but the cold set of Hugh's jaw silenced him. He knew he could not hold him.

Sensing Cleve's feeling his wife raised her voice despairingly: "Hugh, please!"

This Hugh could not stand. He rushed out of the room.

Cleve turned to Sally. His concern was now for her.

"The boy's going, Sally," he said. "I know him. The best thing we can do is control ourselves and make the parting pleasant."

As always she tried to follow his advice. When Hugh returned to the house she met him with dry eyes, and not until the buggy taking him to the depot in Granville had disappeared down the road the next morning did she throw herself on her bed and give way to her grief.

Part Two

A COLD wind whistled through the bare trees around the Winton house, picked up some dry leaves and hurled them against the shuttered windows, blew impotently at the barred door, and hurried away over the bleak fields. Hugh Winton, returning from two years of war on a gray December day, stood in the yard and listened to this dirge which the wind sang over his empty house. The experience of those two years sat solidly on him, stamping his features with some of its hardness, dulling his blue eyes with a too close acquaintance with pain, and checking in his throat a rising torrent of grief which welled up at sight of this desolate, voiceless place.

Two years had hardened him. Many things he had seen in that time, the cities with their burden of life, the limitless wastes of the sea, the lands beyond with their screaming skies and violent, ragged horizons, their strange peoples wailing, laughing, starving, loving, dying—raw, upheaved stretches of the world, with men who crawled in them and died like rats, men wounded, mutilated, mad. He had seen these things, had endured them somehow, but they had not prepared him for his homecoming; some of the hardness deserted his features, his blue eyes warmed with grief, and like a child he wept, unashamed.

He had fled this house, had fled sorrow, and now he had returned, and it was to sorrow he had returned, to a deserted house from which death had taken Cleve and Sally. Although influenza had struck them during the first year of his absence and they had been dead now for more than a year, the sight of the silent house, the storm-swept devastation of the yard, and the bleak fields impressed him now for the first time with the full significance of their passing. Alone once again in his own home, his house rather, for of his home nothing remained but the walls and the memories which they housed, he wandered from room to room as if by searching he might find behind the next door something which lived and had a welcoming voice. He found only silence and dust.

Other than this dust the house was very much as his parents had left it. The chairs in the living room were placed orderly around the cold fireplace, as though some pleasant company had left them there before an evening fire, had mounted the curved staircase, gone to their respective bedrooms, and had not returned. Beneath the flowing cloth which covered the dining room table he saw the dust-rimmed shape of dishes, the high pinnacle of the preserves bowl, the lesser mound of the sugar bowl near it, and around the edges the faint outlines of plates. On the sideboard stood a bowl of wax peaches, furred with dust.

He walked on through the dining room into the kitchen, laid his hand on the cold stove, withdrew it quickly, strode to the side door, unlatched it, and passed out into the back yard. A few sticks of wood lay rotting at the woodpile. He selected the firmest among them and searched for an ax. Although he raked the bark on the floor of the wood-shed and searched the cleft in the old elm, he could not find one. At length he threw the stick back on the pile from which he had taken it, walked around the house, and gathered an armful of sticks from the wind-smashed limbs which littered the ground. He took these into the living room and started a fire.

Sitting there before the fire he was unable to bring his

mind to the task of rehabilitation which confronted him. It clung, instead, to a dreary review of his misery, pervading him with a clairvoyant sadness which told him that there was something symbolic about his parents' death, something more than the simple return of two human beings to the hungry dust; he felt that with them had died a manner of living which he could not revive, a plenteous, deep-loamed, fruitful way. The old house stood a monument to the fertile past, to Cleve, to Old Robert, to their frugality and profligacy, their customs and faiths, and to the dissolution of their hardy civilization. Perhaps it were best to leave it so, to go out into the world again, and to forget it. That had been Cleve's wish, that had been his advice, and that was what his own heart, saddened by the ruin and disorder around him, bade him do, but only for a moment. The fields would live again, would flourish, and flourishing bring joy and life back from the deep soil to which they had fled. Perhaps the stillness of the house was not unlike the bleached grass which covered them now, just a magician's veil under which new life was generating. He could revive those bleak fields, he knew it, and drawing courage from this knowledge, he told himself that he could make the old rooms ring with the music of voices again. What of the world to which Cleve had directed him? No place awaited him there. No friend yearned for his coming. There were sorrow and disappointment there as well as here, and it was alien sorrow and alien death, in the end, that awaited him there. His home was here, and he would live in it.

2

Hugh found the resumption of his life on the farm less difficult than he had feared it would be. Characteristically, he had visualized the task of rebuilding purely as a labor of his own, but when he had made a beginning, he found many hands eager to help him. It was the end of the year, croppers were exercising their annual discontent and seeking new homes, and there was plenty of time in which to make all preparations for a crop. Cleve had left money in the bank, that sum laid by for Hugh's education, and this, he found, was far more than he needed to finance a crop. His expenses, he judged, should not be much greater than if the farm had been in continual operation. Horses and mules he did not have to buy, because the neighbors were keeping and working those which Cleve had owned at his death, having agreed among themselves to take care of his property until Hugh returned. They had collected the implements and stored them from the weather, and had even kept an accounting of corn which they had taken from the croppers as Cleve's share.

As soon as the news of his return had spread through the neighborhood, and it became known that he was going to remain on the farm, older men, some of them his father's friends, some strangers, came to give him advice and encouragement. His nearest neighbors, the Galloways, paid him no visits, nor did he go to their house. Old Henry was still alive, he learned. Lonnie was with him, not yet married, and together they were locked in an avaricious struggle with the earth. He heard nothing about Helen, asked nothing.

Many people came to help him, and all went away glad that they had come because his gratitude was evident, even without words. But that was his greatest trouble, they helped him and went away. There was not one among them all of whom he could say, "Here is my friend to whom I have returned, who shares my homecoming, and loves me." His childhood had been singularly devoid of companionship, and now he regretted it. The nearest answer to this need came in the black shape of Dave beating at his door one morning before he awoke.

"Let me in, Cap'n," he cried eagerly, "let me see how you looks."

"Come on in, Dave," Hugh shouted, just as eagerly. "Push the door; it's not locked."

Dave entered, his face cleft by a broad happy grin.

"I 'clare! I 'clare! Efen you ain't growed to be ur reg'lar man sho' 'nuff. Cap'n, I'm glad to see you, 'fore Gawd I is."

"It's good to see you, too, Dave. You are the first real homefolks I've seen," Hugh said without hiding all the bitterness he felt.

His grief was not lost upon Dave. He shed his warm, dark affection upon him in a smile of understanding.

"Hit's bad 'bout yo folks, hit sho is," he said solemnly. "But," he added, "hit's natchall. Old folks has to poke urlong, 'pears like."

"Well, where are you living, Dave?"

"Whar is I livin'?"

"Whose land? You are working, aren't you?"

"Don't be standin' dar astin' me no question like dat. What you reckon I'm bustin' yo doah down dis time-ur-day fur? I ain't stopped walkin' fur a minute since I done hyead you wus home."

"Came home yourself, did you?" asked Hugh, flattered in spite of himself.

"Yassuh, I done come home. What you want me to start doin'?"

"Can you cook?"

"Cap'n, you know I ain't no kitchen nigger."

"Well, can you find me a cook?"

"Dat's sho one thing we gwiner need. Lemme see. Dar's my sister. She ain't no bad cook."

"Can you get her?"

"Sho I kin. Hab her heah fo night."

"Go get her then."

Dave backed to the door. There he hesitated, looked at Hugh, looked at the floor, made no progress.

"Is dar any danguh uf findin' ur little sumpin' t'eat 'roun heah dis mawnin'?" he asked. " 'Pears like I'm powerful hongry atter walkin' so fur."

"I suppose so. One of the cropper's wives gets my meals."

"I'll jest drap in de kitchen," said Dave, "an' tell her to put de little pot in de big un."

At the end of the week, with Annie installed in the kitchen and a store of groceries, meats, flour, molasses, sugar, and coffee convenient to her hands, Hugh dispatched Dave to invite men to a "cutting frolic." Several white men responded to his request, some sent negroes in their places, some came and brought their negroes with them. At least twenty men had assembled at his house by noon, and when they left for the woods Annie was already immersed in prodigal preparations for their evening meal.

Hugh remembered that Cleve had talked to him of clearing the entire bottom and hill opposite Spring Hill, and had directed him to see that this was done, but he had left the farm shortly after their conversation. Although the whole farm had lain fallow for a year, he thought it wise to open some new land, to turn some of the old fields back into timber, and to build, as Cleve had ordered, a new barn. Therefore, he led the axemen to the woods beyond Spring Hill, taking along a cross-cut saw to use on the trees he had marked for barn logs.

Dave had suggested the saw.

"Hit will save us ur lot uf work," he had pointed out, "efen we square dem butts when dey is cut."

"Right!" Hugh had answered, pleased. Dave was not lazy, but he believed in conserving his efforts.

These trees Hugh felled first, putting two men to work sawing their butts smooth and cutting the proper lengths from their trunks. By mid-afternoon the sun had drawn resin from the fresh stumps and had spread it over their yellow surfaces in little honey-colored beads, like syrup on pancakes.

Wood enough to supply the farm for a year lay strewn on the hill at sunset, stripped of its branches, its trunks cut into segments, its brush piled neatly for burning when it had become dry and sapless. Later, at their convenience, he and Dave would split these segments, stack them to dry, and remove the stumps and roots.

Among the men who remained for supper was one who was almost a stranger to Hugh, a young man, Eugene Clay. Hugh had seen him at church when he was a boy and Cleve had pointed out the Clay farm from the Granville road, but they had never been more than bare acquaintances. Eugene was older than Hugh, but like him lately returned from France. This fact established a bond between them immediately. At the supper table they exchanged war experiences, and before the meal was finished Hugh felt himself warm to this stranger, felt that he would like him greatly, and this pleased him, for he wanted a friend desperately.

Eugene was tall and leanly built, blonde, with a long sober face, saved from ugliness only by the splendor of his wide gray eyes. He did not look of a class with the other farmers present, honest, hard-working, dull-tongued men, and he talked decidedly unlike them; his talk seemed bookish beside theirs, but it was only an unaffected, native eloquence, re-inforced by wide reading, which gave it this tone. Conversation languished over the heavy meal, and soon no one spoke except to punctuate Hugh and Eugene's dialogue with a lethargic question or a drawled exclamation of approval, amazement, incredulity, wonder, lust and laughter.

They talked of many things; the war had shown them many things, and Eugene had found something memorable in all its events, and in the over-zealous passions which composed its recreational activities. He liked to talk, and he did it well, holding the attention of his listeners not only by the smooth clarity of his speech, but by the peculiar trick of selecting one among their group and addressing himself to that one particularly, calling him by name at intervals and apparently ignoring the others. Fascinated by the rapt attention which he drew from the person whom he had selected as a conversational target, the others listened, watching the two men, as if they were actors in a play. He spoke without flourishes or gesticulation, the crisp timbre of his voice betraying little emotion; his eyes, however, were very articulate, full of dark light, and glinting, sardonic laughter. When he spoke of something which interested him greatly, they moved like stage lights among his words, shadowing them here with dark gloom, here with a burning gray zeal.

He had asked Hugh if his clearing new land indicated an intention to farm on a larger scale than his father had, and this question had led to a discussion of tobacco prices, a matter which occupied general attention. Eugene talked about prices for some time:

"I remember, Hugh," he said, "a day when I was very small. I had accompanied my father to Granville where he had some tobacco to be sold. I had never seen a sale before, but this day I watched it with something like mature interest, because my father had promised me a rifle if his tobacco made a certain average. I had the rifle picked out. A twenty-two repeater it was, and my heart was set on it.

"I was old enough to understand the system of selling, old enough to see that he didn't have a thing to do with establishing the price, and I was young enough to feel the grave injustice of it all. Time had not inured me to such unfairness. Of course my desire for the rifle was the pivot upon which my emotions turned. All I could see was this: I wanted something badly, and whether I got it or not rested upon an indirect decision made by strangers whom I had never seen, who had never seen me, and who, in short, cared not a damn about me. I could see the dependence of those farmers more clearly than they could themselves, because they were blinded by resignation and by the habit of being resigned. I wasn't.

"Well, to make a long story short, I didn't get the rifle. And I have never forgotten my loss. I still think that something ought to be done about it. That something could be done. That auctioneer's unintelligible jargon could have been translated, 'You don't get the rifle, you don't get the rifle.' I tell you, Hugh, now that we are men, it means, 'You don't get a new car, you don't pay your fertilizer bill, you don't do this, and you don't do that.' It's a bad state of affairs and no mistake."

Hugh recalled Cleve's bitter prophecies along this line.

"My own father had little faith in the future of tobacco farming," he said. "He wanted me to go to college, to get away from the farm, and I would have done it, I suppose, if I hadn't gone to war."

"You may wish you hadn't gone to war," said Eugene. "The Allies wouldn't have missed you. You may wish you had gone to college, unless there is a change."

"What kind of change?"

"I should have said, 'unless we make a change,' because the tobacco buying companies aren't going to get soft-hearted. They'll go on taking the stuff at their own prices as long as we let them. You can't blame them."

"I don't see how we can change that."

"I do," Eugene replied. "I see a way. You have seen something of the world, Hugh. You have seen something of men. You have seen them die for no better reason than that they got in the way of a bullet. Was it their destiny to stop bullets? How many could have given an intelligent reason for not running to shelter? I did it many times. No, they were brave and foolish, that is to say, they were ashamed somebody would see them running. That's about what bravery is. Men will run toward death, throw themselves on it, but when it comes to a simple matter of improving their way of living by a little thinking and enduring a few hardships, they act like a bunch of children. What could men of this type do if they united in an effort to change the method of tobacco selling? An effort of this kind offers, not death in a mud-hole, but life lightened by some relief from economic uncertainty. Is this worth striving for, or is it better to brace ourselves against conditions as they are, and content ourselves with talking about how bad they are?"

"I have seen the things you mention," Hugh responded, "but I fail to see exactly what they have to do with tobacco prices."

"Naturally, you don't," Eugene replied. "I haven't finished with the things I've seen. The war isn't the only thing they had in Europe. People do things differently in that part of the world, do them better. While we were encamped near London, I learned, for instance, that it was not the English farmers near the city who enjoyed its best markets, but Danish farmers across the sea. I ate butter there, butter made in Denmark and sold in London for a better price than an English farmer could obtain. The Danes were organized. They had uniform, well-graded products. They had London marketing agencies, and they made money."

"Denmark is a small country," Hugh objected.

"Virginia and the two Carolinas aren't but so big. Most of the tobacco which goes into cigarettes is grown within a three-hundred-mile radius of Granville. That's a small slice of the world, a small slice, indeed."

"How in hell would you ever get them working together?"

"It could be done," Eugene assured him. "You haven't thought about it before. That's why it seems impossible."

Addressing the group, suddenly, he cried:

"None of you has thought of it. You would rather endure a situation than try to change it. That's the cursed part of man's ability to endure. Why, in five years we could control every pound of tobacco grown in the bright belt, if we went about it courageously. But it would take a lot of courage, and a world of patience."

"And a world of money, too," said one of the group. "Don't forget that."

"That could be arranged," Eugene stated. "Governmental subsidies could be obtained. Once under way with a fair chance of success, banking houses would finance it. They would have to finance it as a matter of self-protection, if for no other reason. Other farmers have done it. They have done it here in America. The fruit growers in the West have an organization, and it works."

Although most of the men present had read of the agitation for a co-operative plan of selling tobacco it had existed in their minds only as a kind of dream told in the newspapers. As Eugene had said, they were enduring their troubles sustained only by the hope that sometime, somehow, times would be better. Listening to him they felt, for the first time, that they might make things better. His words clothed the cold theories of the farm magazines with a warm reality. They discussed the proposition far into the night. Many of them were skeptical. It was radical, therefore unfeasible.

"I can't see," Eugene said in conclusion, "that we would stand to lose much, even if it were a fore-ordained failure. We are headed for ruin as it is."

3

In Cleve's time the family had not owned an automobile. Hugh found before the winter had passed that he would need one, that he would have to get one unless he wanted to bury himself on the farm and shut himself up, hermit fashion, in his silent house when the day's work was done. Therefore, he paid scant attention to that small voice of caution which warned him to preserve the surplus Cleve had left in the bank, glossed this concern over with his confidence and hope in the soil, and bought a Buick roadster. It was only ten miles to Granville, where he could refresh his mind with a movie whenever he felt like doing so. The Clay farm lay between his home and Granville, and often he picked up Eugene and took him along. Their friendship grew as the year passed.

Coming to Eugene's home one evening in early June, he found him with his long face buried in a farm magazine, reading a report of various farmers' organizations which had attained some success in co-operative work. When Hugh had taken a seat he read parts of it to him, interpolating at intervals with remarks pertinent to their own farming.

"I tell you, Hugh," he exclaimed, "we have got to come to it. It's our only hope, and a good one, at that."

Since Hugh had never had full charge of a crop before, since he had never handled the money and paid the bills, his interest in prices had been indirect. Eugene's concern seemed exaggerated to him.

"Let's not come to it tonight," he said; "I've been farming all day. I'm tired of it. That's why I'm here. How would a run to town strike you?"

"My folks are there now," Eugene replied; "gone to meet Nancy. She's coming home from school."

"Nancy? Of course, your kid sister. She was just a kid when I left home. I remember her, though."

"She's darn near a woman now. Finishes school next year."

"Fine. But let's get along. I wonder what she looks like."

"She's a fine looking girl," Eugene said, simply.

During the ride to town Eugene revived the subject of co-operative marketing. He seemed obsessed by the plan.

"For the life of me, I can't see why this thing has such a grip on your imagination," Hugh grumbled, "since I know that you aren't suffering for money. You don't look like a man to worry yourself to death over other people's troubles. Tell me, why are you so preoccupied with it?"

"You are right to some extent. The little misfortunes of people whom I barely know don't bother me. For instance, I don't give a damn if the French never get the holes plugged in their cathedrals. But this thing is different. It's nearer home than you think. Then, too, it's so vast, so reasonable, that it appeals to my sense of achievement."

"So, ambition, and not brotherly love, is the bee in your bonnet?"

Eugene replied with mock seriousness.

"What does that matter? My motive wouldn't make any difference if I were successful. I suspect that back of most political and social upheavals you will find a few powerful personal ambitions. Time brings discontent to a ferment, a strong man sees it, and rides the storm to fame. Napoleon kicked up quite a disturbance while making a name for himself."

"People like you and Napoleon," Hugh taunted, "get us ordinary folks into some pretty bad messes."

"Lay off, Hugh, lay off," Eugene laughed. "I'll go to work in the interest of the down-trodden farmer, but I warn you that people who get their impetus from watching other people suffer never get very far.

"I was taught differently."

"Your education is deficient in many respects. Your opinion is quite wrong, but also quite natural. As you say, you were taught that. We all were, but, believe me, there's nothing to it."

"Why?"

"I'll tell you. There's too much suffering, too many forms. One loses purpose and perspective in merely observing the sorrows of outraged humanity. It's a life's work in itself. After all, we see so much of it that it becomes common and unimpressive. As a matter of fact, people are so prone to optimism that they delude themselves into thinking most misfortunes are minor blessings. That's God's gift to incompetency. We see a man who has lost a leg, and remark, 'It could have been worse; he could have lost them both.' In the end we have convinced ourselves, and the poor man as well, that he came off pretty lucky. He even becomes proud of the wooden leg."

"In truth, now," Hugh demanded, "couldn't most things have been worse than they were?"

"Theoretically, yes. It's possible to imagine a man with more boils than Job, for instance, plus a worse complication of domestic and economic affairs."

"I don't know where this poor devil is," laughed Hugh, "or what's ailing him, but he is sure in one hell of a fix."

"He's pretty low, I'll grant you," said Eugene; "but I'll bet you that he is deriving some comfort from the conviction that it could have been worse."

"Well, couldn't it?"

"No!" said Eugene, emphatically, "it couldn't. He's got nothing to rejoice in except the fact that he still lives and suffers."

"Most people are glad to be alive."

"I wouldn't be if I were in his position."

"You must believe that there are peace and reward in the hereafter."

"I'm not remotely interested in the hereafter," replied Eugene, "I'm only interested in selling my tobacco for what it's worth."

"Tobacco again! I thought that I had talked you off that subject. Well, if you can't forget it, tell me, weren't prices good last year?"

"Yes," Eugene replied, "they were. Bait, largely. And the war was just over, too. A farmer's memory is only one year long, you know. All of them are working late Saturday night and early Sunday morning trying to make a whopper crop this year. And if they succeed ... watch out."

"You think the companies will take it for nothing?"

"I know it."

"We'll see," said Hugh.

The little town of Granville, spread like a blanket of stars over the hillside beyond them, was still awake, but in a dusty, melancholy manner. Where the road became Prison Street, long lines of maples cast shadows on the sidewalks. Along these dim sidewalks traffic was occasional and leisurely. Shielded by groves of cedar and maple, crouching, sometimes, behind an inner wall of boxwood, were the great houses of the town, houses of wood, white, gleaming spectrally in the moonlight, and massive structures of ancient brick, all marked with an antiquated dignity and the clannishness of age. Each had been built at some distance from the street, a fact which gave them the appearance of withdrawal from the activities of the thoroughfare, the clangor of the world, and the sweaty business of the rabble which composed it. It was conceivable that within their walls, secluded from the bustle of the street, there survived the traditions and person-ages of another and less agitated age. Night is kind. Viewed in the unromantic glare of midday, one would have seen, emerging from these hallowed houses, men hurrying about the trivial affairs of daily trade, merchants bent on making ends meet, doctors rushing to the dead and yet unborn, lawyers confounding right and wrong, and a few dazed individuals, who long since had given up the struggle, content to eke out existence on whiskey and mortgages.

Prison Street intersected Main, forming a commercial core from which the business section of Granville radiated, the most important business houses being very near their point of juncture. Built so near the intersection that, had it been nearer, it would have squatted in the street, stood the Farmer's Bank. This had been the only bank until a few years before the war, when a group of ambitious citizens had established, one block distant, the rival Bank of Granville. Although one bank could handle the financial business of the county, one bank could not please all customers, particularly, a bank grown somewhat autocratic with age and individuality. From its founding the Bank of Granville had done a flourishing, though rather unreliable business, drawing many of its customers from the ranks of those who bore some real or fancied grudge against its more conservative neighbor, people who felt that they were exercising a revenge upon the old bank by giving their business to the new. And they were.

Townsmen, as well as visitors from the country, congregated around the drug stores at night. Hugh and Eugene parked the car and walked down the street to Stone's Drug Store. A pimply-faced youth with tight slick hair, and obviously enamored of his reflection in the huge mirror at his back, mixed them two coca-colas with a flourishing syncopation of spoons and carbonated water. At the end of the fountain, flanking the window, was a long bench, occupied at this moment by two old men whose discussion held the attention of several young idlers. This was the town's forum, and the old men two of its most indefatigable senators. Here

Republicans delivered philippics against Democrats, Democrats against Republicans. Here the affairs of the cook, the
county, the state, the nation, the world, and the Kingdom of
Heaven, were investigated, censured, exaggerated, enjoyed,
and settled.

The more loquacious of the two senators, Squire Thompson, had held his position of magistrate for ten years through
the indulgence of an amused citizenry, who accepted his
ridiculous applications of the law as a comic institution
worthy of preservation. Among the most notable of his decisions, they treasured the one in which he had exculpated
the defendant, and delivered a drunken sentence against the
deputy sheriff. Questioned concerning this unorthodox procedure, the besotted and ill-informed old scoundrel explained
that he didn't recognize the deputy, who was newly appointed, and that he always fined anyone who had the misfortune to come into his court. He boasted that no one ever
left his court unfined, and this claim was largely true, since
most who were brought before him were negroes as ignorant
of the limitations of the law as he was of its application. He
fined them indiscriminately, alike guilty and innocent, explaining that the court must have its costs. "I declare you
innocent," he would say, "three dollars, and you may go; the
court must have its costs." They paid gladly. It was worth it
to escape the proximity of the law.

They knew Squire Thompson. His outrageous decisions,
achieving an epic fabulousness with retelling, were familiar
throughout the county, uglily remarkable, as was the person
of the Squire, with his fat, formless body, and his obscene
bald head, full of foolish facts and half-cracked laws. In
Granville everybody knew everybody else, their families,
their fortune, their friends, their yellow ghosts if there were
any.

Better known in the county than Squire Thompson, and

far better loved, was Dumont Clay, Eugene's father. His life had been a long conflict between two selves, the sweet, sensitive nature which he had inherited from his mother being constantly at war with the wild blood which had characterized his father's people—"nigger-fighters and bull-drivers" he called them. His mother had been a gentlewoman. His father had lectured him on this fact often. Recovering from some violent drinking spell, he would try to expiate his sin by pointing a finger of holy horror at his own behavior, addressing Dumont's attention to a catalogue of evils that followed in the wake of drink.

"Watch yourself, boy," he would admonish, "because you have bad blood, mean, fighting blood. Listen to your mother. Would to God, I had!" he would wail. "She's an aristocrat, right on back to the Ark, but you and I, you and I, we're common, just low-down, wild-eyed, cock-fighting common. They hanged your granddaddy, hanged him for piracy, and God knows how many other things."

Such a man had been Dumont's father, and he thought there was never another like him.

Dumont, in his turn, impressed by his father's lectures, had proved his blood by spending most of his young manhood in drunkenness. He slipped from grace several times a year even after he got married, but he never became quite drunk enough to submerge his lovable nature. Indeed, his inebriety usually took the form of prodigal generosity and good humor. "He would give away the coat on his back," they said of him. In their childhood, Eugene and Nancy had hailed these benders with something like joy, a fearful delight, repressed only by their mother's solicitous alarm. It was Dumont's custom then to come home from market with his wagon loaded with presents for them, for their frightened mother, for the last little black on the farm. The negroes, sighting his wagon coming, would shout with naïve delight,

"Christmas is coming." This exclamation was a signal for general highheartedness for everybody except his wife, but she never scolded him. She had regarded his drinking as an affliction, and had tried to handle it with the same care she would have given an actual physical disability. In time she cured him. He was a sober and subdued man at the time Hugh came to know him, but there still danced in his eyes a riotous, pagan laughter.

Although the hour was late when Hugh and Eugene returned from Granville, the Clays were still awake. At Eugene's request Hugh entered the house to meet Nancy. His memory of her as a child was very indistinct, composed of no characteristic features or facts, nothing more than a vague recollection that there had been such a child, and it was of a child he was thinking as he accompanied Eugene into the house. He found a woman, tall, dark, and beautiful. His face must have shown some surprise and confusion, because she demanded, "Don't you like me grown up?"

"That's hardly a fair question to put to a man who just grew up himself," he answered. "Give me time."

"Time you may have, sir," she laughed; "all summer. But," she added, "your request is far from flattering."

"I'm no flatterer," said Hugh.

"I'm not actually soliciting it," she informed him a bit acidly, and turned to her father and mother who hovered around her as if she were a recovered treasure.

Eugene greeted her rather coldly, Hugh thought, but then he was not effusive about anything.

Hugh watched her talking to her father. Her loveliness seemed to come from some secret source within her. It lived happy, gay, dancing in her eyes, in her smile, in the elastic grace of her straight young body. "She is lovely like a candle flame," he thought, "clean and vivid like a flame," and as he continued to watch her, his mind extended the simile, for he thought that like a flame her beauty might be snuffed out suddenly, but that it would not diminish, or wither away.

"What have you old soldiers been doing tonight?" she asked Eugene.

"After having saved the world for democracy," he replied, "if you can remember what the war was about, we have been hearing tonight why we shouldn't have done it."

"Sounds like a riddle to me."

"It was. Squire Thompson's talks on politics are the world's worst riddles."

"I'm glad you got away before I was put to bed."

Because of the lateness of the hour Hugh excused himself.

"You must come again," she told him at the door.

"I've been practically a boarder at your house this spring," he answered.

She said no more, and he found no excuse for remaining longer at the door, although he was aware of a positive disinclination to hurry.

Home again, he found the spacious gloom of the old house more depressing than usual.

4

The farm was a fine thing in the early splendor of morning, glistening with dew and sunlight. None of the fatigue or weariness of yesterday remained; everything was charged with the bright energy of a new day. Even the horses, idle in the barn-lot now during the weeding season, were full of playful energy, nipping each other with well simulated viciousness, and scampering around the lot for the pure pleasure of speed. The mules, however, were enjoying their leisure with the same stoical restraint which they display toward labor. They were not deluded by this temporary freedom from work. They nibbled the damp grass, or stood immobile and sullen, apart from the high-hearted horses, like barnyard outcasts, as indeed they are, for theirs is a life of toil and plodding, of industry but seldom brightened by pleasure. But they are wise, wiser than horses, because, like people who have endured oppression for a long time, they do not lose their heads in the stress of imminent danger. A horse caught in quicksand will sink himself deeper, and break his high heart in violent frantic efforts to escape. A mule moves cautiously, extricates himself with patient care. They have the simple, self-centered wisdom of peasants. Rarely do they show affection for each other or for their masters.

Aunt Mathy, in her long cataloguing of his grandfather's doings, had told Hugh how Old Robert made a round of the farm each morning before breakfast as punctiliously as if he had been performing some ritual upon which the success of the day depended. Hugh came to do this same thing except when the weather was too wet. It was always reassuring to see the plants rising green and full of brave strength acquired in the night, rising toward the sun before which they had withered and drooped in the late hours of the preceding day, each bearing upon its leaves a little shield of moisture. It was a sweet free pleasure to walk under the cedars behind the barns, to drink, on hands and knees, at the spring in the hollow, and to breathe the fragrant air of morning, touched with the tang of spring. Wet corn smelled like watermelon. The odor of clover made him strange dreams ... dreams of pleasant valleys where the sunlight was heavy and powerful, where happiness floated toward one like a song on the air. One did not grope for it and search the horizon for its coming. One waited and it came. Clover held the promise of peace, effortless and endless. It was a strange thought for a busy morning.

His fields gave him pleasure, too. Nature had provided

those other things, but these growing fields were his; he had made them. Each tobacco plant, each of the three hundred thousand hills, had been placed by his hands or by hands which he had directed. They grew and prospered because he watched them, cared for them, saw that they lacked neither nourishment nor attention. Those acres of uniform plants, well-kept and free of grass, those long, curving rows of corn, already knee-high and full of generous sap, that wide field of crimson clover, they were all his, and they filled him with a pride of possession and accomplishment. When, at times, Eugene's gloomy prophecies hung like a dark cloud over these beautiful fields, he was grateful that price was not the sole end of farming, that there was compensation in the work itself, that poor prices couldn't spoil the meat on his table, the fruit in his orchard. He felt, as he had when a child, that within the farm he had a refuge. It was his castle, his stronghold, his place of security from the storms of an outside world.

Indeed, there still clung to the place from the time of Old Robert certain feudal aspects, some marks of strength and dignity which time had not effaced. The woods which ran to Sligo lay like a wall along the northern boundaries of his land, a wall beyond which no other white families lived. His house was strong and sturdy, and it was beautiful, too, he thought. His grandmother had brought boxwood from her home and rooted it in the yard, and his own mother had trained roses along its solid sides, and these still grew and entwined themselves with the house. Cleve had not been one to allow any minor fault or break to go unheeded. It was still a good strong house.

The road to Granville, the main road, began beyond the border of the farm; no strange traffic severed his land, no strangers wandered over it without a purpose, and the rough trail which wound through his fields to Sligo was little more than a path, and he knew those who went along it. The store and the blacksmith shop, where, at sober intervals, Ed Dixon still plied his trade, were the nearest houses to his own, and even between his house and these stretched another arm of woods.

The store had been a source of great profit to its owner at one time, but now its function of local postoffice was about all that kept it alive. Before the advent of good roads and automobiles trade had been brisk at the store; now everybody traded in Granville. Prosperity is a kind of see-saw; some must always hold down the low end.

Coming to the store one morning Hugh took his paper from the box, peered in to see if there were any letters, and started away without paying any attention to the few cars standing at the building's front. He was concerned with some problem at the farm and he wished to return quickly. He had gone not more than a hundred yards, however, when he heard a car leave the building and approach him. Turning aside to allow it to pass, he saw that it was the Clay car, driven by Nancy. She stopped beside him.

"Care to ride, Mister?" she hailed.

"Mr. Winton," he laughed, "Mr. Hugh Winton."

She slipped the machine into second gear and roared down the dusty road toward the farm, creating a great din of unnecessary noise. When the motor had reached its maximum speed in that gear, she threw it into high, turned toward him, and settled in her seat with the air of having accomplished, dexterously, a rather difficult feat.

"Well, you got off to a good start," Hugh observed.

"Yes, it's so much fun. When it roars away like that I imagine that I'm a pilot taking off, that soon I'll be in the air, away on the wings of the wind."

"A gully in the road, or a rock, may convert your fancy into a reality sometime."

"Let's talk of something else. I left home to get away from Gene. He's forever preaching about calamities coming, too. What's wrong with young men, now, anyway? Why, when Daddy was forty-five he had more fun than Christmas, and over practically nothing, too."

Hugh suspected that Eugene's preoccupation with selling problems had made a deeper impression on Nancy than her bantering words indicated, had worried her and left her natural happiness of spirit a bit disturbed and puzzled over his stern young sobriety. He could understand that. She was too young, and far too lovely, to be moping around about the price of tobacco.

"You won't find me such a moody fellow," he told her. "Gene says that I'm too light-hearted to ever amount to much. And he may be right."

She made no answer to this, being concerned with steering the car up the rough, rutted ascent to his house. She swung around the well and brought the machine to a halt in the yard.

"Are you merely bringing me home," Hugh asked, "or are you paying me a call?"

"Neither, exactly," she answered, smiling, "but since I'm here may I have a few roses for my pains?"

She did not wait for his consent, but jumped out of the car, and hurried toward the porch, exclaiming, like a child, at the beauty of the roses.

"What a lovely old place you have here, Hugh!" she cried; "such a grand old house, so many roses. Don't you feel a little bit selfish?"

"As a matter of fact I get mighty lonesome at times. My house is too big and too empty."

"And you won't even miss these roses?" she asked. "See, I have an armful." It was her way to keep on talking, not pausing for him to answer her questions. "Oh! it is a lovely place, boxwood odor, climbing roses, everything. I can just imagine cow-bells in the hollow at dusk, buttermilk cooling in the kitchen, candles on your table."

"I use a lamp on the table," Hugh managed to get in.

"Should be candles, at least six. The house wasn't made for lamps."

She continued talking ecstatically, picking here and there a full-blown rose, leaving Hugh wondering if she were talking to him or to the air.

Gathering the roses which she had laid on the steps as she chose them, she carried them to the car, thanked him, and turned to give the house a final admiring glance.

"My! I would like to live here," she sighed.

Hugh knew that her words had no double meaning, that she had spoken in simple tribute to the charm of the old place, yet she had ignored him so completely while admiring it and gathering her roses, that he determined to impose himself upon her attention by implying that he had understood differently.

"I think I would like that, too," he told her.

"You took advantage of me," she said blushing; "it wasn't a nice jest."

"It wasn't a jest," he replied. "Does that make it any nicer?"

"Decidedly not. The sentiment might have been all right under proper circumstances."

"Name your circumstances."

"Forget it," she advised.

"The circumstances," he persisted, "were, simply: You liked my house, and I liked your liking it."

"Sounds simple enough, doesn't it?"

"Does it?"

"I think so," she said firmly.

"Then so must I, I suppose. Perhaps I was rude, but such

an intention was so far from my mind, that it took some time to realize it. I'm sorry. But you know I didn't mean to offend you, not really, don't you?"

"I'm sure you didn't," she replied graciously. "Perhaps you've become a flatterer, after all. I'll consider it a compliment."

"You won't go wrong. That's all I meant."

"That's all I remember, then. Come to see us soon."

"I will," Hugh answered hastily, "I'll come tomorrow evening. That is, if you wish. I'll come and bring you more roses."

"These will have withered by that time," she said meaningly. "It's a promise."

He watched her car until it passed out of sight, thinking how little it had meant when she came, how much it meant to see her leave. Sometimes the dull fabric of existence was seared by moments as hot and brief as a bullet. Hope and fear lived within the narrow borders of a smile. Hers, as she left, had been indulgent and personal, had been worth risking her anger, and worth his apology. He strode into his house happily, and walked down the long hall whistling, unmindful of its length and emptiness.

5

The Clay family was a queer one. Although it had, as a family, strong and distinctive characteristics, its members were all unlike, set in sharp and glaring juxtaposition in their whims, their loves, even in their secret, unspoken loyalties. There was a devil and an angel wrestling in Dumont. His wife was in alliance with the angel. Eugene's soul was inscrutable; one never got a peep inside him unless he opened his mouth, and what he had to say seemed tinged always with a sardonic, unfortunately twisted view of the world, or perhaps a too accurate understanding of it. Of them all, only Nancy had a genuinely happy disposition. At least it could be said that she appeared to be pleased with the world, although at times a hard, flinty pride sharpened her tongue and could bend it to an unbelievable bitterness. Few people knew this, however; she hardly knew it herself.

Of the two children Nancy had always been the favorite in her parents' affections, perhaps because she was more like them in her gay disposition than was Eugene. He had been a strange child, often stilled by queer, unchildlike meditation. His failure to respond to their impulsive petting and caresses had puzzled and alarmed Dumont and his wife for years, and with the birth of Nancy, who before she could walk, showed pleasure in accepting and returning these domestic tokens of affection, they had almost unconsciously transferred their demonstrative love to her. Eugene had observed this, considered it in his silent fashion, and had even felt some jealousy of the baby, for he had not objected to their caresses; he simply couldn't return them with the impulsiveness with which they were given. As Nancy continued to monopolize their affection as she grew older, he came to think it proper because she was the younger, their baby, and later when she was no longer very young, he decided that it was natural that a girl should receive some family favoritism. Although Nancy herself had never fully penetrated his sardonic mask, this lack of understanding had not been an impediment in the growth of a mutual love between them. She seemed to know, as her parents did not, that behind the expressionless mask by which strangers knew him, the real Eugene existed, kind, tender, and a little baffled by all natural things. In this belief she differed from Dumont. He had made a remark once which demonstrated this pointedly, a remark which she never forgot, because, apparently, it was so true of Eugene, and in reality, not true at all, she felt.

It had been a custom in the family to make the children kneel and say their prayers before going to bed. At first they had repeated a child's prayer which their mother taught them, but later they knelt and composed their own, silently. One night Dumont had asked Nancy for whom and what she had prayed, and when she had enumerated for him all the members of the family and the negroes about the house, he had praised her for her comprehensive concern, had turned to Eugene and demanded, "And you, what did you pray for?"

From the depths of his bed Eugene had replied with unfitting levity, "I kept my eyes shut and let Nancy do the praying."

This answer had amused her mother, she remembered, but it had angered Dumont. It was this night that he had said among many things:

"Gene, you aren't human; you are more like a monkey. Monkeys watch people and imitate them almost perfectly, but they do so without any human feeling or comprehension. That's you. You wash your face, you comb your hair, you kneel in prayer, but you do all these things just because you see them done. They are not a part of you. You are as perfect as a little machine, and as cold."

Eugene hadn't said anything.

Nancy had understood then what her father meant. Even now it was credible that Eugene fitted himself into the form of things, observed little social customs, and moved politely along the surface of society without having his actions dictated at any time by an inner feeling. His very physical appearance lent itself to strengthen this impression. His cold gray eyes, his only feature which ever betrayed emotion, were generally more contemplative than animated. That long face was like some impassive thing carved from stone, carved with a mind for strength only, but a strangely stubborn and bitter strength.

Now that Dumont was getting old his thoughts dwelt largely on the days and the colorful events of his youth, and it was always to Nancy, never to Eugene, that he talked of these days. He told many splendid stories, told them repeatedly, but she never tired of them. A great many of these tales involved his own father, whom he thought had been a man of uncommon good sense. He illustrated this belief by little anecdotes about happenings in which his father had shown a superior capacity for dealing with situations. Once years before when she had worn herself into a frenzy trying to work a problem in geometry, Dumont had taken the book from her hands, turned the pages, and found, several pages behind the day's assignment, a corollary upon which the solution of her problem depended. That her father who hadn't touched a text-book in twenty years, should work a problem so easily, had embarrassed her greatly. But he had only laughed at her and declared:

"There's more than one way to kill a cat. That's all you have to know. My own father," he reminisced, "taught me that in a way I shall never forget."

"What was that, Daddy?"

"When I was a young fellow," Dumont recounted, "I was pretty hot-headed. There was a man whom I decided I ought to kill. My reasons are not necessarily a part of this story; anyway, I decided to kill him, and set out to do it one day. I met my father and he saw, immediately, that something was wrong.

" 'What's bothering you, Dumont?' he demanded.

" 'Nothing, Father.'

" 'You know better than to lie to me. What is it?'

" 'Father, there is a man I must kill. The world is too small for both of us.'

" 'Is there no other way to handle it? Must you kill him, son?'

" 'Yes. I have made up my mind. Nothing can stop me.'

" 'Dumont, I love you, boy. You are my only child. They will hang you if you do this.'

" 'I don't care. I'll hang happy.'

" 'Well,' the old man growled, 'if nothing can stop you, I'll go with you. We'll both kill the scoundrel.'

" 'But, Father, they'll hang you, too.'

" 'I don't care. If they hang you, I want to hang, too. Come on, let's get the killing done.'

"That," Dumont concluded, "was the only way he could have stopped me. I knew that he would have gone with me, but I rather doubt that either of us would have been hanged. A charge of murder depended altogether upon the character of the dead man in those days. Somebody finally killed this bird, anyway; I am sorry it couldn't have been me."

"What had he done to you, Daddy?" Nancy had asked.

"Run along," he had replied gruffly, "I might have known that you would ask that."

"Well, what was it?"

She never found out, although she plied him persistently. One day he told her, "It all happened before I met your mother. I wouldn't want her to know anything about it."

Upon this piece of information she had established many scarlet romances, but she never learned anything more of the affair from Dumont.

It was through this close association with her father that Nancy gained an insight into a peculiarly masculine side of men, into their likes and dislikes which have no relation to their emotions in respect to women, and this same alliance with him contributed to her long delay in falling in love.

She looked for her father's image in the young men of her acquaintance, did not find it, did not look again. These same young men she frightened and appalled with her frankness, her superimposed masculinity of tongue, and her apparent aloofness from the hot promptings of their hearts. There was little deception about her, too little for her own good; her charm consisted of an intense love of life, and of an impetuous unwillingness to have it molded, patterned, or frustrated in any respect.

During her summer vacations there had been several young men, most of them from Granville, who had paid her admiring attention, young men attracted by her high-colored beauty, who came several times and went away, all of them somewhat puzzled, having found in her armor of good-natured companionship no opening through which to send a weak shaft of sentimentality. At nineteen she had never been in love, although she had given many men a friendly, sexless admiration. Hugh's first visit to her home after her return from school, the sight of him, a stranger, had aroused an awareness of possibilities which the sight of other men had not. She found that she had remembered his appearance distinctly, and willingly. His handsome dark face, the attractive mingling of humor and seriousness in his manner, recurred sporadically in her memory and provoked her strangely. She found herself thinking of him often after the day she had taken him home, after the evening he had spent at her house following his promise to bring her roses. There was something about him which would not allow her to dismiss him as just another pleasant companion, something which impressed her without any effort on his part, because when he had called he had said nothing reminiscent of the rather romantic turn of events at his home that day she had gathered roses. He had repeated his calls during the lengthening summer, but he continued to give her only a friendly, interesting, but nevertheless rather impersonal companionship, almost similar to that which she had extended all her previous beaux.

Before summer ended she tired of his strange behavior. She thought it strange, although what she desired in him was what she had discouraged in every other young man she had known. It was studied cruelty on his part, she decided, for by this time she thought herself in love with him, and secretly she yearned for some overtures of admiration from him. The manner of her upbringing, that unrestrained manifestation of affection which existed in her family, made it difficult for her to be conventionally indifferent toward him, when she wanted only to be tender, generous. She pondered for a long time over his sudden retreat into his shell of deferential indifference when it seemed one night that he was at last going to make a declaration of feeling for her.

They had returned from a drive to Granville and were seated in his car before her house. The night was gorgeous, radiant with the splendor of a full moon, fragrant with the odor of honeysuckle, and she had felt superbly in harmony with its dusky velvet beauty. It had seemed very natural and sweet, very much a part of the night that he should want to kiss her then, and when he did she had been happy for a moment, but when he had not attempted to repeat the caress, had remained full of silence and whatever he had in his heart, her joy had turned to a repentant bewilderment which he did nothing to relieve. She had remained in the car only a few minutes before bidding him good night and going into the house, decidedly uncomfortable, feeling that she had been foolish. There was nothing of the conqueror in his bearing when she saw him again, however, and with time this experience which had been an embarrassing question in her heart became only a question.

Nancy came nearer being jealous over Eugene's friendship with Hugh than over anything which had been tangent to their lives. No one in the family seemed to think that she might love him, might want to be alone with him at times. Often he came before she finished dressing, and when she came down to meet him, she would find him talking to Dumont and Eugene, and sometimes she was forced to take part in this four-sided conversation for an hour or more. This itself didn't annoy her half as much as Hugh's apparent lack of eagerness to bring the strictly masculine party to an end.

Dumont liked him very much. He liked to enlist Hugh's aid in ridiculing Eugene for his sober ways. Once she overheard them upbraiding him.

"Eugene's got one serious fault," her father said; "he's got too much blue blood, and not enough red. I've got blue blood, too, but I'm a damned sight prouder of the red."

"He's a heathen, nevertheless," said Hugh.

"I'll tell you," Dumont whispered, "don't let your mother know I advised it, but you ought to get drunk once. If you get enough whiskey in your system you may turn out to be a human being after all."

Eugene had replied rather shortly, "I might turn out to be a devil just as easily. My blue blood isn't the only thing I inherited from you, I'm afraid."

There was one thing, however, on which Dumont and his son were entirely in accord. Eugene had converted his father and Hugh to his theories about tobacco selling. Nancy was proud of him when he talked on this subject, and it seemed all that he wanted to talk about. He made everyone believe that a farmer's co-operative association would put an end to price troubles. She, too, was an ardent convert to his belief, but she could not refrain from wishing that he wouldn't monopolize Hugh's visits with endless discussions of it. Nor could she understand why Hugh was content to sit and discuss these same things over and over, while she waited like an impatient child. In her heart she knew that it was not for this alone that he continued to come there, but it might as well be, she reflected sometimes, a little despairingly.

Hugh took his time in deciding that he loved Nancy. That unfortunate affair with Helen was still raw in his memory, and it had taught him that this was not a matter with which to trifle. Indeed, now that it was over and buried in the past, he wondered how he could have forgotten her, how his hurt had healed, because it was largely through thinking of Nancy that he now thought of Helen at all, calling her to mind through comparison. It was a bit shameful, he thought, certainly nothing of which to be proud, this easy recovery from what had seemed at the time an agony of loss.

He had learned to distrust his emotions where women were concerned. A few brief but terribly comprehensive experiences with them during the war accounted for this somewhat. There he had known women who wore their sex like a sword half-sheathed in its scabbard, women who concealed under the thin graces of ladies the naked souls of harlots. But they had been beautiful, too, beautiful and desirable. Full of wine he had not found it hard to imagine that he loved them. The morning generally disillusioned him, bringing with its sober air an emotional hangover, a blurred recollection of wet lips in the dark and a conjunction of hot flesh, altogether meaningless and stale, now that day had come. He even forgot their names. But Helen, that had been different. Yet he had forgotten her, had forgotten the pain of losing her; it was easy to forget, so easy for things to lose their charm. His own experience made him fear that nothing was enduringly lovely, and he wanted to be sure about Nancy, to know. It would be better to know fully that he wanted her, to know that and to lose her, than to marry her and then discover that he had been mistaken.

Yet it was hard to restrain himself when every time he saw her he wanted to cry out that he loved her. The nearness of her beauty and her generous presence made a cautious, scrutinizing consideration almost impossible. He was not happy in maintaining silence, not happy in subjecting her to what amounted to a long examination. This made him feel that he was unpardonably egotistical. Surely, she looked good enough for anybody. It was late in the summer, however, before he declared his love in earnest.

He realized that he was living in an era of change, a time of crumbling faiths and customs, a period of discarding. When he had gone from Miss Alice's little one-room school to the new high school, he had marveled at the elaborate efficiency of the building. All the people of the neighborhood had been proud of the new school, as they had been proud of the hard clay roads which had been constructed to accommodate the increasing automobile traffic. These things made it manifest to the passing world, they felt, that they had set here some permanent monuments to their progressive spirits.

But progress is never permanent, they had learned. Their fine school and their roads were out of date now, and inadequate. Children were gathered into busses and transported to school now, thereby increasing the attendance, and making it far more constant than in the days when the weather had been sufficient excuse for anything. There were more children each year and more busses, and at length the new school was an old school and it would no longer serve its purpose. The proposed rebuilding and enlarging made its appearance in the form of an increased tax levy for the coming year. Simultaneously, the county would begin a new road-building program, replacing the sand-clay roads with concrete ones, more permanent ribbons of progress across the old bosom of the earth.

There had been some talk of cutting a new road by Hugh's farm, through the Sligo wilderness to the Virginia line. Hugh first heard of this from Dumont Clay who had learned of it in Granville. Dumont thought it would be a good thing.

"It will increase the value of your land," he said.

"Yes, it will do that, theoretically," Eugene interposed in his critical manner, "but actually it will only increase the tax rate on his land. It won't increase the price of his tobacco, so it seems to me that the road would be a detriment to his farm."

Hugh felt, oddly, that to disturb the peaceful wastes of Sligo with a shining new road would be almost sacrilegious, like holding a picnic in a graveyard. But he said nothing, listened to Dumont and Eugene.

"You are just like Nicodemus, Gene," the old man argued. "We had a negro once who said, 'Nicodemus wus all right, 'ceptin' he didn't b'lieve nuthin' he see, nuthin' he heah.' That's you all over. You don't believe anything you hear, and if something is shown you, by God, you suspect that it's a sleight of hand. Everybody knows that the accessibility of a farm to a road determines the land's value to some extent. Everybody knows that."

"Everybody except me," said Eugene. "I think it's a sleight of hand."

"Be sensible," Dumont ordered.

"Hugh has a road already," Eugene protested, "but mind you, I'm not even agreeing that having a road is a good thing. When you say that a road enhances the value of property, you mean that a buyer would consider the proximity of a road in bidding for the land, would give more money for it than he would if there were no road. But Hugh doesn't want to sell his farm; he wants to live on it. And since he's going to live on it the value is only theoretical, isn't it? The increase in taxes is a biting reality, however."

"There's something in that, I suppose," Dumont conceded. "I've said, myself, that some of our farmers would be better off if they couldn't get into Granville so easily. Some of them stay there all of their spare time instead of 'tending to odd jobs at home."

"I've noticed that, too," Hugh remarked, thinking how recently it was that farmers went to town only on business; "when I was a kid some of them didn't leave the farm during the whole of the summer."

"Their farms are not home to them as they once were," Eugene said; "they are more like places of business, like factories, places where they make their living, but where they do not wish to tarry when work is done. They find the simple pleasures of the farm dull in comparison with the more eventful streets. They must learn that the farm is, first of all, a place to live, a place from which to draw a full living from the land itself, rather than to draw so many dollars to buy a living elsewhere. It's not in the nature of things that one crop should support the whole farm, and a great many urban pleasures to boot."

Dumont was finding it dangerous to argue with his son. Eugene put him on the defensive with a few cool questions and often took his own words from his mouth, to turn them in some bland, diabolical fashion against him. It was safer to agree with him. Eugene was talking to Hugh now.

"In Granville you can hear strangers talk of the apparent prosperity of the country, but it really means little. They draw their conclusions from the roads and schools, things seen as they hurry by, things for which we have indebted ourselves. A country's debt is a poor measure of its prosperity. These strangers don't see the broken farmers a mile away from the road, some of them ragged, and hungry too, I suspect."

"I understand you, but that's because I know you," Hugh interrupted. "These same strangers hearing you would believe that you are opposed to progress."

"No, I'm no mossback. I simply am not sure what progress is. Somehow I think that progress, like charity, should begin at home. They rake all these kids in, red from the hills, pack them in these upholstered schools, and send them back at night to sleep in a ramshackle frame shanty. After all, we live at home, not on the road or in the school, and these taxes don't make our homes any better."

"I imagine," Dumont observed, "that they figure an education will enable these boys and girls to improve their homes."

"It won't, however," Eugene objected. "It will merely make the sensitive ones see how squalid they are. The others will not be affected one way or another. The smart ones will take one look at the dear old homestead and leave. Education shouldn't be regarded as a leveling process. Nature made draft horses, and draft men, and sometimes it is wise to leave nature alone."

Hugh agreed with Eugene that sometimes it was wise to leave nature alone. That was what he felt about the proposed road. A new road leading to some point far beyond the confines of Sligo, a road with all its foreign burden, would destroy that remoteness and peace which made the farm dear to him. Sligo, too, had secrets, traditions and memories which should be inviolate. Nature had shown its hand there once, had exerted its wild force through the length of the valley, had snatched it back from men and covered their works with mould and ashes.

"I hope they don't run a road through my land to the river," he said; "there's really no need. There's no reason why anyone should want to go into that country, and those who are already in it wouldn't know what to do if they came out."

"They probably will never put a road through there," Eugene judged; "most of these plans originate in Granville, and I can see no reason why the merchants of Granville would lend their approval to the building of a road which would provide a short cut to the Virginia markets. There's darned little that a road could bring out of those woods."

The river had been Sligo's highway once, a highway with a wilderness at one end, at the other, an ocean. Men had mastered it, but their victory had been brief. It had yielded to them and crushed them when they were passive with victory. These new roads brought certain destructive forces with them, as well as some advantages. They, too, some day, might mark a bleak trail through a bleaker country.

6

Hugh's visits to the Clay home had become very frequent now, because Nancy's holidays were drawing near their close and there had been an uneasy formality in her manner lately which warned him of the urgency of dropping his attitude of studied indifference before it became a barrier which his natural impulses would find difficult to overcome. Her generous nature was no mask, he felt, yet he suspected that beneath it she guarded a pride which might prove as inflexible as iron.

Above the low hum of his motor as they drove away from her home, her voice came to him startlingly cool. He felt irritated and self-conscious, and angry with himself that it was so difficult now to throw off the artificial relation which he had built between them. With that sullen procrastination which had always characterized his behavior when he found himself in an unpleasant position of his own creation, he drove several miles before exerting himself to break the tension between them. She did nothing to help him, nothing to hinder him. Apparently she was engaged in a courteous battle with boredom. Finally, when it seemed that if he waited another moment he could never speak at all, he halted the car and cut off the motor. It gave a final explosive sigh, like some enormous weary animal, and became silent.

From the hill-top on which they had stopped the lights of Granville were visible. Far away and beyond them the earth and the sky mingled in star-flecked distance. He felt speechless, and despite Nancy's presence a sense of solitude baffled him, for she seemed preoccupied with an inscrutable contemplation of distance and the night.

He took her hand. She allowed it to lie limply in his, and it told him nothing. Finding that the possession of this hand had not helped him, he sought the other. She yielded this one also, and turned to him, a small interrogative smile on her lips.

"Well?"

"Nancy . . ."

"What is it, Hugh?"

"It's nothing new, but tonight it is strangely difficult."

Her fingers tightened in his slightly, but she said nothing.

"But I suppose I made it difficult," he continued.

"I suppose so," she said; "whatever it is, I'm sure I had nothing to do with it."

She was making him ridiculous now, but he had earned it. She said nothing more, left him to thresh his way out alone. Suddenly, he pulled her toward him, his hands holding her arms feverishly. She did not resist him, but seemed to consent out of curiosity more than eagerness.

"You aren't helping me a lot by looking at me so coldly," he protested.

"I'm listening, though," she replied, "if you have anything to say."

"I simply want to say that I love you," he cried. "I've wanted to tell you all summer."

"Why didn't you?"

"That's what I'd like to know."

"I wish you hadn't waited," she said, leaning toward him. "Summers are short at best."

"You mean?"

"What could I possibly mean, dear?" she asked, taking his face in her hands. "You must have known that I loved you the night I kissed you."

It seemed to Hugh, during the long while that he held her there, that the still peace of the night was a benediction upon them, that the earth and the sky knew their love and composed a sanctuary for it, softly making them a part of its vast goodness.

7

Autumn came early that year, came like a thief in the night from Sligo, it seemed, for along the river where the air was thick and damp after sundown, the frosts were heavier than in the upperlands. The nights became cooler, the leaves began to lose their summer green, and the severity of the frosts made fall a none too gentle prelude to winter. There were fair windy days, and dark, drizzling days, cold in the mornings, hot and sultry at noon, as if nature were in the throes of seasonal indecision, flirting at the same time with winter and summer. Some nights the sky was angry and overcast, tracked by flying thin clouds; some nights a harvest moon hung there, like a great ball of white gold. But even on these clear nights the earth was not resigned to the departure of summer. Winds moaned in the lowlands, shrieked on the hilltops, and cried around the gnarled branches of lonely old trees. Old people shook their heads, rubbed their prophetic joints, and averred that it would be a hard winter.

These forecasts alarmed Hugh little. It had been a good year, a full, fruitful year. His fallowed land had stored up secret wealth which was transformed and visible now in his heavy waxen tobacco, in the bulging corn crib, and in the neat stacks of hay behind the stable. The tobacco was unusually good. A heavy, broad-leaved crop, it had cured brightly, making few sand lugs, few tips, and many golden wrappers. There had never been a better crop on the farm. His fields had fulfilled that promise he had read in them on the bitter day of his homecoming. And their faithfulness, he felt, was the beginning of the realization of that other promise, his promise to fill with the music of voices those empty rooms of his house. The rich stacks of tobacco, awaiting stripping in his pack-barn, were so many bulwarks upon which that hope rested. He was ready for the winter, and ready for another year. He owed no money and his storehouses were filled.

The opening prices on the Granville market were disheartening, so low indeed that many feared they would not be able to pay the expenses of their crops unless the market improved. All except Eugene expected some improvement. Hugh held his own tobacco off the market until the middle of November, there being a belief among the farmers that prices always rose as the weather grew colder. They had nothing to support this belief, but it was a hope and they clung to it from year to year. It was a good thing to say to each other at times like this. There was a slight rise in prices during November, but it lasted only a few days, and then the market settled to a steady, low level, and fearing that he was wasting time by waiting, Hugh began to strip his tobacco and throw it on the auction floor with reckless haste. Other farmers were doing the same thing. They were all disheartened now, and they wanted to be rid of the heartbreaking stuff over which they had expended a year's toil and care to such a poor end. In fact, the town endured each day a convulsion of industry. It was the largest crop the warehouses had ever handled. Draymen worked all night hauling the previous day's sales from the floors, making room for the incoming wagons. Sales began as soon as there was light enough to judge the tobacco, and continued often until dusk. There was little rest for anyone.

Hugh stood with Eugene one day and watched a sale. His own tobacco was on the other side of the floor where the buyers would not reach it for hours, although they were working feverishly, crowding around the auctioneer, yelping feebly in response to his deep baying voice, making funny little signs when they wished to bid, buying by crossing their fingers, cocking their hats, or batting their eyes. One of them held a bundle of tobacco in his hands, running trained, sensitive fingers over its silken leaves, and making, meanwhile, a derogatory appraisal of it, in order to discourage competitive bidding. "Thin as silk," he proclaimed, spreading a leaf so that the sunlight filtered through it; "no body to it, at all." He bought the pile with a convulsive wink. They passed on to the next pile treading the bought tobacco under their feet as if it were so much trash.

"Dollar an' ur quarter, dollar an' ur quarter, dollar an' ur half," sang the auctioneer; a hundred pounds of tobacco sold for a price that wouldn't have bought that much cabbage. An old negro man stood by the pile after they had passed on down the row, lifting the fat bundles in his huge black hands, examining them as if he expected to find that they had undergone a ruinous metamorphosis in the short while they had lain there. He picked up several bundles, held them close to his incredulous eyes, finally threw the last one down with a gesture of dejection, walked across the floor, and sat on the tongue of a wagon, holding his woolly gray head in his hands, a figure of dumb despair. He and others like him did not see beyond the buyers, did not see that they were helpless, driven, too, and bound by the urgency of making a living to their part in the gigantic brazen robbery. Their price range had been set for them and they could not go higher than it stipulated; in fact, they were coaxed by bonuses and inducements of one kind and another to stay beneath its maximum figures. It was like the law. These buyers were the executioners. They carried out the sentence which their masters imposed, steeling their hearts, and trying to convince themselves that they were the innocent agents of a system beyond them and above them. But a condemned man does not love his executioner; the executioner, perhaps, comes to despise his victims.

About the floor were standing other farmers whose tobacco had been sold, most of them standing silent and alone, each ashamed to let his neighbor know how low his price had been, each feeling that he had been singled out for a particularly low price. They all looked dumb and defeated, standing there dazed and finding nothing worth talking about, like men who, having sustained the wrath of a tornado, regard the ruin of what had been their homes scattered about their feet, or like men who, broken and worn-out, watch some battle which had thrown them wounded and helpless from its angry center move away from them. A few had some fight left in them. Some cursed, swearing great empty oaths. Some took their tobacco from the floor, loaded it on their wagons, and departed. They would try the Virginia markets, but this was just an angry gesture, and they knew it. The Virginia markets were no better than any other. One or two with little courage and many debts, wept openly. A negro sat sprawled in the middle of his tobacco and nursed the fat bundles foolishly, crying to God what a shame it was.

A heavy pungent smell of horses and tobacco and hurrying men filled the house. Noise followed the buyers from one end of the floor to the other, like a slow roll of thunder, low and menacing. A wave of nausea swept over Hugh. He turned to Eugene.

"Let's go outside," he said; "they won't reach my stuff for hours."

Outside the street was warm and almost empty. A few negroes sat basking in the sun against the brick wall of the warehouse, eating huge slices of yellow cheese, sandwiched between large cakes. Country negroes always ate cheese and cakes when they came to town. One strummed lazily on a battered guitar, singing a low accompaniment about coming home early in the morning and finding his door locked from the inside, a song ending in the melodious threat that he wasn't coming home no more, no more, baby chile, no more.

"By God! they are pouring it to us this time," said Eugene, his eyes cold and clouded.

"The buyers say that the companies don't want tobacco, that they have more than they can store now," Hugh replied, feeling far more hopeless than he cared to show.

This information seemed to anger Eugene. His cold face snapped like a turtle's. He bit his words off and spat them out as if he hated their sound.

"It's a damned lie, a Goddamned weak-kneed excuse. The Georgia market was short. Half a crop in South Carolina. I've heard that before, the lying, thieving rogues."

He walked a block without speaking, as if he were ashamed of the violent outburst, so unnatural of him. They walked on through the business part of town. The streets were crowded with people who had made their sales and were spending what money they had received. They saw whole families emerging from the stores, first the father, then the mother, followed by a brood of curious-eyed children, all laden with bulging bundles, new clothes for the winter. In the spring, about Easter, they would file back again to be outfitted for the summer, this time on credit. In every group there were small children whose pride in their new possessions overcame them as soon as they were on the street; they tore holes in the paper bundles, removed the tops from their shoe-boxes, and examined their contents eagerly. One little fellow wore his new shoes, carried the old ones in the box. He walked along, his head bowed, his eyes fastened upon his shining new shoes.

"You and I, Hugh," Eugene said suddenly, "we can't comprehend what these poor devils are up against. We didn't make our crops on credit. We paid as we went, fertilizer, labor, and repairs. We may have nothing when the crop is sold, but, at least, we won't be in debt."

"No, I can go for another year yet," Hugh answered, thinking that this was poor consolation for the loss of the present year.

"But not another, I think," said Eugene grimly.

They turned into a restaurant where they ate a rather tasteless meal, neither making any effort at conversation. Afterwards they sat, their elbows hunched on the table, and smoked cigarettes. Hugh felt no desire to talk; he was apathetic and listless, drugged by an objectless anger, which, though he did not know it, clouded his dark face with a scowl. He thought of Nancy, of their last week together, and of their coming marriage in the spring. Unhappily, he wondered whether she could endure hardships and privations cheerfully. And then he was angry for thinking in this fashion, for allowing his mind to accept the present condition as a permanent one and plan adjustments to it, instead of rebelling against it. And sitting there, oblivious of his surroundings, his mind wandered back through old years to a field of crimson clover, and to a girl who had cried to the arched night that love was impossible, like a star. He shook himself, blew a great cloud of smoke, and rose from the table.

He ate supper at the Clay home that night. Dumont liked him and approved the match between him and Nancy, but it was her mother who actually welcomed him into the family, cooking cakes for him to take home, taking a maternal interest in him, and showing her favor in effective womanly ways. She was generous like Nancy.

Heralded by the trumpeting of shrill winds, winter came that night, driving sharp, needle-pointed sleet before it. As he walked to the house after putting his car in the garage, Hugh felt it on his brown cheeks and on the back of his neck like a thousand little spears. When he awoke in the morning his window was covered with thin ice, and when he raised it he saw stretched, far and wide, a strange glazed world, cold and motionless. Before night, dark, scurrying clouds marshaled themselves into a belligerent mass, and under the cover of darkness they lashed the cold earth again; screaming like unleashed furies the winds hurled snow into every crevice and corner, deep in cellar doorways, and high and heavy in the branches of trees. Then, as if the elements had set out to do their worst, followed days of murky cold, unrelieved by even a glimpse of the sun, and starless, moonless nights, during which the earth became like a great, hard-packed snowball.

8

On a dark rainy evening in late May, Hugh met the train which brought Nancy home from college. He had not seen her since Christmas, and he waited impatiently for her train, pacing up and down beside the tracks getting a peculiar satisfaction from the sound of the wet gravel crunching beneath his feet. It allayed his impatience somewhat. Christmas had been such a short week, hardly allowing them time to wear off the strangeness of being together again. When they had separated at the close of the holidays, it was in the secure knowledge that both of them would wait impatiently for the spring which was to be the time of their marriage. It spoke in the warmth of her kisses, in those speechless moments when she had clung to him with fierce gentleness.

The whistle of the approaching train split the heavy night air like the shriek of an enraged beast, jerking him up from his impatient pacing, excited and eager-eyed. Hugh distinguished Nancy easily among the other passengers alighting from the train. She stood waiting for him, gay and colorful against the drab surroundings. He was almost rude in his eagerness to get her away from the eyes of the station-yard. She crept near him in the car as they left the town, holding his arm with both hands and talking volubly, interspersing inquiries about her family with swift, brushing, little kisses which kindled flames in his cheek. They were soon home, where he had to relinquish her to the welcoming of her family, and to the irking space of supper, a veritable feast, during which he had to content himself with an occasional smile and a furtive handclasp under the table. Dumont and her mother took pity on him later in the evening, however, and retired to their room, leaving him and Nancy alone except for Eugene, who soon wandered off to bed, too, his long face showing no appreciation of their emotions.

He had asked her to set a date for their wedding in his last letter. There had not been time for an answer by mail, and now he was eager to have it from her lips.

"You haven't answered my letter," he said, when Eugene had gone.

She put her arms about him, drew his ear close, and whispered, "I am the answer."

"Does that mean tomorrow?"

"Certainly not. Nor next week. Next month—maybe. The last of the month."

"I think the first week of June will be far better. That's when I want it."

"Why the first week of June?"

"Because it's sooner," he told her soberly.

They were married the last week of June at her father's house. One would have thought it Dumont's own wedding from the interest he took in it. He invited all his cronies to the wedding supper, inspected all the gifts with the eager avidity of a child, and made a little speech at the table, a speech prompted by a rare indulgence in wine, in which he eulogized the beauty of his daughter, and publicly charged Hugh with eternal care of the treasure he had bestowed upon him.

They went to the sea on their honeymoon, although Hugh would have liked to take her straight to his own house. He was not fully happy until she came to him under his own roof. Annie had decorated the house for their homecoming, filling everything that faintly resembled a vase with roses from the yard.

"My! I feel like I'm in a hothouse," Nancy exclaimed as they entered.

"Jest wait 'til you sees upstars," Annie interjected proudly.

She had reserved the freshest and largest roses for their room. It glowed with their gorgeous color and fragrance. Hugh remembered her first roses from his house.

"Do you still like my house?" he asked.

"I love it," she whispered to him in the dark, lying with his face drawn into the soft hollow of her throat, "but it's terribly old, isn't it? And it's frightfully large and strong, like you."

"I don't frighten you, do I?"

"No, but you could. Will you always be kind to me?"

"Always."

"And you'll love me always, too, and be faithful?"

"Forever," he vowed passionately. "If not, I hope you'll shoot me."

"I will," she assured him, kissing him with breathless intensity.

Above them a soft shower pattered on the roof for a few minutes, and then the night was silent as before.

9

Raising his eyes at the end of the furrow Hugh measured the sun's height above the blue slopes of Sligo.

"Another hour's light," he judged.

He mopped the sweat from his face, then swung the plow to the next row. As he turned, his eyes swept the horizon until they rested on the clump of trees which sheltered his home. His plowlines fell slackly across the beam and his thoughts fled homeward. His eyes, tracking the nostalgic paths of old Sligo haunted by the memories of a hundred years, had brought him home, and suddenly like a light breaking out of darkness the full meaning of the word *home* illuminated his mind. Nancy was waiting there. Again the house had light and warmth and voices, all that he had promised himself on that bleak December day. A furious eagerness to be at the house seized him.

"To hell with the next row," he exclaimed.

He ripped the gear from the mule. Jamming his hat tight on his head he mounted the animal with a bound and set it loping toward the house.

Nancy, standing in the yard enjoying the long shadows of evening, was treated to the sight of her impetuous lover galloping up astride a sweaty mule. She greeted him with peals of laughter. A belated sense of his ridiculous appearance creased his dark face with a grin.

"Did you think the house was on fire?" she asked.

"No, not the house. Me. I was suddenly fired with the wonder of having you here. I rushed home before the dream could end."

She flashed him a swift smile.

She was so fresh and clean that he kissed her gingerly, refusing himself the pleasure of drawing her close against his sweat-soaked body.

He held her at arm's length. "I must get cleaned up," he said hungrily.

She clung to him with her eyes. "Oh, Hugh," she whispered, "please do."

Later, after supper, a gentle-fingered summer rain strummed the roof. The whole world receded into the drizzling darkness, leaving only Nancy and the deep peace of her love.

Hugh was up before the sun rose. Nancy stirred in the bed.

"Wait for me," she yawned.

"Stay in bed. Annie can look after my breakfast."

"No. I'll see you at breakfast."

At the breakfast table he protested against her getting up when he did, but she laughed at his protests.

"Perhaps I made a mistake to marry a farmer, but I won't make the mistake of not being a farmer's wife," she told him.

"You are a fine wife. That's why I don't want you getting up with the cows. You'll look like a farmer's wife before you are forty."

"Well, if I lie in bed, I'll be fat and forty, so what's the difference?"

"I'll certainly leave you if you ever get fat."

"Wouldn't you love me then?"

"I like you just as you are."

"You like me?"

"I love you."

"That's better. Enough to come around the table and kiss me? No. You mustn't lean across. Be polite and come around."

"I was in a hurry to take advantage of your offer."

It was delightful to have her ask him to kiss her.

"Your coffee is getting cold," she warned him.

"It doesn't matter."

"Well, mine is getting cold then."

"That's different. I'm afraid that I had forgotten all about breakfast."

"I'm afraid you had."

"Do you know, Hugh," she asked when he was seated, "that you never kissed me before at breakfast?"

"You never asked me before."

"Hugh! how cruel."

"I always wanted to."

"You always may," she assured him.

He hardly ever saw her between breakfast and noon unless she came to the fields where he was working. Lately she had started bringing him water about ten o'clock by which time the sun had dispelled the last cool vestige of night.

"Where shall I find you if I bring water today?" she called as he left the yard.

"Long Level," he answered, "where the rows curl up and scorch about ten."

Long Level. It was a name held over from childhood, a time when names had more meaning somehow, when they were very necessary. Each field, each plantation road, every little stream had borne a name in those days, exactly as if the farm had been a world within itself, beyond its borders a vast and nameless nothing. Long Level was not a level at all, but a great sloping swell of land, rising on one side from an open meadow and rolling from its summit to a wooded hollow on the other side. The rows in this field were long and curving, spread like a net to catch the rays of the sun. From no part of the hill except the crest could it be seen in its entirety; this fact, he remembered, created in the mind of one working there the illusion that only a small part remained to be covered. How many times he had snatched that false comfort on those burning days when the sun had cut his back like a fire-dipped whip.

Nancy came earlier than he had expected. He tied his plow-lines to the handles, and walked toward her where she waited for him in the shade.

"Sit here in the shade a while," she begged when he had finished drinking.

"I can see that my work is over for the morning," he grumbled.

"No, you may go back to your plowing in a bit. I won't keep you long. In fact, I think I'll take my shoes off and walk in the fresh furrow behind you."

"I have spells like that, too, only I'd like to lie by a creek with my feet in the water."

"Why do we want to do those things," she asked seriously, "and why don't we?"

"Because it would be silly."

"It wouldn't be silly if one wanted to badly, would it?"

"You wouldn't want to badly unless it were very silly."

"Hugh, you can say the meanest things. That's two today."

"Oh, I'm mean all right."

"I believe you are, for a fact."

"Are you joking?"

"No."

"Really?"

"Yes. Something tells me that you have a devil in you. You've got him tied, now, no doubt, but he's there and some day he'll get me."

"If you are serious," he questioned her, puzzled, "please tell me why you believe that?"

"I believe it."

"But why?"

"I just feel it."

"The devil!"

"Yes."

"I mean the devil you do."

"Well, I do."

"Maybe you do," he said crossly, "I'm beginning to feel it myself now."

"I think I'll go back to the house," rising in mock alarm.

"I wonder what foolishness in your head started this anyway?"

"Kiss me and forgive," she said lifting her face, and after a moment, "and again and forget it."

But Hugh had forgotten. Lifting her in his arms he bore her away from the edge of the field into the cooler depths of the woods, where he deposited her on a carpet of clean pine needles, and stretched himself beside her, holding her so fiercely that she felt herself the captive of a wild forest lover.

The tall pines swayed in passive harmony with the ambient breeze, and far, far above their topmost branches stretched an infinity of azure peace. Hugh held her more gently now. She could feel his warm breath on her cheek, but he spoke no word, apparently satisfied with her nearness. A sensation of calm, unanxious joy surged through her, a strange feeling of slow, throbbing peace, which was not entirely the product of her own body and senses, for it seemed that she had drawn into herself not only the pulsing strength of the man at her side but the heat of the good sun, the fragrance of the green pines, and some of the tonic of dazzling blue distance. Life seemed so good and tangible at this moment, that simply by lifting her arms she felt she could draw it all to her and embrace it.

10

On the church grounds and along the streets of Granville Hugh had heard, all summer, rumblings of resentment and rebellion against the price situation which the past marketing season had left so bitterly impressed upon the minds of farmers. As fall and the opening of the markets drew near, it became apparent that there existed a formless current of dissatisfaction strong enough to produce some kind of economic revolution if its diverse elements could be brought under leadership and focused upon a purpose.

On Saturday afternoon the town of Granville became a forum for the country people; farmers assembled in little groups on the street corners and on the courthouse square, commiserating each other, fretting over the conditions of the times, and reminding each other of the bounty of other years, of other years grown unduly beautiful in their memories by this time. Few expected better prices, and few had any plan with which to combat their troubles; most of them expressed a bitter resignation and confused their plight with what they thought was a period of national adversity, not realizing that the prices from which they suffered were man-made and deliberate, were not the penalty of hard times, but an economic oppression, planned and executed against them.

There were men like Eugene Clay, however, who knew that prosperity was rampant in the north and in the west, and that under the natural laws of trade it should be true in their own country. They knew the source of their troubles, and they thought they knew how to check these troubles at their source. They held that only organized selling could bring relief, and lately their opinions had attracted a wide attention. Even those men who thought themselves victims of a natural adversity listened to this talk of organization, but they were not certain that it was the right answer, and moreover, for many reasons, they were afraid of it. With suspicions born of an isolated way of living, they feared that any movement requiring the combined efforts of all was doomed to failure, and there was a great deal of wisdom in this fear.

The newspapers, fattening on cigarette advertisements, were reluctant to support a movement designed to injure their rich clients; their editors discouraged the plan, stressed the strong individualism of the farmer, and cast their doubt upon a plan which called for unity. The townspeople, merchants who suffered and prospered as the farmer did, were sympathetic, but they, too, were afraid that the farmers would not be able to see the thing through, feared that they would only make their condition worse by the attempt, and over the matter they shook their many heads. Their opinion carried much weight, because the average farmer saw in the town merchant a man who had succeeded in a more complex business than that of farming, a man more familiar than he with the intricacies of commerce.

Granville had become a town of considerable size and activity, linked by good roads with other growing towns which had once been remote villages, distant by a day's drive. The merchants of the town were not compelled now to look only to the country for their customers. New industries had appeared, mills built by northern capital had sprung up at their doorsteps, and a steady stream of money tinkled into their cash-registers from these humming mills. It was good business, too, business that came, money in hand, not whining for a year's credit. Many poor farmers worn out by the frustration of the farm had turned to the mills with something like hope. There a lack of freedom was offset by a lack of uncertainty, and a paucity of leisure by some relief from worry about daily bread. Between those families who deserted the farm for the mills and those who still clung to the unequal struggle of wrestling a living from the soil, arose a mutual hostility born of a mutual disrespect. Country people, proud of their liberty, regarded mill slaves as the scum of the earth, judging that the barren freedom of rural life was preferable to the awful security of the mill for which one paid the price of a name. And mindful of this, those who had fled to the mills, when they encountered members of that group to which they had belonged formerly, were resentful of the resentment which once had been their own, and they comforted themselves by thinking how much better it was to have money in their pockets instead of nothing but an outraged hope in their hearts. At this time only the tenant whites were moving to the mill. Those who had land mortgaged it, sustained by the belief that more fruitful years would restore them to prosperity. They gave liens on the future.

This exodus from the country had not attained, as yet, the size or force of a movement; there was nothing remarkable about it, nothing to brand it as more than the casual surrender of a few individuals who had never been particularly successful, just the inevitable fate of a few farmers who had been outdistanced by time and circumstance. No one seemed to realize that here was the first weakening at the flanks, that these deserters had seen with the clarity of cowardice an oncoming defeat which those who were still fighting did not have time to suspect.

11

Notwithstanding the rigorous vigilance which it demanded, the tobacco curing season was a happy phase of the summer's work. The nights of watching the flues were pieced out with many snatches of sleep and many confused awakenings, and they seemed very long. The days were long, too, and fiery hot, but against these discomforts there was the sweet satisfaction of harvest to sustain the weary watcher, no more fear of storm, of sudden hail, of dreaded blight. The fierce flames, curling hungrily up the flues, set a seal of fire on all these. The crop was made, cut, and cured, and every summer fear floated away tranquilly upon the spiralling smoke.

Hugh was tired of it, nevertheless. For a month he had watched those flues, night and day, played the heat up in one barn, lowered it in another, until it seemed that life had become an enormous thermometer, and he a heat-stricken midget at the beck and call of the fluctuating mercury. He hadn't slept in a bed for weeks; indeed, he had hardly slept at all, for those stolen naps while stretched on a cot between the flues were fitful and full of apprehensive dreams. He had seen Nancy only at meals and during some short hours in the afternoons when she had come to the pine grove which sheltered the barns. She never stayed very long because the air was full of soot, it was hot and contaminating. She was tired of it, too, tired of living alone in the old house while her husband led the life of a red-eyed savage, as she vividly described it.

So it was with that feeling of relief which comes when the end of a good fight is in view that Hugh sat propped against the side of the barn. All day he had kept to the shade as much as possible, moving his chair around the barn, following its shadow as the sun swung across the sky. This was the last barn, the very last. All the others had been killed out, and even now the flues of this one were crackling with the last sticks of wood that he intended to put in them. He would watch it until midnight, until the fires had burned down to a shallow bed of coals, until he had pushed these remaining embers far toward the end of the flues; then he could brush the ashes from his hands in a fine gesture of completion, and the month of vigil would be ended. It was a pleasant thought. The fact that it was Saturday afternoon added a final touch of harmony to this sense of completion. He sat and dreamed of the comforts of a clean bed and un-interrupted sleep.

The sound of voices approaching from the direction of the house suddenly shattered his reverie, and a moment later Eugene came around the corner of the barn, bringing with him a stranger.

"Hello," said Eugene.

The stranger bowed. He was a tall man with a dark face, and hair that had grayed prematurely. He had the look of a man who had seen many far places and had been somewhat dissatisfied in all of them.

His name was Maxon, Eugene explained. He was an agent of the farmer's co-operative association of which Eugene had talked all summer. Maxon lost no time in idle pleasantries but set about his business as soon as an introduction had been made. The farmers in other parts of the state were already organized, he said, and the proximity of the selling season made it imperative that steps be taken immediately toward local organization. He had a pleasant manner.

"Our hope lies in numbers," he stated. "We have guarded against premature launching of the project by incorporating in every contract the stipulation that it does not become effective until a decided majority of the growers have become pledged members of the association. In that way we will know where we are when we start."

"How are you financed?" Hugh asked.

"A very proper question," observed Maxon, "and one that is easily answered. Although we expect to earn our operating costs through handling charges, just as the warehouses do, the initiation fees plus some loans which we have already secured will enable us to make a start. From that time on it will simply be a matter of taking the tobacco into the pool and selling it. We will have the bulk of the tobacco. We can demand a fair price. Those two things being true, it should be easy to obtain additional backing, should we need it. As I have said the association will demand handling charges just as the warehouses do."

"Of course," agreed Hugh, "and will you use the warehouses as they are used now?"

"Not exactly," he replied. "You will offer your tobacco on a warehouse floor, as you have always done. It will be graded there by association graders, a value will be set upon it, and you will receive your money. There will be no auction."

"Are you a farmer, Mr. Maxon?" Hugh asked.

The question appeared to nettle the man, but he displayed no irritation in his answer.

"No, I am not a farmer. I'm employed by the pool. I'm an organizer, a salesman, I suppose."

"That's all right. Go ahead."

For the better part of an hour Maxon talked. Eugene lent his persuasive wits often. There was no doubt concerning his earnestness, and although Hugh had heard it all before, repetition failed to dim the glorious prospects which Eugene had painted.

Although his friendship for Eugene advocated an immediate support of the plan, Hugh hesitated. The pledge was one which he wished to give only after mature consideration. The contract which Maxon presented could not be entered into lightly. Its terms were definite and absolute, calling for an unwavering allegiance to the association for the period of five years. That meant delivering all the tobacco he would raise for the coming five years into the co-operative pool even should its operation prove unsatisfactory. It was a most stringent demand, and one for which he would receive only some promises based upon a hopeful experiment. He hesitated.

Both Eugene and Maxon seemed to understand that his hesitancy was due to honest deliberation, to a proper recognition of the seriousness of pledging his support, for neither advanced any new arguments, but waited patiently for him to speak his mind. It was evident that he was weighing it as a moral obligation as well as a business venture. Could he honestly swear loyalty to something which had yet to prove its right to loyalty? It was fine and splendid in conception, but what would it be in execution? He did not know. He could not. No one could. Calm, deliberate judgment was a faculty which Hugh was slowly acquiring. Two years earlier he would have accepted or refused the proposition on a basis of pure idealism; now he pondered it.

"I am still not entirely satisfied that we can go from scratch," he said at length. "We may exhaust our facilities for borrowing before we complete our arrangements for selling. It's rank foolishness not to anticipate the toughest sort of fight from the established tobacco companies, for our success must mean their defeat. And although we are engaged in a fight with these people, nevertheless, they are our best customers. Although we farmers deliver our tobacco into the pool, the pool must sell to no others than these same manufacturers. They already have enormous surpluses of raw tobacco, I understand, which will enable them to go for a long time without taking more off our hands, if the scrap comes to that. They have money, too. We can hardly hope to finance the manufacturing end in addition to the costs of pooling."

"That's exactly what we hope to do eventually," said Maxon.

"That could develop into an abuse on a par with the present system," Hugh exclaimed.

"How?" Eugene demanded quickly.

"That would be the most powerful kind of monopoly, wouldn't it? If the organization fell into the hands of unscrupulous men, the farmer would be the victim of a centralized enemy, instead of several competitive ones."

"A far cry that is," Eugene objected.

"Well, if the idea occurred to me it may occur to others," Hugh rejoined with undeniable logic.

"It seems to me," Maxon broke in, "that while all these evils could possibly develop, they have no proper bearing as arguments against the pool, because it is to oppose, and to end these very evils that we have started our campaign. Should the association degenerate into all that you have mentioned, it would have created no new abuses. We have, now, just the sort of economic tyranny of which you speak in the form of tobacco companies. You are absolutely at their mercy. You can hope for nothing from them. Should the association prove to be a sword turned against its makers, it will be, nevertheless, the only weapon worthy of a name that has ever been lifted against the tobacco companies. They have ridden roughshod over everything without having a finger lifted against them."

"If it's just a case of swapping horses it won't mean much," Hugh argued.

"No theory is perfect," Eugene observed, "as long as it is only a theory. Your objections are the kind that any thinking man could make against any untried plan, but you shouldn't allow them to cloud your estimate of the whole. Of course we can't guarantee anything. Our accomplishment must rest entirely on our vision, on our loyalty, and on our hope. The history of the association will be, whatever it is, not so much a test of the plan, as a measure of the men who put their efforts behind it. The conception is practical and simple, with every promise of success. Its outcome resolves itself, finally, into a question of courage."

"It will take more than courage," said Hugh; "courage is a common quality, and often as not it gets us nothing more than a bad beating. You know that."

"We won't discuss it," returned Eugene, visibly angry.

Maxon showed some embarrassment at this exchange of words between the two. He had expected an easy convert in Hugh, since he was familiar with their relationship; moreover, Eugene had predicted that he would sign readily. Puzzled, and feeling that the conversation had taken on the color of a family affair, he withdrew and left the two men to themselves.

Eugene regarded Hugh bitterly from the depths of his cold eyes.

"You have disappointed me," he said.

"Have I? Well, get set for a surprise. I think I'll join. Your last flight of oratory was too much for me."

Maxon was visibly mystified when Eugene called him back with the contract, but he had been dealing with strangers too long to allow his lack of understanding to delay its execution. That was his job, and when the gods threw him a blind gift, he took it unquestioningly.

"Yes sir, sign here," he said. "Thank you," and it was done.

Before leaving, both Maxon and Eugene begged Hugh

to accompany them in their campaign during the coming
week, and since the crop was housed he willingly agreed to
go along.

On Monday morning he joined them at the Clay home.
They set off in Eugene's automobile, working toward Granville, having decided to organize that part of the county
first, and to visit the sparsely settled Sligo section later.
Eugene's voice was vibrant with suppressed excitement,
although his long face betrayed no feeling. Success had rewarded their efforts of the past week, giving them confidence
for the work ahead of them, and to Eugene who was new at
it, a valuable basis of experience. It soon became evident that
securing a contract afforded Eugene a greater pleasure than
it did Maxon. He worked hard and conscientiously, but it
was only a job to him. To Eugene it was an adventuresome
crusade.

At first Hugh did little talking. However, many farmers
were persuaded to sign because of his presence, because he
was there to state that it had seemed a good thing to him, that
he had signed. Before the day had ended he developed a
strong dislike for his role of exhibit. The second day he
solicited contracts with the earnestness of a veteran of the
road.

When they reviewed their work at the end of each day it
was gratifying to find that they were securing contracts
from more than half the farmers on whom they called. Some
gave them quick and positive refusals, some had to be
harangued for a long time before they would sign. In many
cases they left blank forms to be signed and sent in at
pleasure. This was necessary in those cases where farmers
disliked the appearance of having been out-argued, of having had decisions forced upon them. Sometimes they followed this same policy in dealing with ignorant men, who,
though they failed to comprehend the intricate wording of

the contracts, were disarmed by having them left to their unruffled persual. Their greatest difficulty arose with the men who could not read. These men, who signed by making their mark, had to accept the contract purely on faith. Maxon would have been utterly helpless in these cases without the assistance of Eugene and Hugh, who were recognized and trusted by most of those upon whom they called.

Some men displayed an amazingly apathetic unconcern, others an adamant imperviousness to reason, contending that only fools would try to change the existing order. Things just changed, they believed, men didn't change them. It was all a matter of God's will or accident, and what was good enough for Paul and Silas was good enough for Tom, Dick, and Harry. There were men, they discovered, who lived absolutely in the present. The past, in the sense of monitory history, had no existence in their minds whatever. They apprehended no future; they signed no contracts. Far be it from them to meddle with the course of nature.

The utter lack of response which they encountered from the natives of the Sligo valley was at once amusing and pathetic. They farmed in an undisciplined fashion, content to take what the land would produce in the summer and in winter to hunt with their lean, black hounds.

In other parts of the state other farmers were enlisting their neighbors; originating in the south, the movement had spread northward, had covered the state, and had made some progress in Virginia. Almost overnight "The Co-ops" became the outstanding object of public attention. Their activities were heralded by word of mouth and by the press, by friend and foe. They elicited much sympathy and much abuse. Every man who had the remotest connection with the existing order of tobacco selling, whether he were buyer, warehouseman, or speculator, joined in vilifying the organization; they fought it with propaganda and with ridi-

cule. They were fighting for their jobs. Soon the very
intensity of their resistance affirmed the fact that they
feared the Co-ops as a powerful foe. Ridicule gave way to
deadly, earnest opposition.

Long before the markets opened, before the association
had ever handled a pound of tobacco as a functioning business, the people of the county had divided themselves into
two distinct factions, with all the accompanying factional
attributes, political hatred, militant loyalty, and a fecundity
of argumentativeness, which, until this time, nothing less
than a war or a presidential election could have evoked. A
spirit born of the late war permeated the co-operative group.
They felt themselves crusaders for the right, fighting an up-
hill but valorous battle against the entrenched forces of
adversity. Those farmers who refused to ally themselves with
their cause were "slackers." Those who openly opposed them
were traitors.

They felt these distinctions keenly. Nothing could be
worse they held, than a farmer who tried to defeat his
brothers in their first battle against economic tyrants. But
there were many who opposed them, most of them big farmers, men who owed their success to the pursuit of a studied
caution; it was altogether against their nature to plunge
headlong into this radical movement. These men were the
opponents whom Eugene feared above all others, because he
knew that the force of their opposition was doubled by the
fact that they were farmers. They were unfriendly to a
plan which boasted their own interests. It was only natural,
therefore, that their attitude should create fear and suspicion
in the minds of lesser farmers, people who had often looked
to these men for guidance. Many of them, through virtue of
their extensive lands, were able to dictate the loyalties of
hundreds of small tenant farmers. It was easy to combat the
arguments of the buyers and warehousemen; indeed, their

activities afforded a fulcrum with which to bolster up the courage of the Co-ops, since it was logical to declare that they were fighting for self-preservation, that the intensity of their opposition bespoke the power of the new order. But it was difficult to explain away the defiance of these unconverted farmers. It was easier and perhaps best to call them traitors. Betrayal was a common human frailty, and most people had some acquaintance with it.

The forum in Stone's drug store resounded with this battle. Squire Thompson, bloated with that stupidity which thinks all others stupid, held forth there daily. His role was purely that of a spectator, at least it should have been, because he owned no land and had no profitable connection with a tobacco company, but the store was a favorite loitering place of the buyers and their talk had given him a smattering of prejudicial information. He absorbed this flow of propaganda, stained it with the vindictive pus of his own ignorance, and slavered it upon any who would listen, unaware of how acidly it stung the raw feelings of some of his hearers.

Dumont Clay came into the store one morning, ordered a coca-cola, and stood at the fountain savoring its sharp flavor. The Squire was in the middle of one of his blasts and from the bench where his great bulk rested he could not see Dumont.

"The association will never handle a pound of tobacco," he prophesied; "y'all will see I'm right. 'Taint nuthin but a slick scheme to collect a million dollars in entrance fees, and that'll be all. The only farmers it'll ever benefit is them that's organizin' it, sich as that crazy Eugene Clay."

Dumont had not finished his drink. He never finished it. Stepping from behind the fountain he confronted the Squire, stood over him in contemptuous silence for a moment, then threw the icy sludge from his glass full in the

Squire's gaping face. Without a word he turned and paid for his drink and walked out of the store.

The final effort of the campaign to secure members took place in the courthouse at Granville. It was to be a big day and farmers began to pour into the town early in the morning, although the speech-making had been advertised for the afternoon. Perhaps the announcement that there would be a free barbecue explained these early arrivals. By eleven o'clock the streets were crowded with farmers of every class and description, prosperous ones arrayed in their Sunday clothes, poor ones in faded blue overalls and wilted straw hats, some alert and eager for all the patches on their pants, and some whose faces were as washed out as the frayed shirts upon their backs.

It seemed to Hugh that the barbecue, which was served in one of the warehouses, was a meaty hurdle for the exercise of primitive appetites. A cosmic hunger moved the hot crowd. It surged by the tables in long mouth-watering lines, each individual equipped with a paper tray, a cheap tin spoon, and a clamorous impatience to have his dish filled. Behind the tables stood ten sweating negroes, serving the hot seasoned meat into the waiting trays. The warehouse hummed with a monstrous eating noise, punctuated now and then by the shrill cry of some participant who had been building up an appetite since early morning with hard corn whiskey. Within an hour all the food had been consumed. Nothing was left of the feast except several baskets of bones, and of the crowd only a few little town negroes, waiting to gnaw the succulent bones.

The well-fed crowd moved to the courthouse in a mass and filled it, seats, aisles, and windows; many could not get in. Maxon opened the meeting by making a talk similar to those he had been making to scattered individuals during the past few weeks, very similar to them, except for the fact that addressing a crowd gave a shade of self-conscious dignity to his speech. It was evident, however, that he had mastered the technique of talking to farmers. He spoke in their native phrases which he had picked up in associating with them. He used the ancient parable of the bundle of sticks. When he had finished his talk, he turned the meeting into an open forum, by asking a man lately recruited to speak to his assembled comrades. Other farmers followed this man's example, and for hours they talked to each other in the plain effective language of their own kind.

It was peculiar, Hugh thought, that the crowd responded most heartily to a speech which failed to appeal to him. A middle-aged man, Ralph Jackson, whom he knew slightly, was the speaker. Possibly the fact that he had never heard any save political speeches accounted for the manner of his talk, because it was full of bombast, and by some rhetorical legerdemain he contrived to bombard his hearers with a volley of patriotic allusions which bore no normal relation to the subject under discussion. But he managed it almost plausibly. He recounted the struggles of the Continentals, and how they were saved through unity. He swept from victory at Yorktown to campaign a while with Lee, surrendered, not without glory, at Appomattox, and finally in a fine flare of verbiage, he routed the Germans in a victory ingloriously easy of attainment. They had the blood of conquerors in their veins, he assured them. His speech accomplished a great deal, for fired by his assurance that they were a race of indomitables, the very backbone of the country, they signed the contracts as fast as pens and forms could be supplied. Charged with the electric power of mass feeling they shouted confidently that their purpose was achieved. A few weeks more, now, and the opening markets would tell the tale.

12

The prospect of fall and the opening markets was one
which farmers held before them all summer, a sort of annual
lollypop to assuage the bitter taste of labor and self-denial.
Hugh knew, for the first time this year, the full meaning
of this dependence on the fall markets. He had departed
from the custom of the country in financing his crop as it
was made, paying for his fertilizer when he bought it, and
paying cash for his croppers' food and clothes instead of
allowing them to charge it at the store. In the end any credit
advanced to one of his workers would have been his liability,
therefore he undertook no additional risks by paying for
what they consumed and taking his chance of reimbursing
himself from the proceeds of their crops. The pursuit of
this policy had already resulted in the utter depletion of his
ready money, and hardly any of it had been spent in the
gratification of personal wants, he realized, as he checked
his accounts. He had bought no clothes for himself and only
a few insignificant purchases had been made for Nancy.
This latter discovery struck him with a force akin to embarrassment. Shirts and overalls for Dave, May money for
all the negroes, (the first Sunday in May and a great dressing up for church) a doctor's bill for Henry Lawson when
his wife had presented him with his latest son, long lists
of fatback and flour, a little Saturday money under all the
names, something for all of them, and nothing for Nancy.
It was a formidable sum when totalled, a year's living for
twenty hands, and for his own wife only a few household
expenditures. True, she had come well supplied with everything when he had married her, but neither that nor her
silence about her wants should have allowed him to go so
long without making any inquiries about her needs. He

closed the ledger, put it back in the safe, and walked to the house, thoughtfully.

The mute accusation of the ledger followed him to the supper table, and when it continued to rankle his mind as he and Nancy withdrew to the living room he sought to free himself of a growing sense of shame by talking to her about his neglect.

"What do you suppose I found from my records this afternoon?" he asked.

"That we owe a lot of money?"

"No."

"That a lot of money is owed us?"

"Quite a lot for one year, but something much worse than that."

"Are you serious?" she asked in alarm.

"Quite serious."

"I refuse to ask another question," she pouted, turning her attention to her needle. "What is it, Hugh?"

"I find there, in black and white, that I don't love you anymore, that I never did, it seems."

"That is serious, really; let's burn the book."

"No, we'll try to correct it. Next year, no, next week, we'll buy you new clothes, and give you money and everything, which, according to that book, you have been without since I married you."

"Oh, I haven't been so bad off, but now that you have brought the subject up, as a good husband should," she added with smiling malevolence, "look at this," displaying the frayed border of a petticoat, "and at this," she cried, tracing a run in her stocking.

"I'm looking," he said; "that's right, go ahead and rub it in."

"No, really, I need nothing. I'm very happy just to have you back after that miserable month of tobacco curing. I'll never spend another month alone at night, listening to owls screech and ghosts walk."

"Ghosts glide, honey, and there are no ghosts in my house, anyway."

"Of course there are, Hugh. Didn't Aunt Mathy tell you that?"

"Did you encounter a gentleman ghost," Hugh asked, "a gentleman ghost who grabbed you in two strong arms, hugged you, and kissed you with a whiskey breath, and a long, loud laugh?"

"I did not," Nancy protested, "but who is he?"

"That's my grandfather. Give him my regards if you meet him."

"Oh yes. I've heard that he was a powerful hand with the ladies."

"How families degenerate!"

"I'll degenerate you, if I ever hear of your imitating him."

"I'll see that you don't hear of it."

"What do you think about Eugene?" Nancy asked suddenly.

"I wasn't thinking about him. I see no connection between Eugene and ghosts."

"We were talking about ladies, I believe."

"They never cross my mind now."

"Nor his, I'm afraid. I wish he would get interested in some good girl."

"Let him alone. He's having the time of his life. He's in love with the Co-ops."

"Really, I wish he were married."

"You think well of matrimony, don't you?"

"I think Eugene's going to need someone who is very near and dear if the Co-ops fail. He's too wrapped up in it."

"Yes," Hugh agreed, "it would go pretty hard with him

if it fell through. It's a sort of holy cause with him, and he's high priest. He couldn't stand its failure as well as a lot of weaker people could. We shouldn't talk of failure though. And yet . . ."

"What were you about to say?"

"I was just thinking that if it had not been for Gene I doubt that I would have signed. Of course I'm loyal and I believe in it to the utmost, but honestly, Nancy, all these big farmers who refuse to consider it aren't fools. They have good reasons. I believe they distrust it because the rank and file are so whole-heartedly for it—poor whites, especially, and all those folks who look for the easiest way out of trouble. Of course we have a lot of members, but what sort of folks are they, most of them, I mean? How far can we rely upon them? Everybody is too sure that the battle is won to suit me."

"Naturally, you are anxious, but don't worry too much; Gene says we are getting stronger every day, and number is power, after all."

Hugh said nothing to discourage her. They had discussed improvements for the house and he thought he read in her optimism the hope of their quick realization. The Clay home had running water and she had missed it sorely since their marriage.

"Daddy's going to put in lights this fall," she said as though she had read Hugh's mind.

"Once you told me candles were just the thing for this house."

"Oh, that," she laughed, "that observation belongs to the romantic past. Now that we are old married people, lights would be mighty nice."

"Lights couldn't make you any lovelier."

"I could see much better, though."

"We'll see," said Hugh. He wanted to give her these things,

but he was afraid to count too heavily on the price of tobacco.

Hugh was one of many who were afraid to be too hopeful. Even the inhabitants of Granville, people who had only an indirect interest in the affairs of the farmer, were awaiting the opening of the market with a dubious expectancy. One felt that these merchants and townspeople, the non-combatants, as it were, watched the rivalry between the Co-ops and the old tobacco companies as spectators of a game, watched with bated breath, quelling in their bosoms a shout as yet unformed, ready to spring forth in acclaim of victory, equally ready to deride defeat.

The first few days of marketing drew sympathetic approval from the merchants, because the Co-ops valued the tobacco at prices which had been considered fair even in the best years. Many farmers were unhappy and alarmed, however, because the association paid them in cash only about forty per cent of the estimated value of their tobacco. They compared the notes which they held for their balances with the high prices being paid on the auction floors, for price was the most effective weapon which the companies had to turn upon their young rival. As the season lengthened price became a deadly weapon indeed, because the hand-to-mouth, spring-to-fall credit basis on which most farmers lived had been supported by a quick release of cash during the short selling season. The notes issued by the association began to throw this rusty machine out of gear. Many of the poorest farmers were simply unable to wait for the maturity of their notes, and the lure of the ready cash on the auction floor was irresistible.

The actual operation of the Co-operative Association proceeded with far less friction than one would have supposed. The work differed but slightly from that of the open warehouses. The tobacco was handled in the same way. Arrange-

ments for storing and redrying were identical on both sides.
Since the employees of the new order were all men experienced in tobacco, the mere handling and bookkeeping were
attended to with ease. The auctioneer and the babel of the
buyers were gone, however; other than this, one would have
noticed no change. The farmers still drove their wagons into
the gaping buildings, unloaded their contents upon the
floors, displayed long rows of yellow bundles, and still
renewed old acquaintances on the floor or gathered in little
groups beneath the wide roof to wear away the time with
conversation and much reflective expectoration. Some
chewed store tobacco; some used the raw, home-made twist.
Both kinds served admirably as conversational auxiliaries.
Nothing emphasized a well-seasoned observation like the
proper use of tobacco juice. Proficiency in this respect
allowed a speaker to drive home the truth of a remark with
a silencing flourish which transcended the narrow limits
of oratory and bespoke something of the finer art of drama-
turgy.

Maxon had departed shortly after the markets opened,
and Hugh now limited his activities to the simple ones of
being a loyal member and delivering all his tobacco as he had
agreed to do. The organizing days were over. No more cam-
paigns for members would be conducted, not for the present
at any rate. Next year there might be further solicitation,
but for the time being they were content to rest upon their
laurels, to utilize the fruits of their first victory. Eugene continued to work toward further organization, however, in
addition to his duties as manager of the local receiving warehouse, an office which had been bestowed upon him in recognition of his work as an organizer. His capability for this
position, rather than the use to which he put it, was doubtful,
because he was not satisfied to confine his activities to the
management of the warehouse. He must always be after a

new member, always haranguing some recalcitrant country-
man. He visualized a time when all tobacco would come
through the hands of the Co-ops, when the warehouses of
the open markets would be spectral halls of a departed re-
gime. He spent a great part of his time in visionary preparation for the advent of this day; but to the idealism of a
dreamer he brought a strong practical hand. The farmers
accepted him as their leader. Only a few criticized him, and
these criticisms were directed chiefly at his youth. His ad-
mirers contended that if this were a fault he would outgrow
it, and they supported him with a kind of paternal loyalty,
seeing in his accomplishments, perhaps, some lost dream of
their youth.

And these same men were badly in need of leadership.
Their victory, if at this stage it could be called that, had come
upon them so quickly that they were hardly conscious of its
significance, hardly capable of retaining the rewards it had
brought them. Moreover, like all easy things it was tainted
with the germ of complacence. It had not been attained
through hardship and valor; no long enduring courage had
brought it to pass. It was a conquest of revolution with all
the hysterical inefficiency of such a conquest. These men had
simply set out to do a thing in a new fashion, and because
they had not failed, they thought they had made a full success. The majority of the members were in no position to
appraise their progress; they saw that the association fulfilled its surface promises, it took their tobacco and paid them
a fair price for it, and with that they were satisfied and not
overly curious about its future. It seemed to be working
satisfactorily, and from that they inferred that it would do
so always.

Eugene knew, however, that so far their operations were
buoyed by the excitement and energy of youth. It still had
the fascination of a game and a gamble. The fair promises

of its possibilities cloaked the small mishaps and mistakes attendant upon its daily activity, but optimism was not enough and he knew it. Nor was loyalty from its members enough. They were fighting money and brains, and as the days passed, each shedding a little more light upon the wide scope of their undertaking, he realized that only with money and brains could the fight be won. The pool's possession of the tobacco meant little unless they could find quick and profitable markets for their holdings, and as Hugh had pointed out earlier, these quick and profitable markets were none other than the old, established tobacco companies. The costs of storing their holdings while negotiating with the manufacturers were enormous. Their problem was still one of selling. The fact that the manufacturers possessed a surplus of raw tobacco from which they could go on manufacturing for some time, perhaps years, made this problem extremely difficult, because these companies would be, at best, unwilling buyers.

For a time it seemed that the foreign markets offered a solution, but negotiations with them demonstrated that their needs would be far beneath the pool's mounting holdings. Nevertheless, the Co-ops continued to operate, continued to take in tobacco, and to give in return so much cash, and so much in short term notes. So far these notes had been paid when they fell due; long since the alarm which had greeted their appearance had given way to a grumbling but unsuspicious acceptance. A banking arrangement, covered by the pool's holdings had been made to discount these notes, and now the holders were not compelled to wait for their maturity. There was nothing like ready money to ease the mind of a farmer, to inspire his respect and loyalty. The officials of the association knew this; they also knew that they couldn't go on buying tobacco and storing it indefinitely. Many of the wiser farmers knew this, too. Eugene knew it from long hours of sleepless pondering, but there was nothing he could do but keep working and hope that some unforeseen turn of events would come to their aid.

It was well for the peace of mind of the co-operative farmers around Granville that nature had masked the workings of Eugene's mind behind that long, inscrutable face, that in those cold gray eyes there was seldom any shadow of what lay behind them. Among them all, only Hugh knew when at last the selling season was over, and spring was marshaling her advance guards along every brook and hedgerow, that Eugene's early confidence had given way to a terrible will to succeed, that his hope had suffered before an ever-vigilant awareness of the difficulties ahead of them, and that the fine mettle of his first optimism had become the strained tension of close combat. Eugene talked freely to him.

"It was ever so with rebels," he said; "we must wrest power from the mighty by those same weapons with which they dominate us. We are long on courage, but short on ammunition."

Hugh was not much consolation. "I feared it from the first," he said.

"It isn't as if we had already lost anything," Eugene continued a shade more optimistically; "we still have the tobacco. We have that. It represents money, too, plenty of money. The question is: How soon can we convert it into cash?"

"If we were only able to manufacture," Hugh offered.

"That's out," said Eugene, shaking his head. "It would take millions to compete with advertised brands of cigarettes, the advertising alone, I mean. If we could only persuade farmers to reduce their crops, to grow foodstuffs instead of tobacco, to settle down to a homespun existence for a few years, long enough to dissipate that surplus which the companies have, we would be invincible. But look what's happening. Every farmer who sells on the open market is increasing his crop, because it just isn't in human nature to resist the high prices with which the companies are trying to lure our members away. They have turned one set of farmers against the other, and now it seems that next year's market will be glutted. The manufacturers can just file the stuff away for future reference. A crop failure would be a blessing in disguise."

"People are sure getting ready for a whale of a crop," Hugh observed dismally. "The Galloways are even breaking new ground. I saw Lonnie and the old man down by the big woods yesterday, grubbing, and burning brush like a house afire."

"They'll pay for it later," Eugene prophesied.

13

Eugene's wish for a crop failure came near fulfillment, and perhaps in the way that he had meant it this short crop was a good thing. The cigarette companies accumulated no surplus from the far southern markets, because both in Georgia and South Carolina the first months of summer had been hot and excessively dry, leaving a lean and withered crop to face the devastating heat of July. Upon this starved and perishing country nature then released a flood of rains, the pent-up showers of the drought it seemed, a wanton display of liberality which did more harm than good. A great part of the tobacco was drowned, and that which survived was black and heavy, full of green spots after it had been cured, hard to keep free of mould, and almost without value.

The northern belt boasted far better crops. By the end of July the farmers around Granville, having brought their

tobacco through the growing season with no lack of rainfall, saw magnificent green fields slowly ripening under the
burning sun. They felt that it was time to be jubilant, time
to congratulate each other that they had escaped the numer-
ous perils which June and July usually held for them. But
they were to learn again the foolishness of anticipating the
elements, the utter lack of reason for judging one day by
another.

Hugh stood in the yard one sweltering July afternoon
and scanned the sky. For the past week the weather had been
sultry and sullen and although behind him the sun hung
like a door to hell in the sky, a heavy black and yellow cloud
hovered over Sligo. He watched it form, thickening and
spreading, shadowing his land. The sun still blazed at his
back but from the dark horizon before him a sinister cold
breath came.

His heart stood still. Hail. He knew what was coming
and turned toward the house sick with helplessness. He sank
into a chair on the porch and buried his face in his hands.

Nancy found him there so dazed that she had to speak
to him twice before he noticed her.

She shook his shoulder. "What is it, Hugh?"

"Hail," he said not raising his eyes.

"I must get my chickens in," she cried, and ran into the
yard.

The sight of Nancy driving an old hen and her brood
across the yard was almost funny to him as he thought of
his acres of frail yellow leaves and the swift, cold harvester
sweeping toward them.

A gust of wind whirled a cloud of dust in the yard and a
sheet of rain settled it before his eyes. He got up and went
in the house and as he walked down the hall he heard the
staccato beat of hail on the roof.

Nancy came in through the back of the house and joined

him in the hall. She led him into the sitting room, made him sit down, and stood with her arm around his shoulders. She racked her brain for something to say to him, but she knew as well as he that nothing could restore his fields. They could look toward them no longer. They now had to look within themselves for strength to stand the loss.

"Have courage, Hugh," she begged.

It was for courage alone that he had been fighting since the first chill of the cloud had reached him, and now he felt it coming to him steadying him against the storm outside.

He got up and pulled her close. "I can stand it," he told her, "if you stick by me."

She kissed him.

Above them the din abated suddenly, a few last hailstones bounced across the roof, and the air was quiet.

She let him go out to the fields alone.

Hugh went in the faint hope that some of the fields might have escaped the path of the storm. But none had escaped. The storm had stripped the tobacco in the rows, leaving naked stalks and shredded leaves in its wake. The breathtaking terror of hail was not the destruction he saw at his feet; it was the awful speed and suddenness of its force, like a dark swoop of death from the sky, that sickened his heart.

Tobacco, growing, drugged his mind just as it did when smoked in a pipe; in it he saw not only a testimonial to labor and patience, but the very meat and bread of the coming year. Some contended that it was just as well for it to be destroyed by hail as to be sold for nothing on the auction floor, but this was not true, because its broad leaves were so many green promises, and even though a promise be broken it was better than nothing.

Nancy marvelled at the calmness with which Hugh went about salvaging what he could from his crop, cutting that which had not been destroyed completely, and gleaning from the mud those leaves worth saving. She thought it was a miracle of courage in his heart, and not a fear which sustained him. Had she known how bewildered he was, how utterly without resources he felt, she herself would have been frightened. The truth of the matter was that his silence was the result of consternation and shock, a mute awe before the solemnity of the ruin of his fields. It was a sight to breed fear, for in a few moments all of one year's labor had perished, and with it most of his hopes and plans for the coming year. In addition to the unpaid bills of the current summer, he was now faced with the inevitable prospect of having to make the next crop on credit. To the burden of providing for himself and Nancy was added the responsibility of taking care of the farm's negroes. They turned to him with the pathetic helplessness of children; he dared not weaken or show dismay before the mute appeal in their eyes. Nevertheless, his brain reeled through an agonizing cycle of fears that tormented him throughout the day and far into the desperate hours of the night. The knowledge that his position was not altogether unbearable (had not Cleve been through the same thing in his time), that credit could be obtained, was not sufficient to ease his mind, because it is not enough simply to live, when by simply living one draws heavily on the future, pays today's toll with tomorrow's debt, and balances the good fortunes of the future against the evil ones of the present.

Eugene read hope into their present plight, and because it was less saddening to agree with him than to differ, Hugh tried to see things his way. Both knew that the widespread disaster would reduce the manufacturers' surplus and thereby strengthen the pool's position. That nature had done something for farmers, which, though bitter, was necessary, and quite impossible had it been left to their own volition, was obviously one way of looking at the situation; Eugene made the most of this argument, and under his cold logic many farmers endured their troubles in a spirit of sacrifice rather than in one of unrequiting hardship.

It was through this very experience, through his unrelenting battle to survive until another crop could be made, that Hugh came to know how fully he loved the farm and how completely it was second nature to him. Not once was his mind tempted by thoughts of escape, by plans to take up some foreign and less imperilled mode of living. Every effort, every thought, was concentrated on overcoming this year of failure, on seeing another crop flourishing in his fields, on keeping intact and untarnished his heritage of land.

Hugh felt that this land which had nourished his fathers was held in obligation to them and to the yet unborn. He felt honor-bound to preserve the land in its entirety, to take from it only its gift of sustenance in order that he might pass it on still free and fertile. Hugh felt that it was wrong to sell a part to save a part unless it be a last and desperate measure. Cleve had felt the same way, yet he had been forced to sell some. If each generation must pare away part of its acres in order to retain the plantation, in time it would all be gone, and with it the family as well.

By dint of patience and economy that were nearly superhuman, Hugh got through the winter months without encumbering the farm with a mortgage. He used his good name, stretched his credit far and wide, using his name always as security, never the land. He brought his crop to harvest and even to market in this fashion, loyal as yet to the Co-ops who were entering their third year of operation.

Not until his tobacco lay on the warehouse floor did the high courage which had borne him along during the past two years falter, but when he had parted with his first load of tobacco and held in his hand only a trifling amount of money and a long-term note, his heart grew sick with disappointment and apprehension.

Nancy grew to dread his returns from Granville on those days when he had delivered tobacco to the association, because there was little that she could say, reasonably, which would cheer him. They had lived on hope for two years, and now that the time for the fruition of this hope had come and almost passed without satisfying them, there was no further source of consolation, should it fail them. Beyond this were certain vague possibilities of which she dared not think at all.

"Don't give up, Hugh," she begged, "don't give up before you see what the winter markets will do. Tobacco sells better then, doesn't it?"

"I can't pay my bills with these damned notes," he answered bitterly, "no matter what value they place on the stuff. I need money, not promises; I've had enough of promises."

"There's money in the open markets," she hinted.

He looked at her in amazement. This was the first time that anything like this had ever been said between them. Slowly he answered her, like a man who regrets his decision.

"You know I can't do that."

"Well," she replied in defense of her suggestion, "the Co-ops haven't done what you believed they would do, not what was promised. They have broken their promises. Why should you suffer to keep yours?"

"They haven't broken their promises, dear; they have simply been unable to keep them. That doesn't relieve me. Maybe they still have a chance."

"What shall we do, then?"

"I don't know."

"But there must be something, some way. I hope . . ."

"Hope! I've heard the word 'til I'm sick of it."

"But, Hugh, without some sort of courage . . ."

"And courage, too," he cried. "What is courage? What can it do but tempt us on in the face of ruin. What good is courage to a condemned man? Although he walk straight and hold a high head the gallows is still there ahead of him."

"It's something to hold a high head," she told him.

But her reason told her there was no good to be derived from repeating these words to him, for now they seemed to be without meaning, to be the shrivelled carcasses of things which had once held life. And so she began to talk of other things, of the land and how rich it was, and of years of plenty, so many fair promises ahead of them. As winter wore on with no better returns from tobacco, she made much of the fact that they still held the land, unmortgaged.

"We still have the land," she would say, and sometimes when Hugh did not feel the terrible emptiness of his possession, he would answer, even proudly,

"Yes, we still have the land."

Another year passed and in that year Nancy gave him a son. When the doctor allowed him to go to her room, and he had seen his son and had read in its mother's face the white agony of having one, all his troubles seemed lessened thereby, so much so, that in this new responsibility there was a rebirth of confidence and joy in life. His fields appeared richer when he saw them again, and once more it was a pleasure to walk through them and handle the broad green leaves. He had a son now, a son, who should know this farm as he knew it, and love it, and some day, perhaps, bend it to his will.

When the markets opened again he went with a full harvest, and again he returned with empty pockets. This was the last year that the Co-ops operated, and long before the year was ended, both he and Eugene knew that it would be the last year. The association was crumbling daily, suffering not only from the attacks of its enemies but from the desertion of its members and the general discontent of all who held its slow notes. The banks had long since ceased to discount them. The prolonged failure of the association to redeem them hinted at something worse than an inability to dispose of the tobacco which was supposed to protect them. Suspicion was directed toward the high officials of the pool, and slowly evidences of corruption crept down the line, until every farmer who had supported the organization began to feel that he had been duped, that his sacrifices had been polluted, and that to make more would be useless. The organization had weathered the attacks of the old tobacco companies, it had withstood the disasters of inexperience, it had even generated a war-like loyalty among its members, but it tottered under the disintegrating force of scandal. Honorable men began to desert it, openly, and without anyone criticizing their withdrawal. Even those members who supported it to the very end did so with no hope of gain, but simply because they could make no compromise with loyalty or their bond. Its failure was complete and far-reaching in its effects, for many had supported it not only with their tobacco, but with the savings of other years, and there were some large landowners who had mortgaged their property to borrow for the upkeep of tenants in order that these same tenants might strengthen the pool with their crops and be able to live while they waited for payment. These men held, when the pool went into receivership, nothing but batches of notes to show for their loyalty and labor.

Although Hugh went about sowing plant-beds and breaking land when winter broke with an air of knowing what he was doing, the future was nevertheless very dark and doubtful, and sometimes he felt that the only reasonable foundation he had for beginning a crop lay in the wisdom of being prepared to continue, should a way of continuing present itself. It was impossible to live in the same house with him and not feel some of the anxiety which tortured him. But Nancy had other things to think of now, having become more of a mother than a wife, being so wrapped up in the care of her baby that the farm was only a background upon which her more important interests manifested themselves. Therefore to Hugh's mutterings and complaints she invariably replied, "But we still have the land," until, if one had asked her a moment later, she would not have known what she had said.

14

In February when the croppers began to dig into the warm hillsides, and later in March when they took the great turning-plows into the fields, Hugh ordered them about their tasks with the same attention and discipline which had always marked his supervision of their work. He set aside fields for Dave, who had taken a wife and wished to have a crop of his own, and he appointed a share of the land to every cropper, dividing it among them fairly, giving each one a strip of rich lowland for corn and fields of sandy loam for tobacco. He designated the fields which he intended for his own crop, and he, too, dug his own plant-bed in the side of a sun-swept hill, and he broke his fields with the turning-plow. They made the land ready for a crop, as they had always done, but they, themselves, were not ready when they first took the plows from the sheds, nor when they had broken the land.

Hugh had made no arrangements for fertilizer because he had been ashamed to go to the fertilizer merchants in Granville and ask for another year's credit; he had paid them nothing on the previous year's account. There was hardly a store in Granville at which he did not owe something. All those debts had had their beginning in the terrible year of hail, and since that time they had mounted steadily until the dissolution of the Co-ops and the certainty that their notes were almost worthless had brought his plunge into debt to a sudden halt. He knew without asking that his creditors could go no further, that from the cropper on his land to the wholesaler who supplied the stores there stretched a line of credit which was taut and ready to snap under any additional burden. There had been a time when he could have gone to the banks in Granville and borrowed money on his land. Other farmers had done that. He had been tempted to do it in the year of hail. Finally, when all sources of securing provisions on credit had been closed, he had approached the bank, but despite the fact that his land was unencumbered, his request had been refused. The banks, as well as those individuals who made a practice of lending money, they who had grown fat off the diurnal distress of the farmer, turned a deaf ear to the cries about them and sent their money on safe and foreign missions.

Nevertheless, Hugh persisted in the folly of beginning a crop, buoyed by nothing more than a hope that time would bring some turn for the better. There are certain practical limitations to delusions, however, and these were drawing closer about him every day, closer and faster, and he saw nothing that he could do. He could only wait while there was still time for waiting, and walk in his fields, wondering.

He hated to burden Nancy with his worries, but he had to talk to some one. They were not troubles which he could discuss with the negroes, not even with Dave.

He watched her sitting beside the crib where little Dumont lay sleeping and in the soft light her face seemed as peaceful as the child's.

"Nancy," he began, "there's something I must tell you."

His words seemed to pull her from a deep reverie.

"What?" she answered dreamily.

"The bank turned me down, you know. I must have fertilizer within the month, and I'm really at my wit's end."

"Everything will turn out all right," she said.

Her answer was so stupid it angered him. She could not have understood him. This was no time for aphorisms. He studied her calm face turned toward the child, and silently he recalled the senseless optimisms which she had fed him for months now when he tried to talk to her. He had tried to excuse her behavior because she was preoccupied with the care of the baby, but he loved the child, too, and he knew that love was no excuse for burying his head in its crib while the world crept upon him. That she could sit there and wilfully blind herself to the imminence of his ruin instead of standing by him and fighting it doggedly, hurt and angered him so that he could not trust himself to speak to her further. He got up and left the house and walked out in the night.

His tired brain struggled for an explanation of her attitude. As he thought on it he began to see things which had been before him for months. She had never professed love for the farm, and her loyalty had been to him rather than to it. She had turned to little Dumont with all her emotion, because in him she saw something which was her own, something which responded to her love. The farm was different, Hugh was forced to admit; it took everything and gave her nothing.

Why, he asked himself fairly, should she feel differently? He had not married her to make her miserable, but she could not have been very happy these last few years. Perhaps he should be grateful that she had not upbraided him for his failure. It was selfish to ask her to bear with him, if she could escape his torment. Let the blow strike her when it must;

there was no good in holding it over her like a threat to shadow her days.

But his trouble was too intense to be borne alone, and when he returned to the house he longed to smash the dreamy wall she had built between herself and reality. Pride alone prevented him from turning to her again that night, pride and the hope that she might come uncalled from her dream.

His orders to go ahead with work had been reason enough for the negroes. They were not tormented by the future. It had always taken care of itself, nor did they doubt that Hugh would provide the fertilizer, the food, and the clothes, as he had always done. That was his duty, not theirs. They feared the perverse seasons, hail, and blight, but they were blithely unconcerned about the ability of the landlord to take care of them. The store was still there, stocked with bread and meat, and the land was still rich and tractable. White folks knew how to handle matters of management; a negro's work was in the fields; the white man took care of them, and they took care of the fields. It was a partnership well established by time and experience. They were not worried. Hugh kept them busy, not even telling Dave that he saw no way of continuing. If it came to the worst they could make enough to eat. The lowlands would grow corn without fertilizer, and corn would grow hogs, and corn and hogs would hold them for a while, anyway.

When the warm showers of April had softened the land and a crop of grass had taken root in the turned fields, the negroes began to question each other covertly, and to study Hugh when he was not looking, wondering why he delayed. Their plants were ready for the fields, and they knew that the fields should be ready for the plants, bedded, fertilized, and in readiness for the first planting season. Alarmed by the flight of time, unwilling to be forced to admit to the negroes that he could not finance the crop, Hugh made another plea to the bank. Again he was refused, but in a manner which left him some hope. The Granville bankers directed him to a land bank in the city of Bullsgate, thirty miles distant. This bank, recently formed, dealt exclusively in loans on land, he was told. He wrote to them, stating his needs and describing his property. Within a week he received a reply. They would send an agent, they wrote, who would appraise his farm, and advance the loan that his appraisal warranted. This was the first encouraging thing that had happened to him in a long time, and it gave him a pleasure altogether out of proportion to the conservative promise of the letter. He waited impatiently for the agent's coming, torn between hope and anxiety, afraid to be too hopeful, afraid not to be.

Nancy's calm and unenthusiastic reception of the letter's message fortified his suspicion that she had tired of the farm, and had withdrawn her active interest from his work. She didn't belittle the significance of the letter's promise; she even expressed gratitude for the relief it gave him, but her attitude was only one of acquiescence, as though he had recalled her for a moment to an enterprise of which she had despaired long before. That she had not been thrilled by this marvel of good fortune which had come in the nick of time amazed and hurt him, and yet her passivity was very much in keeping with the lack of concern she had shown for his affairs all the previous winter. Had he confronted her with an accusation of spiritual desertion, as the suspicion in his heart warranted, she could have rested her defense, he realized, on the simple contention that he had agonized himself unnecessarily, that his plight had never been as serious as he had imagined, and that knowing this she had wisely refrained from aggravating his fears by participating in them. She could have maintained that her behavior had been the wisest kind of loyalty, the kind a calm mother gives a sick, frightened child. The whole miserable story would have borne out her testimony. And yet he knew it was not so. He knew that his concern had been real and terrible, and that the proximity of ruin had been real and terrible, too.

Gratitude is not so much the product of an action as of a need. A man suffers and he is grateful for an end of suffering. Therefore, Hugh could not consider the bank's agent anything other than a deliverer, although nature had not cast him in that mould; Hugh saw, when he came, a man who eyed him shrewdly, who walked about the farm and dug into the loam with his heel with the air of one who knew exactly what he was doing. He spent half a day in his survey of the fields and woods, the houses and barns. He even made Hugh point out all the boundaries and their markers. When he had finished his inspection, he turned to Hugh.

"Can't you see your way out on less than five thousand?" he asked. "That's a lot of money."

"I owe a lot," said Hugh.

"Need you pay it all now?"

"My creditors are pressing me, and I'd like to take care of them."

For a moment the agent dropped his professional hardness, and a look of experienced kindness softened his eyes.

"Take my advice," he said, "and leave your creditors to worry a little while longer. You didn't wish these debts on them. There's no point in one man sacrificing himself to pay a debt when ten men are stalling. When everybody stalls it amounts to darned near the same thing as when everybody pays. A man is entitled to self-protection. This farm is all you have in the world, isn't it?"

"Yes," Hugh answered.

"I wouldn't endanger it too heavily, then."

"But these men gave me credit, and in good faith, too. I can't let them down. Most of them are my friends. After all, five thousand isn't much money. One good crop could clear that much."

"Well, I can let you have it. You're the judge. You've got to pay it back. The land is well worth the loan."

The loan was made to cover such a long period of time that Hugh could not conceive of the impossibility of repaying it. The payments were to be made semi-annually in sums which reduced the principal and interest simultaneously. These payments would continue for thirty years. A brief calculation showed Hugh that he would pay back more than twice the amount of the original loan, but when it was considered by the year it did not appear frightening. Anyway, he had to have the money. He could not imagine a time when he would be unable to scratch together four hundred dollars a year.

"That does look mighty small," the agent agreed, "but let me warn you that the bank will take no excuses when the payments are due. They don't regard this loan as an investment in land. It's money lending, and as such the semi-annual payments are not to be regarded lightly."

Within a few days Hugh received the bank's check. Armed with it he paid off old bills, bought fertilizer, and hurried the croppers on with the work of preparing the fields for the plants. He was saved.

Part Three

HENRY GALLOWAY had been fleeing all his life, putting more years and more land between him and the
poverty of his birth. It had been a flight with no fixed goal,
no dream of finished attainment, no hope of relaxation; it
had been enough to escape and keep moving.

When he reviewed the course of his long flight, it seemed
now that it had been a curved one and that it was leading him
back toward the point from which he had started. The future
reared itself before him like a wall, and he was uncurious
about what lay beyond it. He thought of his life as a story
that was told. He tied his days in a tight little bundle and
sat upon them waiting.

The land no longer pleased him. Times were hard, prices
were lower than he had ever seen them, and the farm threatened to engulf his life's effort in a flood of debt. Lonnie was
no good, and Helen had been dumped back on him to feed
while James took himself to a mill job in Granville.

When he had been younger old Henry had lain in his bed
each morning and planned the day's work, and with the first
light of day he would be about his work eagerly, sure of what
he was doing and of where it was leading him. It had been
pleasant to lie there while the others were sleeping and devise
a task for every hour of the day, to conserve his time, and
not to waste any of it. And when he had returned to his bed
at night, the fulfillment of the day's labor had rested like a

balm upon him and had eased his sleeping. Now he tossed restlessly when he should have been sleeping, and when he awoke his troubles were waiting in the dark, waiting to pounce upon him and confuse his thoughts before the day had started. It was no longer a pleasure to send his mind out among the growing crops. They grew to no purpose. His fields had failed him. His foolish children were a curse and a shame to his age.. There was nowhere that he could turn for a moment's reassurance or peace. Work itself no longer comforted him because it held no sure promise of reward, and it failed to bring dreamless sleep as it once had done. It only aggravated the pains which age had brought to his body. His body was failing him, too. He faced the day as tired as he had been when he went to bed.

The habits of a lifetime sat solidly upon Henry Galloway. He might have found some relief in lying in his bed and surrendering to the pains which bound his joints, in permitting his worries to overwhelm him. Defeat is not as bitter as a purposeless resistance. But old Henry didn't know how to surrender, he didn't know how to allow the world to sweep over him and away from him. When he had finished the morning review of his miseries, he thrust his withered white legs from beneath the sheets, groped in the dark for his shoes, and went about his dressing, groaning with stiffness.

It was dark in the still room, and he dressed himself with some difficulty, fumbling for the chair which held his clothes, and supporting himself awkwardly with one hand while his legs were guided into the stiff channels of his trousers. Lacing his shoes gave him more trouble than anything else. He could get his feet into them without bending, but to lace them almost broke his back, and this operation he prefaced with a groan and terminated with a weary grunt. Then he lighted the kerosene lamp, moved it from the mantel to the dresser, and called his wife. His voice snatched her from sleep as completely as though he had snatched a drifting stick from a stream.

"Yes, Henry," she answered, rising from the bed as she spoke.

"Git dressed," he ordered, and left the room.

The narrow black tunnel of the hall led him to the kitchen. Entering it he paused long enough to light another kerosene lamp, then from a box behind the stove he drew some strips of lightwood, crossed them in the flue of the stove, and applied a match to the fat resin. The flame spluttered and spread and soon licked the cold walls of the flue. He fed a few dry sticks of pine to the little blaze, watched them until he saw that they were burning briskly, then took two tin buckets from the table, stepped out of the house, walked to Lonnie's window and called him. A sluggish grunt responded to his call. He filled his two buckets at the well and returned to the window, where Lonnie's heavy breathing told him that he was still sleeping.

"Git up, Lonnie," he yelled, "day's breaking."

Lonnie would awake this time. He had to call him twice every morning, had to assure him that the night was really over.

All his movements were marked with the precision of long repetition, and it would have angered him if the members of his family had not gauged themselves to conform with his actions. As he bore the two buckets from Lonnie's window to the kitchen door, he bore them with the expectation of having his wife meet him at the door and relieve him of his burden. He was not disappointed. She took the buckets from his hands, and with no word to her he turned and walked toward the stable. According to his calculations, Lonnie would come along the path behind him after an interval of about two minutes, therefore he left the lot-gate open for him, and without pausing made his way to the corn-crib, unlocked the door, and counted thirty ears of corn into the basket which rested near the door. Swinging the basket from his left elbow he trudged toward the stable. As he had expected, he heard Lonnie inside, filling the troughs with hay. He entered the granary and spoke to his son. Lonnie returned his greeting in a voice still heavy with sleep. It was like that every morning. Lonnie never showed any life until he came to the breakfast table. From his basket old Henry counted out five ears into each of the six troughs. Five ears were enough for a mule now that there was no work to be done save a little light cultivation. He returned the empty basket to the crib, locked the door, tried the lock to satisfy himself that it was fast, and retraced his steps to the house.

Stooping at the woodpile, he loaded his arms with stove-wood, and resumed his steps toward the kitchen. Lonnie had reached it before him, and stood now, jammed against the wall near the stove, waiting for breakfast. Old Henry remembered that he had taken most of the cut wood from the woodpile. For the first time since getting out of his bed he departed from established routine. The memory of the exhausted woodpile drove him to this violation.

"Hit's gittin' pretty light, now, Lonnie," he observed, "light enough to cut wood. Go and cut 'till your breakfast is ready."

Lonnie moved obediently out of the room, although he felt that he had been deprived of a short period of idleness which by right did not come under his father's dominion.

Helen had joined her mother in the kitchen and was helping with the cooking, washing some strips of bacon in a pan of cold water. Her mother stood over the stove, watching it, as though it were a voracious monster which would consume the biscuits she had just put in it if her eyes deserted it for a moment.

Old Henry poked among the pots and pans and moved the coffee-pot to a point where it would come to boil quickly. In this movement he had again departed from the ordinary course of his morning activities. His wife followed his gnarled hand with curiosity.

"What you want, Henry?" she demanded. "Breakfast will be ready in a minute."

"I ain't zactly hankerin' fer breakfast," her husband responded; "jest thought I'd try a cup of coffee. 'Pears like I can't git started right this morning."

"Is it that pain in your side again?" Helen asked.

"Yes," he replied, "least I reckon hit's the same pain, only hit seems to be up in my chest now."

"Let me mix you a little soda-water before you drink your coffee," offered his wife. "It's just indigestion, maybe."

" 'Tain't indigestion," he growled.

"Well, soda-water can't hurt you," she persisted.

"Something tells me soda-water ain't gonna do hit no good."

"Drink this anyway."

"I don't want hit!" he shouted in sudden exasperation, and hurried out the door.

His wife shook her head and resumed guard over the stove.

Old Henry went to the well, drew a bucket of water, and drank deeply. But the pain in his chest burned as fiercely as before. Tugging at the chain had almost exhausted him; the pain ate at his bosom like a ragged saw. His breath came in short gasps as though he had been running, and although the morning dew still cooled the air, perspiration stood in great clammy drops on his forehead. He wiped it off with his sleeve, and sat down on the base of the well.

The rising sun shone on the woodpile where Lonnie was swinging the heavy ax. Old Henry watched him, almost enviously. How easily the ax rolled up his arm, paused in the air, and fell, glistening in the sun. Lonnie wrenched it from the wood with one hand, carried it above his head indolently, then brought it smashing into the wood again. Each blow added another stick to the pile before him. He tossed them there with a careless snap of his back as he bent and straightened with the ax. Old Henry watched him and thought how good it was to be young and strong and hungry in the morning. Lonnie thought nothing about it, went on smashing the wood.

Helen came to the kitchen door and said that breakfast was ready. Lonnie dropped his ax and hurried toward the kitchen. Old Henry remained on the platform of the well.

"Ain't you coming to breakfast?" Lonnie asked.

"Naw. Hurry and git yourn. Then we'll set off to the fields."

He sat on the well until Lonnie had finished his meal.

"Bring me them scraps from the kitchen," the old man commanded, "and that bucket of slops left from last night."

"I'll feed the hogs," Lonnie offered. He could see that his father was ill.

"I'll feed 'em," was all his father said.

He took the two buckets and walked down the path which led by the stable to the pig-lot. At the crib he stopped and stirred the mess with a stick. It was not thick enough, he decided. Into the thin dishwater he measured a quart of bran and an equal amount of ship-stuff, and stirred it into the water. He wiped the stick on the rim of the bucket, pulling it across the rim sharply to prevent it from bringing the clinging mixture out with it. The naked stick he put back in the crib, locked the door, tried the lock, and picked up his buckets again. His arms trembled with the weight of his burden and the sudden exertion of lifting them again caused the pain to burn his heart like a jet of flame, but he continued along the path stubbornly, stumbling under his load and sloshing the dirty stuff on his trousers at each step.

At the pen he set the buckets down and waited to regain his breath before lifting them over the rails to the trough. This pause was the third departure from the strict procession of his habits, and the hogs considered it with outraged patience. They squealed and grunted, pushed each other aside, and stood in the trough, trying to come over the fence to their breakfast. Old Henry eyed them coldly and moved the buckets back from the fence, not yet feeling strong enough to lift them above the rail. The pain still tore at him, he panted like a wind-broken horse, and the cries of the hunger-maddened hogs were like files in his ears. Finally, since it appeared that waiting did him no good, he raised one bucket to the top rail. The pigs were all in the trough now, and he had to pour part of the slops over their backs before they would move. As soon as the first little rivulet ran the length of the trough they buried their noses in the stuff, and fell to eating with a gluttonous smacking of their jowls. The old man reached for the other bucket, and had lifted it almost to the top rail when a sudden surge of pain warned him not to struggle with it longer. He heaved it to the top, nevertheless, and bent over the rail to pour the slops into the trough. At this moment the bucket slipped from his hands, and its contents flowed over the backs of the hogs and to the ground. Old Henry tried to straighten, but the pain slowly drew him double over the rail. For a moment he struggled, his face apoplectic with agony, then all struggle and pain went out of his face, and his body fell limply into the shape of a half-closed jackknife and hung upon the fence. His head sagged lower and lower and finally came to rest in the trough, where the hogs had almost finished their feeding.

2

The three years which had passed between the failure of the Co-ops and the death of Henry Galloway had written themselves bitterly into Hugh Winton's face, had entrenched themselves across his forehead and shadowed his ready smile with a dark grimness. There was a look of perplexity about him, and neither his smile nor his laugh could dispel it entirely.

Three years before, he had borrowed five thousand dollars and made several excellent resolutions. He had resolved to bend every effort toward a speedy removal of the loan and to be on his guard against everything that might thwart him in this good intention. First, he had wiped out every debt that stood against him and had composed a program which was designed to obviate the possibility of falling in debt again. He had determined to adhere to a policy of paying for merchandise as he bought it. He had swapped all his little debts for one great one, and upon this one he had concentrated his efforts. He had made a new start with a clean slate except for his obligation to the bank, and this obligation, he felt, was on a basis which he could handle. Back of all his resolutions was a purpose greater than any of them; he had determined to overcome Nancy's silent antipathy for the life into which he had brought her, and to win from her an honest, full-measured love. On the strength of these resolutions, and through the possibility of realizing the purposes for which they had been formed, he had made himself happy for a while. Indeed, he had lost nothing, he assured himself. The farm was still his (he could keep that mortgage going forever, if necessary), and Nancy was still his, only she seemed to have forgotten it. Well, it was up to him to make her remember. Those years when fear had boarded at their table had been enough to drive her to doubt and indifference. He could forgive her for that. Indeed, he had never accused her of failing him, but a silent barrier separated them, and he had set himself the task of removing this. It had seemed to him, three years before, that his life was rushing toward chaos, and that fate had given him a chance to drag it back from the very brink of ruin. That had been three years before, and he was now no nearer the realization of his purposes than he had been then.

In making his resolutions and in following them, he had been guided by a belief in compensatory justice. He had believed that a man's accomplishments were inseparably related to his efforts, that they bore the relation of cause and effect, and that in the long run this relation was always justified. He had realized, of course, that the circumstances which had brought him to the plight in which the land bank found him were not ones of his own making, yet this knowledge had not bound him with a sense of fatalism. He had refused to believe that his life would always be the prey of forces outside his own control. He made an honest effort to rationalize the failures of the past, had excused them as his share of human hard luck, and had steadfastly refused to consider them auguries of the future. The simple truth was that he had found himself in a desperate situation, but with one hope left to him; and he had blinded himself to those things which did not contribute to his optimism. That had been three years before.

In no year since then had he made more than enough to pay the land bank and permit him to start another crop. Farming had become like a bad habit which was practiced with little reason and no profit. His life had been as barren of luxuries as the croppers' had been; their way of living had been preferable, he thought, because they got as much as they had ever had, and it was through his worrying and

skimping that they got it. The payments to the land bank
had become so important in his impoverished budget that he
began to lose his sense of ownership and came to feel that he
was a tenant on his own land.

Eugene assured him that it was natural enough that he
should feel that way. Nancy made frequent visits to her parents' home, and while Old Dumont played with the baby,
Eugene vented his sardonic lectures upon Hugh. Once Eugene had amused him; now the cruel clarity of his observa-
tions hurt him.

"Yes," Eugene said, "you feel like a tenant, because you
are one. About five out of every ten farmers are in the same
fix, farming the bank's land, and paying dear for the privi-
lege."

"But the land is only mortgaged to the bank. In thirty
years . . ."

"You mean that you have sold your life's right."

"Sold nothing," Hugh cried; "in thirty years . . ."

"In thirty years," Eugene repeated, "you will be dead."

"If prices come back," Hugh persisted, unruffled by the
prospect of the grave, "if prices come back, I may knock the
whole loan off in a year or two."

"Prices aren't coming back, Hugh. You may as well forget
that. Why don't you look around for something else to do?
Get a job."

"And leave the farm?"

"Why not?"

Hugh could think of no reason that would satify Eugene's
question. Therefore, because he could not translate his feeling for the farm into words he answered in a blustering way,
depending upon noise instead of reason to give emphasis to
his reply:

"No, by God, I'll stay! When I leave the farm, they'll put
me off!"

"They will never do that," said Eugene; "the land must have tenants. When the bank forecloses, you can stay and work the land for them."

"Eugene," Hugh exclaimed hotly, "you had better understand, now, that I don't appreciate the way you are talking. The farm means too much to me to be made the butt of your jokes."

"I'm not joking," Eugene rejoined, unperturbed; "the hold that these land banks have upon the land is the first step toward a system of peonage. Consider this: you are a good farmer, yet you are hardly making a living. Let's suppose that you fail to meet your payments to the bank. The bank will foreclose, then, as a matter of course. There will be no buyers for the land, because other farmers will be losing theirs, and those who are not indebted do not want more land. It will remain in the hands of the bank, I think, and you will remain on the land as a tenant—unless you find employment in the mills at Granville."

"You can talk pretty gaily about it," Hugh accused him, "since your land isn't mortgaged. You didn't grow the tobacco I did while we were trying to build the association. You didn't stand the losses I stood, and on top of all that, you drew a good salary while superintending our ruin. Don't forget that we peons paid that salary."

"Don't throw that in my face," Eugene returned; "I worked just as hard to put the association over as you did."

"I don't like your cold-blooded prophecies."

"I'm sorry," Eugene said in a milder voice; "I underestimated your love for your land, I'm afraid. Forget it, will you?"

They parted amiably to all appearances, but Hugh did not forget what Eugene had said. He resented the cruelty of some of his remarks but he could not deny their truth. On the way home he spoke to Nancy about his conversation with her brother, and for the first time she expressed her own feelings about the farm. Without storming, and without reproaches, she made it clear that she had despaired of it. He heard her in silence, and neither spoke of the matter again for several days. It came up again, however, one night when she asked him to drive her to the Clay farm.

"Gene's heartless, Nancy," he complained, "I really don't like to go there now."

"Not heartless," she replied with a sudden sharpness, "but sensible. He knows what he is talking about. Why don't you give up the farm and get something else?"

"Has he been putting that into your head, too?" Hugh demanded angrily.

"We talked about it some," she admitted.

"So! you and your brother are going to make something out of me."

"Really, Hugh, what can be said for farming now?"

"I've known for a long time that there was nothing in it for you."

"Have I complained before?"

"No."

"And I am not complaining now," she continued; "but I do hate to see you waste your life—and mine, too."

"I've done my best, Nancy. It hasn't made me happy to see you suffer. But I've done my best."

"I know it, Hugh. I know that you have done your best, but your effort has been wasted. I'm afraid that it will always be wasted here. You see," she added shrewdly, "there's the child to think of, his future."

"Do you think I don't love the child?"

"No. But to love isn't enough. We've got to plan for him, and for ourselves. The farm is taking the best years of your life, and none of us is getting anything for it."

"I must ask you to give me credit for knowing all these

things, Nancy. But I know what I want. I want the farm mine again, clear of debt, and prospering."

"What if I want more than that?"

"Nancy, let me tell you once and forever that I am not going to leave the farm, not for you, not for the child, not for anybody. I mean that. Unless you can reconcile yourself to staying here with me, you are free to do anything you think better. Is that clear?"

"Too clear," she replied evenly; "have you something better in mind for me?"

"I hope you'll stay," he stated a little contritely.

"I'll stay," she replied, and suddenly bursting into tears she left him and went into the room where little Dumont lay sleeping.

Dumont was a merry little fellow with an inquisitiveness about that part of the farm which lay away from the house that kept his mother in a state of constant alarm. He was old enough to escape her sight quickly and hide himself in the woods behind the barns before she missed him. He was altogether too friendly and fearless and cursed with a passion for horses and mules which caused Nancy to tremble with terror whenever she found him gone from the yard. She had discovered him once, trailing one of the patient horses, having a splendid time hanging on to the animal's tail with all his little strength. He was far too young to discriminate between horses and mules, and this faculty of discrimination, she knew, might be a matter of life and death. Horses are like dogs in that they make allowances for the pranks of children. They have been man's companions for ages, but mules are still aliens. The child's healthy love of the open and the creatures of the farm delighted Hugh, who thought Nancy too fearful a guardian. But this was a matter on which she refused to listen to him at all; she handled the boy as though he were altogether her own, as if his relation to Hugh were a careless and meaningless one.

Now that Dumont was old enough to take notice of things and draw some conclusions in his little head, Hugh feared that the air of constraint between Nancy and himself could not escape the child much longer, and that having witnessed it he would become influenced by it. He imagined that Dumont would grow up in this passive alliance against him and come to suffer his love as Nancy now appeared to suffer it. As yet there was nothing in the boy's behavior which indicated that he was aware of the growing tension between them, and it was true that Nancy made no wilful effort to curb his affection for his father, but her insistence on keeping the child at her skirts as much as possible and her refusal to allow him to go to the fields made Hugh uneasy. From such subtle beginnings a definite estrangement could grow; therefore, he took the boy with him sometimes in spite of her protests. Dumont was always eager to accompany him, a fact which left his mother no reasonable arguments for forbidding it. At these times she resorted to tears; Hugh took him along, nevertheless. Like that other bitterness which was so long in coming to words between them, this silent wrangling over the child existed as a shameful secret in their hearts, but both knew the other's mind, although they never exposed their jealousy in direct conversation. Fortunately, the child knew nothing of this, but he would sense it later, Hugh knew, and then the three of them would be involved in its wickedness, and of the three, the child, who alone was innocent, would endure the bitterest hurt. This very prospect urged Hugh to make another attempt at reconciliation with Nancy, and he bared his heart to her, bringing all his fears into light. She listened patiently, but impassively.

"It's unnatural for us to live like this," he concluded, "and God knows what it will do to the child. That's the worst part of it. Nancy, we must make a change. Can't you have patience with me," he cried, "for the child's sake?"

The trouble, Nancy knew, was that Hugh called to her for something she did not have. He thought she was withholding her love and co-operation, but in her heart she felt there was nothing further to give to a manner of life in which she no longer believed.

"Can't you?" he was asking.

"How can he fail to see it, too?" she thought. The long, barren years behind them ground down upon her memory and under their weight she cried out in pain and resentment, "It's no use, Hugh. This life deadens me. I can't give it any more. I can't be different."

"Don't you think we would all be happier if you tried?"

"I suppose so," she said listlessly.

"Can't you?"

He simply would not, could not see. And it wasn't fair. Not to her. Not to little Dumont. She felt her tongue sharpen with anger. "No," she cried, "I can't! I may hate myself for saying it, but you must know that I feel that you are condemning us all to some terrible end . . . to ruin . . . degradation. I can't escape because of you."

"Nancy, don't say that. Don't blame it all on me. God knows I've tried. . . ."

Shame flooded her. But she had said it. And it was true. She was silent.

"Your love is dead," he accused.

"No," she said, "it's just . . . just changed." She let it go at that.

He said no more to her.

For a while following this conversation it was apparent that Nancy was consciously exerting herself to be congenial, that she was trying to inject into their life some semblance of that spontaneous joy which had characterized the early days of their marriage, but her efforts succeeded only in demonstrating to Hugh how far apart they had drifted, and how futile it was to hope for a return of their former happiness. In the end it angered him, hurt his pride, and hardened him to the realization that he must adjust himself to living with her coldly.

In the end his appeal to her and her inability to comply amounted to an open declaration of war. That very thing which he had feared and tried to forestall by his attempt at reconciliation was made hideously alive by his failure to revive her loyalty. It was as though in admitting it they had created it, had given its nebulous danger a ferocious reality. Not only had he failed to better the situation by his appeal, but he had deprived it of whatever graciousness silence had lent it. Their admitted incompatibility had made the child's affection a challenge; now both accepted it openly. Hugh knew, and the knowledge sickened him, that the very wickedness and perversity of this contest was the only bond which held him and Nancy longer, that their lives met only in their love for the boy, and that there they clashed. The unsuspecting object of their struggle went about his prattling and playing with an innocence which cried shame and reproof upon them both, but neither had the courage to surrender him to the other freely.

Nancy wanted to keep Dumont with her at the house during the day, and in the evenings when Hugh had returned from the fields she put him to bed early and kept him there until Hugh had departed for the fields the following morning. When Hugh took the boy with him in spite of her protests, she endured it with such bitterness that it made him sorry for her, made him feel that he was doing her a needless wrong. His part in this inhuman game called for moves so cruelly obvious, for gestures so flagrantly inconsiderate of her, that he himself was constantly aware of their brutality.

It was easy for her to combat him without the appearance of doing so. The normal care of the child, his early dismissal to bed and his late awakening, all these were things which he could not forbid without making a fool of himself. The dubious courtesy of silence which they extended each other, their refusal to charge each other with design and cruelty, every aspect of their mute struggle, intensified the conflict, aggravated it, and set them hopelessly apart. As the summer lengthened both realized that they were living in a hell of their own making, but neither saw any way of emerging from it except separately and divergently. Finally, both felt that they acted with justice, Nancy believing that loyalty to her child forbade her surrendering to Hugh and to a future in which she had no confidence, and Hugh believing that in his stubborn fidelity to the land he was insuring the future for himself and for the child.

The strain of this wretched life bore heavily upon them both. It began to mark Nancy with an austerity and dullness unfitting to her youth. To Hugh it seemed that the flame to which he had once compared her beauty had died, and yet the memory of it burned him still, and the need of her love tore at his heart even when he knew he was hurting her most. This, too, he endured in silence.

One hot July day, just before they were ready to begin cutting tobacco, Hugh left Dave and the other negroes repairing the barns, went by the house and took Dumont with him on a tour of the fields. He intended to select the tobacco which should be cut first, and had decided at the last moment that the boy would enjoy going with him. He was not mistaken. The little fellow expressed immediate approval by trotting away at his father's heels. As they went down the sandy road, Dumont amused himself by running ahead of Hugh and sitting in the sand until he almost overtook him. He was evidently playing some sort of game of staying ahead of his father, because he never waited quite long enough for Hugh to come up to him, laughing loudly when he was within a few steps of him, and jumping to his sturdy legs and hastening off again. Whatever this game might have been, it afforded him the wildest amusement as long as Hugh stuck to the road, where the soft sand was easy on the boy's bare feet, but when Hugh left the road and turned across a new-mown hayfield, Dumont discovered that the stubble not only prohibited running, but even made walking painful. Hugh noticed his discomfort and picked him up in his arms.

"Want to ride my back and play horse, son?" he asked.

Dumont clasped his arms around his neck eagerly, stuck his legs beneath Hugh's armpits, and clicked his tongue, as he had heard the negroes do, in an imperious command to move forward. Hugh went slowly for a few steps, but this was not Dumont's idea of playing horse. He clicked his tongue more commandingly and spurred Hugh in the side with his heels. His mount responded by galloping across the field, drawing up at the other side out of breath from his exertion and the boy's tight hold on his throat.

"Here we are," Hugh panted.

"Come up, horse!" ordered Dumont, digging his heels into Hugh's sides.

"Horse is tired," Hugh complained.

"Come up, horse!" urged the boy.

Hugh stooped to the ground, assumed an equine position, and began to jump up and down on all fours, josting his rider until it seemed that he must topple off. Dumont kept his seat, however. Finally, Hugh rolled to his side in the soft sand and deposited Dumont in the sand flat on his back. Hugh shook himself, jumped to his feet, and ran around the prostrate horseman.

"That'll teach you not to ride your horse too hard, young fellow," he laughed.

Dumont regarded him critically from his position in the sand. "Me whup horse," he stated, rising.

Hugh ran from him. The boy pursued him armed with a long weed he had snatched from the ground. Nearby was a cornfield in which Hugh concealed himself. So intent had Dumont been upon his chase, running with his eyes on the ground, that he failed to note the manner of Hugh's disappearance. When he looked up and did not see his father, he halted suddenly, looked around him in every direction, and wailed one long frightened word: "Daddy?"

Hugh came out of the tall corn immediately. "What is it, son?" he asked.

"I wus lost," Dumont stated firmly.

"Did you lose your horse, too?" Hugh inquired sympathetically.

"That's all right," the boy told him with an incredibly straight face, "horse no 'count. Git tired too quick."

"Suppose you just walk along with me, then," Hugh suggested gravely.

Hugh had to take him up again when they came to the tobacco fields, for the plants towered above his head and the gum from their leaves stuck to his clothes. As they moved from field to field he made him walk, but keeping up with Hugh's rapid strides soon tired him, and he asked to be carried, and not until they were almost back to the house did he ask to be set upon the ground again.

His adventures of the afternoon occupied his mind until bedtime, and when Nancy suggested bed, he objected, saying that he wanted to sleep with his father.

"No, you must sleep with Mother," she commanded.

Dumont pondered for a moment, then, suddenly, his face lighted with a solution.

"We bof sleep wid Daddy!" he exclaimed.

Nancy picked him up in her arms and rushed from the

room, and he never knew what consternation and shame his simple statement had produced.

3

That summer marked the failure of Hugh's good intentions. Long before it had passed he was forced to set out on the wearisome task of providing credit for the croppers. In town and at the near-by country stores he established small accounts, endeavoring to obtain the necessities of life by diversification of his requests. No one man would now undertake the risk of supplying all his needs; he asked many, and somehow he at last got together enough to feed all the negroes.

The crops were good. Barring hail there was nothing which could harm the tobacco while it ripened in the fields, and they were prepared to harvest it fast enough to prevent the sun scalding it. It was a splendid crop and only lack of judgment in curing could spoil it now, but so much damage could be done to a good cutting of tobacco by faulty regulation of heat in the barn that Hugh decided to cure it all himself rather than leave any to the care of the negroes. He knew too well how they spent their nights around the barns, how easily they became careless in the pursuit of pleasure, and how vulnerable they were to sleep. Therefore he went to the fields only during the first day's cutting. After that he remained at the barns, sleeping intermittently during the day. His mind functioned like an alarm clock, allowing him to sleep for an hour after he had stoked all the flues and removed the fallen leaves from the vicinity of the pipes, awakening him in time to trim up the fires before the heat in the barns abated. He turned the management of the field forces over to Dave whom he regarded as the most reliable of the

negroes, and he never left the barns himself except to go to
hurried meals at the house.

He had no regular hours for meals, but went when he could
best spare the time. Therefore he saw little of Nancy and
Dumont, finding often that they had eaten their meal and
had left his cold on the table. But the boy managed to slip
away to the barns sometimes. Hugh taught him all those
things which had endeared the barns to his own childhood.
They roasted corn and sweet potatoes in the flues, cooled
watermelons in the spring, and passed the sultry hours of
the afternoon stretched drowsily beneath the pines. Hugh
showed him the small conical depressions in the silt at the
mouths of the flues where the doodle-bugs made their homes,
and he taught him the song which brought the bug scurrying
from its subterranean dwelling. The boy spent an entire afternoon crouched before the mouth of the flue singing:

"Doodle-bug, Doodle-bug, your house is on fire."

And from all the little cavities the doleful refrain brought,
eventually, a small agitated creature, and always when
amazement had stilled the boy, the creature dug back beneath the dust. Hugh did not explain that any repeated
sound would have produced the same effect; he allowed Dumont to enjoy it in all of its marvelousness. The boy's reason
balked at each performance, and the appearance of each bug
was nothing less than a miracle to him.

Sometimes Dumont stayed at the barns after dark and the
negroes petted him and told him tales which they had tried
out on their own children. There was one especial story which
he asked for night after night, a strange story about a group
of children who lived on the border of a great forest which
harbored a monster who called one child after another to
him, and no one ever saw them again. No one had seen the
monster either. They had only heard him calling from the
depths of the forest, and they had seen the children go into

the woods in response to that call, and none of them came back. The story ended with the monster calling the last child whose name was Renee. When the negro, imitating the beast, called "Renee!" in a long shivering wail, all frightful things became possible in the darkness. The story was unlike other negro tales. It bore no kinship to the simple and rather benevolent "hants" of which they told; it was a horrible alien thing, and their simple and factual account of it increased its horror. Dumont was always ready to go to the house when he had heard it, and he insisted that a strong bodyguard accompany him through the darkness.

An event took place during the third week of curing, however, which terminated Dumont's visits to the barns. Nancy had consented to his going there reluctantly all the while, and she listened with growing disapproval to his account of his pleasures there. His report of Renee's fate and the terrible impression which her history had made upon him aroused her particularly. The boy had gone to sleep many nights clutching her in fear that the monster might call him. She knew that it was wrong to excite his mind with tales of this kind, but the thing which prompted her refusal to allow him to visit the barns again came about from Hugh's own carelessness.

Dumont had begged to go with the negroes to the field, and Hugh had consented. After an hour had passed and they had not returned Hugh became nervous. A quarter of an hour and still they did not come. He laid his ear to the ground and listened for the wagon, but he heard nothing. His anxiety increased with each minute, until, unable to endure the suspense longer, he set off in the direction the wagon had taken. About half way to the field he met them, and Dumont was safe enough although he had been in grave danger. He had insisted, the driver explained, upon riding on top the loaded wagon. The wagon had turned over on the side of a steep hill, spilling the boy to the ground and the tobacco after him. He had escaped serious injury through virtue of pure luck; falling he had landed in a ditch, and in that way had escaped the full force of the load which came after him. As it was, he was pretty badly scratched and his clothes were torn.

In his relief Hugh curbed his anger at the careless driver. As soon as the wagon had been unloaded and sent back to the field, he turned his attention to the boy who was happily engaged with frightening the credulous doodle-bugs. Dumont followed him to the spring and submitted to having his face washed and his clothes brushed, but Hugh saw that these operations would not conceal the scratches in his skin nor the rents in his clothes. He looked him over dejectedly.

"You're a little wreck," he sighed finally.

"Suh?" said Dumont.

"I wouldn't tell Mother about the wagon if I were you," Hugh advised him.

"How come?"

" 'Cause it would frighten her. You don't want to frighten her, do you?"

"Nawsuh."

"Tell her you crawled into a briar-patch, then. That won't scare her."

"All right."

When Hugh saw Nancy again she lost little time in taking him to task angrily.

"You are a fine one," she exclaimed, "allowing him to chase young rabbits through a briar-patch while you sleep!"

Hugh realized that Dumont had taken the raw story which he had supplied and developed it artfully.

"Yes, I let him get away," he admitted.

"Suppose he had crawled upon a moccasin. You ought to be ashamed of your carelessness."

"I am ashamed," Hugh replied listlessly.

"You certainly ought to be."

"Since no harm came to him, why not forget it? Don't make it any worse than it was."

"I'll see that it gets no worse," Nancy stormed. "He's made his last little trip to the barns!"

Hugh was willing to let the matter drop, since he had come off pretty lightly under the circumstances, he thought.

4

Dumont came to the barns no more after his unfortunate adventure with the wagon. Hugh missed his cheerful company and found that those long drowsy hours of the afternoons which formerly he had devoted to amusing the boy plagued him now with their emptiness and teased his mind into bitter ruminations over the cause of the child's absence. Nancy's detention of the boy at the house and his own enforced stay at the barns gave him a taste of what it must be like to find himself removed from his family permanently. He speculated on this prospect, knowing that a continuation of his lack of harmony with Nancy must bring them eventually to separation and to a battle over the boy. Day after day he turned the sorry business in his mind, trying to thresh it out from its beginning, trying to understand Nancy's withdrawal from him, and seeking what faults of his own had reared discord between them. In the reason for this searching lay, perhaps, the reason for their failure—for they had failed, both of them, he decided. They had failed in allowing themselves to become so far estranged before admitting it, in awakening to it when it was too late, just as though some secret disease had spread through their veins, had laid firm hold upon them, and had asserted itself only when no skill could halt it. Had she been a different sort of woman, one of no restraint, a blatant, quarrelsome wife, one who laid her complaints and worries before him with his daily food, then, he told himself, they might have talked the thing to death when it was young. But it had grown secretly and in the dark and it had a strange baffling strength.

The way they were living was wrong and foolish, Hugh realized with a weary disgust, and it had to be ended soon, somehow, some way.

These thoughts gave him no rest but seethed in his mind constantly, and from the recesses of his memory they dragged out to torture him the first full days of his marriage, the fecund nights and the soft showers above them, Nancy and her lips searching for his in the darkness, the warm flow of her body toward him, and the glory of their mornings together. And the days throbbing with life, their life; the farm throbbing, too, their farm, their tobacco, sucking its green blood from the earth, spreading proudly before them, filling their fields. The hot sun and a good thirst, the end of a row and Nancy waiting with water, Nancy waiting, waiting. It had been so, day after day, night after night, days burnished with sunshine, and days with no sun, nights when a slow moon stirred the clouds, and nights with only clouds.

Fed by these memories his desire turned into a resolution to end their stupid selfishness, to make an end of it. There was no reason in Nancy's attitude, he decided, and he had been foolish to attack it with reasoning, with talking, and with patience. He had allowed her to grow strong in the belief that they were at impossible loggerheads. Tension had become a habit between them, and out of their love for the child they had created something utterly foreign to love, had made a mockery and shame of it. There was no sense in humoring the situation longer, no point in barricading it with more time. Nancy was his wife and she must live with him as one. Upon this objective he fixed his attention as he busied himself with his last barns. He planned to return to his house armed with a purpose and to assert himself as its master.

Friday night he fired the barns heavily, choking the flues with split pine and long branches of oak and hickory, building a fire which would burn fiercely, yet hold a steadily mounting heat; the tobacco could stand it, because he had driven all the sap from it by days of slowly increased temperature. It was ready to be killed out. Most of the night he was awake, driving the temperatures higher and higher, and morning found the barns crackling inside from the blast, so hot that he had to shield his face and run in when he wanted to read the thermometer. The dry plants swayed from the tiers like leaves in the wind, and the pipes at the end of the flues were red hot. He stoked all the flues again, loading them this time with pine alone; pine would hold the heat where he wanted it, would burn quickly, and by noon there would be only ashes in the flues, and he could leave the barns without further fear of fire. At noon he left the barns, their fires dying.

From the moment he entered the house Nancy marked the change in his bearing toward her, regarded it in silent amazement. He spoke to Dumont and waited on him at table with an air that suggested that in attending to the boy's wants he was serving the mother as well. He tried to engage her in conversation, mentioned his success with curing, and maintained a barrage of light talk, apparently unsubdued by her noncommital answers. He conducted himself as though he had returned from a long absence to his home as it had been four years before, as if the happenings of that intervening period existed, if at all, only as a bad dream, a dream whose evil memory he tried to dispel by plunging into reality. When he had finished his dinner he took Dumont into the sitting room while Nancy helped Annie clear the table. He was there playing with the boy when she came back from the kitchen, and when she sought to get Dumont upstairs to sleep, Hugh carried him up the steps and deposited him upon his bed for her. He left her in the room with the sleeping boy.

From her room he went directly to the kitchen and filled two huge pitchers with hot water which he took to his room. There he set stolidly about shaving and removing the stains of tobacco from his skin. He lathered his face assiduously, first rubbing the soap in with his fingers, then covering it with soft bubbly stuff from the brush. The razor left a clean bronze path behind it as he drew it through his heavy beard. Afterwards he bathed, working long to remove the resinous stains from his fingers and nails. He was not entirely successful. Bathed, he set his room in order, cleaned his razor, placed it back in its berth in the bureau, stretched himself upon the bed, relaxed in a feeling of comfort and cleanliness, and surrendered gratefully to sleep.

The sun had set when he awoke. He lay still thinking that it was morning, but quickly a memory of the day recurred and he got up to dress. At the window he paused and breathed deeply of the cool evening air, conscious, for the first time in weeks, of a sensation of genuine refreshment. Dusk mantled the yard beneath him, dimmed the line of cedars beyond the well, and had almost erased the horizon, above which a few early stars flickered feebly. Across this nebulous gray plain the call of a whippoorwill floated to him from the woods, and faintly, a second later, came the distant whoop of a great owl, silvered by the night air.

He found Nancy and Dumont at the supper table.

"I thought you needed sleep," she explained, "so I didn't call you."

"That's all right," he assured her, "I did need it."

Sleep had left him no desire for food. He ate lightly, drank a cup of coffee, and excused himself from the table.

Down the dark path he made his way to the barns. The fires had died completely, but it was still very hot inside. He decided to leave the doors shut for the night, to open them to the air the following morning. He spent some time in this inspection. When he returned to the house the ascending moon had dispersed the darkness somewhat.

Nancy was reading a story to Dumont. He sat on the floor at her feet, supporting his chin in his hands, listening with an air of absorbed interest. When the story was finished he repeated it to his mother, embossing it here and there with rich details of his own invention. Hugh thought of the briar-patch and rabbit episode. Nancy read another story, and Hugh watched her and the boy, conscious that on the first night of his return from the barns he was sitting alone in his own house, not as one of the family. He was an outsider. The storybook formed a little enterprise of amusement which occupied Nancy and Dumont, and at the same time excluded him, excluded him, like most of Nancy's maneuvers, without advertising her intention. He found a newspaper and scanned it, left them to their storytelling. Soon Dumont's chin slipped through his fingers and nestled sleepily on his chest; he propped it up repeatedly, tried hard to put off his bedtime by playing the attentive listener, but it was no use. His head sank lower and lower and finally he gave up the fight and sank in a defeated heap upon the floor.

After putting him to bed Nancy came back to see that the kitchen doors were locked. Hugh locked the front hall and waited for her at the foot of the stairs. Soon she came walking in the dark.

As they mounted the stairs he passed his arm around her. Had she been a stranger this gesture would not have cost him more courage, and her response was certainly that of one who was a stranger to the motive which had impelled him. She bore his caressing arm with a frigid indifference, made no attempt to remove it, neither hastened nor abated her calm ascent of the stairs, ignored him completely. Nevertheless, he persisted, and as they reached his door on the second hallway he guided her toward his room, and because she sought to free herself from his clasp, they halted before the door. He thrust it open with his left hand and spoke for the first time since they had left the foot of the staircase.

"I want you to stay with me tonight."

"No," she gasped, struggling against him, "no, not tonight."

Even as she struggled in his arms Hugh felt how far apart they were. The emotional reunion he sought had become a clash of wills as soon as he touched her, and he knew suddenly that she could feel in his touch no love, no desire, but only the fleshless force of the purpose which drove him. He saw profoundly how ugly and graceless his actions were and yet the scene seemed to fit into the pattern his whole life composed now and with the same stubborn strength which sustained him against the unyielding land he picked her up and strode into his room, savagely slamming the door behind him with his foot.

"Tonight," he said as he released her. "I see no need of waiting."

"You can't know what you are doing!" she cried.

"I know quite well what I'm doing; I should have done it long ago."

"Hugh, you can't force me," she cried angrily; "you aren't fool enough for that!"

"I'm not going to try to force you," he answered calmly, "but I am going to submit a choice to you. You must live with me as a wife, or not live here at all. One or the other. God knows I have had patience with you, when I saw no need of patience. I've worked for you, humored you, and what have I got in return? I'll tell you. I'm a stranger in my own house, in my own family, at my own table. I've tried to talk you into being a wife, I've argued, almost begged, but now I'm through with arguing, with begging. I'm asking for no reasons, no explanations, simply this: either live with me as a wife or put an end to the whole sham. Take your choice."

"Don't yell so," she warned him, "you'll disturb the baby."

"I don't give a damn if I rouse the neighbors," he shouted.

Her calm reference to the boy chilled his anger, halted the rush of his hot retort, and gave him time to regret the angry turn the affair had taken. He had not planned it so; he had hoped to plead with her successfully, but she had not given him a chance. He regarded her dumbly and helplessly, felt himself losing that sense of mastery which his anger had given him. She moved to the window and looked out into the darkness. He followed her.

"Well, what are you going to do?" he demanded.

"First," she replied, not turning her head, "I'm going to see about the baby." She looked long into the night before continuing. "And then," she said, "I'm coming back here, if you still want me."

"Go then," Hugh said quickly.

Hugh prepared himself for bed and awaited her return, but it was now a prospect which gave him no pleasure. Instead of anticipating her coming as though he were a groom awaiting his bride, he found himself nervous and unhappy, and in his mind the memories of their early marriage marshaled themselves reproachfully; their remoteness taunted him. It was like thinking of life from the grave, because it had been so long since he had been free emotionally, he had buried love so deep in the hard clay of his body, that it lived now only in the pageant of memory.

Nancy's footsteps coming along the hall fell on his ears with a regular deliberative measure, sounding not eagerness and haste, but, rather, resignation. She entered the room without speaking and crept in beside him silently. Silhouetted in the moonlight from the window he could see her tense profile. She lay quite still, so still that he could hear her breathing, so still that in the dim light he could see her bosom rising and falling rapidly, as though she controlled a struggle there. He laid his palm along her cheek, turned her face toward him, and called her name softly.

"I am here, Hugh," she replied simply.

He sought to pull her nearer him, but she resisted with the inertia of a lifeless body. She waited for him. Slowly, beseechingly, he sent his arm around her body, begging his way across her shoulders and down her trembling side. As he drew her nearer her body tautened like a bow, she evaded his kiss, and her limbs refused him. He held her close nevertheless, entreating her, trying to break her resistance in his encircling arms. Suddenly she relaxed and lay limp in his embrace. For a second he thought that all resistance had gone out of her, but his relief died quickly; she was weeping, weeping submissively and helplessly. He released her and withdrew his arm. She continued to sob. He listened, torn between amazement and a slowly rising disgust with himself.

"Go to your room, Nancy," he ordered with as much gentleness as he could summon to his voice.

"I am willing, Hugh," she wailed.

"Go to your room!" he shouted, beside himself, "and go quickly!"

She stumbled from the room, holding her hands over her face like a grief-stricken child. He closed the door behind her, walked to the window, and shoved it to the top savagely. A sick confusion of thought blinded his actions, but soon calmness returned to him, calmness and a certainty of defeat and sadness. He stared listlessly across the treetops as if in the star-strewn sky he might read some answer to his problem, but the sky was serene and untroubled and un-answering.

5

Despite his resolute watchfulness Hugh was piling up small debts again. No amount of economy could bridge the gap between necessity and income, and now that fall had come and the croppers had exhausted their sparse gardens, each month added something to their charge accounts at the stores. As for the payments to the land bank, stretched out before him down the years, there was nothing he could do except adjust himself to them stoically and pay them as he paid his taxes. His economies could never alter these; they were arranged, cut and dried, fixed. In time he had come to regard them with the same complacence that a man feels for a wooden leg.

During the summer he had accumulated debts in spite of his efforts to spread his resources over the summer months. Some of them were unavoidable, unexpected, demands which slipped upon him and left him no chance for compromise. There had been sickness in a cropper's family. Dave's wife was amazingly fecund, swelling with the seasons, and not even the negroes could get along without a doctor these days. There were other debts which he had made in sheer despera-tion and disgust, through his unwillingness to engage in hag-gling with the negroes over the small expenses which were necessary to their simple pleasures. Their desire to dress up in the spring, their demands for spending money for the few great festive days of the year, and their childish exuberance at Christmas, these were things which touched him deeply, which went behind his reason and tugged at old memories and left him helpless. The negroes rewarded him with no particular gratitude for satisfying these wants. He knew that. In their opinion he was merely fulfilling his duty, a duty which was older than he, one which his grandfather and Cleve had observed, one so old, indeed, that it had become a tacit part of the croppers' contract, as much a part of it as the provision of leisure on Saturday afternoons. He had done his duty.

Against this formidable array of little debts he had the disposition of the croppers' tobacco and the dubious fortunes of the winter markets. He decided that it would be best to pay all his small debts as fast as he sold tobacco, to pay them and refrain from considering the proceeds of the crop as his own until he had cleared up all the accounts. Then he would pay the land bank, and whatever was left he could spend with a clear conscience. Prices were poor, so low, that when a curing had been sold and the money divided between the cropper, the creditors, and himself, it seemed to have undergone a process of infinite disintegration and to have lost in this multiple distribution whatever purchasing power it had represented in the beginning. It did no good to stack the receipted bills beside the bill of sale and check one against the other; the money was gone.

The date of payment to the land bank drew near and he had laid aside nothing with which to meet it. There was some tobacco left unsold, but not enough, and knowing that it was not enough he made no hurry to sell it. He had made a mistake to pay his open accounts. Of all his creditors the bank alone was in a position to force payment, and as a matter of self-preservation he should have paid it first. At length the payment date came and passed, and soon there came letters from the bank, and shortly an agent, all threatening and demanding not reasons but money. Hugh showed the agent the tobacco bulked in the pack-barn, and it looked good enough packed in the barn to satisfy the man that the note could be paid within a few days. He made a few more grave threats and went away. Hugh sold the tobacco and spent its proceeds on clothes for Nancy and the boy. Its price would not have paid the note anyway.

With the new year the croppers, knowing the ways of the farm from long service there, set about preparations for another crop, finding tasks and executing them of their own accord. Some dug plant-beds; others took their grubbing-hoes and cleared the edges of the fields where the border brush threatened to creep out on the open land. Hugh said little to them, gave little advice, so consumed was he with a sense of the futility of their efforts. He felt a foolish detachment from their proceedings, a thing which had its origin not so much in his failure with the land as in his failure to placate Nancy. Her continued coldness, which he had not tried to remove since that night when she had come to him weeping, now stood like a wall about her, shutting him out and shadowing his consciousness with the conviction that she had no need of him, that her life was in no sense a part of his own. He was alone, and on the whole farm there was no one to whom he could turn with an open heart.

He thought of the coming year in an apathetic fashion, dulled by the certainty that there was no way of carrying on, and strangely this certainty of defeat gave him less grief than he had experienced when things had stood very much the same with him in that winter before he had secured the loan from the bank. He had seen no way of making a crop that year, yet he had begun the year's work diligently, had agonized himself in a search for aid, and had refused to let hope die. There had been some reason in trying then. The breach between him and Nancy had not seemed insurmountable, and his hope had never been utterly outraged. Now

when he himself censured his weakened courage and his resignation to defeat, his arguments were sadly lacking in conviction, all tainted with the belief that his actions mattered
little to anyone. He was alone. It was the bank's move, and
he waited for it, idling.

A sense of failure crept through his veins like a deadly
virus, paralyzing his will and stilling hope. There was nothing ahead, nothing except some final action by the bank
which would publicize the failure which he had already admitted to himself. That was all there was now and he waited
for it just as one who is dying of an incurable disease waits
lazily and hopelessly for death. From the wreckage of his
courage and hope there emerged slowly, not a desire to revive them, but a wish to justify his failure, to explain it,
to have someone listen while he recounted his trials and his
long suffering battle with adversity; there could have been
no other end, he had left nothing undone, and he wanted
desperately the satisfaction of telling people that this was so,
and of convincing them that there was some sense in wandering idly about his farm while other people were working
and in paying no more attention to his fields than if they
had been a wilderness. He spent little time at the house because he could not tell these things to Nancy. She would
have listened silently, and whether she believed or cared
greatly, he would not have known.

He stayed in the fields, sitting for hours sometimes in the
same spot watching the negroes grubbing, watching them
get ready for a crop which would never be planted. They
stuck to their work, easing it with laughter and play, agi-
tating their minds little over his strange behavior, character-
izing it among themselves as "white folk's foolishness," a
thing which did not concern them much. Their crops had
been sold, their bills had been paid, and they were not
hungry.

Hugh knew that the progress of despair was a finite thing. He knew that his heart riding a failing tide of hope must sink eventually to some hard rock of bottom from which it would not rise again. He could feel it now like a sluggish weight upon his stomach. He also knew that in the past he had risen from the bedrock of despair, not through hope, but through following some course of action adopted in desperate revolt against spiritual inertia. Something like this happened to him, now, sitting idly at the edge of his fields, looking across them at the blue fringe of a world in which he no longer believed.

That blue fringe upon which he gazed was the deep woods of Sligo basking in the thin, oblique rays of the late winter sun. The borders of his own land lay near the limits of his view, and included a large part of the heavy timber, great pines and oaks which had flourished in the time of his grandfather. He realized with a feeling akin to amazement that never before had he considered these trees as his own, as personal possessions which he could dispose of for a price. The discovery moved him mightily, gave his mind nourishment for the first time in months. He seized the idea hungrily, turned it over and over, exploiting it for the last drop of relief it would give him. He took it with him to bed that night, and for the first time in many nights his mind was able to project itself along this slim tangent of hope, instead of beating itself around an endless circle of defeat.

By morning his thoughts had charged him with an energy and purpose so different from the dull resignation which had weighted him that to those who had seen him lately he must have presented the appearance of a man slightly drunk. Nancy noticed the change when she set his breakfast before him, and though she served him silently and masked her curiosity behind that frigid indifference which had become her feeling for him, he thought this plan too good to keep.

Excited by this new prospect of relief, he forgot momentarily what a range of coldness lay between them, and over his coffee he told her impulsively of his plan to sell the timber.

"I tell you, Nancy," he cried enthusiastically, "I believe this will give me the chance I need. Just one good crop may put me ahead."

She cleared the table, saying nothing, but regarding him with the practical tolerance one displays for the wild dreams of children. He went on with his talking, unabashed by her lack of interest.

"Yes," he continued, "one good year is all I need. Why, I may even get some money ahead."

"You and your plans," Nancy commented wearily, "you and all your plans can only postpone the end a little longer. You can't sell timber forever."

Had he not been engrossed with his own ideas Hugh would have heard with surprise Nancy's cynical retort. Usually she refrained from any expression about his work. Rather defensively he asked: "It's the only thing I can do, isn't it?"

"I suppose it is," she replied. There was something like pity in the look she gave him as he left the room, but he did not see that.

All the farm negroes felt, as Aunt Mathy had felt, a sense of farm geography and history, and the events which marked its days were registered in their minds as matters of great importance. They had watched Hugh idling and brooding when he should have been drilling fertilizer and they remarked with relief the sudden end of that "spell" which had shadowed him all winter. He appeared one fine morning and laughed with them as had been his custom and sent them about their duties with his old force and discipline.

Things had been going badly without his leadership and they welcomed its return. Only Dave had felt some inkling of what had been going on in Hugh's mind all winter, and

he was so relieved to see an order of discipline established
once more that he began to spur the lagging negroes whose
laziness he had almost come to ignore. They responded readily and with good humor, for that dark "spell" which had
gripped Hugh cast a shadow into their own lives; they were
not unaware of that lean sorrow which seemed to rise from
the very fields.

They knew courage and revered it. They knew that it was
better to meet adversity and wrestle with it than to lie down
abjectly and wait for the worst. When in their conversations
they talked about the fearful things of life, it was not of
sickrooms and the colorless comings of death that they told,
but of young bucks and wild women, the swift clean swish
of razors, and of ends that have some sort of victory in them.

There was something of the color of a military pageant in
the way they marched to the edge of the Sligo woods, all
armed with glistening axes. The sound of their axes seeking
the hearts of the Sligo giants had a valiant ring.

Each day strengthened Hugh's belief that he had found a
way out of his difficulties. Before he had sent the negroes
into the woods he had arranged to supply the foundation
timbers for another mill which was going up in Granville.
The contractor was a local man; he knew Hugh well and
had been glad to give the order. How simple everything was
now that his plan was in action! Soon the great trees would
be ready for the sawmill, all of them, and then they would
be so many strong square pillars with which to prop up his
world which had been so near tumbling. His activity elated
him. He had little time for doubting and worrying; indeed,
he looked back on the winter's despondency as if it were an
unbelievable thing, a sickness of the mind, from which, fortunately, he had recovered. This rebirth of activity nurtured
other hopes. True, Nancy lent his work no encouragement,
but his optimism was all-embracing; it knew no limits. It

had a peculiar logic of its own, one that saw only those things which contributed toward its own ends. It reduced all of life's difficulties to the simplest of equations, a beautiful balance in which desires were arranged as the equals of efforts, and success became a mathematical certainty. Since Nancy's indifference had originated in the barrenness of his labor, he thought that successful labor must just as surely end her coldness. Happiness smiled at him, beckoned him, and he was eager to follow; even the distant sight of it charmed him, made pursuit a delight.

He was never without this feeling these days and he let his soul revel in it, asking nothing from Nancy, nothing from life but this wonderful sensation of opportunity reborn. It warmed like sunshine, firing him at times with an ecstasy of effort, descending again like a gentle shower of peace upon his thirsty heart. It was as good as being free to stand in the middle of his woes and know that they were smaller than he, to know that he feared them no longer, and that one by one he could rout them. His mind flew back across a barren stretch of years to a day when living had been principally a sensation of being alive, just that, a luxurious embracing of air and sunshine and hunger. Life had been good to him when he was a boy. It had been everything that he wanted; there had been no denials. He had wanted so little. He had not forgotten that youthful sense of rightness, of order, that wonderful co-ordination of earth and body that had been his without seeking—it had just been so, he had simply found himself in the middle of it, and it could be true again, he told himself. That was what he wanted. That was what he wanted for little Dumont, all of that.

He contented himself with the prospect of happiness, unwilling to endanger it by a too precipitate rush of eagerness, yet he kept it ahead of him like a banner which lent zeal and meaning to his work. At length the last great log was snaked from the hillside and lashed to the wagon which bore it away to the sawmill. Gathering their axes and pikes the negroes walked behind the wagon; in the distance they resembled a funeral procession.

Dave remained with Hugh, whose eyes turned from the little band winding down the hollow and rested on the bare hill above them. It lay before them, its nakedness unrelieved by a single young tree. The trees which they had cut had been too firmly rooted, too long masters of sun and soil to allow any encroaching growth about their feet. Their stumps climbed impotently for a few feet, their great yellow faces turned toward the sky like a vast field of sunflowers.

"A new-ground for next year," said Hugh.

Dave said nothing, but he faced Hugh and a slow smile of understanding and approval passed between them.

6

Old Henry's death had been the beginning of an era of freedom for the Galloway household. Freedom had its faults. Nothing worse could have happened to Lonnie. At first he took his ease with little thought of consequences, but there soon penetrated his sleepy brain an awareness of what his behavior was bringing to pass among the other workers of the farm. He saw soon that the croppers were idling as he was, sleeping late in the mornings, and spending too much of the night in pleasure. He took steps to end this spreading idleness. His father's training had engraved certain things in his mind, and while he had not practiced them, neither had he forgotten them. He knew what should be done to the crops, he knew when these things should be done, and how they should be done, and this was all he needed to know, he reasoned. The negroes could do the work. He set himself, therefore, the task of giving them instructions daily, laying out the next day's work for them when they gathered at the stable lot late at dusk. This arrangement did some good, but it failed to accomplish all that he had hoped of it. He bore its shortcomings with resignation, however, having decided that nothing short of early rising on his own part could better the situation. What he lost through their undirected efforts, he gained in the deep comfort of sleep.

At first it appeared that Lonnie paid for his ease only a small loss accumulating from the undisciplined efforts of his negroes, a little loss of time here, grass left too long in one field, suckers left too long in another, there a ragged clump of weeds or a tottering fence. But in time these things amounted to an astounding total of negligence and waste, but as is the way of such things, it came about so slowly that it failed to astound Lonnie, failed to shame him into a policy of correction. Indeed, within a year it seemed that Old Henry's ghost must have been hovering over the fields by night, taking from them the neat fences, the well-trimmed hedgerows, and all the little evidences of industry by which he had marked the farm as his own.

Lonnie had felt some respect for his father. He could see that the old man had been right about a lot of things. He had been right in driving the negroes. He had insisted that they work and it had been a good thing. They should work. The old man had maintained the mastery of his own house; his word had been law, and here again he had been right, Lonnie thought. So he bullied Helen about her housework and no doubt would have bullied his mother had she not been so old and feeble that she kept to her room most of the time. He seldom saw her except at meals.

Helen bore his trumpetings stoically, unimpressed by them because she had never been impressed by Lonnie; she harbored no illusion about him, indeed by this time she held few illusions about anything. She certainly had none as far as her marriage was concerned, but here she composed herself with the knowledge that she had no right to expect much from it. It had been a mad thing to do, and she was fortunate in having nothing more to contend with than James' ineffectual, pitiable devotion. He was not cruel, anything but that. He was weak, almost cringing, and he wanted only to be good and have her love him. She succeeded in feeling terribly sorry for him. Each weekend he came from the mill and while he was with her she gave freely of the shameful pity which he roused in her, and all the time she hoped that he did not know what moved her. He deserved no hurt, and as far as she was able she shielded him. He seemed to misunderstand sufficiently. At times she wondered if she knew what she really did feel for her husband; it was true that she felt nothing going out from herself to him, rather she felt that she was submitting to his affection, accepting it for no better reason than to avoid hurting him. She derived no happiness from seeing him, yet she was not unglad when he came on Saturday. Indeed, she looked forward to his coming since it broke the week-long monotony, and gave her some relief from Lonnie's sullen arrogance. Lonnie disgusted her; James never did, although she had known disgust with herself over him.

He begged her to walk with him in the woods when he came. "It's nice to get in the woods after a week in the mill," he explained. She consented, and they went along the path which led toward the Winton farm. James displayed a childish eagerness about their aimless walk. He was happy, apparently unburdened by memories of the mill which she knew he disliked. He forgot easily. Until Monday he was free, and his freedom was not spoiled by the prospect of resuming work then. He had put that out of his mind. Things touched him lightly. Even when they had lost their land he had not seemed greatly troubled. "We made a poor living on it anyway," he had said, and she had been amazed at the ease with which he bore his loss. At the time she had thought him brave. Now she wondered.

Down the path where the creek crossed there was a large moss-grown rock, and it was to this that James was leading her. She knew. He loved the spot. He would coax her to leap the stream and climb upon the rock, where he might lie beside her and pour out his weekly tale of love, and cover her face with his kisses, his eyes shining meanwhile with the unquestioning trust and happiness of a child, while she felt nothing except what an awful liar she was.

He was still overcome with the wonder of his love when they returned to the house. It shone in his face and his slight body radiated a fever of excitement and desire. With difficulty she persuaded him to allow her to go into the kitchen alone; she started supper there, conscious of a heavy unhappiness over this false elation which she generated in poor James.

Lonnie lumbered in before she had put the biscuits in the stove. It was dark in the hallway but she knew his heavy step. She knew that he would be ravenously hungry, as usual, and before he spoke she composed herself for the grumblings which the delay in the meal would bring from him. He paused in the doorway and surveyed the dim kitchen. At the moment she was placing a pan of uncooked biscuits in the stove, and Lonnie's attention settled upon the little lumps of dough in the pan she held.

"Can't you ever have a meal on time?" he demanded, settling his great bulk against the door-jamb with the evident intention of threshing the matter out thoroughly.

"Supper will be ready before you know it," she replied evenly. "Can't you wait in the yard where it's cool? James is out there."

"Is he here again?"

"Yes."

"I suppose that accounts for your being late."

"We went for a walk."

"It's a wonder that you remembered to come back a'tall."

"You aren't hurrying supper a bit by standing there jaw-ing about it. Now go on and leave me alone or I won't make another move."

"You won't?"

"That's what I said," Helen replied, and suiting her action to her words she went to the open window, propped her elbows on the sill, and gazed out into the yard.

"All this is his doin'," Lonnie stormed, but he left the kitchen.

Lonnie would not join James in the yard, Helen knew, for he had no use for James. Poor, weak James! How terribly apparent his weakness was against the brutal backdrop of Lonnie's strength, for Lonnie had strength of a kind, she mused, the strength of boorishness and selfishness through which he was able to take what he wanted without feeling any of that suppressed bitterness which their way of living engendered in her. Lonnie's appetites were all primitive, and the primitive life of the farm, their coarse food, their hours and days undiffering, and the long black nights satis-fied him. She could hear him washing his face on the back porch, spluttering into the water as he lifted it in his hands, bathing himself with a tremendous sloshing and blowing, like a pig in a puddle, she thought. That was right, like a pig in a puddle. It would be just as well if Lonnie had a stall in the stable. He could eat there. The other beasts did. And he could sleep there, and that was what he cared for more than anything else. Momentarily she was ashamed of her thoughts, but the continued sound of his violent ablutions dispelled this feeling.

"Gimme a towel," he shouted from the dark doorway.

She drew one from the closet and thrust it toward him, but his eyes were filled with soap and he did not see it.

"Hand it here!" he yelled.

She thrust it into his groping hands and he dried his face, still puffing and blowing. Yes, the stable would be good enough for him, she concluded as she returned to the hot stove.

The meal was ready now and she moved into the dining room to clear the table for it. Lonnie was there before her, and he had taken the cover from the table. It lay in a crumpled heap on the sideboard where he had thrown it. He had already seated himself at his customary place, and was waiting impatiently for her to set the food before him, cleaning his nails meanwhile with the prong of a fork. She stood watching him, flooded with hot shame.

"Don't do that, Lonnie," she protested.

"Don't do what?" he asked in honest amazement.

"Don't sit there cleaning your nails with that fork."

"How come?" he demanded; "it's my fork, ain't it?"

"Yes, it's your fork and your fingers," she answered, "but that doesn't make it any better."

Lonnie made no reply. Indeed, he couldn't, for at this moment he had his fingers in his mouth, attempting to remove a stubborn hangnail with his teeth. Successful in his attempt, he spat the offending bit of skin on the floor, and viewed his finger with satisfaction.

"Don't be a fool," he advised Helen as she placed a dish of meat before him; "farmers can't be dudes."

She ignored this observation and continued to bring the food in from the kitchen. Lonnie helped himself from the dishes as she set them on the table. This, too, annoyed her.

"Lonnie," she began, "can't you wait until the others come to the table?"

"I'm here, ain't I?" he demanded. "If the others want to eat, let 'em come. I ain't holding them."

Having delivered his opinion on this matter, Lonnie gave his undivided attention to the meal, nor did he halt for so much as a casual greeting when his mother and James came in response to Helen's call.

James mumbled a brief hello as he took his seat, but it came something short of a greeting. He, too, fell to eating silently, helping himself to those dishes within his reach. Lonnie paid no attention to him. Old Mrs. Galloway, whose reach was constrained by age and rheumatism, passed her empty plate to her son, who, pausing first to fill his mouth, loaded the plate from the various dishes and passed it back to her without making a single inquiry as to her desires. She accepted it and began to peck at its contents.

Helen did not take a place at the table, but busied herself refilling the dishes which Lonnie emptied, supplying hot biscuits, and keeping Lonnie's cup filled with coffee. Lonnie was eating with less haste now, though with none the less deliberation. At first he had heaped his plate with a great bulk of food as though his stomach were a vessel into which he must put first an adequate ballast before undertaking to load it with a selected cargo. Now he was packing it with some discrimination for taste and quality. Into it went a liberal portion of preserves well-wedged with buttered biscuits. Against this he laid away a store of molasses into which he had mixed a huge slab of butter. He sopped the last dark stain from his plate with a rapid flourish of a biscuit, drained his coffee cup, drew the back of his hand across his mouth, and emitted a noise between that of a sigh and a belch. It suggested at the same time repletion and regret. Nevertheless he leaned back in his chair and surveyed the wreckage at his end of the table with a greasy satisfaction. From his shirt pocket he drew an elaborate toothpick, carved from the quill of a turkey feather, and set about dislodging the remnants of his meal from his strong yellow teeth. This operation engaged him for some time, and he pursued it methodically, thrusting his thumb and forefinger into his mouth at intervals to remove some obstinate particle of food. At length he returned the toothpick to his pocket and gave his attention to those who had not dispatched their meal with his speed and thoroughness.

Helen came to the table. James was eating slowly and apologetically, it seemed, but James was apologetic about most things. His only defense against the world lay in his soft supplicating eyes, which, like the eyes of a timid dog, were sad and crying out constantly against violence.

"Make out your meal, James," Lonnie said, speaking to him for the first time since James had come to the table; "go right on eating. Don't let me stop you."

"I'm doing all right," James smiled.

"Just help yourself," Lonnie continued; "it don't cost you nothing, you know."

James laid down his fork and tried to continue smiling, but his effort produced only a sickly grin.

"I've had enough, I believe," he said lamely, crossing his knife above his fork.

"Make out your meal," Lonnie persisted derisively, "you don't get a chance to but once a week."

"I'm not hungry, not any more," James protested.

"I know damned well you ain't now," Lonnie sneered.

Helen had listened to Lonnie baiting James with growing anger. This was as much her house as it was his, and the food was even more hers, she felt, since she had done the work of preparing it.

"Don't pay any attention to him, James," she interjected; "eat all you want, and don't let his manners make you feel that you are not welcome."

"You shut up," Lonnie shouted at her; "whose house do you think this is?"

Old Mrs. Galloway stirred her coffee and looked from one to the other, her eyes beseeching peace, although she feared to ask for it. James' eyes, too, sought first Helen's and then Lonnie's, and rested finally upon the empty white plate before him.

"Looks like you been givin' me a lot of lip lately," Lonnie growled.

"Let's not quarrel," Helen begged, knowing the futility of exchanging words with him.

But Lonnie had no desire to drop the matter.

"I think this has been going on long enough to deserve some talking," he said. "I ain't the first one in this house to get tired of this eternal visiting."

"Lonnie, please . . ."

"You shut up and listen to me."

"Stop talking to her like that!" cried James, rising and trembling visibly. "I don't have to come here to eat, and I don't have to stand for your talking to her like that." The sound of his voice gave him courage and he stared at Lonnie defiantly.

"She's my sister, ain't she?" he bellowed.

"Well, she's my wife, and you've said enough to her."

Lonnie's reply to this statement was to reach across the corner of the table and collar James. The feel of weaker flesh in his hands sent an electric thrill through his body. James tore at the hand throttling him, but Lonnie was too strong for him. Slowly he twisted the collar until it became a veritable noose about poor James' neck, cutting off the air from his lungs, and soon he hung limp and gasping across the table.

Old Mrs. Galloway had tried to rise from her chair, had failed in her effort, and now she sat slumped in her place, too weak to do anything other than cry out in terror and protest. For a moment Helen herself was paralyzed by the horror of the scene, but none too soon she rushed around the table and threw herself against Lonnie, trying with all her strength to tear that terrible hand from James' throat. Lonnie shook her off like a feather, thrust her away from him with one hand, and after giving James' collar a final wrench, he slung him against the floor viciously, and strode out of the room without looking back.

Whether James had been choked into insensibility or whether the fall had knocked him senseless, she did not know. She knew only that he lay quite still upon the floor, that the color of his face was that of no living thing, and that apparently he was lifeless. Bending above him she loosened his collar frantically and thrust her hands under his shirt trying to detect a heartbeat. A faint pulsation rewarded her anxious fingers. This restored her calmness somewhat, and lent her the presence of mind to fetch some water from the kitchen and bathe James' face and throat. In a few seconds he moved his head slightly, and after a moment he opened his eyes, but his first consciousness was of that terror from which he had escaped, and immediately he was struggling against her. His efforts exhausted him quickly and he lay upon the floor staring at her vacantly. Although he was still too weak to speak, Helen could read both shame and relief in his eyes. As soon as he was able to stand she guided him into her room and he sank willingly upon the bed. She lifted his feet from the floor and removed his shoes, speaking soothingly to him, meanwhile, as she would have spoken to a child. She realized that for the first time he had taken a man's part by her, and despite the pitiableness of his effort it stirred her pride and gratitude. James was trying to talk. She bent above him tenderly.

"Helen," he whispered.

"Yes?"

"Helen, I tried to stop him."

"I know," she assured him, "you shouldn't have done it. He's a beast."

"Will he come back?" James asked anxiously.

"No, not tonight," she replied, and leaving him for a moment she bolted the door. She returned to the bed and lay beside James. He made no attempt to talk. Soon she thought that he must be sleeping, and she laid an exploring palm along his cheek. Her fingers found it warm and wet.

7

The dissolution of Hugh's dream of reestablishing himself through the sale of the timber began with a chance remark which fell from the lips of a stranger. He had come to Granville bent upon discovering when the sawmill would have his lumber ready for delivery to the contractor. Upon this information depended his arrangements for fertilizer. Already it was high time that it was in the ground. Many farmers had started planting, but on his farm not a single field had been bedded. The negroes had begun their covert questioning and troubled watching again. There was not much time left. These thoughts hastened him along the street toward the mill, yet he went hopefully; everything would come out all right. The lumber was at the mill, the contractor had ordered it, and only time stood between him and the money he would derive from its sale. This comforting conviction filtered through his mind like a ray of sunlight, silvering those dark doubts which still hovered in the back of his head. He walked along admiring this peaceful mental horizon which he had created from a few trees and a sawmill.

A group of dingy individuals covered with the fuzz-like down of the cotton mill blocked the sidewalk as they huddled around one of their number who was talking excitedly. They paid no attention to Hugh, their eyes being riveted on the one who was doing the talking. As Hugh skirted the huddle a remark from its center struck like a bolt of lightning straight into the silvery nebulous dream which filled his mind. Like thunder the words still dinned at his ears.

"But I tell you there ain't gonna be no new mill!" the man had said.

"Ain't?" repeated a listener dully.

"Naw."

"How come?" demanded another of the fuzzy ones.

" 'Pression," their informant stated simply.

Hugh stood and listened. There was no use to ask questions. There were questioners enough, and all of them just as concerned as he was, he realized.

"I had counted on working there," a third worker said sadly, " 'specially since two days a week is all I can get in the old mill. I had counted on it right smart," he added walking away, his eyes fastened on his shuffling feet.

The man's place was filled quickly, and the gloomy drone continued unabated. Hugh joined the group, pushing himself into the lint-covered crowd, searching for the oracle of evil whose dismal chant still rang in his ears. He saw a little man, covered like his companions with gray down, only his covering seemed to be a part of him which had adhered to his frail body during a long course of sad, bleak years. His face was gray, too, and gray was his hair protruding from the eaves of his weather-scarred cap, and down his sallow cheeks clung the feathery dust of the mill, like a growth of parasitical whiskers.

The little man found a morbid pleasure in relating this sad tale. He was a newsbringer, and he fulfilled his office with no dull comprehension of the weight of his tidings, reading the force of his message in the drooping faces of his hearers.

"You'll find it up at the office," he explained, "tacked up on the bulletin board, a notice what says 'Work on the new mill has been postponed temp'rarily.' I seen it. That 'temp'-rarily' means from now on, in case y'all don't know," he added. Silence settled upon the gathering, and the little man moved fleetly down the street.

Hugh found himself standing like one of the workers, overcome by the same gloom which bound them.

"It's hell, ain't it?" one of them asked turning toward him, but when he saw that Hugh did not belong to his company he walked off without waiting for an answer. Silently Hugh left the gray men.

What to do now?

Finding no ready answer to this tremendous question, he continued toward the sawmill, wearily, like a pilgrim robbed of his faith in Mecca. The mill was idle, too. A sour clerk in the clapboard office pointed out his lumber stacked neatly at one side of the yard. He viewed it dejectedly, too hopeless to be angered by its bright yellow impotence. The clerk had heard the news, too. It meant his job, he said. All the lumber in the yard had been destined for the mill and none of it had been paid for and none of it would be now, he supposed.

"But the notice said 'temporarily'," Hugh stammered, grasping for a straw.

"What notice?"

"The notice on the bulletin board," Hugh explained weakly.

"I don't know what you are talking 'bout," said the clerk, eyeing him suspiciously. "I don't know anything 'bout any notice. All I know is what the boss said. He said there wasn't going to be no new mill, and took himself off to get drunk."

"See you later about my lumber," said Hugh turning on his heel.

"Uh huh," the man mumbled without looking at him.

What to do?

Back along the hot street went Hugh, trudging aimlessly now. It was a beautiful day, and its glory fell about him like a shining shower of mockery. He felt terribly alone, felt the restraining walls of his own flesh. He could feel his heart feeding its nervous flood through his purposeless limbs, pounding madly at its labor of sustaining a bitterness which he wished passionately had never had a beginning. Life! The gift of life! He dug the old phrase from his memory and examined it contemptuously. It rang with hollowness. A sentence, that's what life was. It had battered his proud spirit, put chains on its gay feet and consigned it to grovel in the dirt of despair. And worst of all it had locked this broken, shamed thing in the fleshy walls of his own heart, and he had to endure its aching because this vile prisoner was also himself. He despised the cringing prisoner, he poured all of the contempt of an industrious man upon the crying little coward, but it moved him not at all. He had been beaten too long, and too badly. He lay flat on his belly in his dark cell and cried to the world, "Go ahead, kick me." That was the soul that he bore along the streets of Granville, and he was heartily ashamed of its company.

Was there anything that he could do? He put the question to the prisoner.

Without raising its head, it answered promptly, "No, there is nothing."

A man bent on some business with a farmer seated in his wagon at the curb ran against Hugh. The impact knocked a sack of potatoes from his arms. It burst on the pavement. Like a swarm of freed mice the potatoes scattered and made their way across the sloping sidewalk, and hopped, one by one, into the gutter.

"Watch where you are going," shouted the hurrying one as he pursued the fleeing potatoes.

"Go to hell," Hugh replied, and marched on his way.

The potato-herder opened his mouth for some fitting vilification, but his eyes measured the width of Hugh's retreating shoulders and he restrained himself.

"Clodhopper!" he whispered to the potatoes as he bent above them.

On his way back to the farm Hugh composed himself to the extent that he resolved to apply reason to his present plight instead of just sitting down and waiting for things to happen to him. At first he told Nancy nothing of his disappointment. He was ashamed for her to learn of it. She had shown no interest in the outcome of his lumber deal, had regarded it as just another senseless feature of the senseless business of farming, and she cared little about it one way or the other. Hugh knew this and kept his bad news to himself.

The best thing to be done, he had decided, would be to write to the bank and tell them the whole story, explain how he had planned to carry on through the sale of the timber, and explain further that there was now no way of going ahead. He did this, closing his letter with a rather defiant plea for aid. "None of the fields have been prepared for planting," he wrote, "and there isn't a smell of fertilizer on the place. I suppose the land is yours now, and there ought to be some fertilizer in it right away."

"That'll bring 'em hotfootin' it," he commented grimly, as he sealed the envelope.

Nancy watched him address the letter. Perhaps he had been successful in the lumber deal after all.

"That," she asked, indicating the letter, "is it a payment to the bank?"

Hugh shook his head. His silence appeared to provoke her curiosity.

"Didn't you get your money?"

He shook his head again. No need of going into details. She cared nothing about it, anyway.

"What happened?" she pressed him.

"They've discontinued work on the mill," he answered. "They don't need the lumber now."

He thought a shade of sympathy crept into her voice. "But they will resume building, won't they?"

"Probably," he replied, striving for lightness; "the notice said 'temporarily'."

8

The transition from farm owner to farm tenant was accomplished without any momentous fanfare. Even at the hour when the bank was engaged in the meticulous mockery of a sale before the courthouse door in Granville Hugh was impressed, not so much with the finality of what they were doing, as with the utter casualness of its execution. Nothing emphasized this more than the fact that he did not attend the sale. He knew exactly what was going on, he knew how brief and spiritless and how seemingly unimportant the whole procedure had appeared, without actually witnessing it. The courthouse door at Granville had become, by this time, a theatre where these sordid dramas were enacted daily. Its patronage was transient and inconsequential and the actors themselves no longer evinced any enthusiasm for their parts. The worst that could be said about the sale was that it was the culmination of a long fear. The fear had been the worst part. It had struck now and he set about adjusting himself to the changes it had brought.

These changes, like the real meaning of the sale, were largely invisible ones. The farm appeared just as it had before. Nothing had changed in the soil, nor in the houses that stood on it. They all kept their fixed places, preserving a stolid indifference to the emotions of their inhabitants. Outwardly everything was as it should be. Thrown across the fields his eye returned him no distorted or irreconcilable view, but when his vision was extended and became not seeing but thinking, then the fields, the woods, the houses, all became a chaotic blur.

As far as he could tell the sale made no difference to Nancy. As sick as his own thoughts were at the time he was still able to admit that her attitude was eminently sensible. They had never had more than a precarious living from the land, and their chances of obtaining that were as good as ever, in fact their chances were better if anything, because they were not burdened now with providing a living for the negroes. It had been a long time since he knew what Nancy thought, but he was certain that she did not resort to the weak defense of resignation; she had a stronger one. She despised the farm and everything connected with it, and long ago hatred had silenced her.

Hugh made an earnest effort to organize his thoughts sensibly. He tried to convince himself that what had taken place had actually been for his good. This was true in a sense. Not only had he lost his land, but with it he had lost the woes of ownership, taxes, interest on debts, and an unremunerative responsibility. But a review of these equivocal advantages failed to sustain him long. He had lost much more than that, and like a well-fed dog his mind sniffed contemptuously at all these dry bones, sniffed contemptuously and returned to him begging for a succulent morsel. He had nothing to offer it.

Now that he was living in a state which he had contemplated with fear and abhorrence for years he found that existence, physically speaking, was very much as it had been before. The bank was not unkind. Its agent, who visited the farm periodically giving instructions and orders, did so with a visible appreciation of what taking orders must mean to him. The man advised tactfully. He spoke guardedly, and Hugh was filled at the same time with resentment and gratitude. The negroes still came to Hugh for orders, although the bank saw that their living was provided. For them there had been no change. They still had shelter and food, and someone to "boss 'em around," and that left them little to worry about.

All these things were as they should be. The stupendous change which he had to face, Hugh realized, was that he was now without a sustaining purpose, that he had nothing to look forward to other than the mechanical execution of the tasks which revolved with the days. He had planned his future around a single theme ... the resuscitation of Nancy's love. His efforts to save the farm had been but a part of that purpose. He had looked to the farm to restore her to him, as he had looked to it for everything else, and now for the first time he held no illusions about the possibility of reclaiming her. He dismissed the thought lightly, too lightly. He even found himself wondering if his desire for her, and what he had told himself was a burning need, had not degenerated into nothing more than a stubborn purpose. Well, it was no longer even a purpose. That was finished, too. He thought about her without pain, and her beauty now moved him no more than the impossible beauty of a dream.

Rapidly he became willing to drift aimlessly from one day to another, finding dullness and a partially self-imposed stupor more bearable than a pack of crying wants and no quarry in sight.

9

Little Dumont remembered the barns. He had prattled of
them during the winter, recalling with vast excitement the
marvelous doodle-bugs and the alarm which he had stimu-
lated among them, laughing as he told of their tumbling
terror at the cry of fire. Pensively he had hungered for the
corn and potatoes which Hugh had cooked for him in the
great flues, and to Nancy's exasperation, the tragic tale of
Renee had fastened upon him, and its memory seemed to
give him a terrifying delight. He told the story to himself in
the long evenings before the fire, related it bravely enough
there in the light, but later when Nancy had put him to bed
and darkened his room he begged her to stay with him. In
the dark Dumont found it altogether plausible that the
monster would tire of Renee's solitary company, and he
strained his ears for that unearthly call which had led to
Renee's undoing. But this was a terror of the night. He had
no fears by day.

The whole wide farm was his domain, and he roamed it
with a masterful confidence. The woods which sheltered the
barns were his headquarters; here his far-flung expeditions
toward the mystery of deep Sligo began, and here they always ended. The barns were his frontier posts, back of them
the house and safety and beyond them the woods, the world,
and the curious rim of the sky. Here, while he was sleeping,
reposed his wooden guns and horses and all the priceless
accoutrements of his adventurous wanderings. Here also
was a fairyland lake where, tired of his wanderings, he might
rest his turbulent spirit in sailing calm ships upon its placid
surface. In reality the lake consisted of a ragged hole in the
ground, formed by excavations for flue clay and filled with
an accumulation of winter rainwater, but to Dumont it was

a lake and he sailed ships upon it frequently. It was his custom to kneel at the water's edge and send a block of wood drifting upon a voyage, then to rush around to the opposite shore and launch an enemy vessel. When this was done expertly the two men-of-war always sailed into each other's dangerous proximity, whereupon he pelted them both, impartially, with a broadside of pebbles. Notwithstanding the necessity of acting as gunner for both combatants there were some very satisfactory and destructive engagements in these waters, and Dumont's imagination suffered not at all from a confusion of loyalties.

Gradually the spring sun lifted the water from this basin until the clay banks towered two feet above the surface of the pool. The bank was white and hard and crumbly, and one day a section of it dislodged itself beneath Dumont and he tumbled into the water behind it, suffering a wetting such as he had never experienced except in the safety of his bath. The water was cold, very cold, and beneath it he found no footing except the treacherous white clay. He floundered and fell prostrate several times before he made his escape, strangling on the dirty water as he struggled and screamed. Safe on the banks he took stock of his plight amid his slowly subsiding coughs and splutterings.

His clothes were soaked and clung to his body with a persistent iciness that set him shivering in spite of his previous warmth in the April sun. He had not known that water could be so cold, and on the heels of this observation came a late recollection of his mother's warnings about water. She had warned him about everything, and about water particularly. This memory added heavily to his distress, and he made his way slowly toward the house, his head full of remorse over his disobedience and his body tingling with a chill unlike any cold which he had known before. This was not cold which wrapped itself about one openly and cleanly. Instead it had got inside him somehow, and now it ran through his flesh with a nauseous shivering. He was sick, he was scared, and his hesitant return home became quickly a panic-stricken flight which landed him in Nancy's room a frightened wreck of a little boy.

Between his coughs Nancy got a garbled account of the accident. She put him to bed immediately and set to work with a hot water bottle and a course of household remedies, but the child grew steadily worse. By sunset he ran a high fever and carried on a delirious monologue. Even in her frenzied anxiety she tried to make sense of what he was saying. She heard the name "Renee" but it was not uttered in fear. There was some talk of boats and a battle, the names of the distant fields, and finally, only an incomprehensible, feverish muttering. Then she sent for Hugh.

He came running. Nancy was walking from the bed to the door, from the door to the bed, almost out of her wits. Brushing by her he reached the bed where the boy lay tossing and muttering. The sight held him so that for a moment he was unaware of Nancy at his side.

"Have you sent for the doctor?" he demanded.

"Not yet," she cried; "send for him, please. It happened only a little while ago. He fell in the water. It's pneumonia, I know. Oh, get the doctor, Hugh. Hurry!"

There was a telephone at the store. Hugh sent Dave there to 'phone for Dr. Allen, and returned to the room to find Nancy still walking wildly.

"Is he coming?" she asked abstractedly.

"I sent Dave to 'phone."

"I shouldn't have let him leave the house. Oh, I knew it! I knew something would happen."

"Where did it happen?" Hugh asked.

"At the barns, I think. He was almost out of his head when he got to the house. But it must have been at the barns.

He hadn't had time to get far. I had hardly missed him when he came in like this ... Oh, God have mercy on me!"

"Control yourself, Nancy," Hugh begged. "Even if it is pneumonia, there's no need to be scared. There are many things worse than that."

"But look at the little darling," she cried. "I blame myself for it. I should have watched him."

"Don't blame yourself. That's foolish. Please try to be quiet and wait until the doctor sees him. You may be alarmed unnecessarily."

Nancy sat down on the edge of the bed and laid her hand across the boy's brow. Touching him seemed to quiet her somewhat, although her lips trembled in a silent convulsion of grief.

"You stay with him," Hugh advised. "I'm going to see that the negroes take care of the stock."

An hour passed before the doctor arrived. When he came Hugh followed him into the room and watched his examination with mounting alarm. It was too brief, almost casual, he thought. Unconsciously the doctor shook his head as he rose from the bedside. Hugh and Nancy stood like two prisoners awaiting a verdict.

"It's pneumonia," he announced tersely, "and it's advancing very rapidly. He must have had an especially violent exposure."

Nancy began to sob, and sank back upon the bed.

"Now, that will never do," the doctor warned her. "You can't help him that way. You must summon all your strength and courage and nurse him as he ought to be nursed if you want to save him."

She rallied at his words. He was promising her recovery for the boy if she would help him. With a great effort she held herself silent.

"Your child can get well," he continued gently. "Pneumonia is an unpredictable, but not necessarily a fatal, disease."

Nancy hung on his words, gleaning them for hope. He gave her full instructions regarding the boy's care, and suggested that she secure the services of a negro nurse. "You must look after yourself, too, you know," he added.

"You know I can't leave him, Doctor," she protested; "sleep is out of the question."

"You must sleep," he commanded. "See that she sleeps, Hugh."

Hugh followed him into the yard and between them there was no false gentleness.

"Your child is very ill, Hugh, very ill, but don't despair. You must help Nancy keep up her courage. You owe it to the boy to nurse him with hope. That's all I can tell you now. It will be days before I can say more."

"You'll return in the morning?" Hugh asked.

"Yes, but don't bother to call me unless there is a pronounced change. I shall come every day for a while."

There followed a week of long days and longer nights, a week of agonized waiting. Dr. Allen had told Nancy that the disease would turn suddenly at the crisis, that not until this period would he be able to predict its outcome. She waited for this time in awful suspense, dreading its coming, yet finding in it her only source of hope. Hugh tried to cheer her with a philosophy which he himself did not feel.

"It's useless to break yourself with worry now," he said. "In a way it's just as though the disease does not begin until the period of crisis, for then he will either recover quickly, or..."

He did not finish. Nancy was sobbing afresh.

"I can't bear it, Hugh," she cried between her sobs. "If he says then that there is no hope, I can't sit here waiting for..."

"Nancy, you mustn't give way like that, not before the boy."

Her violent grief could not possibly have had any effect upon the child, for he still lay in a stupor, muttering feverishly of some fantasy which burned in his brain. He had had only one lucid interval during the week and then he had not spoken. Nancy knew from the vast questioning in his eyes that he was conscious. Their perplexity had almost torn out her heart before he lapsed again into delirium.

In the hall outside the sickroom Hugh met Dr. Allen. "What change?" he asked eagerly.

"None, that I can see," Hugh answered.

"This is the day," the doctor whispered, as he laid his hand on the door-knob.

Hugh thought that his examination was more scrupulous than on the other days. Before, he had seemed to perform his routine explorations with little doubt as to what he would find. Today there was an awful eagerness in his face as he bent above the boy with his stethoscope. What messages this instrument brought to his ears or how he translated them Hugh did not know, but he did know that their meaning could be read in the doctor's face, and he watched it with breathless intensity. He moved the stethoscope from one position to another, tracking the boy's chest and sides as if he communicated with many foreboding voices and left each hurriedly in hope of a kinder message from the next. Finally it seemed to Hugh that for an eternity he studied the boy's pulse, holding the wan little wrist in his heavy, sensitive hand. Gently he lowered the wrist back to the bed, and silently placed his stethoscope in the bag beside his chair. He sat there studying the unconscious child with grave perplexity.

Hugh was choking with questions, but out of concern for Nancy he restrained himself. She did not know, as he did, that a definite turn was expected now, but all the examinations were ordeals to her, and she begged the doctor to speak.

"I can't say anything yet," he stated, shaking his head.

Hugh followed him into the hall, fearing that he was withholding his opinion in front of Nancy. But he still shook his head.

"I can form no definite conclusion yet," the doctor said. "But sometime today I will know. I shall remain here."

All that afternoon they waited, and far into the night. Nancy was almost at the point of collapse, but she refused to leave the room. She understood from the doctor's prolonged stay that he expected the crisis of which he had told her earlier, and in the face of this nothing could induce her to leave the bedside. As midnight drew near she sank into a chair and rested her head on the bed. Her eyes closed wearily, but she was not sleeping. Hugh was not asleep either, although he had been persuaded to go to his room.

Precisely at midnight Dr. Allen began another meticulous examination. Suddenly he drew his stethoscope from the boy's laboring chest, and concentrated his attention upon the tiny wrist. Again with a desperate gentleness he relaxed it.

"Will you call Hugh?" he asked rising.

"Tell me doctor," Nancy gasped, "tell me!"

"I'll call him," was his only answer.

In a moment he returned with Hugh. As soon as they were in the room he began to gather his instruments and place them in his bag methodically. When he had finished this he turned to Hugh with a terrible briefness and said, "Stay with her, Hugh. I'm afraid you won't need me longer."

"Doctor, what do you mean?" Nancy screamed. "You can't leave him now!"

"It's out of my hands now," he replied simply.

She clung to him as he left the room, crying for assistance that was beyond him, but he hurried away like one who flies from an old and invincible enemy. Despairingly, she turned back into the room to wait without hope.

Morning came clear and beautiful. From her post beside the bed Nancy watched it creep in through the window and bathe the bed in its warm brilliance. Little Dumont's pale cheeks and the fine blue lines along his temples were like lifeless wax in its bright path. He still lived, but this itself was torture now. Her grief had become too deep for physical manifestation. Dry-eyed and mute she watched her son. Through the open window she could hear Hugh talking to a negro about some matter of the fields. In spite of her own calmness she wondered how he could speak so calmly to the negro.

Hugh had not left the house for days. Each morning he sent the hands to the fields, and each night he directed their feeding of the stock. Morning and evening he answered their sympathetic inquiries about little Dumont. This morning he could not bring himself to tell them that he was going to die. His tongue refused to form the words. Instead he said to them all, "He is no better."

It sounded hopeful somehow, thought Nancy.

Hugh came back into the room directly. Nancy acknowledged his presence by silently clasping his hand. He closed his fingers around her smaller ones and settled himself at her side. For some time neither spoke, then in a tone of surprising control and evenness Nancy said, "Hugh, you must go to town."

"Why?" he asked in amazement.

Her composure almost deserted her when she tried to answer.

"We have nothing," she groaned, "nothing fit to bury him."

"God, Nancy, I can't do it!"

"You must."

"I can't do it," he repeated.

"You wouldn't want anyone else to do it, would you?"

"No," he wept.

"Go then," she said quietly.

An hour later Hugh found himself in one of the new department stores in Granville. The place was crowded, and for some time he stood dumbly watching others make purchases. His own mission appalled him. Finally a salesgirl leaned over the counter and addressed him.

"Something for you, Mister?" she asked with a mechanical smile.

"Yes," Hugh answered.

She waited for him to go on, her smile changing to a pout before his clod-like dumbness.

"Well, what do you want?" she demanded finally.

"Boys' clothes," he stated.

"Fifth counter on your left," she directed and turned her back.

Hugh found the counter and another steronyped smile behind it.

"Something for you, Mister?" he heard again.

"I want a suit for a little boy," he repeated dully.

"All-rightie," chirped the smile, "and how old is the little boy?"

"Five," Hugh told her.

"Five, five, five, Ummmmm. Here we are. Something nice for summer, light yet durable, and easy to wash."

She held up a cheap play-suit for his inspection.

"No, that won't do. I want something nice. The best."

"Oh, something for Sunday perhaps."

"Yes."

She rummaged beneath the counter and came up with an

assortment of boxes. From one of these she drew a suit of fine linen.

"Here," she exclaimed, rising, "is the very thing. You see, it's two-piece with a double-breasted jacket. He'll look like a little man in this."

"That'll do," said Hugh; "wrap it up."

"He'll look cute in that," she said as she thrust him the bundle.

Hugh paid her and walked away, blinded with tears. The girl watched him go in wide-eyed astonishment.

"Of all things," she said.

10

Like a proud tree suddenly wrenched from the soil, its roots tracing the thin air, was Nancy after Dumont's death. She had sunk her life in that of her child, and of her pride and stubbornness nothing remained. She had become a woman who wept and invited pity, and in her tears Hugh soon saw that there was some contrition and much late understanding. They still stood apart but her grief afforded a bridge on which he might cross to her. Hugh saw this, yet he hesitated.

This had not become apparent to him all at once. At the funeral they had been united not in sympathy but in sorrow, and immediately afterward, in fact as he brought her home, he felt the chill of their established coldness settling back upon them, and he was strangely reluctant to resist it although he found something horrible in hugging his sorrow to himself in silence, this sorrow which had had its inception in a mutual love. They rode home in silence, and silently they parted when they reached the house, Hugh taking himself to the fields and Nancy to her room.

Annie set a cold meal before him when he returned at night but he found that he could not eat it.

"Take some coffee up to Mrs. Winton," he commanded her; "I don't suppose she feels like eating either."

But he did not go himself to see. He walked away from the house again seeking some nameless comfort from the vast solitude of the night. A subtle breath of spring caressed the air and all around him the fields seemed heavy with an expectant peace as if knowingly they had opened their pores for the descent of a seasonal magic. He felt some of the lust of spring touch his own heart, and he felt that it is always better to be alive than to be dead, although he could not have said why this was true. He returned to the house, not comforted, but strengthened in some strange way.

Mechanically he locked the doors and went up to his room. Before his door he paused and thought of Nancy beyond the thin wall on his left, and was impelled to offer her his sympathy. For a second he yielded to the impulse. He took a step toward her door. Then he checked himself and turned resolutely into his own room. They had been apart too long; his sympathy would have meant no more to her than the conventional mumbling of a stranger, he decided. But even after he had undressed for bed he could not satisfy himself that he was right, and he finally dropped off to sleep still debating whether she had any need of him.

Each night for a week he tried to settle this question. A change in her bearing was becoming more obvious daily. He could not say why he knew this, he could not put his finger on any thing she had done or said, and yet he knew that her silence was no longer the bitter accusation it had once been; it seemed now to be an eloquent appeal. She made the first move.

He was sitting on the edge of his bed thinking of her lone battle with grief in the darkness across the hall when he heard her coming along the passage between their rooms. She halted at his door and rapped upon it, hesitatingly, he thought. He arose and opened the door. They stood there for a moment, saying nothing. It seemed that a certain astonishment fixed them both in their tracks. Then he took her hand and led her through the door.

"I'm so miserable alone," she said as though her presence demanded explanation.

"So am I," he answered. "I was coming to see about you, if you hadn't come here."

"I knew that," she said simply, and suddenly he knew that she did know it, that he would have gone to her.

She said nothing more, but sat upon the bed tracing some meaningless pattern with her nervous fingers.

"We've been pretty foolish," she said finally.

"Yes we have," he agreed.

The firm smooth lines of a girl were visible beneath her gown, but her face had something of the agony of eternity in it, although tears had not obliterated her beauty entirely. She was still lovely, even in her grief, but her beauty stirred in him no feeling other than pity. He wondered if this would have been true had there been no shield of sorrow between them.

"I suppose it takes things like this to show people what fools they are," she mused.

"Do you repent the way we have lived?" he asked suddenly. The sound of his own question surprised him, as though he heard himself saying a cruel thing to a child. But she answered without bitterness.

"No, not exactly," she replied truthfully; "I haven't reached repentance yet. It's such a shock, so overwhelming . . . this sudden realization that I need you."

"Are you sure," he asked gravely, "are you sure that it isn't a need that another could fill?"

"I am not sure of anything yet," she answered in the judicious manner of one who has exhausted all elemental emotions. "I am not sure, but does that matter greatly to you?"

"No," he replied, "not greatly." And he knew that he spoke the truth.

Suddenly he knew that he was free of all bitterness toward her, and all at once he felt that magnanimous and impersonal concern for her which the sorrow of a stranger can arouse.

"Don't judge me too harshly, Hugh," she said as if prefacing an apology for the cruelty of their past.

"I am not bitter about the past," he answered slowly, like a man who puts an unspoken credo into words; and moving to her side he took her hands in his. They were limp and cold, but he felt that she drew some comfort from the contact. "Somehow, it was never bitterness that I felt," he resumed. "It was amazement and hurt, and then a tolerance that you will never understand. This came late. I don't understand it fully myself. But whatever it is," he added, "I have no desire to hurt you further. I mean that I can forget the past if that will make your sorrow any easier to bear."

"It will, Hugh," she sobbed, "it will. You are kinder than I deserve."

"It's not a question of what you deserve," he said with unintentional sharpness. Quickly he added, "It's simply a matter of trying to understand."

"There has been too little understanding between us," she mused.

For a moment he felt a desire to take advantage of her humility, but a quick surge of shame smothered the impulse. This was no time to upbraid her. Indeed, he saw with a flash of clarity that there was no reason to do so now or ever.

Restraint had done its work upon him pretty well.

Nancy pursued a silent questioning. Grief sat upon her like an inquisitor, torturing her with sharp plunges into the secret depths of her soul. "Could it have been a punishment?" she asked, weeping again.

"I don't know," he answered frankly.

"I'm afraid it was," she sobbed convulsively.

"God isn't vindictive."

"Life is then," she shuddered.

"It's the same thing," he thought to himself, but to her he spoke compassionately: "Don't complicate your troubles. They are bad enough without convincing yourself that you deserve them."

She still sat on the side of his bed. Thinking that she would go to her room soon he released her hands, and eased beneath the cover, but she appeared reluctant to leave him. Finally, because it seemed cruel not to, he asked her if she wished to remain with him. Without hesitation she replied that she did.

She extinguished the light and crept in beside him. He moved far to one side, conscious that the memory of the last time she had lain in his bed lay with them like a profane ghost. He could not shake it off. It was there between them, and he could not get around it with any little sympathetic caress. He lay silent far on his side of the bed. His concern proved needless, however, for soon she moved near him and clung to his shoulder. He said nothing more to her and soon a merciful sleep settled upon her weariness.

After that night she continued to sleep in his room. But she was like a small child who seeks company because of a fear, and he began to feel toward her as if she were a child; she threw herself so trustingly upon his strength that he felt nothing more than a desire to deserve and reward that trust.

Even when she clung to him in the dark, even when he kissed her now, he felt only a bewildering sense of compassion. She seemed to expect nothing more.

On the whole, he decided, their present way of living was just as strange and unreasonable as their long indifference had been. It was true that no wilful coldness showed itself between them, but there was a coldness, nevertheless, nor could it have been otherwise, since that which had united them was death itself. Love feeds upon life, not shadows, and to Hugh it seemed that their very life had become a thing of shadows.

II

Lately Nancy spent much time at her parents' home. She went there at least twice a month, and on her last visit she had remained a week. Hugh regarded these prolonged stays suspiciously. The thought that she simply wouldn't return from one of them was strong in his mind, but in truth he worried over it very little, and did nothing whatever to hinder her. When she expressed a desire to visit her old home he took her there obligingly, and there she remained until she came back of her own accord. Eugene usually brought her back to the farm. Hugh had been at the house when he came the last time, and he could not fail to observe Eugene's unhealthy pallor and the complete absence of good humor which marked him with a positive bitterness. After he left, Nancy confided that he had been drinking heavily, that he sat in his room in a drunken stupor for days at a time. It had been going on for months, she said, and her mother was nearly crazy. Eugene seemed to ignore her suffering. He just drank more when she upbraided him, just drank and sulked, if that intense contemplation of the bare walls of his room could be called sulking. It looked more like madness, Nancy said sorrowfully. When he wasn't sulking he talked with a forced gaiety, and this, too, coming from Eugene, sounded like madness. Yet hardly a week had passed before she wanted to go back to the Clay farm. Hugh took her there, and returned home without seeing Eugene. He had been drunk in his room again, he supposed.

As the lengthening spring gradually eased the sharpness of his grief for Dumont, Hugh felt his spirit sink again into that stagnating languor, that terrible unfeelingness which had been upon him at the time the boy died. He struggled against it angrily. He was ashamed that he no longer cared about things, ashamed that he had to counterfeit an interest in matters that formerly would have sent his blood hot or cold instantly. What if he had lost everything? What if his fields were now another's? He had demanded the best of his negroes while these fields had been his. And they had responded. Was he to prove a lesser man than his laziest negro? With such flagellating questions he drove himself to work, but there was no satisfaction in anything he did, and he could not impose upon himself the conviction that what he was doing amounted to anything at all. Like the negroes he was concerned with nothing more than making a hand-to-mouth living, he had no purpose beyond that, and every empty minute of his day cried what a bare purpose this was. Some faculties of feeling he had lost altogether, and this too shamed him, but his shame did not restore them to him. Among the greatest of these losses was his inability to get at the inherent goodness of things; now there was no magic in the sun, hunger was merely a recurrent twinge, and the wind blowing from the pines brought him no message.

Out of sheer boredom he took to hunting for a while each afternoon. He had no hope of getting any game beyond a few young rabbits which could be found in the meadows.

It was some kind of excitement that he wanted, and for this reason he often borrowed a hound from Dave and engaged in long yelping chases instead of simply shooting the rabbits where he found them. In the fall there is some sense in hunting rabbits with hounds, but in the spring all one really needs is a rock.

Sometimes Dave accompanied him, and if he was impressed with the folly of chasing rabbits a mile when they could be shot with less trouble, he kept his thoughts to himself. Obediently he took command of a knoll to which Hugh directed him. Hugh posted himself on another elevation, and in time the hound, true to his training, would bring a rabbit within range of one of them. Eventually the fleeing animal would be solemnly shot, and Hugh would try to imagine that he had derived some amusement from it. Dave made no pretense that he was amused. It was a serious business with him; fresh young rabbits assuaged the bitter taste of collards. Hugh allowed him to keep all they killed, and Dave was grateful. "I gut some pretty good drinkin' liquor at de house," he told Hugh as they plodded across the fields.

Hugh remained silent.

"Tain't fur by my place," Dave persisted; "I drinks ur little evy night fo supper."

Hugh paused to grind a clod to dust beneath his heel. "This corn ought to be harrowed," he said.

"Ur little dram don't hurt nobidy," Dave advised, eagerly hospitable.

"I never cared much for whiskey," Hugh said finally.

"Hit's good fur you," Dave protested, but he did not press Hugh further that day.

Later in the week they hunted together again, and as they walked homeward across the bottom, Dave brought the subject up again.

"Dis heah is regular cawn mash," he declared firmly. "Tain't no ole sorry shugah liquor. Hit's good, sho 'nuff."

"You are pretty sure of it," Hugh grunted.

"I made hit," said Dave.

"The hell you did!" Hugh shouted, stopping and looking at him.

Dave hung his head and concentrated his attention upon forming some marks in the soil with his big bare toes.

"What are you thinking about—making whiskey on this land?" Hugh demanded.

"Oh," answered the culprit hopefully, "don't let that bofer you. I makes hit down on de Galloway side."

"Why do you make it at all?"

"Well, Cap'n," Dave countered, "you know de bank ain't lookin' atter us like you uster. Ur nigger is gut to look atter hisself dese days."

"I see," Hugh said and dropped the matter.

At the point where he took the path to his cabin Dave hesitated.

"Want me to fetch you ur dram?" he offered.

"No," Hugh replied with a grim smile; "since you are doing the honors, I'll go with you."

"Jest have ur seat," said Dave indicating a wobbly cane chair when they had come to the cabin. He disappeared in the pines behind his dwelling, was gone a few minutes, and returned with a jar in his hands. He was very proud of the white stuff. "Hit's purty, ain't hit?" he asked, shaking the jar to demonstrate how nicely it beaded.

Hugh took the jar and drank deeply, gasped, and returned the container to Dave who stood evidently awaiting some comment of approval.

"It's strong enough!" Hugh said, cooling his throat with a deep breath.

"Ain't it!" Dave exclaimed raising the jar to his mouth.

He, too, drank deeply and smacked his lips when he had finished.

Indeed, it was good whiskey, Hugh realized. Already he felt as if a warm electric sponge were expanding in his stomach. A creeping pleasure tingled in his limbs. His tongue felt thick but supple. "You're right, Dave," he praised, "it's good."

From that day their evening drink followed their hunting as a matter of course, except that it soon became two drinks, then three, and finally a slight drunkenness each evening. Eventually Hugh began to take a little home with him, for a night-cap he told himself. He offered to pay Dave for this, but the negro refused his money.

"Hit don't cost me nothin'," he explained.

It seemed that Nancy was going to stay for good this time. She had been gone more than a week now. Well, let her stay, damn it, let her stay. Hugh was about drunk. Let her stay if she wanted to. It was all the same whether she stayed or not. Hugh knew that he was nearly drunk, but this last observation was pretty sober. It summed the whole business up concisely, he thought. That last night-cap was putting ideas into his head instead of dispelling them. He administered himself a larger one. Let her stay—for that matter, by God, he would—he would—but sleep had his brain at last.

He was sick in the morning, but by noon he had sweated it off, and by midafternoon the prospect of an hour's hunt and a few drinks afterwards—just a few today—appealed to him. The more he thought of this the more enticing it became. That had been a good idea he had hit upon—that of hunting every afternoon. He was beginning to get a kick out of it. And the whiskey—that had brightened things up a bit, too. It certainly was better than moping around like a sick hound. He felt genuinely grateful to Dave. Dave had always

been a good negro. At first Hugh had censured himself for
sitting and drinking with Dave, but now he seldom thought
of it. They had grown up together, hadn't they?

Earlier than usual he unhitched his mule and rode him to
the house. He waited impatiently for the animal to finish
drinking, finally pulled his head from the trough and led him
to the stable lot. "Go fill your belly with grass," he advised
when he had unbridled him and sent him scampering into
the lot with a smart smack of plowlines across his high brown
rump. The mule lay on his back in the dust before the gate,
pawed the air, and rolled from side to side. When he arose
he shook his hide like a blanket and walked sedately toward
the grassy bottom. Hugh whistled for Dave's dog, and
walked to get his gun.

He let the hound run at will today. Soon they were far
from the house. The hound skirted every bramble and
thicket, thrust his expert nose into every opening between
the briars, but with no success. All at once he stopped,
apparently for cogitation. Hugh allowed him plenty of time.
The dog pursued his own ideas for a moment, and suddenly
it appeared that some radical idea had been born in his head,
for deserting the meadow he loped off toward the woods and
disappeared in their shadow. Hugh followed. Deep in the
woods he heard the dog bay. In a moment he bayed more
confidently, and shortly afterward he broke into a running
medley of verification. Hugh hurried. Soon it became apparent that the dog was leading him down the stream which ran
between his place and the Galloway place. His rapid pace
quickly brought him out of the woods and into the meadow
below the Galloway house. From the meadow the land
swelled toward the house which, crouching against the sky at
the crest of the knoll, seemed to hold the surrounding country in a sombre malignant gaze. Crossing the bottom, Hugh
took a stand halfway up the slope and turning his back on

the old house he watched the dog's movements below. The hound had undertaken a tough job, for the bramble along the stream was as dense as jungle growth, affording many thorny tunnels into which rabbits could squeeze with no possibility of a dog following. The dog sniffed at these, howled hopelessly, and persisted in a frantic search for some opening into the thicket. Hugh sat down and watched him coursing up and down the bottom, his snaky black tail waving behind him like a bleak pennant.

Lost as he was in following the dog's fruitless maneuvers, Hugh took no notice of the deepening shadows, and it was not until a few large drops of rain thumped his hat brim that he realized the approach of a storm. It had come with the belligerent quickness of all spring clouds, like an angry blob thrown over the horizon, and soon a gray curtain of rain swept across the meadow and up the slope. There was no shelter nearer than the Galloway house and with only a moment's consideration Hugh ran up the hill toward it. The storm followed close on his heels. As he reached the porch he felt several damp clinging spots on his back where the rain-drops had plastered his shirt to his body. He paused for a moment and surveyed the downpour across the bottom, but only for a moment, for suddenly the storm broke with such force over the house that the porch afforded no shelter whatever, and somewhat unwillingly he rapped on the door. Only then did he consider that he was coming face-to-face with an old and possibly unfinished adventure. No one answered his knock. He beat on the door again, harder. The rain whipped about his legs so fiercely now that he stood with his hand on the knob half-minded to enter if his last rapping brought no answer, and even as he debated this intention he felt the knob turn in his hand, and an instant later he saw Helen standing before him. During his wait at the door his mind had formed several speculative images of the woman he had expected to find. The woman who admitted him into the dark hallway corresponded to none of these images, however.

"Why Hugh!" she exclaimed, as though a day and not twelve years stood between them.

There was little of the girl of the clover patch about her. Time had taken away most of her girlishness, but it had compensated for this robbery by the gift of a wholesome maturity; she was, Hugh perceived, when his eyes became accustomed to the dark room, somewhat larger than she had been, but it was a graceful largeness. Pride of endurance had engraved itself upon her features without marring them, and strength graced her body with a firm sweetness.

She scrutinized him closely, too. "You haven't changed much," she said finally.

"Oh, yes I have," he contradicted quickly; "it's been a thousand years since we . . . since I was a boy."

She made some reply, but a tremendous blast of thunder obliterated her voice. It obliterated the twelve years between them, too, as far as Hugh was concerned. Suddenly their old relationship flamed in his mind and his eyes sought her hungrily and possessively. She dropped hers under his frank gaze.

"And so you married James Carroll," he said in abrupt compliance with his thoughts.

"And you married Nancy Clay," she returned as though they were accusing each other of misdeeds of the remote past.

Perhaps it was the closeness of the room, or the roaring wall of rain outside which gave them the sense of isolation from everything except their frustrated past, but Hugh ascribed his mood to no particular reason; he was conscious only of the fact that between them there was only a vast blank of time; otherwise they were as they had been. He saw a woman whom he had once loved, one whom he had lost through a grotesque misjudgment of values, and for the first time he realized that he had lost something which he would never cease to want.

"What a hell of a mess we made!" he blurted out under the strength of this late realization.

"We?"

"Yes, *we*."

"You assume a lot."

"Assume nothing. I know what you felt."

"Well," she weakened, "it will do no good to talk of it now."

"It will do good!" he cried. "It'll do me good to confess what an arrogant fool I was. I loved you, Helen. I came to tell you, but you were gone, and since that time there has been no opportunity. Indeed, not until now did I realize that I would ever again want one, but I do, Helen, I do."

"Let the past stay buried," she begged him.

"But it isn't buried. We aren't buried. We're alive, Helen! We're alive!" and he repeated it exultantly, like one who had stepped from the grim obscurity of the grave into the certain light of day. "We're alive!" he shouted, "and what a difference that makes!" In his eagerness he had moved nearer her, and now he reached out his arms in a gesture of sudden gladness and expectancy.

Again some protest came to her lips, but it was lost in another deafening crash of thunder. Before it had died away Hugh folded her in his arms. She struggled, but his tenacity was as wildly unreasonable as his sudden declaration of passion had been, and soon like a great wave it enveloped her in its power and they were lost beneath it to all except each other's nearness. He found her lips and so absorbed was he in the ecstasy of finding them that he was not conscious that she was bound to him only by the strength of a kiss.

"Hugh, this can't be!" she cried.

He kissed her again, but this time she drew away and

slipped from his arms to a chair. He fell to his knees beside her and brought his face near hers, but the sight of her tears and her trembling lips restrained him.

"Why do you cry?" he asked.

"You shouldn't have done it, Hugh," she wept unreservedly. "You shouldn't have come here. It was cruel. It was better to have left things as they were. Now it's too late."

"It's not too late for me," he cried stubbornly.

"It's madness."

"No it isn't. It might be happiness—for both of us. You haven't been happy, have you, Helen?"

"James is good to me," she parried.

"But you haven't been happy?" he persisted.

"No, Hugh, I haven't been happy."

"Nor have I, Helen. For five years I haven't known what it was."

And suddenly he was pouring out all the pent-up sorrow and disappointment that had burdened his heart so long. Helen heard him with growing sympathy; his story cemented them in a fellowship of sorrow, and as he talked she drew him to her with compassionate tenderness.

"I'm sorry, Hugh, so sorry."

She held him to her bosom and stroked his bowed head. Out of this gentleness she became aware of a burning longing for him smoldering deep within her, and when he lifted his face she evaded him no longer. Under his caresses the aching rapture of her lost youth cried in her heart again, and when he suggested that she meet him at their old trysting place she heard herself calmly consenting.

"Tomorrow, then," he said.

"Tomorrow," she repeated, like an echo down the years. With a sudden concreteness of intention she pointed out that she could not come at dusk as she had done long ago. "Expect me later, after Lonnie has gone to bed," she said.

At this moment the sound of heavy footsteps on the porch brought them to their feet, and directly Lonnie strode into the room. He surveyed them both sullenly, his dark face a ferment of suspicion and spitefulness, but he confined his words to a mumbled greeting. Hugh offered no explanation of his presence, and since the rain had abated he made a hasty departure from what had become an embarrassing silence.

At home he found Nancy back again. He accepted her return with a casual greeting.

12

The morning sun fell pleasantly upon Hugh's bed. Nancy had left it and he was quite alone with his anticipation of what the day held. There was no pressing task which called him to the fields, there was no immediate necessity whatever which distracted his mind from its pleasant work, so he lay and allowed his imagination to deal long and lazily with the prospect of resuming relations with Helen. Some difficulties presented themselves; some qualms reared their anxious heads, but he subdued these eagerly. Compared to the rather morbid habit of mood which he had suffered lately, his disposition this morning was gay, exuberant, apprehensive only of pleasure. Jacob, at the end of his long service for Rachel, must have spent a similar morning, for Rachel had been in his heart first and longer.

Nancy brought tender eyes to the breakfast table, but they were not tender with any promise; they were eyes with something to ask. She was not long in asking it.

"Will you do something for me?" she began.

"That all depends," Hugh replied in the cautious formula of childhood.

"Seriously."

"All right."

"It's Gene," she said. "He's getting worse, and unless something is done it's going to kill Mother, not to mention what it's doing to him."

"What can I possibly do about it?"

"I want you to try reasoning with him."

The manner in which he had been spending his evenings while she had been away was a fine preparation for this task, Hugh thought ironically. Nancy's request tickled him evilly, but he maintained a grave face.

"I'll see what can be done," he said soberly.

"Today?" she urged.

"Might as well. I haven't anything else to do."

"Don't regard it that way. It's worrying me to death."

"Do you think I could do better," he asked sourly, "if I postponed seeing him until some day when I have a thousand other things to do?"

Nancy ignored his ill-humored question, and he regretted it instantly himself. When he had finished his meal she put the matter forward again.

"You will go today, won't you?"

"Yes," he answered kindly, "right now. As soon as I can saddle a horse."

"Oh, thanks," she murmured, almost humbly.

At the Clay home he found that Nancy had not exaggerated the distress that Eugene was causing his mother. Mrs. Clay was pale and hollow-eyed, and he could see that she was not far from tears when she greeted him. Old Dumont himself sat in an unbecoming state of melancholy, as if Eugene's condition were his own suffering conscience; perhaps it was as near that as anything outside a man's own head can ever be. He had been a pretty wild one in his time, and his aged features were stamped now with a sad blend of sorrow and guilt.

"He's at it again," Mrs. Clay confided, as she led Hugh toward Eugene's room. "I won't go in," she said brokenly at the door, "I can't bear to see him."

Hugh entered the room alone. Eugene sat propped in bed, his eyes searching the emptiness beyond the open window. Hugh closed the door and stood watching him, and it was a sorry sight. Eugene was not one of those in whom whiskey produces a spurious appearance of well-being. It had drained his face to the point of emaciation, it had dulled his fine eyes, and his hard bitter mouth was harder and more bitter than ever.

"Be seated . . . Priest," Eugene commanded, favoring him with a cold glance.

"Priest?"

"You came to convert me, I take it."

"I came to tell you I think you're a damned fool," Hugh responded hotly.

"Any priest would agree with you," Eugene conceded, "but that's beside the point. Granted that I am a fool . . . we'll forget the expletive—granted that I am a drunken fool, just what is that to you?"

"To me, frankly nothing," Hugh blazed; "but it's a lot to your people. Your mother couldn't look any worse if you were dead."

"Will you have a drink?" Eugene asked abruptly, reaching for a jar standing by his bed.

"I don't mind," Hugh responded, pouring a small drink into a glass.

Eugene watched him closely. "You don't down the stuff like a novice," he judged; "a true priest should strangle and gasp. This lacks a lot of being the wine of the holy communion, you know."

"The taste of whiskey is not new to me," Hugh rejoined, "but I'm no drunkard."

"Well, I am, and it's better so. Drunkard or madman, what is your choice?"

"Is it that bad?"

"I'm not positive. To discover involves becoming sober, and I'm afraid to become sober."

"You're in no danger of that at present," Hugh pointed out.

"True. I watch that closely. As I have said, I fear it. Therefore, I guard against it. But it becomes more difficult."

"Oh, undoubtedly," Hugh said wearily.

"You seem to doubt it."

"It's immaterial," he replied. "Enough of this pointless talk. I promised Nancy that I would try to reason with you, and for her sake and your mother's I will."

"Reason away, then," urged Eugene.

"Can't you consider them?"

"I have considered them."

"And they don't matter?"

"They do. But evidently you know nothing of my need for whiskey, nothing of my dread of soberness; in short, you know nothing about it, hence you're in no position to be reasonable about it."

"No, all I know is that you are young, practically unobligated, possessed of a fine farm, free of debt, and absolutely blind to your opportunities and responsibilities."

"Oh, the farm. Well, I'm not doing so badly there. You mention that I still have the farm. Doesn't that strike you as a rather remarkable achievement? I still have the farm, but only because I made up my mind to quit farming. To farm requires to borrow, and to borrow, eventually, to lose the land. That's right, isn't it? I have decided to make the land support me in a more leisurely fashion. This is a big farm, you know, quite a large farm, indeed. Each year I shall grow enough to eat, and each year I shall sell enough land to pay the taxes and buy myself a suit of clothes. I'll live here like a rat in a cake of cheese, nibbling a little off the edges when I must, and retiring to the hole in the center, my home, until necessity drives me forth again.

"You certainly are drunk."

"Nevertheless, that's a mighty sober and long-headed way of farming. I intend to follow it at any rate," Eugene concluded.

Whiskey had not impaired the keenness of that sarcastic mind, Hugh perceived. It had simply rendered its sharp edge suicidal. Perhaps, when in soberness it turned to devour its owner, it became, as Eugene had intimated, maddening. Perhaps behind that long face a torment of self-analysis made the relief afforded by whiskey necessary. Hugh knew from his own experience how little one man can know of another's inner misery, and he saw that Eugene had no intention of exposing his inmost perplexity to the futile balm of conversation. And for this he respected him, although his respect was an admission of defeat in the mission which had brought him there. He could do nothing, so he got up to go.

"Another drink," offered Eugene; "I share my joys."

"But not your sorrows," Hugh observed pertinently.

"No," said Eugene, with his first grim smile, "I drown those."

Hugh left the house quickly, unwilling to expose himself longer than necessary to the pitiable spectacle presented by the two old people. Before their misery the sympathy which he felt for Eugene dissolved, and as he rode out of the yard he was conscious only of a profound disgust for the drunken man. This feeling, too, he soon shook off, and gave his mind whole-heartedly to the prospect of seeing Helen later in the day.

Not for a second did he doubt that she would come, nor was it her promise alone which supported him in this conviction. Had he been capable of analyzing his own mind, capable of examining the latent foundations of his beliefs, it would have surprised him to discover that few of them rested upon the hard rock of reason, but upon an integral reliance upon the justice of his desires. Time and misfortune and the utter rout of his hopes had not fully disillusioned him; at this hour he could still believe that the chief business of the future was to compensate for the unhappiness of the past. Hugh was a plain man; his thoughts were plain and forcible, and that is how his life would have been had its mastery not got out of his hands. So it was largely out of a belief in justice, out of a feeling for the instinctive rightness of life, that he expected Helen to meet him. She would come because there had never been more between them than a barrier of time; that was removed now and she would come. No groom ever awaited his bride with more fervor than Hugh awaited Helen, nor with an easier conscience. A few more hours, the swift fall of darkness, the late moon and beneath it a long-delayed delight. Hugh dreamed of all this as he rode along, and all of it gave him nothing but satisfaction.

Wrapped in this reverie, lulled physically by the undulating motion of the horse and the languorous hot sun, he gave little attention to the fields bordering the road or to the few automobiles which hummed past him. Indeed, by the time he reached the store and entered the wooded road which led to the farm a drowsiness bent his head, and his hand rested upon the pommel of his saddle exerting no check upon the reins. Once or twice he nodded, slumped drowsily in the saddle, recovered himself foolishly and righted himself in his seat, but in the following moment his eyes would droop heavily again. Once the figure of a man far down the road arrested his attention for a brief instant as he straightened in the saddle before he slumped again into a happy doze.

When he awoke it was with a rude jolt which almost shook

him from his seat. This time his eyes opened wide, for standing at his horse's head, with his hand on the rein, was a man. Fully awake Hugh stared at him while a hot anger flooded his body. The man was Lonnie Galloway.

"Take your hand off that rein," Hugh ordered sharply.

Lonnie's only answer was to give the rein a vicious jerk. Unused to such treatment the horse quivered with surprise and pain.

"Do you hear me, fool?" roared Hugh.

"You and me have got some talkin' to do, before you go any further," Lonnie drawled insolently. "You ain't foolin' me none 'bout Helen. I know 'bout y'all." An ugly cunning gleamed in his eyes as he spoke.

Hugh heard him impatiently and with no intention of debating the matter, for he was far too angry to think of anything other than that this stupid fool was detaining him.

"Once more, Lonnie, take your hands off that bridle."

"We ain't done talkin' yet," said Lonnie tightening his hold on the rein as he spoke.

Rage lifted Hugh out of the saddle and before Lonnie had time to follow his swift movements he had swung from the stirrup and stood at the horse's head. For an instant his attention was riveted upon Lonnie's detaining hand at the bit, and as if this sight galvanized his anger, without a word of warning he shot a powerful blow at Lonnie's sneering face. The lower part of that face seemed to recede an inch or two under the force of his flying fist, and Lonnie fell heavily to the ground. As he fell, the full force of his body, through that hand which still clung to the bit, tore again at the tender mouth of the horse. The animal reared in fright and one descending hoof struck the prostrate man. All of this happened seemingly as a part of the blow which Hugh had delivered; indeed, he had stepped back a little to set himself for another blow when Lonnie should arise, but Lonnie didn't arise. He lay quite still, and Hugh moved cautiously nearer. He extended one foot and prodded the inert figure, but Lonnie made no movement. Really alarmed now, Hugh bent and examined him closely. Lonnie had fallen with one side of his face to the ground, and as Hugh turned him he saw spreading through the sand, like slow red ink through a blotter, a pool of blood. This blood came, he found, from a small spurting hole in Lonnie's temple, from such a hole as might have been made by the sharp heel of a horseshoe. Failing to detect any signs of life in Lonnie's face, Hugh tore open his shirt and laid his ear over his heart. A terrible stillness reigned within. At length he closed the shirt clumsily and staggered to the edge of the road where he sat down on the hard dirt bank and gazed with fascinated incredulity upon what had been a living man only a few seconds before.

Down the road a short distance the horse had halted and was grazing peaceably. It was a gentle, toil-worn animal, and its fright subsided quickly. A large fly which seemed to have sprung from nowhere buzzed around the still body lying in the road and came to rest finally at the border of that little rivulet of blood which the sun was drying along Lonnie's temple.

Sickened by this foul visitor Hugh got up from the bank long enough to rip a piece of cloth from Lonnie's shirt and drape it over the wound in his head. Then he resumed his seat and made an effort to collect his scattered wits. But about all he could do was to gaze with growing horror at that terribly mute figure in the road.

Hugh had reason, later, to realize that he had no clear conception of the passage of time. The thing was timeless somehow, like a horrible dream, and like one in a dream he stared fixedly at the dead body sprawled in the roadway. Slowly his senses focused upon the frightful implications of his position, and seeking a way to clear himself he came to no conclusion. It was impossible to charge a horse with murder. It was equally impossible to prove that the hole in Lonnie's head hadn't been made with any one of a thousand hard instruments, a stone, a club, a pocket-knife clenched in the fist.

Suddenly he realized that he was not alone. Into the line of his vision there came a pair of feet—so silently had they come in the soft sand that he had not heard them approaching. The feet came to a dead halt, and Hugh knew that their owner, like him, was staring at the thing in the road. Slowly he raised his eyes. They came to rest upon the goggling face of a young negro man. He was not unknown to Hugh. The boy was some sort of relative of one of the families on the farm, and being a lazy shiftless scamp, he had existed for the past few weeks upon nothing more than the advantages of this relationship. Undoubtedly he would have prolonged his visiting indefinitely had not Hugh taken the matter into his own hands and ordered him off the place. That had been the day before. Well, here he was again, and Hugh was indeed sorry to see him. A portentous questioning seethed in the negro's eyes, but Hugh wasted no time in explanations.

"Don't stand there like a knot on a log," he shouted; "go to the store and phone for a doctor."

The negro moved off, giving the body a wide berth.

"Hey!" Hugh yelled after him, "you might as well tell them to send the sheriff, too."

Then he settled himself upon the bank to wait resolutely for their coming.

13

Some weeks had passed and Hugh was again upon the Granville road. This time Nancy was seated by him in the rusty, ragged remains of that Buick he had bought upon his return from the war. The car still ran, and its doing so was a tribute to many things. That anyone should ride in such an out-moded vehicle proclaimed the poverty of its passengers. That the machine was capable of transporting passengers was a tribute to Hugh's stolid patience. And above all, its slow and shame-faced progress bespoke the spirit of its driver, dull with the awful dullness of a thing which had once been bright.

Their mission, like their conveyance, was a sorry one. They were going to Granville where today Hugh faced trial for the murder of Lonnie Galloway.

As they passed the spot where Lonnie had met his death, Hugh relived the whole ghastly business. He remembered his anger and the fierce blow. Again he saw the terrified horse rear and plunge, and though there had been a great rain since, he imagined that beneath the hot white sand Lonnie's blood was sinking deeper and wider into the spongy earth. Once more he waited for the sheriff to come, and once more he heard himself telling his unbelievable tale of how the thing had happened.

"It doesn't sound very good, Hugh," the sheriff had said when he concluded. That was all—"It doesn't sound very good." But he said it with such a terrible simplicity of meaning.

They had taken him directly to Granville. Nancy had thought that he was spending the day with Eugene, and had known nothing of the tragedy until he told her upon his return late in the day. In Granville they had questioned him briefly, and had listened rather cynically, he thought, to his account of the affair. It sounded weaker even to him each time he was forced to relate it. But the fact that he had not fled, that he himself had notified the sheriff and the doctor, they counted in his favor, although some of them were of the opinion that this was nothing more than a premeditated piece of smartness.

The verdict of the magistrate's court had been that the implication of guilt warranted holding him for trial before a superior court. He had realized the futility of protesting what he himself felt was a reasonable judgment and had made his arrangements for bond and returned home in time to acquaint Nancy of his predicament before sunset.

So had ended his day of promise.

Since that day Nancy's encouragement and her show of loyalty had been a sore trial to him. She seemed to exult in being loyal, as though she found some delight in being able to rescue something useful from the junk-heap of their emotions. The fact that the whole situation had grown out of a planned infidelity to her made her attitude all the harder to bear. True, it would have been merely a technical infidelity, it could have been nothing more under the circumstances, and yet women were unpredictable. She had been different since the boy's death. Even before the present difficulty a change in her attitude had been perceptible, and in his heart Hugh could not say that she did not love him. Perhaps this late solicitude had some elements of passion in it. Once she had been warm enough, but it had been a flame, even then, which wanted fanning. What she hid in her heart would remain a secret until he sought it with ardor, and for that he no longer had any inclination. As a final mockery, none of these complications had succeeded in freeing him of a burning desire for Helen. He still wanted her, and he wanted her with the fierceness of a passion which had slept for a bitter fruitless period. He had not seen her since Lonnie's death.

Murder trials were rare events in Granville. People still talked of the last public hanging, that of a negro thirty years ago, as if it were one of the splendid realities of a glamorous dead age. No one expected to see Hugh hanged publicly; indeed, only a few expected to see him found guilty, but there were many who did not know him, many who had no interest in his fate, and what the court served up to them be it acquittal or conviction, was entirely beside the point; they were not seeking justice, but entertainment.

When Hugh entered the old courtroom he found the stage set and awaiting his appearance. The judge had not taken his place upon the bench, but behind the worn rail which restrained the eager spectators, he saw the local fraternity of lawyers, the sheriff, the clerk, and a rather pompous stranger whom he judged was the district attorney. Seated at a table, withdrawn from the others, was Fleming Kane, his own lawyer. Kane had evidently been searching the doorway for his arrival, because he rose and placed two chairs for him and Nancy as they came down the aisle.

Fleming Kane was an old man. His memory and his sense of politeness extended back to the time of Hugh's grandfather. His hair was white, and white was the neat little bow tucked beneath his collar. A faded mustache hid his mouth, but his eyes were clear and comprehending. Attached to a black ribbon which emerged from his starched bosom was a pince-nez which he held in his long thin fingers. This he seldom carried to his eyes; its function was oratorical. He waved it before his spell-bound juries. Fleming Kane, in dress and manner, seemed a bit theatrical in this bustling courtroom. It was not so. The times had changed; Fleming Kane had not.

With an ancient and easy grace he drew a chair for Nancy. Then he directed Hugh to a chair next his own.

Rarely in his long career had Fleming Kane prepared to defend a client whom he respected yet failed to believe. Often he defended those whom he disbelieved completely, but in those cases his respect had been confined to the tortuous duties of his profession. Many times during the past few weeks he had drained Hugh's story through the fine sieve of his long experience, and each time there remained the same debris of doubt.

At the preliminary hearing before the magistrate Hugh had told of his encounter with Lonnie exactly as it had occurred except for the mention of Helen's name and her bearing upon the tragedy. The omission of this important factor had not increased the plausibility of his story, he knew, yet he could not see how it would help to name her. So to the repeated query: "But why did Lonnie halt you?" he had replied obdurately, "He must have been drunk." And that had been all that Fleming Kane was able to get from him.

The old lawyer made a final effort. "Within a few minutes, Hugh," he whispered, "you will be in the hands of the prosecution. Undoubtedly, you will be faced with this same question; in fact, you will be hounded with it. And under that hounding you may find yourself giving answers which so far you have restrained. It will be too late for me to help you then. I am entitled to know every fact, no matter how trivial it may seem to you. Otherwise, I am fighting in the dark." He tapped emphatically upon the table with his pince-nez. "For the last time," he begged, "can't you give me some reason for Lonnie's act? It will help me."

Hugh was touched. "There was a reason," he admitted, "but it won't help you any."

"Hugh, I must know that reason."

Hugh shook his head. "No, that reason won't hurt you either."

At this moment the judge made his appearance and put an end to another anxious protest from the old lawyer.

An expectant hush settled over the courtroom. With a gravity of mien which appeared alien to human affairs the judge took his seat and devoted his attention to some papers lying before him. A visitor from Mars would have been forced to conclude that the man was both deaf and blind, and that he would have been surprised, even angered, to discover that a thousand eyes hung upon his movements. The crowd which filled the benches, being commonplace inhabitants of this earth, found nothing amazing in the judge's deportment. Guardedly they readjusted their feet, moved their many heads to the right or to the left of the heads in front of them, and cleared their throats nervously. Betrayed into awareness by these mundane noises the judge raised his head and ordered the court to proceed with its business. The clerk called the court to order and the crowd gave itself another cautious shuffling.

Hugh had not feared to be examined. In his mind the case had resolved itself into nothing more than a repetition of the magistrate's trial with the exception that here they would be forced to believe his story or not to believe it, and to say one thing or the other definitely. Except for the added decorum of the superior court he had not expected the two trials to differ greatly, because it was to be a trial without witnesses, either for or against him. Therefore, he took the stand with composure.

The name of the state's attorney was Hines. He faced Hugh, a corpulent, red-faced, politically flavored individual, charged with that strange energy of the obese. Already he had subjected the jury to a merciless questioning, discharging every man who admitted the possession of any information about the case. Satisfied that no man of the twelve had an idea in his head, he was ready for Hugh.

After the usual identifying questions had been asked and answered, he invited Hugh to tell the jury just what had happened. Hugh told them. Hines heard him out with complacent irony. Then he proceeded to question Hugh:

"You say that you had been to the home of your wife's parents?"

"Yes."

"And you were returning peacefully along your way, when, for no cause whatever, Lonnie Galloway halted you?"

"Yes."

"What did he say—he said something, didn't he?"

"Yes. He said, 'You and me have got some talkin' to do.' "

"And what did you say?"

"I reminded him to turn my bridle loose."

"You reminded him?"

"I had warned him before."

"But you didn't ask him what he wanted to talk about?"

"I did not."

"You didn't want to talk to him, did you?"

"No. I didn't want to talk to him."

"And why not?"

"As I have said, he was drunk."

"If he had been sober would you have talked to him?"

"Not if he had approached me in the way he did."

"What would you have done?"

"Just what I did, I suppose."

"You would have killed him?"

"I didn't kill him."

"The man is dead and you were the only one with him."

"He met his death from the blow of the horse's hoof."

"Because he was drunk?"

"Principally because of that."

"You weren't drunk yourself that morning, were you?"

"No."

"You hadn't even had a drink?"

"Yes, I had taken a drink."

"Just one?"

"Just one."

"You had had a drink, but you were not drunk?"

"No, I wasn't drunk."

"One drink never makes you drunk, does it?"

"Never."

"How many drinks does it usually take to make you drunk?"

"I am not a drunkard."

"I didn't ask you that."

"That's my answer, anyway."

It seemed to Hugh that Hines was proceeding with the air of one who carried a tremendous ace up his sleeve. There was nothing in any answer he had given, he felt, which should suffuse that fat face with elation, yet elation was what he saw there.

His eyes roved across the sea of faces. Those of the jury were imponderable; they had taken on some of the judge's gravity. The spectators showed only an itching impatience at the long pause. Nothing wrong there. Nancy's face sent him a message of loyalty and approval, shadowed by no fear. But the wise old face of Fleming Kane betrayed a poorly concealed apprehension and bewilderment. Something was wrong and suddenly Hugh knew what it was. Seated at the front of the negro section, convenient to call, he saw the negro boy whom he had sent to call the sheriff after the accident. So there was to be a witness and a hostile one at that.

Hines returned to the attack. "Do you wish to add anything to what you have stated?" he asked with perspiring unction.

"Nothing," Hugh replied.

"You have told the truth, the whole truth, and nothing but the truth?"

Hugh nodded.

"You may come down," said Hines, and very deliberately he watched Hugh as he left the witness stand and crossed to

the table where Nancy and Fleming Kane sat. Then Hines
faced the jury.

"Before I call my next witness," he began, and paused
portentously, "before I call my next witness, allow me to
direct your attention, gentlemen, to the fact that I have permitted the defendant to tell his story as he wanted to tell it.
He had an opportunity to tell it without prompting and
without interruption, and most of all he had a sworn opportunity to tell it with truth. I propose to show that he did not
do that."

When he had completed this statement, Hines walked
back to his table and settled his huge frame in a chair, turned,
and whispered to the sheriff. The sheriff arose and in a loud
voice called, "Jerry Graves, Jerry Graves, if Jerry Graves is
in this court let him come and be sworn."

That was the negro's name, Hugh remembered. An instant later he saw the boy making his way toward the front.
The clerk administered the oath to him, and Hines motioned
him to the chair.

"What do you know about that?" asked Fleming Kane
under his breath.

"He happened along after the accident," Hugh replied.

"Where was he while it was taking place?"

"I don't know."

"We'll soon find out, I fear," said the old man.

Before examining the witness Hines turned his eyes toward Hugh's table, reading their faces for signs of discom-
fiture. But Hugh betrayed no alarm. Apparently disappointed he began questioning the negro.

"You are Jerry Graves?"

"Yassuh."

"Where do you live, Jerry?"

"I jest lives around."

"Where do you call your home, Jerry?"

"I gut some kinfolks on de Winton place."

"Do you visit your kinfolks once in a while?"

"Yassuh."

"Had you been there just prior to the event under discussion?"

"Suh?"

"Where were you on the day that Lonnie Galloway was killed?"

"I wus dar."

"Where?"

"I wus on de Winton place."

"Well, Jerry, do you know anything about this affair?"

"Yassuh."

"Will you tell the jury what you know."

"Well, I hyead 'em."

"What did you hear, Jerry?"

"I hyead Mr. Hugh an' Mr. Lonnie talkin'."

"Just where were you at this time, Jerry?"

"I wus in de bushes by de side of de road."

"What were you doing there, Jerry?"

"Nothin' but restin'."

"You were lying there in the shade resting?"

"Yassuh."

"Could you see the men in the road?"

"Nawsuh, not widout gittin' up I couldn't."

"Did you get up, Jerry?"

"Nawsuh, not at fust I didn't."

"Did you hear Lonnie Galloway speak to Mr. Winton?"

"Yassuh."

"Tell the jury what he said, Jerry."

"He say, 'You an' me gut some talkin' to do.' "

"That isn't all he said, is it?"

"Nawsuh, he say, 'I know 'bout y'all.' "

"Did he mention any name? Think hard now."

"Yassuh, he say, 'You an' Helen ain't foolin' me none.' "

"Helen is the sister of the deceased, isn't she?"

At this point Fleming Kane jumped to his feet and cried vigorously, "I object."

"Objection sustained," said the judge.

"But, your Honor," protested Hines, "I am trying to establish the identity of Helen, and thereby some motive for the crime."

"The words of the dead may not be construed," said the judge sharply.

Visibly chagrined, Hines returned to the witness. "Did you see anything that took place in the road?"

"Nawsuh."

"Did you hear a blow struck?"

"Yassuh. I hyead sumpin'."

"And then all was quiet?"

"Hit sho wus."

"You thought this silence ominous?"

"Suh?"

"This sudden quiet made you wonder what had happened, didn't it?"

"Yassuh."

"Did you get up off your back then and investigate?"

"Yassuh. I peeped out at de road den."

"And what did you see?"

"I seed Mr. Lonnie stretched out daid, an' Mr. Hugh settin' dar lookin' at him."

"That's all you can tell us, Jerry?"

"Yassuh, dat's all."

Turning to Fleming Kane, Hines said, "You may examine the witness."

And then Fleming Kane did a very strange thing. "I have no desire to waste the time of this court with a superfluous and irrelevant examination," he said. "With the exception of a reputed statement which is not admissible as evidence, your witness has done nothing more than corroborate my client's testimony, word for word. I am satisfied with your examination of the witness," he concluded.

An appreciative murmur of amusement ran through the crowd, and the deep red face of Hines took on a slightly purple shade. He bowed awkwardly and sank to his seat.

Hugh approved the decision of his lawyer and turned to Nancy to whisper some pleased comment, but what he had to say died in his throat. She met his eyes with a cold suspicious stare, and he turned away quickly fearing that others would see the look she gave him. Fleming Kane sat wrapped in thought, his fingers busy with his pince-nez. Hines shot a bewildered glance in his direction, but the old lawyer took no notice of his interrogative red countenance.

Silence ruled the court for a moment. It was an embarrassing silence for Hines. Rising he addressed the judge, "Your Honor," he cried, "since my opponent has the time of this court so much at heart, perhaps he will be kind enough to place his client upon the stand and proceed to ask him what questions he thinks he ought to answer."

Fleming Kane had merely pricked Hines before. Like a skilled swordsman he had feinted for a vulnerable opening, and now with the sure, leisurely grace of a master he administered his final stroke. "I am sufficiently satisfied with your examination of my client," he said, withering Hines with a wise old smile. Then he turned incisively to the jury, conveying the impression that one could not assume a wordy seriousness about so simple a matter. He pointed out that no motive had been established, no witness had been found to say that murder had been done, and no reasonable doubts could be held concerning Hugh's testimony. "This is true," he declared, "because Jerry Graves, Jerry Graves who unknown to us witnessed the accident, bore out my client's

testimony, word for word. Furthermore, Jerry Graves found
Hugh Winton with empty hands. He did not have in his
possession any death-dealing instrument, nor had he had
time to dispose of one before Jerry appeared from his browsy
retreat where he sought comfort from his eternal enemy, the
good sun."

Pausing here he punctuated the air with his emphatic
pince-nez. "Even if you believed in your hearts that Hugh
Winton committed the murder—and you don't believe it—
even if you believed firmly that murder was committed,
under the evidence as brought forth in this trial you can't
return a verdict of guilty. Why? Because your verdict would
be nothing more than a guess; and the Law, my friends, does
not smile upon guess-work, nor upon guessors," he concluded
with an unmistakable bow in the direction of Hines.

What Hines had to say didn't amount to much, and he
said it apparently crushed by that conviction himself.

The jury retired, remained for twenty minutes, then filed
back in to render a verdict: "Not guilty."

14

Lost as he was in the hubbub which followed the announcement of the verdict (people were congratulating him
and Fleming Kane, as if between them they had won a very
clever game), Hugh failed to notice at first that Nancy was
not sharing these plaudits with them, and when he did think
of her he could not find her in the crowd which had gathered
around him, nor did a hurried scanning of the aisles pouring
their torrent of humanity toward the narrow doors reveal
her to his sight. She was gone from the building.

He extricated himself from the clamorous group around
Fleming Kane's table and went in search of her.

Outside the crowd had dispersed into many affable little knots, each occupied with the formulation of its private verdict, though to what purpose they were engaged so earnestly, none could have said. Hugh heard their devious opinions as he skirted the huddles looking for Nancy. He associated her disappearance with that cold stare she had given him at the close of Jerry Graves' testimony, and when he finally found her leaving the courthouse square with Eugene, none of that warmth and loyalty which had recently lighted her face remained. Her expression was empty of feeling except for its message of rather surprised accusation.

Halting at the sound of his voice, she surveyed him coldly. "I'm going home with Eugene," she announced.

"All right," he heard himself say.

They stood there and looked at each other for a long speechless moment. Eugene waited for them impassively. Finally Nancy said, "I'm going home to stay, Hugh."

"Is it because of that negro's tale?" he asked, but it was only out of some queer sense of politeness that he asked it. His feeling that Nancy could never penetrate his heart again burned in his mind at this moment like a great truth. Her words had no deeper effect than to move him to surprise that she cared whether he and Helen were lovers.

"That had something to do with it," Nancy admitted.

"It's not true."

He saw that she did not believe him, but he saw that she wanted to believe.

"There's nothing to that," he reaffirmed. Again it was only a wish to let her down easily which made him speak.

"I don't believe you, Hugh."

"Believe it or not as you wish, Nancy. But remember this. It may be the last thing I ever have to say to you. Even if it were true, what right have you to accuse me? I'm not saying that it is true, or that it might have been, but if it were,

I wouldn't be ashamed of it—not after the kind of wife you have made me. No," he finished, "you should be the last one to blame me."

For a moment he thought that she would break under the impact of his bitterness, for a moment it seemed that some gentle wind of memory had blown a freshness and longing into her cold face. For a fractional bit of time the truth of his charge tore through her reserve and left the nakedness and hunger of her soul exposed, and then decision emptied her eyes of their pain. She turned from him and walked away with Eugene.

He watched her go, not sorry, not glad.

Dusk had almost obscured the outlines of his house when Hugh returned to it. It loomed there before him, huge, empty, and profoundly silent. Being utterly without any wish to enter it, he sat in his car and watched the day die.

A wave of fire from the setting sun still laved the distant shore of the Sligo woods, just as on a million other dying days. He watched the horizon sweep, closing like a dark torrent on the fiery rim of the sun, watched until the black circle was complete, until the circle itself vanished under the blacker onrush of night, and still he sat in the same place lost in a fathomless reverie. Finally, he climbed from the car and walked to the house, but even at the door he halted, turned, and retraced his steps.

Back at the car he halted again, stood undecided for a moment, then strolled off slowly down the path which led to Dave's cabin.